Sinai
Prospect

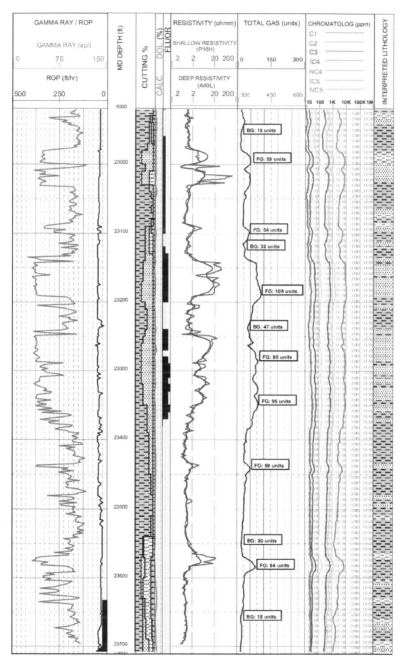

Mud Log

Mud logs are created during drilling by examining rock chips brought from the bottom of the borehole to the surface by circulating mud. Gas detectors record the level of any gas or oil brought up in the mud. Mud logs provide the first record of what type of rock the bit is drilling through, and what fluids occupy the pore spaces between grains.

SINAI
PROSPECT

A NOVEL

What makes the desert beautiful is that
somewhere it hides a well.
Antoine de Saint-Exupery

BY

JEFF LELEK

STEAMBOAT PRESS
COLORADO

SINAI PROSPECT
Copyright © 2020 by Steamboat Press

Printed in the United States of America

Contents

MAP OF THE MIDDLE EAST

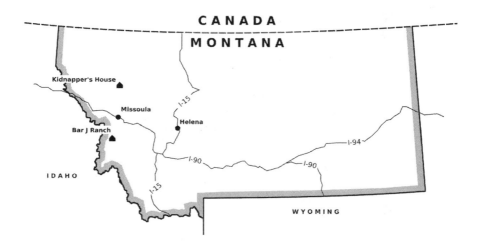

MAP OF MONTANA

CHARACTERS IN JAKE'S WORLD

Jake Tillard—*Geologist*
Gussie Tillard—*Jake's daughter*
Libby Joyce—*Jake's girlfriend*

BAR J RANCH—MONTANA

Lester Heiser—*Ranch foreman*
Marv Tillard—*Jake's Dad*

WINTHAM & ASSOCIATES

Chester Grant—*Partner*
Gary White—*Partner*
Charles Alfred Lister III—*Partner*

EGYPT

Barney Wilcrow—*Jake's Boss*
Layla—*Gussie's nanny*
Mohammed—*The Bedouin*
Salah el Gindi—*Jake's partner*

U. S. FRIENDS AND COLLEAGUES

Jack Webber—*President of Big Rock Oil*
Larry "Snake" Holt—*Lawyer*

CHARACTERS IN THE OUTSIDE WORLD

GENERAL INVESTMENTS, LTD.—NEW YORK CITY

Osama abdel Fatah—*Head Representative*

Aly Hakim—*Finance*

Taha Shaarawi—*Technical Expert*

U.S. POLITICIANS

Nancy Clancy—*Secretary of State*

Dick Steer—*Ambassador to Egypt*

Gordon Foley—*Ambassador to Israel*

ISRAEL

Yaroun Herschel—*Minster of Security*

Daniel Moses Ran—*Minister of Infrastructure*

Benjamin Shapiro—*Prime Minister*

Irma Levi—*Shapiro's right hand*

Mekele Abebe—*Ethiopian Coptic priest*

Vasily Kirchoff—*INOC Chairman*

Yosef Kettler—*businessman*

Simeon Friedman—*construction mogul*

Ruth Karsh—*Istourism chief*

Saad Bardi—*antique store owner*

EGYPT

Maged Khafagy—*EGPC Chairman*

Hesham Ibrahim—*EGPC Contracts*

Gen. Mohammed Latif—*State Department*

Moustafa Hanify—*Chairman Egypt Gas*

Karim Nabet—*Business mogul, Triton Oil*

Ashrah abdel Amr—*Bid committee member*

MONTANA

Moustafa Badry—*chief kidnapper*

Ashraf—*nasty kidnapper*

Mohammed Tawik—*kidnapper*

Joe Faraday—*State trooper*

"Hickey" Fischer—*Hell's Angel*

Randy—*SWAT team leader*

U.S. FEDS AND ASSOCIATES

Gen. Richard A. Radisson—*State Department*

Stan Kawinski—*CIA operative*

Brad Marshall—*agent in Montana*

Vince Mantero—*agent in Houston*

Paul Wheaton—*Jesuit professor*

Prologue

THE WHITE HOUSE
WASHINGTON

From: The Office of the President
Subject: Project Stable
Date: March 22, 1995 8:26 PM EST
To: The Secretary of State

COPY NUMBER 2
TOTAL COPIES 5

TOP SECRET   TOP SECRET   TOP SECRET   TOP SECRET

Nancy,

Have read latest files.
Believe path too risky.
Shut down all operations on Stable.
Mothball project.

President of the United States of America

Book One
Transition

CHAPTER 1

THE hairs on Jake's neck and forearms stood straight out. He heard a crackling sound then the lightning bolt grounded fifty yards away. Sinister clouds closed in. Rain and hail began to fall.

"Mohammed?" Jake asked in broken Arabic.

The Bedouin gazed north as Jake Tillard studied his face. Mediterranean complexion; not too dark. Black hair short but still curly. Northern Sinai tribes shared this trait with Semitic people from the Levant. His long face fit his tall body. The thin aquiline nose set him apart from people in Cairo, more reminiscent of the true Arab from modern day Saudi Arabia.

"*Mesh tamam*. Not good," came the shout in Arabic, barely discernible through the wind that howled between the barren mountains surrounding them.

"Right. Let's go", Jake said in Arabic. He tried to use the local language whenever he could. Mohammed's English was elementary.

Jake was at work in the mountains of the northern Sinai, halfway between Cairo and Israel. With the help of local Bedouin, he was mapping the geology on Gebel Halal. Several hundred miles to the north a low-pressure front had stalled in the Mediterranean. This system birthed a wind running southeast, trying to escape, sucking up moisture for miles before hitting land. The storm likely did not extend more than a hundred miles east of them, where Israel began. It certainly did not extend a hundred miles west, to Cairo.

Here, rain swept across the desert in huge sheets. Rains like this were rare in the northern Sinai. The wind was not. Winds came every year with such constancy that each storm had a name and date. Today was September 20, and El Muknissa was right on schedule. According to the list Jake consulted before leaving Cairo the week before, El Muknissa would last four days, would surely carry rain, and would unleash winds from forty to forty five miles an hour.

The khamasin winds were named after the Arabic word for fifty, as they occur over a fifty-day period. They bring mostly sand, with only seven of the twenty-one named storms predicted to bring rain.

"*Y'alla*, go fast," Mohammed shouted while maintaining his footing on the sandy surface dissolving under his feet.

Another lightning flash came moments later as they picked up their daypacks. Jake counted to eight before the thunder arrived.

"Two miles", he had to cup his hands like a megaphone so Mohammed would hear him.

They were near the top of Gebel Halal, almost a mile from their Suburban. After covering half that distance in the first ten minutes the sky opened up, releasing sheets of water that made them gasp for air. Despite the long khaki-colored poncho flapping around him, Jake was soaked to the core. The temperature had dropped twenty degrees and the wind chill approached freezing. Jake and Mohammed trudged on.

Mohammed accepted the weather without question, without complaint. Bedouin could walk all day across the desert in August without breaking a sweat. Neither did they mind freezing temperatures and relentless rain. They were compliant, accepting the challenges Mother Nature bestowed.

Tall, lanky Mohammed led the retreat, with Jake struggling to keep his sand-colored galabeya in sight. His robe blew madly around his legs, and Jake wondered how he avoided tripping. The sandstone changed to slippery limestone and the grade was steeper. They were on a dip slope of the rock, walking on an ancient sea bottom turned to stone, elevated two thousand feet, and tilted twenty degrees. The footing could not have been worse. Sand blew across the landscape and littered the ground, acting as tiny ball bearings beneath their feet. There was a constant risk for boots to slip into cracks and twist an ankle. It slowed Jake down. Years of fieldwork had made Jake sure-footed, but he had turned forty-five a couple years ago.

The Bedouin was soon out of sight. After plowing on for another five minutes Jake saw the vehicle. Making a mental note never to get a tan field car again, he yanked open the driver's door, threw his pack in the back seat on top of the other field gear, and slouched down in the seat. Mohammed had already settled into his.

"The wadi fill up," said the Bedouin in colloquial Arabic. "Ten minutes we are stuck."

It had been raining for less than half an hour, but already the runoff was rising in the half-mile wide, normally dry creek bed below the Suburban. Wadi Araba was the main watercourse in the Sinai, draining the northern half of the peninsula to the Mediterranean. The wadi was famous in the area, and mentioned in the Bible.

Gebel Halal was also famous. The mountain resembled a volcano, which it was not. Its shape was a big cone with the top missing. One theory held that Halal was the mountain of Moses. God removed its top and reduced the mountain's elevation because of Moses' pride in getting so close to God. Jake had studied aerial photographs of the mountain, flew over it, and hiked on top of it. He agreed. Gebel Halal looked like someone removed its top. It is a most unusual geomorphic feature. He had been to St. Katherine's monastery in the southern Sinai where most people thought Moses had received the tablets. Gebel Halal made more sense. He thought it a good sign, perhaps indicative of oil riches below.

Jake cranked the ignition, put the truck in four-wheel low, and eased across the wadi. The flat plateau to the southwest had disappeared under water. It was two miles to asphalt, and touch and go whether they would reach it today—or at all.

The year before a swollen lesser wadi had washed an entire bus off the pavement, water carrying it a hundred yards until it butted up against a cut bank. Seven of the twenty-one passengers died, including three small children. The road itself had been ripped up for a hundred yards, its pieces carried away to become part of the desert floor. Floods like this also carried old land mines around, depositing them in unpredictable spots.

"To the left" advised the Bedouin.

"How can you see anything in this rain?"

Mohammed didn't reply. Traditionally, his nomadic people traveled by foot or by camel. They tended goat herds or smuggled illegal goods across country borders they didn't recognize nor care about. Regardless of the mode of transport, it was crucial to see depressions before a camel's leg or a car's wheel dropped into one.

The windshield wipers swept back and forth as fast as they could yet Jake could hardly see the front of the hood. A flash of lightning and a simultaneous crack of thunder made both men flinch. Water rose to the base of the doors.

Mohammed pointed with his whole arm, shouting in staccato, guttural Arabic. "There, to the right! Asphalt."

Jake swung the SUV up the bank towards pavement. The truck spun its wheels and bounced over some large rocks before settling onto the road. He shoved the transfer stick forward, putting the Suburban into four-wheel high.

"Tell me, *habibi*, how can you see the desert floor through the water?"

"*Mesh arif*" — I don't know. I feel it. I grew up crawling on the desert. My life is walking through it. Sleeping on it. I know the desert. I hear its voice."

He was never sure he understood exactly what Mohammed was saying. The Bedouin's Arabic was different than the dialect Jake spoke. Not that Jake's was very good. Not as good as his French. More on par with his Spanish.

From Jake's experience, the Bedouin culture had similarities to the Native American culture, which Jake had studied as an anthropology student in college. They related intimately to their surroundings. Trees, mountains, and rivers were part of their extended family.

Mohammed flicked on the cab light to organize his pack. He had a notebook, but could not read or write. Jake looked at him, studying his face again, especially his eyes, the most memorable part of his ruggedly handsome face. They were dark brown like most of his countrymen, but it was their depth, their infinite and mysterious depth, that drew you in. Jake wondered as he drove just what this Bedouin had been through in his roughly sixty years on earth. A few wars, tribal spats, run-ins with authorities.

The Bedouin were as interesting as the pygmies, the Bushmen, the Eskimo, and countless other indigenous peoples. Centuries of nomadic drifting about Near Eastern deserts had created a Darwinian breed capable of surviving the harshest conditions. Someone once referred to them as camels without humps. They are a proud, humorous, colorful, and independent people.

Jake loved them.

Whenever he did fieldwork in the desert, he hired one of these 'locals' to help. Normally he drove into an area and asked the first group he saw who would be the best one to serve as his guide. After much discussion and several cups of tea brewed over an open fire and served in small glasses with no handles, one individual always emerged as the clear choice. If Jake was lucky, it was the most capable. If not it was the most political. In any case, the choice was final.

A Bedouin provided benefits from guide to communicator to Sherpa-like porter. In the Sinai, the most important role was navigating safely through old mine fields and scattered war debris. Four skirmishes beginning with W.W.II and ending with Operation Badr in 1973 had created a weapons junkyard in a truly spectacular landscape. Anywhere else, countryside like this would provide raw material for national parks. Here 'foreigners' were prohibited from venturing off the pavement for fear they would be blown up. In spite of this, tourists were blown up on a regular basis.

Fourteen years ago, one of Jake's geological colleagues and best friends was doing fieldwork in the central Sinai when his Jeep rolled over a mine. The blast killed his Egyptian driver instantly. A camel driver found Jake's friend two days later with only moderate leg and buttock wounds.

The rain slowed for a minute and then suddenly stopped altogether. Five miles down the road the asphalt wasn't even wet. As fierce as it was, the rain was localized. A typical desert storm. The moon came out and its near-full circle lit up the desert. Jake could see small hills to the north, and smooth sinuous sand dunes to the south. A couple of rusted military vehicles, remnants of the '67 Battle of Abu-Ageila, looked like they were parked at the side of the road. Scattered lights of a small village twinkled in the distance.

Jake looked at his friend. "I'll drop you in Nahkl, OK?"

"You go Cairo tonight?"

"After I gas up."

"Then I get out after village. A few kilometers."

Although Jake had done fieldwork in the southwestern United States and Siberia, nothing had prepared him for the barren dryness of the Egyptian desert. The Western Desert that stretches between Cairo and Libya was even more arid than the Sinai, but the Sinai was bad enough.

Several years ago, Jake had a conversation with one of his guides about the eating habits of the Bedouin. Essentially they subsisted on milk, dairy products, bread, and fruit. They ate meat once a year, normally to celebrate the Bairam, or end of the holy month of Ramadan. With this they seemed to thrive. In contrast to their urban equivalents they were always thin, healthy, and fit, commonly living long lives.

Jake and Mohammed had tea in Nahkl while Jake finished making notes in his field journal. The trip had yielded positive geological results. Twenty minutes down the road Mohammed pointed and Jake pulled over. Getting out of the truck, the tall man left without a backward glance and began walking into the vast empty dessert.

"I'll see you in a week, OK?" Jake called out, hoping to get some type of response before he lost his friend to the blackness of the dessert beyond.

Mohammed turned around, paused, and called out in Jake's direction, "For how long will you need me?"

"I just need to pick up my supplies and rock samples at your place. I don't have the space to take them now."

The Bedouin nodded and replied *"Masalama."* With that he continued walking north. Miles from nowhere. Jake watched for a few minutes, then shook his head and drove on.

CHAPTER 2

DOZENS of swallows chirped in the purple Jacaranda trees as an oversized ruby sun fell into a level horizon. A paranoid lizard scurried across the pink granite boulder, stopped to stick its head up, and flicked its long green tongue. It looked around, expecting nothing, but cautious nevertheless. Overhead one solitary cloud interrupted the deepening indigo sky. A soft balmy breeze wafted down the Nile, warmly caressing everything in its path.

From below the cliff, the sounds of a fisherman thrashing the side of a boat with fishing nets wafted up through the crisp, dry air. Every now and then a voice punctured the air with monotonous yet soothing verses from the Quran.

"Alhamdu lillah rabbi al aalameena.' 'Maliki yawmi al deeni."

"This is soooo breathtaking. I can't believe I'm actually here." Kathleen leaned back on the bench and stared out over the Nile, watching the setting sun. She let herself relax, rolling her neck from side to side.

Jake met Kathleen the day before. Vice President and COO of Venture LLC out of Calgary, she was at the conference to invest in oil and gas ventures.

Jake had not heard her, being engrossed in self-analysis, helped along by his third gin and tonic. Since arriving in Aswan two days earlier for the Egyptian Exploration Prospect Event, Jake had worked nonstop trying to interest investors in his company's oil properties in Egypt. The truth was his management did not want as much risk as they already had. They wanted a partner who could infuse cash into their current Egyptian ventures and lessen their vulnerability. Although Mubarak seemed to be holding things together, the company had upped its risk assessment of Egypt. Jake thought this was a knee-jerk reaction.

Jake was distracted these days in silent reflection, ruminating on the current state of his personal life. This current round of deep introspection was brought on by memories of his last trip to Aswan, with Paula, his second wife, just before she died. Paula had been the love of his life, his soul mate, and the mother of his daughter.

He also worried about the direction of his career. It had been five years since he had an economic discovery. Geologists who don't find oil don't win. They don't even get to stay in the race. Jake was depressed.

"Don't you think it's magnificent," Kathleen tried again, staring at him, expecting a comment in return. Her long dark hair blew in the breeze; her jersey skirt gently caressed her.

"You mean the view?"

"Not just the view. All of it. This spot. Aswan. Egypt. It's magical."

Jake watched as Kathleen fiddled with her necklace, a simple strand of pearls. After two days of courting conference participants, Venture was the only potential buyer for what Jake had to offer. He and Kathleen had spent several hours going over data, contracts, and project plans. Jake also sensed that Kathleen might have an interest in more than just his prospect portfolio.

Jake looked at her, leaning on the railing, bent slightly forward, and looking down at the Nile. Based on their conversation at breakfast, he surmised that her long dark brown hair came from an Italian ancestry, or possibly from the small amount of American Indian in her past. At five feet ten, she was almost as tall as Jake. She looked younger than her forty-some years, with large expressive chestnut eyes, high cheekbones, ample breasts, and that worked in her favor. It made her look unique, exotic. Kathleen was exceptionally attractive and available. But Jake felt no twinkling of desire. It was too soon.

"Aswan is magical," he finally replied. "It's your first time here, right?"

"Yeah, my first time in Egypt. Do you know what we're looking at?"

"Well, we're on King Farouk's Terrace. Over there is Elephantine Island," Jake pointed, while moving to stand next to Kathleen. "It has a hundred feet of relief which kept it safe from Nile floods before the Russians built the high Dam. There's a Club Med on it now. It seems strange to put a luxury resort next to the poorest people on earth, but whatever. The huge boulders propping up the island inspired its name a century before Christ. Don't they look like a caravan of elephants heading up the river?"

"Hmmm. Sort of. I wouldn't have seen it myself, but I guess they do. What's all that graffiti?"

"The oldest ones are cartouches of kings and nobles etched during Pharaonic times. The cruder ones are Greek inscriptions from travelers who came fifteen hundred years later, like two thousand years ago. Elephantine Island is famous, but can't hold a candle to Kitchener Island over there. Leave it to the Brits. Lord Kitchener imported a collection of plants from around the world, to shade his wife from the harsh sun and heat that plagued her. Some fifty years later his plants evolved into the Aswan Botanical Garden. You should visit."

"How do you know all this stuff?"

"I'm interested in it I guess. I started out studying anthropology in college, but switched to geology. It seemed to me that geology controlled just about everything else on earth. What grows where. Where people settled. Where trade routes developed. What sparked wars. The Industrial Revolution and our current quality of life. Where the best wine was produced. Et cetera. So why not study the basic key to our lives."

"OK," Kathleen said. "I can't top that."

"But you really should visit the botanical garden."

"I'm almost out of time", she sighed with a glance and a playful smile thrown toward Jake.

"Well, then ponder this. See that sandy plain on the other side of the river? That's the far eastern extent of the Sahara. I doubt there's a single living creature between you and the Atlantic coast of Mauritania, thirty five hundred miles west. Just endless sand, rock, and mirages."

"Wow", she sighed again. "That's overwhelming."

Jake took her arm and led her inside, walking past doormen wearing yellow balloon trousers and red vests that cried out 'Mardi Gras'. When she asked him to walk her to her room, he couldn't think of a way out. Incredibly, she stopped in front of room 140, and put the large brass key into the lock.

"Did you know this was the room in which Agatha Christie wrote 'Death on the Nile'?" Jake asked.

Not answering, Kathleen turned and put her arms on his shoulders, admiring his rugged face.

"You know you're incredibly attractive, don't you," she said. "Did you acquire your ponytail at Dartmouth?"

Jake stiffened a bit, feeling awkward.

"No, it came much later. Probably my mid-life crisis. I'm sorry Kathleen, but I need to phone the States. The time zone thing, you know."

He tried to bow out gracefully, but Kathleen was visibly irritated. She probably wasn't used to men putting her off. Jake thought he might be sorry later, but he just wasn't ready.

Jake met Paula in his late thirties after a failed marriage. They married only after she became pregnant with Gussie. Thirty at the time, she gave up her vet practice when she moved to Houston to have the baby. A few years later she reluctantly agreed to move to Egypt. Never embracing the Egyptian expat lifestyle, she had asked Jake to move back to the States. He put it off, unwilling to juggle her wishes with his career. A year ago, crossing the Corniche in Cairo, Paula was fatally injured when a car ran a red light. Jake blamed himself and lived with the guilt on a daily basis.

CHAPTER 3

DUSTY DOYLE made the sign of the cross for the first time since he was an altar boy in Northern Ireland. Despite close calls in several countries, he had not yet been blown up. He suspected his luck had just run out.

Tuesday's sunrise in Egypt's northern Sinai Peninsula started a gorgeous orange-red, thanks to flecks of desert dust kicked up by a moderate northwest wind. Dusty's crew leader Gyorgi Szabo had the Egyptian workers in place early. Roped together five feet from each other, the twenty men spanned a hundred feet shoulder to shoulder. This human chain moved inexorably forward, each man stepping in unison, swinging metal detectors in repetitive swooshing arcs. They hoped to get a signal from relict debris or ordinance before stepping on it. It was boring and dangerous work that paid the equivalent of ten US dollars a day. The men risked their lives continuously, and were happy for the opportunity.

Reacher Oil had contracted Global Clearance Ltd to mine clear several paths through the rocky brown desert. Global was the top international company for ordinance removal, with experience in half the countries of the world. Here they were clearing debris from World War II and one of the Israeli wars.

After safe corridors were staked the geophysical team came in. Dozens of men called "juggies" would string out miles of electrical cable that connected sensitive geophones to central recorders. Trucks with large metal plates then shook the ground every hundred feet, sending shock waves into the earth. These acoustic waves bounced off rock layers and returned to geophones on the surface. The huge amount of digital data collected was later manipulated by computers and analyzed by geophysicists, who constructed a three dimensional picture of the rocks below.

Jake sat on a small rise, back to a boulder, watching the action. Resembling the Marlboro man, his khaki outfit melted into the complexion of the desert. After more than twenty years doing this kind of work, he was good at it. Including the clearance efforts, the seismic shoot, and ultimately a well, he had convinced Reacher Oil Company to set aside twenty-five million dollars for the venture. Most likely their efforts would reveal nothing. Hopefully they would result in an oil field worth hundreds of millions of dollars. Jake loved wildcatting.

As he stood on the rocky knoll he had a good feeling. In two weeks the clearance crew had unearthed two hundred and thirty-eight pieces of debris. Most were harmless objects such as old bullets, mortar shells, guns, knives, or scrap metal. Some were standard ordinance. Two were more problematic. The first of these was an unexploded 100-millimeter shell from World War II, which was moved gently to the pit where everything was detonated weekly.

The other item had commanded more respect from Dusty, who confided to Jake why he hated this particular type of ordinance. Manufactured by the US and used by Israel during the War of Attrition from 1968 to 1970, the CBU 58 A/B cluster bomb was designed to destroy or maim human bodies and light skinned vehicles. Dropped from a plane, a large pod or dispenser carried 650 baseball-sized bomblets, released at a certain pre-set altitude determined by barometric pressure. Scattering in the air, fins caused the bomblets to rotate. They exploded after rotating a pre-set number of times, sending metal shards screaming in all directions. If the settings worked correctly, this happened just above the ground, inflicting maximum damage. If the shells didn't rotate enough they plopped onto the ground and sat there, waiting to rotate further before exploding.

According to the US Government the "dud rate" for cluster bomblets ranged from five to fourteen percent. UN experts estimate as many as one million unexploded bomblets contaminated hundreds of strike sites in Lebanon after the Israel-Lebanon conflict. Since the Israelis used these devices secretly in the Sinai conflicts, there are no estimates for that area.

Dusty hated these bomblets for one reason. To clear them, he had to pick them straight up, and carry them to the ordinance pile. One wrong turn, an unexpected stumble, and they could detonate, claiming a limb or a life. He had seen it happen.

The cluster bomblet, however, was not why Dusty now crossed himself. Today one of the crew towards the north end yelled to stop. Gyorgi, the crew leader from Hungary, waddled over to investigate, then called for Dusty. The metal detectors indicated that something large was buried fairly deep. Two members of the crew carefully started digging, and came upon a large bomb three feet down. As they continued to dig out the middle, ahead of the fins, Dusty hopped in the hole, sat on the bomb, and started to uncover the front, where he could get at the fuse. He couldn't tell exactly what type of bomb it was, but guessed WWII vintage. Just as he was thinking WWII arms were found mostly in Egypt's Western Desert towards Libya, he uncovered the fuse that promptly started smoking when the fresh air hit it. This is when Dusty crossed himself, jumped out of the hole, and shouted for everyone to run. Four seconds later the bomb exploded.

White phosphorus incendiary munitions are not considered chemical weapons under international law, which forbids them only for use against civilians. Used extensively in both World Wars by both sides, they continued to be used in venues like the Gulf War. The most deadly single bombing raid of all time was an incendiary attack known as Operation Meetinghouse, which killed around 100,000 people in Tokyo in one night. Various chemicals are used in incendiary weapons, but white phosphorus is arguably the nastiest. Being a metal, burning phosphorus sticks to the skin and is absorbed into the body, resulting in kidney, liver, and heart damage. On the skin, it keeps burning unless deprived of oxygen or until it is completely burned up.

Only a few feet from the hole when the bomb went off, bits of the canister and its contents flew up and onto Dusty's back. Phosphorus seared off one ear immediately and vaporized his hair. His left arm and shoulder were covered with the ignited metal, quickly burning its way through skin and muscle to the bone.

Jake could hear the scream clearly a hundred yards away. It didn't last long. By the time he reached Dusty, Gyorgi had stopped the burning by throwing a canvas tarp over him. Dusty's head was a bloody mess, what was left of his arm and shoulder had third degree burns. But he was alive. Unconscious but alive.

As bad as that was, Jake noted a potentially more serious problem, and yelled at Gyorgi. It is strict policy never to venture into uncleared land, for obvious reasons. When Dusty saw the fuse smoke and yelled "run", the Egyptian men closest to him did just that. Being roped together, they all ran in the same direction, and were now fifty yards to the north, in uncleared land. One of the men was yelling in Arabic "Help me, help me".

"Shit", Jake muttered, correctly deducing that the man was standing on top of a land mine. By good fortune his fellow workers had not yet yanked him off.

"*Stanna swaya*! Stay put!"

All the men froze in place. Working with the crew's translator, Jake instructed the men to unhitch themselves while Gyorgi cleared and staked a safe path to them. One by one the workers retreated through this path to the larger swath they had cleared earlier.

Like Dusty, Gyorgi had many years of clearance experience, and knew what to do. Jake kept everyone else at a safe distance while the Hungarian worked. Before long he had stabilized the land mine and freed the petrified Egyptians.

Although Dusty was unconscious Jake talked to him, reassuring him. His condition was dire. Being a scientist and realist, Jake weighed the odds and decided they weren't in Dusty's favor.

With no way to communicate from their remote location, Jake administered first aid and loaded Dusty into the back of a Chevy Suburban. The three-hour drive to the Ahmed Hamdy tunnel took only two as Jake pushed the car. Fortunately Dusty was unconscious the entire way. Screeching into the army outpost, and almost getting shot by jumpy guards, he explained the situation and within a half hour watched Dusty being loaded into an army helicopter for a life flight to Cairo. Jake had seen some gruesome injuries during his rodeo days, and knew it would be touch and go.

CHAPTER 4

THE room seemed tight, though it easily accommodated the table and four chairs. Smoke rose in steady, sinuous tendrils from three cigarettes, while the fourth man periodically released a large, billowy cloud from his cigar. The smoke mixed and hung beneath the discolored and cracked plaster ceiling. The white plastic wall clock ticked off time as the base of the cloud sank, coming closer and closer to enveloping their heads. Ventilation was poor. The lighting was worse. A sole fluorescent bulb, up in the cloud, tried its best.

The four had come together at the sudden request of the Minister of Security, Yaroun Herschel, last to arrive. The meeting was odd for two reasons. First, these four individuals did not normally meet. Second, the Minister had been quite explicit that there was to be no publicity.

"Minister if I may," said Simeon Friedman. "Water is the biggest challenge for the future of Israel. Every child knows the River Jordan flows through Syria and Lebanon before it hits Israel. The Arabs could strangle us by taking more for themselves. In the last fifty years, the Dead Sea has shrunk by twenty five percent and the salt works are threatened."

Friedman, an Israeli construction mogul, thought he had anticipated the Minister's goal in calling the meeting.

Minister Herschel looked at Simeon pensively, wondering if the thin frail looking man had the degree of commitment needed for what was coming. Yaroun's informants had been watching Simeon, gathering information about him. He seemed to be losing energy lately.

"My friend, water is a problem. But we sit next to an entire sea. Yes it's salty. But we've used desalination and drip irrigation to turn the desert into vegetable and fruit gardens."

"I know that, but...."

"Energy is another matter. Oh yes, the sun brutalizes our country, and some think it's the answer. But powering Israel with sun and wind is cost prohibitive. The world still runs on fossil fuels. Unfortunately, we have virtually none of our own. In spite of the Israeli National Oil Company, we still import over eighty five percent of our fuel."

Vasily Kirchoff couldn't help speaking out. He had been appointed Chairman of INOC three years ago. He leaned into Herschel.

"In the last two years, INOC has changed direction. We no longer put all our efforts into exploration. We are trying to solve the problem in other ways."

Minister Herschel continued as if he wasn't even interrupted. "Coal from Australia and South Africa, crude from Russia, fuel oil from the world market. We spend too much of our GDP on energy imports. The richest oil fields on earth are next door, and we can't get at them. The Arabs would let their own economies wilt away before they sell us a barrel. They burn their gas rather than send it to us. Politics change slowly. The peace initiative is a joke. We need a game changer."

"We think there is oil offshore in the Mediterranean," said Kirchoff.

The Minister glared at the transplanted Russian, and lit another cigarette. He had never grown used to the dour, aging, heavyset man with the Stalinesque bushy eyebrows and mustache. He remembered when Vasily arrived from the Soviet Union. He had been the number two man in the Soviet Oil Sector. Trained as an engineer, he later received a Soviet-style education in economics. Yaroun thought that was an oxymoron of the grossest kind—Soviet economics. The Minister continued to glower while addressing him in condescending tones.

"You need help, Vasily. You don't have the clout or the means to do anything significant. Your scheme to bring liquefied natural gas from Qatar will never come about. The Qataris have the largest natural gas field on earth, but I'll bet my daughter's virginity they will never send a cubic foot to Israel. At least, not in my lifetime."

Yosef Kettler had been silently watching the antics. Hiding his Napoleonic complex reasonably well for almost eighty years, he had combined cockiness and brains to make a fortune. An Auschwitz survivor who had been in the first wave of Kibbutznicks, he lived on the farm during his formative years, before moving into commerce, manufacturing, and just about every other money making area in the fifty some years since. Arriving just before the Minister, he had not offered a word yet, not even a greeting. He was somewhat nondescript, an old man who could easily disappear in any setting. He leaned over the table and talked so quietly the other three strained to listen.

"Vat you vant Yaroun?" he said dispensing with the title. Yaroun had never liked Kettler. Although each of them had been ruthless in their careers, he felt Kettler had been that way because he enjoyed it. Perhaps a fallout of his prison camp experience.

"Yosef, you don't waste words. Neither will I. I want an assured source of energy. Israel won't get nuclear; the world won't allow it. If our eastern neighbors sent us their product, what security would that provide? Quite frankly, I don't know how to solve this problem. That's why I brought you all here."

Yosef tilted his head back, and an extra large cloud of yellow smoke rose only a couple feet before disappearing into the dense layer above. None of the other participants knew that Yosef and Yaroun had already spoken. That they had essentially orchestrated this meeting's agenda. That they hatched this scheme in support of a larger agenda.

"Does the Prime Minister know ve meet?" Yosef stared into the eyes of the head of State Security and did not back down. Few men could get away with this.

"No."

Vasily and Simeon melted into the background. A chill ran through Simeon. Vasily shuddered with déjà vu. This was reminiscent of older days in Russia. Days he wanted to forget.

"Yaroun, I vill give it tought."

Yosef sat back and massaged his temple with his left hand. Suddenly, he looked straight at the Minister again with an intensity rare in modern men.

"If dere is something to do, I vill do it. You vant to be informed?"

"No. You take care of it. Just get me a status report every so often. Let me know if you need any funds."

"I'm a rich man," Yosef said. "I have no living children. Vat I have is my heritage, my country. I can tink of nothing better to spend my money on den Israel. Vat if I need your help in oder areas?"

Minister Yaroun took a small notebook and Mont Blanc pen from the inside pocket of his suit coat. He scribbled something, tore off the sheet of paper, and gave it to Yosef after folding it one time.

Yosef looked at it before slipping the paper into his pocket. The name meant nothing to him, and the phone number had an odd prefix he could not associate with any district. The strangest thing, however, was the word surrounded by quotation marks at the bottom of the paper. '*Baashert*', an old Yiddish word meaning 'destined'. He assumed it was a code of some kind.

The men left one by one, in prearranged order, the Minister first, Yosef Kettler last. Of them all, only Minister Yaroun smiled as he got into his Mercedes. He knew Yosef Kettler better than Yosef knew himself. They had collaborated during the sixty-seven war with Egypt, when Yosef's industrial empire helped thwart war shipments to Egypt, diverting them to the State of Israel. If anyone could bring a supply of energy to Israel, Yosef could. Yaroun knew Yosef wanted one last chance to leave a legacy to the State he helped create. He only wondered how far Yosef would go to get the job done.

CHAPTER 5

THE Suburban passed a "Jordan taxi" on the road descending into Cairo like it was standing still. The black and white Fiat had boxes and suitcases stacked on top at least eight feet high, making it appear precariously top-heavy. Jake had gotten stuck for about two hours at the Ahmed Hamdy tunnel that goes under the Suez Canal. Traffic flow through the tunnel was efficient for a number of years, until salt water began leaking into it. Since then, the authorities closed it at night, and traffic crept through one way at a time during the day.

An hour past the tunnel, and eight hours since the bomb went off, Jake passed the butane bottling plant four miles outside Cairo. The city beneath him was trying to emerge from a cloud of pollution that rivaled the world's worst. Within minutes he dropped three hundred feet from the eastern desert down the Mokattam bluff into the Nile valley. Like Mexico City or Los Angeles, the topographic low that followed the Nile here concentrated the effluent of cars, factories, and burning rubbish. Visibility was under a quarter mile.

Jake turned off the autostrade and traveled down one of Maadi's newer streets. Completed as a four-lane road less than three months ago, it was already reduced to two crooked lanes by large piles of dirt, bricks, and other debris dumped by trucks during the night. Every new expat arriving in Maadi had the impression of a war zone. After a couple of months, they hardly noticed the filth and disorder. After a year, they accepted the mess as normal.

Looking up from changing the CD, Jake swerved to avoid a wild *baladi* dog. Dog packs terrorized the community, threatening rabies with every growl. Every few months the local police would go on a 'shoot' to clean them out of the neighborhood. Each time they culled the wild dog population they killed a few pets along with the *baladi* dogs.

Finally Jake swung into the driveway of his villa, parking under the flame tree, or Royal Poincietta, which had just dropped the last of its red flowers. He walked down a path made of limestone blocks, between hibiscus and bougainvillea, to the patio. It always amazed him that his walk was built of the same stone as the pyramids, quarried from the Mokattam hills through which he had just drove. Close up, one could see the inch long foraminifera fossils, representing a bloom of sea life thirty million years ago. His home was a picturesque two-story stone structure with a wrought iron balcony crowning the entrance. Built during the British heyday, it was beautifully landscaped with flowers bordering sidewalks that meandered through the property. There was a large stone terrace off the back of the house that was great for entertaining but was currently overtaken by Little Tykes toys. This terrace was the domain of his daughter, Augusta, whom everyone called Gussie.

"Daddy!" yelled Gussie as he entered the front door.

The ten year old ran flat out across the living room and flung her arms around her father.

"I missed you."

Luckily, Gussie was small boned and slight, with an appetite befitting a mouse. Her long blond hair swung back and forth as he hugged her.

Layla called from the top of the stairs. "Hello, Mister Jake."

Layla, in her long galabeya and head covering, looked like millions of Muslim women in Cairo, but her grasp of the English language and knowledge of western families made her completely different. She began working for western families when she was seven, and had spent her entire life in the employ of American households. She learned English from the children of those households when she was very young, and spoke and understood it like few non-native speakers. She had been with Jake since he and Paula arrived in Egypt, became a confidant to Gussie before Paula died, and was now her de facto mother. Layla was a skillful cook, did the laundry, and cleaned to an acceptable level if you didn't look too close. Her real gift was keeping the house running smoothly, and keeping Gussie in line. Gussie was precocious and tough to rein in, but Layla found that Gussie was skilled at cooking and loved to help make dinner.

Jake studied her coming down the stairs, her rotund frame ambling along in a very efficient manner considering its breadth. Her sumptuous cooking was something not even she could resist.

The permanent smile on her plump face was contagious. As she descended, Layla was telling Jake what had gone on over the weekend, but got cut off by Gussie who talked so fast he could barely follow.

"Daddy, guess what happened? I won the chess tournament in school. I beat Andy Harper in the last round. Isn't that great?"

"That's super Gus. I knew you could do it."

"And guess what else? I've got a sleep over tonight."

"Just a second partner. Who said you could go on a sleep over? Where is it?"

Jake pretended to be stern, while winking at Layla, who was genuinely pleased watching him interact with his daughter. Gussie was very bright but a bit socially awkward. Jake was inwardly ecstatic that she had a sleepover.

"It's at Sarah's house Daddy. Layla said it would be OK."

"Well then OK Gus. On one condition. That you give your ole' dad another hug."

With that she again plunged herself into his waiting arms. "Are you packed yet?"

"Not yet" she laughed as she ran up the steps. He had been gone only two weeks but it seemed as though Gussie had grown in that short time.

"Mister Jake you need to call Mister Barney," Layla added.

Barney Wilcrow was Jake's boss, the head of the local office. They had worked on and off together for most of their careers, starting out in Casper Wyoming during a boom in the oil industry.

Jake had always been the scientist. He had resisted management, which he regarded as a graveyard for incompetents. He preferred the field but also fiddled with computers after they came along. Jake knew his strengths and knew what he loved.

Barney took the other road. The yellow brick road to stock options and three martini lunches. Although he wasn't as bright as Jake, he had overtaken his friend and contemporary. Maybe a result of his management lifestyle, Barney had become round, bald, and old looking.

Jake remembered being in the middle of Wyoming when Barney decided to deviate from geology. They had been driving across the Wind River Basin, heading for what was to become Jake's fourth discovery well in a row. They were kidding about their boss, Darrell Darkin. Old 'D-squared' had burned out decades before they met him. Rumor had it he could once find oil. By the time they worked with him, he was limited to finding the corner bar and another glass of scotch.

When Barney said he was accepting a promotion to supervisor in Midland, Jake predicted he would transform into a D-squared clone.

They both laughed for miles, telling management jokes. Nevertheless, Barney had gone to Midland, then Odessa, then Houston, Fort Worth, and Cairo. He would no doubt retire to a more materialistic existence than Jake.

'Maybe,' thought Jake, 'I should have taken Barney's road'.

He thought about his recent career. It had been a while since he discovered anything. All his prospects out of Fort Worth came up dry. His years in Cairo had been worse. But that was the nature of the business, he kept telling himself.

Layla brought Jake back to the present.

"Mister Jake, you need to call Mister Barney. He said it is very, very important."

"It might could take a number," Jake drawled, impersonating Barney's west Texas accent and idiomatic speech.

"First I'm gonna take me a bath. Then I'm gonna eat me a real Amurican breakfast. Then I'm gonna take me a nap. And then, lady, if I can muster 'nuf energy, I'll go an' call Barney."

Layla was frustrated.

"He said it was really, really important."

Jake thought perhaps it was a 'security thing'. While he was gone, someone blew up another car in front of the main Misr Bank downtown. He had already scanned the US Embassy security report delivered by his assistant, which Layla had placed on the table by the front door. Several groups of Islamic fundamentalists were wreaking havoc with the economy while vying for power. They warned foreigners to stay away. That seemed to be the only part of the plan working.

For expatriates, it was a mixed blessing. A bit scary, but also convenient. Hotels on the Red Sea were empty, and ran deep discounts for foreign residents. Jake and a group of guys liked to head to the southern tip of the Sinai to scuba dive. Few tourists meant they could rent a dive boat at a good price.

The threats had progressed, however, to a worrying degree. A terrorist group out of Afghanistan had recently warned foreign businesses to stay out of Egypt. Incredibly most of the violence had so far been against Egyptian citizens. But sooner or later it was inevitable an American company or executive would be victimized.

"OK, OK." Jake muttered to himself, dropping the drawl. "The sooner I call, the sooner I can relax."

He dialed the office quickly, hoping no one would answer. It rang only once.

"Reacher Oil. Good morning."

"Hello Nagla. Get me Barney on the phone please."

"Just a minute, Mr. Tillard," said Nagla.

"Wilcrow." Back in the Wyoming days, Barney had not minced words. His foray into management only exacerbated his tendency for brevity.

"Barney, Jake." He could match his old friend in pithiness. "I can't come in now. I've been in the field for two weeks. I'm disgustingly filthy. I'm distraught over the bomb thing and Dusty. I need sleep."

"Jake, come in now. I've got some bad news."

Layla was around enough to know something was up when he put down the phone. She was half American by now, and counted on him to keep up with the outside world. The world beyond what the Egyptian government wanted the locals to know.

"What's wrong, Mr. Jake?"

"I don't know. He wouldn't say over the phone. But he said it was bad news. Could you stay with Gussie for another hour or two, please Layla? I'll call the Gleasons and bring Gussie over a little later."

On the way out, he shed his work shirt on the bedroom floor and donned a clean golf shirt. The office was only two miles away, and the Mercedes covered the distance in no time.

Twenty company expatriates lived in-country, working with over a thousand Egyptian nationals. The expats worked long, hard hours. The nationals did not. Management occupied the original company building, where Jake parked. It was a grand old villa circled by a high wall with bougainvillea creeping along the top. The grounds were well kept, with plenty of trees, and a few old Royal palms trying to maintain a semblance of a row along the south wall.

As the company had put oil fields into production and added staff, the bulk of the technical work moved to a drab six-story building down the street. Most management spent at least half their time there, but it was still nice to be able to retreat to 'the country club,' as they referred to the head office.

The office was nearly deserted. It was a public holiday. Walking into his boss's office, he began looking at pictures on the wall, which he had never studied. A couple contained images of Jake, but most were photos of Barney with dignitaries. One showed him with an older gentleman on a hillside, an Israeli flag in the background. Jake recalled that Barney had worked in Israel before. The man looked familiar, but he couldn't place him.

"Jake, have a drink."

Barney walked in, poured a couple of Bourbons, and handed one to Jake. Embedded in an Islamic culture, Jake knew something was very serious for Barney to be pouring alcohol.

"You and I go back a long way," he drawled.

The pause that followed told Jake this was not a security thing. It was personal. Barney sat on a leather chair facing Jake, his weight causing him to sink lower.

"I've been through this durn thang every which way fur a week. Ain't no good way to say it."

Barney paused and stared down at his plump hands as he fiddled nervously with an oversized ring

"Just spit it out, Barney. What the hell is up?"

They both stood, bourbons in hand. Barney walked over to Jake, reaching up to put his hand on Jake's shoulder.

"Son, your department's bein' eliminated."

In France they say 'un ange passe'. The equivalent of a pregnant pause. The quiet was deafening.

He stared straight at Barney, waiting for something else. He knew the layoff, or rationalization as HR called it, was coming. The Corporation was under pressure to boost earnings and support the stock price. Unfortunately they were doing it by cutting off their best bet for future growth, once again going for the Exploration Department jugular. Then of course there was the Egypt 'thing'.

This was the third time the ax would fall in six years. The first one, when he was in Houston, hit exploration hard, and thirty percent of the department was sent packing. The second one was more fairly distributed, with the exception of the corporate office, which got by again mostly with incentivized early retirements. Of course no one at the very top of the house left. Including the sixty-nine year old COO. Jake wondered how Exploration would fare this time around.

Barney misinterpreted Jake's silence. He had seen this before. The receiver of bad news simply shuts down. The news does not get processed. Barney knew it was still his ball.

"Jake, I got me a fax from the states. I been on the phone with ever one I thought might could help. Bottom line is the company's just doin' away with exploration. The whole dang lot. It just don't pay to look for oil anymore. There's too much of it around, too much on the world market. Too many new countries like Brazil in the game. The price is just too low."

Jake remained silent. He needed to think. He needed to process what had been said.

"God damned," he said, walking toward the window staring out at the maze of buildings and disarray that made up the Cairo skyline, "God damned."

That was all that came out. He paced over to the bookcase and picked up a baseball sized Lucite cube. One of Barney's many mementos of projects he'd worked. It had a tear shaped cavity inside with black oil.

"It's been too long, Barney. The Sinai is gonna pan out. You know it's a good play."

Barney shifted his eyes away. That seemed out of character to Jake. Barney's response took a bit too long.

"Jake, I'm not with you on this one. It's ram pasture, son. Or goat pasture in this case."

Barney had been a big supporter of what Jake was doing out east. This reversal perplexed Jake.

"Shit Barney. Where are they sending me?"

Barney looked at Jake with penetrating eyes.

"I don't know. I asked 'bout other locations, but it's the same everwhere. Haven't found a home for ya yet buddy."

Jake looked out the window again before wheeling around and throwing the little plastic cube across the room. It hit the picture he had been looking at, glass shattering into dozens of shards that dropped onto the carpet. He sat back down.

Neither of them spoke for several minutes. Jake pushed his right hand threw his hair. In spite of his reaction, he realized that he wasn't surprised. After laying off a dozen geologists himself in the last three rounds, he was disillusioned with the whole game. The reengineering, the cost cutting, the Continuous Improvement, the race to please the investment analysts. Lots of words with lots of meetings. And little substance. This was the weariness he had seen in the mirror in Aswan.

"What about the Venture LLC deal? Kathleen was so interested. I got an email a week ago that sounded pretty positive."

"You been in the field, so you wouldna' heard. They came back and said they warn't interested. Somethin' 'bout the wrong fit. I guess that little lady didn't punch her own weight."

"Maybe sleeping with her would've helped," Jake said.

Barney just looked at him.

"So what's exactly happening Barney?"

"Well, all seven of your direct reports are bein' let go. I already gave notice to the contractors to end your Sinai seismic program. Next week you'll need to terminate your other two exploration ventures. I been instructed in no uncertain terms to tell each worker not to show up at the office past today. You know. Confidentiality reasons."

"You didn't tell them yet, did you?"

"Yesterday."

Jake was irritated. He was the senior Exploration man in country, and it was his place to tell his staff. But then he'd been out of touch, and he could hardly expect the world to wait for him.

"Barney, it's my job to tell them."

"Couldn't wait. Global coordination."

Jake's mind was running through the alternatives, but his impulsiveness quickly won.

"Barney, I quit."

Barney put up a weak attempt to talk him out of it. Jake wasn't listening, already thinking about alternatives and options facing him and Gussie. He had some savings built up, but not enough to pack it in. Especially not with raising Gussie, putting her through college, and funding what he hoped was a long and active retirement. While assessing options, he lost track of the fact that Barney was talking.

"Please let Doris and me help. We both feel very bad. Whatever you need, you just ask."

Barney just stared at him.

"We'll help you pack out, of course. If you need help with Gussie, Doris is ready."

"What's the timing?"

"You should vacate the office immediately. Like all your guys. But in terms of packing out, that's up to you. The package this time is pretty much like last time, so you know it well. Hank'll fill you in on the details and your personal situation."

Hank was the local HR guy. Nice enough, but in Jake's eyes just another piece of Corporate overhead dragging down profits.

Instead of going to see Hank, he went to the local watering hole to find his flock. Not many were there, but the couple guys he talked to had worn themselves out talking about the latest turn of fate. He drove home an hour later, even more tired.

When Jake got home again he found Layla hard at work preparing dinner, perspiration evident on her flushed face. He looked at her for a while, distracted by the 'whoop – whoosh, whoop – whoosh of the ceiling fan, rotating unevenly overhead.

"I need to talk to you, Layla?"

"Sure Mr. Jake. What you need?"

"Well," he swallowed, "I have bad news. The company is doing away with exploration." He paused, not wanting to say the next part. "Gussie and I will have to move back to the States." She rushed to sit down, and looked up at him. "But Mr. Jake, why?"

The heavyset woman was visibly shaken. Jake knew that she had grown close to each of the three expat families she had worked for before. Each of them had young girls as well. Layla had told him when he hired her that it became more difficult when each family left. But he sensed this time was proving to be even worse for her. He saw large tears well up in her eyes before she averted her gaze down.

"I'm very, very sorry, Layla. I don't know what else I can say."

"I will never work for an expat family again," she said between sobs. "I can't. When you leave, it will be like my arm is cut off." She covered her face with her hands, the tears breaking through.

He knew it would be a major decision for her not to continue working with expat families. A decision that would have major consequences to her family income and lifestyle. But he knew she was stubborn, and wouldn't put it past her.

He'd forgotten about Gussie's sleepover, but found her packed and ready to go. Jake couldn't tell her the news tonight, so he drove her over to the Gleason's.

Later that afternoon, gin and tonic in hand, he phoned his dad in Montana. Marv was sympathetic and supportive, and Jake realized it was great to have someone just listen.

"I knew you'd quit Reacher sooner or later, son. I'm surprised you lasted this long. When will you move?"

"Soon. Maybe a couple weeks. Let Gussie finish the first term. Then leave for Christmas. I can probably get the air shipment into Houston in early January. The ocean shipment might get there in March. What a mess. This is not what we need, dad. It's been hard lately."

"Yea. Spend Christmas here, OK?"

"I'd like that. But I'll have to spend some time in Houston getting squared away."

"Want me to keep Augusta for a while?"

"Maybe. Maybe not. We're gonna need each other."

"Why don't you bring Layla back with ya? I'm sure that granddaughter of mine would love that."

"Good idea dad. I'll give it some thought. I'm not sure she'd come. And I'm not sure how I'd do it."

"Well, you'll figure it out son. You've always made good decisions. Hang in there."

Jake hung up and took a long sip of his drink. Gussie was still young enough that the mid-school year move wouldn't affect her academically. Emotionally it was a different matter. Most of the other families leaving had older kids. It would be harder on them.

That night Barney met with Dick Steer, the US Ambassador to Egypt, at his home within the Embassy compound.

"Is it done Barney?"

"Yes sir. Jake actually made it simpler than I expected. He quit."

"Not surprising. That boy's gotta bit of a temper and he's altogether too ethical for international work. Well, that's one obstacle out of the way. You stay in the background, OK?"

"Yes sir."

CHAPTER 6

FOUR days later Jake made one last drive to the Sinai, to pick up his things. Coming out of the tunnel beneath the Canal, he left the African continent behind, and entered the barren, rugged Sinai. Its jagged, crimson mountains rose in the distance. Driving over Mitla Pass, he realized how much he loved the desert of this ancient land.

The view from the pass was stunning, the road weaving through miles of limestone and sandstone hills, their eroded shapes creating a surreal image. The hues were subdued, the shapes gently curving, like a Dali landscape. In ten minutes, he dropped down onto the flat desert plain that stretched a hundred miles ahead to Taba. Every so often, a row of trees snaked away, marking an underground water course.

Further east, closer to his field area, splotches of grass and wild flowers appeared, their vivid colors contrasting with the sandy desert floor. In one week the entire palette had changed, courtesy of the storm he had lived through. Interminable brown was now dotted with subtle green.

"Wow," he said aloud. Content to be back in the desert after the events of the last week, he felt calm again.

Mohammed was waiting for him at the usual place. It took only two or three minutes for the Bedouin to determine something was bothering Jake.

"What is difficult?" he asked in Arabic.

'Perceptive son-of-a-bitch,' thought Jake, 'all I need is a Bedouin psychoanalyst.'

Jake tried explaining the layoff to Mohammed, who had never experienced long-term employment, the corporate world, or anything other than personal freedom.

"*Malesh*" he said. 'So what.'

"Still living in your tin box?"

"*Aywa*, when I'm here."

Mohammed's 'home' was an old mud-logging trailer set beneath an Acacia tree. The first time Jake had seen it, he thought it was a good omen. The trailer had been used by an oil company maybe thirty years ago to monitor the drilling progress of wells, recording any concentrations of oil or gas as the bit dug deeper and deeper. These days, mud loggers crammed their trailers full of high tech, computer-driven analytical equipment. Back twenty or thirty years, they weren't so sophisticated. Nevertheless, it was highly unusual for anyone to leave one lying around.

One thing bugged Jake about the trailer. No well had been drilled in this area, at least according to the maps and records that he'd been able to find. Jake assumed the trailer had been abandoned while being transported during the outbreak of one of the wars.

Inside, Mohammed insisted on making tea. He took a roll of paper and ripped off about two feet to serve as a tablecloth, then set two glasses of tea on the paper. The clear small glasses with no handles were so hot from the boiling tea that Jake knew better than to lift his. He looked at it, stared a while, mesmerized by the wisps of steam rising from the tea.

Jake's eyes became unfocused and got that glassy look that had become commonplace during the past week. When they finally refocused, they drifted to the paper tablecloth. He became intrigued by the pattern of graph paper with a faint thin line squirreling its way through it. There was a handwritten date on the paper next to the thin line, 19 May 1967. Fascinated, he slowly lifted his eyebrows.

"Mohammed, where'd you get this paper?"

"In a box. I used some. There's enough left for years."

"Can I see what's left?"

Mohammed dragged a grungy box out from a small closet. Inside were four rolls of graph paper. At the beginning of each roll was a handwritten name. '*Um Haga*'. 'Mother of All'.

"What's interesting, my friend?" Mohammed asked with the glib curiosity he reserved for things foreigners found so interesting, yet to him seemed so dull.

"This house of yours is an old trailer used by geologists when they drill wells. These papers record measurements taken while the well was drilling. As the well got deeper, the mud used to lubricate the drill bit circulated to the bottom of the hole and back. When it reached the top, it was put through a machine to see if any gas or oil was in it. The thin line here records any hydrocarbons encountered."

Mohammed was an intelligent man. Nevertheless, Jake could tell he had no idea of what he was saying.

"The funny thing is our records don't show a well drilled here ever."

"The Israelis were here in the sixties."

"Yes, I know. But did they drill wells out here? There's no record....." his voice trailed off as he considered this.

Jake took a quick look at several areas of the rolls, and the thin line never strayed very far from the zero mark.

'A typical Sinai well,' thought Jake, 'not a sniff of oil.'

Apart from the tiny Sadot gas field close to the border with Gaza, the Sinai had given little indication of having oil or gas. Prospectors for some time had given it their best shot, and a few had tried to make something scientific out of the 'Burning Bush' story in the Bible. Their theory was a naturally occurring methane leak had been set on fire, giving the impression of unnatural combustion. The gas may have leaked up a geologic fault zone, not unlike the San Andreas in California. They tried to use Biblical geography and modern geology and satellite imagery to prospect.

Mohammed looked at Jake with a very serious expression as he loaded the rolls of paper into Jake's hands

"You take them. You'll know what they mean. And you'll know what to do with them."

"*Shukran.* Thank you."

He had no need for the rolls but didn't want to offend Mohammed by rejecting his offer. In reality they were more unwanted baggage. More crap to haul around. He took them to his car, planning to get rid of them in Cairo.

The charts landed on the rear seat, and bounced onto the floor of the Suburban, coming to rest next to the spare water bottles. Jake could not foresee the changes this gesture of Mohammed's would bring. To him. To the Bedouin. And to the world around them.

CHAPTER 7

HUMIDITY swelled the air. The gray sky had little trace of the blue that should have been there. Jake had driven only fifteen miles in the last hour, battling morning traffic on "The Loop".

Jake hated commuting by car, preferring the bus or train. Other cities had mass transit that worked. Why not Houston? City planners tried buses but no one rode them. They tried HOV lanes but almost no one used them. Every few years they discussed light rail, and though city officials took boondoggle trips to inspect rail systems in places like Germany, nothing ever materialized. Commuters lost out, and now those commuters included Jake.

Finally he crawled down the exit ramp, eyes glued to the brake lights in front of him. He tore his eyes free long enough to catch sight of his destination, an office building just past the Galleria shopping center.

Five months out of Cairo he was well practiced for his twenty-first job interview. The economy stank and the industry was stagnant, but he had multiple degrees from prestigious universities and years of practical experience.

Jake experienced all the routine transition stages after his termination. He was a textbook case. Initial euphoria from a sudden sense of freedom, accompanied by an intense optimism fueled with perceptions of endless opportunity. This was followed by depression caused by rejection and self-examination. The ennui that settled in next was a mental game his subconscious constructed to balance the two. Several weeks ago, he moved into a final psychology that stuck with him. Maybe it was the time he spent with Gussie. For whatever reason, he regained confidence, reassessed his value structure, and firmed up an action plan. He knew he could find oil and gas, and he set out to convince someone to help him do it.

About that time he also took stock of his physical condition. Since Cairo he had put on twenty pounds, which even his six foot three inch frame could not hide. He joined a health club and used it every morning after dropping Gussie at school. He relished those drives with his daughter, when they talked about amazing things. One moment they might be sharing observations about things like the shapes of clouds or people's heads. Another, Gussie might be talking about her dreams to become a doctor or an engineer. Jake could not predict what she would end up doing. Gussie excelled at math and was wildly creative at the same time. She was full of optimism and seemed to possess insights far beyond her years.

The Impala almost steered itself into the underground parking lot, stopping next to a black Jaguar with the license plate TEX-MEX. He sat pondering whether the owner made his fortune in Mexican food, or Mexican drugs.

An art deco aluminum-lined elevator took him up two stories to the lobby where a directory sitting on a podium indicated that Webber Oil was on the thirtieth floor, two from the top. Still early, the elevator was empty except for three girls going to the thirty-first. His ears popped on the way up.

Webber Oil's office was decorated with Western art, both traditional and modern. The reception area showed off a half dozen bronzes, including two Remingtons, and a number of paintings, one a Bierstadt of Yellowstone. In the far corner stood a six-foot tall pair of pink and turquoise ceramic cowboy boots. The receptionist stopped speaking into a headset, and offered her help.

"Mr. Webber, please," said Jake.

"Yes sir. You must be Mr. Tillard. Please have a seat. Would you care for coffee?"

"Thanks, black."

Jake preferred milk and sugar, but found most people who considered themselves westerners didn't trust you if you drank your coffee other than black. He wandered, examining the artwork, and wondering if the entire collection was here, or if it continued throughout the office.

"Ah, Mr. Tillard."

The impish little man joined him while inspecting the Bierstadt canvas.

"You are a connoisseur?"

"Not really." Jake paused for a moment. "Mr. Webber?"

"No sir. My name is Arnie Teller. Mr. Webber's personal assistant. I'll take you to his office."

"Please," Jake replied.

Artwork continued down the hall, spilling into Webber's office. The best was obviously here. Arnie Teller said Jack Webber would be along directly, and left Jake to enjoy the art. Walking over to a Remington bronze of horses rearing, he noticed the detail, right down to the intertwined mass of rattlesnakes that had done the spooking.

Jake's eyes moved to a half dozen diplomas arranged on one wall. 'Son of a gun', he thought, 'we are fellow alums'. The University of Montana diploma was almost twenty years older than his, but the coincidence made him think. When Webber entered, Jake was sitting in one of the overstuffed leather chairs. He rose and introduced himself.

"I know who you are, Jake. I heard you speak at a conference a few years back. Even tried discreetly to hire you. But that was back when times were better."

Jake remembered when headhunters would call, anxious to yank him out of his job and deliver him to other employers. Boy had times changed.

"I hope you don't mind coming down here. I wanted us to meet. I'll tell you up front I have no job for you. In fact, I'm struggling right now to keep the company cash flow positive."

"Well, that takes the pressure off," Jake shrugged.

"I don't even look at resumes for exploration people anymore," Jack said. "But your resume got mixed in with a pile vying for our analyst position. Maybe your MBA caught somebody's attention, I don't know. Anyhow I noticed your name and took a look. You've got a gaggle of degrees and a pretty impressive career. You having any luck finding your next role?"

"None at all. Twenty-one interviews so far, and no bites."

"I'm surprised you got that many people to give you the time of day."

"Well, like you said. My resume's impressive."

"Why d'ya leave Reacher?"

"They did away with exploration," Jake said simply.

"They lay you off?"

"Actually I quit. They might have put me somewhere else in the company. But I guess I was pissed off."

"A bit impulsive, don't you think?"

"Maybe. I suppose that's a trait of mine. Along with a general lack of patience."

"Well, at least you consider it a trait and not a problem."

"I suppose that's why it's still a trait I possess." Jake chuckled.

"How's your dad," Jack changed the subject naturally. "I knew him at the university. Fellow Griz. We weren't best friends, but we used to fish some. I sort of remember you from back then. Weren't you a bit of a hellion in high school."

"I did worry my mom some."

"It took some to worry that woman."

Jake began to put together the connection.

"Dad's fine. Since mom died ten years ago, he's pretty much stuck to the ranch. You know, in between ranching he fishes, hunts, keeps to himself."

"Where's the ranch again?"

"The Bitterroot Valley south of Missoula, near Hamilton."

"No wonder he stays put," Jack's eyes twinkled. "I'm envious. God's country for sure."

"It is. I grew up there. The ranch was tough at times, especially in winter. But it taught us values."

Jake thought about his dad, tough as nails, with a sense of justice that didn't tolerate anything other than Christian ideals. His mother was the perfect complement. Loving, forgiving, and fiercely protective of him and his two brothers. He thought how hard it must have been for her growing up in relative wilderness surrounded by tough men.

He remembered when he was eight, how his mother dealt with the wrath of a drunken ranch hand. Drinking was not allowed on the ranch. The man was drunk and out of control in the barn. When his mother came in, the drunk was swinging a chain at another worker. Although she didn't know it yet, the other cowboy had broken up a fight between the drunk and Jake's oldest brother, then fourteen. The chain might have ripped the man's head off had his mom not driven a pitchfork clear through the drunk's thigh, pinning his leg to the barn wall. Not stopping there, she saved his life by then hitting him on the head with a shovel to knock him out, so she could unstick him from the wall, put a tourniquet on the leg, and drive him to a doctor.

Jake learned to protect himself in a wilderness environment. Did his share of fishing and hunting. Developed the ability to respond to unexpected crises. Jack's voice snapped him out of his fog.

"I grew up in Minnesota, but fell in love with your home state during college. The two have a lot in common, but you can't beat the Rockies."

They talked for almost an hour. About Montana. About the oil industry. About families and life in general.

When Jack had to head to a meeting, Jake left the office confused. Thinking about his Montana roots and his career with a large company, there was a disconnect he could not get his head around. He had been looking for another job but Webber made him realize there was another option. For some reason, he felt lighter going down in the elevator than he had in a long while.

He decided to spend some time alone before heading home. Maybe the artwork in Webber's office inspired him, but he was surprised when he pulled up to the Menil Collection. It had been years since he was there.

Put together by Dominique de Menil and her late husband John, the collection was a wonderful mélange of world art. Western Masters including the impressionists, Picasso, and other Europeans. Primitives ranging from Inuit and totem makers of North America, to tribes of Papua New Guinea. It also included Christian icons from the communist bloc, and a large Cy Twombly exhibit.

Moving room to room, he looked at but didn't see the collection, his mind preoccupied with what he wanted out of life. A parallel began to form in his mind between pieces in the museum and his dreams. It suddenly dawned on him why he liked this museum. Quite simply, he loved the variety, and realized his aspirations were similar. He knew he was a happy person. He knew he liked different

things. Like a brick aside the head, it suddenly struck him that he
liked almost everything, as long as it all flowed past in rapid eddies
and whirlpools. He craved variety and the excitement of discovery.
He couldn't foresee how significantly the afternoon would play into
this need.

CHAPTER 8

MIDDAY heat and humidity hit him on the way out the door. Although only a few puffy white cumulus clouds had dotted the sky before he entered the museum, a huge thunderstorm now occupied the northwest sky. Easing into traffic on I45, he pointed the Impala towards the cloud. The first drops hit as he pulled into his driveway twenty minutes later. Power walking the thirty feet from the garage to the back door made him soaked.

Jake remembered the first thunderstorm after returning from Egypt. Gussie woke up terrified and ran screaming to his bed. She'd never seen a thunderstorm before. In all the years in Egypt it only drizzled twice.

He also remembered Layla's reaction to the thunder. Occupying the guesthouse above the garage, she had come running into the main house, her face as white as her headscarf. He'd had to calm them both down.

Jake had been surprised at how quickly Layla agreed to move to Houston with them. She loved Gussie and was quite interested in an adventure to the great United States of America. He'd also been surprised at how easy it was to obtain a three-year visa for her. She had proven herself a godsend in helping Gussie settle into Houston and in keeping the household running.

A bright flash was followed immediately by a very loud crack. The discharge must have been within a few hundred yards. Gussie hugged him.

"Did that one scare you, kiddo?" Jake looked down reassuringly at his daughter.

"Uh-huh."

"It was pretty close."

"Did it hit our house, daddy?"

"No, but it was close. Maybe when it stops raining we can take a walk and see if it hit anything near here."

"Will it come that close again?"

"I don't think so pumpkin. You know what they say. Lightning never strikes the same place twice."

"Do you mean if I know where it hit, I could stand there and be safe?"

"That's what they say. But they're wrong. I'd rather stay in our house where it's dry and safe."

Gussie gave him another hug.

"Did you get a job?" she asked.

"No but how about playing a game with me."

"OK. How about some coloring?"

"That's a deal. I'll get us something to drink. You set it up."

Jake came back with two Brown Cows in tall glasses, the frosted kind with the Carousel ponies dancing around the sides. When they were in Egypt they couldn't get root beer or reliable ice cream, and the treat of both hadn't worn off yet for either of them. Gussie rolled out a very long piece of paper about a foot wide, diligently colored for at least fifteen feet.

"Come on Dad, let's color."

"What's this Gussie?"

"This is my scroll. Remember, like those dead ones we saw in the museum."

Gussie appeared a bit exasperated with her dad and huffed as she painstakingly unrolled her scroll across the floor.

"You mean the Dead Sea Scrolls in Israel?"

"Yeah those ones. In the round building."

A few months before leaving Egypt they drove to Jerusalem for a short vacation. In the Israeli Museum, they saw the Dead Sea manuscripts, displayed around the perimeter of a circular room. It surprised Jake that Gussie remembered.

"But where did you get this one?"

"Layla gave it to me in Egypt. It came out of one of my boxes. I just started coloring it."

Jake got down, picked up a green crayon, and began to color where Gussie had left off. He realized this was one of the mud logs he had gotten from Mohammed in the Sinai. He thought he had thrown them all out but apparently Layla packed this one into Gussie's boxes.

'Well,' he thought, 'at least one will go to good use.'

He continued the job of putting green between the line, which indicated total gas, and the base line of the chart. Glancing down the roll, he noticed in the distance there was more green towards the end. The depth numbers indicated that end was deeper in the hole. Gussie was fairly meticulous in her coloring, usually staying between the lines. Intrigued, he rolled over a few times to get himself down to that part of the chart. Sure enough, she had stayed between the same two lines. The chart recorded a gas increase, something Jake hadn't seen when he unrolled part of the chart in the Sinai. He looked farther down and saw the green expand more, matched by the appearance of blue, red, and pink. He crawled down further, unrolling the chart to the end.

"Daddy, you're not coloring. What are you doing down there? You need to color up here with me."

"Just a minute, Gus."

Jake studied the curves and cocked his head. He knew these logs were old, but the methodology hadn't changed much since the 60's. If he was reading them right, the curves documented not only a gas show, but gas that was rich in heavier hydrocarbons, butane through pentane. Each of Gussie's colors showed a component richer in valuable natural gas liquids than methane. This meant there might be some liquids dissolved in with the gas. That would raise the BTU content and make the gas worth more. There might even be oil. He looked for a scale explaining the curves, but there wasn't one.

'Well, what do you know,' thought Jake. 'Gas in the Sinai.'

Jake had convinced Reacher Oil to explore for gas in the center of the Sinai four years before the company terminated him. Barney had supported the idea in the beginning but had cooled off near the end. Jake headed the project himself, and directed the efforts of a staff which at one time reached ten company people and as many as fifty contractors. They did geologic fieldwork for two years. They ran two extensive seismic programs to image the rock layers underground. They were supposed to drill three wells, but they pulled the plug when the company did away with wildcat exploration.

Now here he was, looking at proof of hydrocarbons in the Sinai. He chuckled, feeling a sense of personal vindication.

Gussie wandered over just as he was laughing.

"What's funny daddy?" asked Gussie with a worried look.

"Nothing, Gus."

"But you're laughing at my coloring."

"Oh, no I'm not. Your coloring is great. Perfect. I was just thinking of something that happened a long time ago. Back when there were dinosaurs."

He picked up the blue crayon and continued to color. Gussie was used to her dad talking about dinosaurs, so she just smiled and picked up a crayon. His mind drifted back to Mohammed, remembering the sadness in the Bedouin's eyes, and remembering his words, "You take them. You'll know what they mean. And you'll know what to do with them."

Jake put down the crayon, and looked at Gussie. He went to the other end of the roll, and looked at the header, finding a key to the curves. Folding the paper just below the header, he took the top of the log down to the bottom of the roll, where he had been coloring blue. When he lined the two up, he could read the values of the curves.

"My God," he said, "it can't be."

"What's wrong, Daddy," Gussie asked. She seemed worried again.

"Nothing, sweet pea," he said in a daze. Gussie continued to look at him. He was entranced.

The header indicated a compressed scale on this log, compared with what was typically used on modern logs. Only a small deviation indicated a fairly large presence of gas. It made sense when he thought about it. Thirty years ago, companies did not want natural gas in places like the Sinai. It had no value. In fact, the government did not allow foreign companies to produce gas for a profit. They looked for oil only. Gas shows were a nuisance.

Jake went to his computer and searched the date on the log. This well was drilled during the late part of the Israeli occupation. The

Israelis had rapidly built up certain parts of the Sinai. They threw up buildings and small settlements wherever they found enough water to irrigate. They sucked oil out of the Gulf of Suez fields as fast as they could. Certainly, they did not want to bother with gas in the middle of the Sinai, on land they might not be able to keep long term.

"Gussie," he said. "I figured out why no one has produced my gas field."

The little girl looked at him with curious eyes, expecting some type of explanation. Her dad was acting strange, in her opinion.

"The Sinai didn't belong to the Egyptians when this well was drilled. The Israelis drilled it, and didn't want the gas. No one in Egypt knows this well was ever drilled. No one knows there is a gas field there."

He paused, his daughter still staring at him.

"I wonder if anyone in Israel remembers?"

The curiosity in his daughter's eyes faded quickly, and she headed off in pursuit of something more fun to do. She had seen her dad absorbed in nonsensical, non-fun things like this before, and wanted no part of it.

Jake read the total gas curve. It was in units, a non-standard calibration unlike the parts per million used today. By rough calculation, he figured the bottom of the well was taking in over 200,000 ppm total gas. The well was almost blowing out.

"Gussie, can I keep this log," Jake asked.

But Gussie had long since fled.

"Gussie," he shouted.

She came back into the room.

"Can I keep this log," he asked again.

"You mean my scroll," she corrected, frowning.

"Yes sweetie, this scroll."

"But I haven't finished it yet. I wanted to finish coloring it before I gave it to you."

"I love it just like it is. Please, may I keep it?"

"OK but I need to finish coloring."

"OK Gus. Help me roll it up. You can finish later."

They carefully rolled up the paper, with the header of the log rolled last, and on the outside. Jake read off the well name, '*Um Haga*'. He remembered reading that name in Mohammed's trailer, along with the date, 19 December 1967. He wrote down the latitude and longitude on a piece of paper, finished rolling the log, and put a rubber band around it. With Gussie two steps behind, he walked down to his office.

He put the log on his desk and went over to the old metal file cabinet he had bought from the company when they had consolidated offices years back. Opening the second drawer, he pulled out a file labeled Sinai maps. When he left Reacher, he didn't take any company documents, but he had accumulated quite a few personal maps, articles, and documents during his career working many different areas.

The Sinai map was one of his 'personal' maps. Over the years Jake had plotted all sorts of different things on it. Oases he had visited on the weekends. Archeological sites he inspected with an amateur Egyptologist friend from the University of Chicago. Good camping sites he, Paula, and Gussie had found. Opening the map to the general area of Mohammed's trailer, he spread it out on the desk. Using a set of metal ten point dividers and a pair of draftsmen's triangles, he plotted the latitude and longitude from the log.

It fell twenty miles east of the trailer. It also fell on one prospect blob he had sketched on the map. Not one of his main leads, but one of the questionable leads he mapped purely from looking at surface drainage patterns. Essentially, it was an area that seemed to divert the water drainage, with runoff flowing around it. A slight topographic high, and a spot to expect a geologic structure under the surface. With no seismic or better evidence for a structure, however, it was one of the leads a company would never invest in drilling.

"Son of a bitch," he said, not realizing Gussie was right beside him.

"Daddy", scolded Gussie. "That's a bad word!"

"Sorry sweetie. You're right. It's just that Daddy found something fascinating on this old piece of paper."

"What?" she asked.

"It's hard to explain. But it's very, very good news."

Jake grinned and shook his head in disbelief. It was hard to believe what he had just found.

"Tell me," she insisted.

"OK. This mud log combined with the work I did in Egypt might lead to a gas field."

"So now you drill a well?" she asked. Gussie looked at him with her brown eyes and a face full of enthusiasm.

"It's not quite that easy, pumpkin. First, I need to put a deal together. Then find some financing. Then get an Egyptian partner. Then get the concession rights from the government. Then shoot some seismic. Then drill a well. Only after all of that can I find a lot of gas. And then we live happily ever after."

"Sounds great," Gussie said, again scurrying off to find something more interesting to do.

Jake pondered the path ahead. He hadn't put a deal together on his own before. He hadn't the faintest clue what to do first. Nevertheless he felt more excited than he had since starting in the industry. The mud log stayed on his desk where he had placed it.

CHAPTER 9

JAKE thought of Gussie as he watched the little girl in the row ahead of him press her face to the window. She saw a blue meandering strip of river, dissecting a maze of a city, with endless brown beyond its edges. This same view captivated Gussie each time she landed in Cairo.

Conversation increased noticeably as their plane cut through the orange pollution haze, the great pyramids of Khufu, Khafre, and Menkaure visible in the waning light of early evening. BA flight 0155 was twenty minutes ahead of schedule; the landing was gentle, and the taxi short. Before the plane stopped, dozens of people leaped up and started hauling bags down from the overhead bins. The steward on the intercom emphatically asked people to sit down, to no avail.

'That steward hasn't flown into the Middle East much,' Jake thought. He found the entire population a contradiction, on one hand intolerant and incapable of waiting, and on the other possessing an infinite patience and ability to wait forever for simple things. After staying in his seat through most of the pushing and shoving, Jake got up, lofted his small shoulder bag, and jostled his way through the remaining passengers exiting the plane. He realized there were parts of the local culture he did not miss.

Jake had been out of Egypt for less than six months, but it seemed an eternity. At the base of the stairs he waited for an Egyptair bus. It took seven minutes from the time he hit the ground to when the bus dropped him at the terminal door, only thirty yards from the plane. Inside Terminal 1, he walked down the familiar corridor between the ever-hopeful duty free stores that never seemed to have much to sell. In front of each sat a young woman, head covered, looking bored, waiting for someone to step into her little store. He heard the heels of the woman in front of him clicking on the highly polished marble floor.

Jake walked down the slight slope from duty free to baggage claim. Before he turned the corner to Passport Control, he spotted Omar, his favorite expediter. With Omar's connections and smooth talk, officials never opened the bags in which Jake had tucked away the odd VCR, computer equipment, or other taxable items he smuggled into the country. He hadn't expected Omar to meet him. His future partner, Salah, was looking after him already.

"*Habibi, izayak?* Friend, how are you?" said Omar. He offered his hand and took Jake's passport. "How is everything? How is your family?"

"Fine, Omar, fine. How are you?"

"*Alhamdulillah.* Thanks for asking. It's good to see you back. How long will you stay?"

"A short time, unfortunately. I miss Cairo. It's nice to be back."

He retrieved his single bag from the conveyor and put it on the trolley Omar had procured. They walked through Customs, Omar waving to everyone he couldn't reach to shake hands, and went down the spiral concrete ramp to a waiting car. Jake tipped his friend twenty Egyptian pounds, a good tip for the short time involved.

As the car moved slowly down Salah Salem Street, Jake gazed out the window at fountains, some of which had water and some of which did not. He rolled down the window and smelled the distinctive stench of burning plastic Baraka water bottles.

Jake would spend most of his time with the man he hoped would be his local partner. Salah el Gindi was an old friend. Well positioned in the Egyptian oil industry, he had cut his teeth in Gupco, the biggest joint operating company in Egypt. With four thousand employees, Gupco was responsible for producing more than half of Egypt's oil during most of the industry's lifetime. El Gindi quit just after becoming a District Production Engineer and moved to the Emirates for seven years producing oil offshore Abu Dhabi. Salah made enough there in seven years to allow him to retire at age fifty. Not interested in taking it easy, he was still very active in his sixties, making deals and consulting. Unlike many engineers, Salah was multi-dimensional. Most of his time was dedicated to buying and selling real estate. Money begat money, and Salah had put his Gulf earnings to work.

Salah had helped Reacher Oil break through red tape several times, mostly for operational problems. He knew important people in the Petroleum Ministry who could make things happen. For this reason alone, Jake considered him the perfect local partner. They were close personal friends as well. A jack Moslem, Salah liked Bourbon and appreciated the American culture, a throwback to his years in the engineering program at the University of Tulsa.

Driving along the Nile, Jake chuckled as he recalled Salah's story of flying between the US and Argentina, sitting beside two beautiful young women from Buenos Aires. Before the food service came, he got his special Moslem meal, consisting of shrimp and steak on the tray. Asked about it, he began to explain Moslem customs and rules to the girls. Next came the beverage cart, and he ordered a glass of wine, confusing the women. Salah professed that Islamic rules are suspended when a Moslem man traveled, then really confused them by offering to share his hotel room for the next few nights, despite a clearly displayed wedding ring. 'Alas,' Salah had told him, 'nothing came of the invitation.'

The next day, Jake's alarm went off at ten, waking him from a deep, jet-lagged sleep. He showered and reached the Marriott coffee shop by eleven, eating feta cheese and olives with baladi bread. Glancing up from his plate, he watched Salah maneuver his six-foot frame through the tables. With fairly light skin, his facial features hinted at European blood not too distant in the ancestral chain. Wearing a Harris Tweed sport coat over a black turtleneck, he commanded attention by his posture, along with the fact that no one else could possibly have worn such attire in the dead heat of Egypt's summer months.

Jake stood up and the two men locked in a bear hug, kissing cheeks.

"*Habibi*," Salah began. "How was your trip?"

"Long but it's good to be back. I missed the feel and smell of it here."

"I don't remember you loving the smell when you were here," Salah laughed.

"Neither do I."

"When I leave, at most for a month, I am always happy to return."

"I know Salah. It's good to see you."

Smiling from their hearts, and talking as much as they smiled, the two men quickly reestablished their friendship.

"I was not surprised to get your fax," Salah said.

"You must have been surprised by what I want to do, no?"

"Not at all. At least not by your interest in doing a deal in Egypt. I am flattered however that you want me as a partner."

"Who else would I ask?" said Jake.

"Dozens of others. But I'm glad you chose me. Your fax had no details."

"I need to discuss those with you in person."

Jake did most of the talking. Salah would not understand the geology, so he talked mainly about funding, logistics, and what would have to happen in Cairo to facilitate a successful project. The only technical aspects he discussed were connected with the mud log, and how his daughter had really been the one to reveal the prospect.

Salah was a process guy. Jake needed two things from him. The legitimacy of an Egyptian partner, and the ability to make things happen. At this first meeting, they didn't bring up compensation or interest splits, Jake knowing he needed to hook Salah on the opportunity itself. Money would be an issue, but it was the chance to be a player that mattered most to Salah.

"Salah, it's noon already. Can we meet again tomorrow?"

"My pleasure, *habibi*. My house?"

"I would like that," Jake smiled. He knew at that point they would be partners.

At two o'clock, Jake kept his appointment with Hesham Ibrahim, the head of leases and contracts with EGPC, the Egyptian General Petroleum Company. Their office was in Maadi, south of Cairo, where Jake had lived. It took three cups of tea and forty minutes to give Jake confidence he had the correct story. New policies precluded EGPC from granting a preemptive lease. Jake had expected to tie up the acreage quickly, and could have done so a year ago. Now he would have to compete against the world, not that anyone else would be interested in the Sinai.

"Five months ago," Hesham explained, "the Petroleum Minister decreed that all open acreage in Egypt would be through competitive bid. His intent was to preempt inside deals. Put a halt to corruption. Now, an interested party can evaluate existing data for any non-leased acreage then nominate an area for the next bid round, which is never more than six months away. They can submit a bid and compete against other companies interested in that block."

"Things have changed," Jake said.

"Yes they have. You've been gone a short time but it's a new world here."

"Go on, Hesham."

"There is a bid round already announced that includes the central Sinai. Our geologists added a large block, although they are not sure anyone will bid. The EGPC is putting out a correction soon that will add another block to the offering, and extend the sale closing date to August 31. I need to know within four days if you want to nominate other acreage, or request changes to the current block outline."

"I might amend the block outline," Jake told him. "I'm working with Salah el Gindi. He'll visit you this week."

"Ah, my old friend Salah," said Hesham. It did not surprise Jake that Hesham and Salah were friends.

Leaving the EGPC building at three-thirty after making the rounds, Jake recalled how amazing it always seemed in that office. Outside offices along the windows housed the *moudeers*, or big bosses. Virtually all of them kept their doors closed, and their miniblinds shut. You could never tell if anyone was inside or not, and if they were, whether they were working, conducting personal business, asleep, or dead. The interior of the building contained cubicles, some with low walls and some with higher walls for the more senior workers. At any given moment, most of the staff chatted with each other, drank tea, or just sat staring into space.

Jake got back in his car and asked the driver to pass by the Reacher Oil office. He didn't want to visit, but felt an urge to look at the building where he had worked four years. Not wanting anyone to know he was around, he sat in the car and looked at the walled office. On the whole,' thought Jake, 'I don't miss it.

The car took him to the Gleason's house. His old friends had been delighted to hear he was back, and had insisted he visit for dinner.

"Hello, Katie," he said when the door opened to reveal a child who had been in Gussie's class. He talked with Katie and her mom Cheryl about Houston until John got home. They stoked up the grill and barbecued pork ribs that Jake had carried frozen from the States. Cheryl refilled their margaritas and they sat down to eat. After dinner she took Katie upstairs to sleep while John and Jake talked about changes since he left.

"My job never changes," said John, who worked for US AID, the organization that oversaw most of the two billion dollars the US government heaped on Egypt every year. "I've got another intern helping to approve small loans to local village businessmen. It's great to see her enthusiasm. I'm afraid I've lost mine."

"Jake, in your industry new stuff's happening. The investment climate's improved so you're seeing new players. Two new major foreign companies have opened offices. Several more are fishing for opportunities. One of these, Everon, has been to the Embassy and AID offices, asking about all aspects of the gas business. Have you heard of them?"

"No," replied Jake.

"You looking for a job? You'd be invaluable to them here."

"I'll think about it," Jake said. But he was thinking they could be competition for the Sinai block.

The rest of the evening covered gossip in Maadi. Two more divorces. Another medical evacuation due to softball injuries. One raging affair that everyone knew about except the poor spouse. A normal year.

Fading fast, Jake made his exit before ten, his car creeping down the Corniche to his hotel. Pondering the day as he brushed his teeth, he thought 'not bad'. Some new information. A score with Salah. Good contacts with the government. It could be a short trip.

The next morning, Jake met Dr. Moustafa Hanify, chairman of Egypt Gas. Jake had liked the old man the few times they had met. This contact was fortuitous, because Salah knew virtually no one in Egypt Gas. Jake wanted to get Moustafa on board early in the game. If he could get the gas company interested, they might influence the EGPC bid committee. If he learned anything in the four years here, it was to lay as much foundation as possible.

Moustafa came out of his office to greet Jake. Tilting slightly to get his enormous bulk through the door, he looked as though someone had pumped him up with a compressor. 'What a suitable build for the head of a gas company', Jake thought.

Moustafa's chest was so large that his arms wouldn't hang at his sides, but angled outwards like a poorly made doll. Jake watched as he waddled across the floor, his hands sweeping back and forth in a futile attempt to keep his mass in balance. His face especially pudgy, his eyelids appeared to droop and shut off the outside world. Moustafa came over and pumped Jake's hand vigorously.

"*Izayak, khawaga*—How are you?"

The term for 'foreigner' sounded nasty, starting with a throat clearing 'kh'. Nevertheless, it was used fondly, sometimes carrying tones of 'rich' and 'clueless', with a distinct dose of 'envy' and 'respect'.

"I am very well, thank you Moustafa. How are you?"

"I am fine. But you look thin."

This was a standard line of the Chairman. He knew he was morbidly obese, and used it to his advantage.

"Compared to you, a bus is small," Jake replied.

The two of them laughed, Moustafa's fat jiggling randomly. Tea and small talk took up the first fifteen minutes, with the last ten devoted to business. Jake asked the Chairman if he would be interested in Sinai gas production, and whether he would support building a pipeline to send it to market.

"Of course," Moustafa said. "All of Egypt wants more resources and production from anywhere. Especially places like the Sinai."

"I thought you would like the idea," Jake said. "I have a plan to find gas in the Sinai."

He chose the word 'find' instead of 'explore'. Dr. Moustafa Hanify did not know a lot about exploration. Jake wanted to gloss over the finding part, and concentrate on the downstream part.

"Is this the dream of a madman? Or am I drinking with a genius?"

Moustafa's fat shook again as he laughed. Jake laughed too, it being impossible not to follow a fat man's lead.

"Neither, Moustafa. I merely have an idea. And I want the chance to spend money pursuing it. I believe I can find gas but the real question is the market. Where can I send it, and will someone buy it."

"Yes most definitely to both of those questions. You know Egypt needs lots of gas. We have dual fired electric power plants waiting for gas. They are burning low quality fuel oil now but can also burn natural gas. We have to import fuel oil, which ends up polluting the air. If anyone finds gas, I can bring it to market."

"What if it's too far from the grid, Moustafa?"

"That is a question of economics. Of market price. Of distance. Of pipeline costs."

"How would Egypt feel about exporting gas to Israel?"

This was Jake's ace card. He had figured out while at Reacher that gas in the central Sinai would be too costly to bring into Egypt's national grid. A project might fly if you could export gas to Israel at a price higher than the internal Egyptian grid delivery price. Israel thirsted for fuel, especially a 'green' fuel like natural gas. Jake was a constant advocate of this possibility in Reacher, but Barney was hesitant, and the head office never warmed to the idea.

"Export to Israel would be difficult," said Moustafa after a long pause. "But with the peace process, maybe not impossible. Egypt has good relations with Israel. Export could make sense. Politically it would be delicate. Perhaps the formation of a Palestinian State could make a gas transmission project palatable. You know we have exported a lot of oil to Israel, after a scheme set up at Camp David."

"Moustafa, I believe exporting gas to Israel is not only possible, but inevitable. I want to help Egypt realize this potential. I want to find gas in the Sinai. I want to build an export pipeline. And with my American connections I want to be the one to integrate the Israelis into your gas grid. Egypt could make a lot of money through such a plan."

That was the seed Jake wanted to plant. The fact he was American would help get in the Israeli door. The major gas player in Egypt now was the Italian company ENI. They could be the major competition for most of the acreage in the bid round. Italy had weak links to Israel. No leverage. The United States did.

They ended their conversation with an air of hopefulness.

"This could be a very big deal," Jake said.

"I won't be around to see it," Moustafa rebutted.

Jake knew Moustafa was a couple of years at most from retirement, if not death. It would be the feather in his cap if he could expand his gas grid outside the country. The industry had talked for years about linking either a gas pipeline network or a power grid between the

Maghreb states of Libya, Tunisia, and Algeria with Egypt, and on eastward to the Levant states of Syria and Lebanon. Some spoke of taking such a link all the way to Turkey. An Egypt-Israel pipe could start a new chapter in regional cooperation.

He knew he had Moustafa thinking. Jake stood up to leave.

"*Maasalama khawaga.*"

"*Maasalama Moustafa.* Until next time."

Jake had not brought up Salah, but at the appropriate time would send a fax to Moustafa. Jake felt good as he walked down the white marble steps outside the Egypt Gas building, the late day sun beating down relentlessly.

At dinner with Salah, it took less than an hour to agree on all terms for their partnership. Jake would provide all upfront money, technical expertise, and operational staff. Salah would handle the government, negotiations, and local issues. Of the percentage not taken by the government, Jake and his funding partners would keep ninety percent and Salah would keep ten. If they were successful, Salah would reimburse his share of the costs out of his portion of the profit stream. If they were not, he did not need to put any money in. It was a great deal for Salah, and he knew it. Jake on the other hand knew he would be able to count on Salah through thick and thin. He could not proceed without an Egyptian. They spent the next three hours plotting a strategy for how to approach the bid round, most of the plan involving Salah working the system through the backdoor. For his part, all Jake had to do was find someone with eight million dollars to put into a high risk, somewhat crazy scheme, in a volatile third world country.

Business done, Jake retired to the Marriot, sleeping late again the next morning before heading to the pool for breakfast. He spent two hours relaxing in the sun. About half of the bathers were Egyptian women with kids, hiding under veils and long black abayas, the other half expats or tourists in swim suits. He longed to get back to civilization and to Gussie.

Taking off at five the next morning it took six hours to get to London, and thirteen after that to land in Houston. It was a great connection.

CHAPTER 10

Tel Aviv
May 24

IT was a public holiday and Daniel Moses Ran was poolside at Tel Aviv's Panorama Hotel. Ran was sixty-nine today, and he reflected on his haphazard path through life. Brought up orthodox in Brooklyn, he attended synagogue parties and Talmud readings. Just as black suits blended together on the streets of his neighborhood, so did little boys with sideburns curling down their necks. Leviticus wrote 'You shall not round off the peyos of your head', and so the men in his neighborhood didn't, more than two centuries later.

Escaping growing restrictions in Poland, Daniel's grandfather immigrated to the US before World War I. He sailed alone aboard the Octavius, a Greek ship sailing from Gdansk, known to the Germans as Danzig. He built the Ran family fortune in New York City from pickles, spending fifteen hours a day making barrel after barrel of pickles from old family recipes. Immigrants in Brooklyn couldn't get enough of them. The salt and other ingredients could have contributed to the old man's premature death from cancer during the first year of the Great Depression.

Daniel's father was terribly affected by his own father's death. Hating pickles, his dream was of the new Jewish homeland. After the formation of Israel in 1948 he plotted to leave a decade later when Daniel was twelve. A confused multi-cultural young man, Daniel returned to the US for college and majored in engineering, intending to build bridges and dams across Western North America. By a twist of fate and lack of job prospects, he joined a Negev kibbutz in the mid seventies. After picking more than enough produce, he migrated into politics and was appointed two years ago as Minister of Infrastructure.

Daniel was still gazing across the Corniche when Yosef Kettler sat down beside him. The older man followed the gaze of the younger before breaking the silence.

"You haf only a few years left," Yosef said in his accented English.

Daniel looked around, seeking an explanation. Yosef smiled and swung his arm through the air like a sorcerer's wand.

"Ven you get old like me, you'll be unable to stare at anyting else when dere are vomen around in bating suits."

Daniel laughed out loud, for the first time that day. Yosef had that effect on people. The ability to make them laugh. Or cry. Or tremble. Depending on his intent.

"Look here," Yosef pointed to a young mother in a black bikini. "She's beautiful. How nice of her to ver a suit dat could not possibly cover her."

"So," Ran changed the subject "I have some results."

"Vat do you have?" Yosef lit a cigar.

"It took a great deal of probing. I almost gave up." He gave a sigh but Yosef didn't react. "I found someone who remembers the Sinai oil campaign. A horde of geologists worked the Gulf of Suez, trying to suck the most oil out before Israel had to give the fields back to Egypt."

Yosef kept staring at the Minister. He had unlimited patience, when it suited him.

"The Sinai was a different story. Most geologists working there were University kids doing basic science. Only two groups were actually exploring."

"Certainly some are left," said Yosef.

"Only one. One whole group was killed in the field during the six-day war. A fluke, really. They were south of El Arish returning from a three-month mapping campaign when they hitched up with a supply convoy for dinner. Apparently just before dinner an Egyptian fighter sprayed them with bullets. A fuel tank blew up killing half the dinner party, including all the geologists."

"Bad luck," Yosef puffed on his Cuban.

"The other group, more experienced, disbanded and spread out. A few have died of old age. A couple others are untraceable. I could only find one."

Daniel watched the older man blow smoke rings, which lasted a few seconds before falling apart in the breeze. He hated the smell of cigars.

"Ver is he?" asked Yosef.

"He owns a winery in the Golan," Daniel replied.

Yosef Kettler laughed at this. He had business interests around the world, and virtually everywhere in Israel. Except the Golan. He thought it a gut cinch that this God-forsaken piece of land would ultimately be extricated from the State of Israel. Most likely by Syria. Perhaps by the Palestinian State, if that ever came about.

"Vat does he know?" Yosef asked.

"He has Alzheimer's."

"Shit," said Yosef. "My legacy derailed by Alzheimer's, and not even mine."

"His memory sometimes works and his grasp of the big picture seems sound. He swears there is an undiscovered gas field out there. He babbles about being on a drilling rig when gas started coming in on them. Sounds like they had to stop the operation because there was too much gas."

"Is dat possible?" asked Yosef.

"In those days, yes. These days they can control it better. Build up the mud weight by adding barite. They could easily hold it off long enough to drill past the gas sand and then put steel pipe across the interval."

"Vy didn't dey try dat back den?"

"Well, two guesses," Daniel said. "One is they didn't have the technology. The other is they didn't want gas and shut down the operation to look for oil elsewhere."

"OK."

"But actually neither of these guesses would be correct."

Daniel waited for the rich old business baron to lean towards him.

"Vat do you mean?"

"The guy in the Golan said the night they took the gas kick, the Egyptians began dropping bombs nearby. They shut down and got the hell out."

"I don't suppose Mr. Alzheimer's knows ver 'dere' is?"

"Of course not. One of those fleeting details."

"So ve are no better off dan ve vere."

"Perhaps a bit better. He mentioned they left a few things behind."

"Vat kind of tings?"

"Stuff like drill pipe, tools, small supplies. Maybe a few pieces of the rig. He wasn't sure."

"Dere's no vay dat shit is still dere," said Yosef. "Egyptians may not do much vell, but dey recycle everyting not nailed to de ground. My guess is everyting's been melted and turned into security bars by now."

"You may be right. But the old guy says he took vacation a few years back and retraced his steps. He swears he came across stuff he recognized from the operation."

"So. All ve need to do is find some oil vell stuff and ve've found my energy source?"

Daniel smiled a wry sardonic little smile.

"I doubt that's all we need to do. It's a first step but the road will be long and rough. Maybe a Bedouin will know something."

"My life has been a series of long and rough roads," Yosef said. "I'm now looking for my yellow brick road"

Yosef Kettler let his eyes wander. They settled on the girl in the black suit again, facing him this time, her bikini top unable to contain her. A smile spread across his face. Daniel couldn't tell if it was due to the girl, or their conversation.

CHAPTER 11

THE Brown Palace had not changed and Jake guessed it never did. He had been a frequent guest back in the boom days. Those golden years when oil coursed through the veins of Denver. Beginning about 1978, oil was the city's pulse. Everyone important, and those who thought they were, stayed at the Brown. Even after the crash in '86, it remained busy.

As sunlight filtered through the windows, Jake sat in the Hogback Room, eating breakfast. The hash browns were as greasy as he remembered; the waitresses as weathered. The major difference, Jake decided, was the clientele. Fewer cowboys. Fewer oilmen. More financial types. More lawyers. More suits and briefcases but just as many boots.

Jake had arrived in Denver the night before, spending only three days in Houston after returning from Cairo. Just enough time for him to organize his presentation, gather business cards, wash his clothes, kiss Gussie, and leave.

The trip from the new Denver International Airport was forty minutes. Its predecessor, Stapleton, had been only fifteen minutes from downtown. The price of progress.

On his way to baggage claim, he had passed under a huge banner welcoming the American Association of Petroleum Geologists to their annual convention. Some seven to nine thousand individuals had registered. Denver drew a crowd.

Jake had submitted an abstract the day before the deadline a few weeks after he left Reacher. At that time, he figured he might as well get a trip to Denver, and make the best of the geologic work he did in the Sinai. His plan was to give a fairly academic talk. Now, after finding the mud log, Jake had a different agenda. He had a deal to peddle.

Leaving the Brown, Jake turned right on the 16th Street pedestrian mall. On the corner was a Hispanic man selling the Denver Post. Three steps beyond was a drunk passed out against the wall. A plastic Dunkin Donuts mug rested near his thigh with a few coins in it. Jake thought the two men illustrated America. One exercised the right to check out. The other his right to work like hell and make a life. Jake turned back and bought a paper.

He waited for an electric shuttle bus to pass before crossing the mall. Noticing the pavement beneath his feet, he remembered when it was laid. The light gray granite was from Stone Mountain in Georgia, the world's largest bald mountain made of granite. The squares were cut in Italy and shipped back. Go figure.

Halfway down the Mall, past Jose O'Houlighan's, Jake ran into Buddy Koop, a Denver institution in the oil community. He had found a ton of oil in his day, and seemed to enjoy every step along the way.

"Buddy! Buddy! Hold up a minute," Jake shouted, sprinting across the mall. Buddy, bald with a handlebar mustache, was decked out in a brown suit, Bolo tie, and cowboy boots. At six foot six and one hundred ninety pounds, Buddy looked like the character he was.

"Well, Jake Tillard. I'll be. What's it been? Ten years? How the hell are ya? Heard ya were livin' with the A-rabs."

"Good, Buddy, I'm good."

Jake remembered that Buddy was a died-in-the-wool Coloradan. At least as much as he could be, being born and raised in Odessa and spending the first part of his adult life in West Texas. Like many in this part of the west, he had little use for the rest of the world, and couldn't understand why anyone would travel abroad, much less live there.

"Yea, I spent time in Egypt. Just returned a few months ago. Good to be back in the U.S."

"Amen, I hear ya. But it's gettin' bad here too. So many damned Hispanics, you'd swear y'as in Tijuana."

"Things change, Buddy."

"Yea, things change. Back for the convention?"

"I am. I'm giving a talk on a promising area in Egypt. Trying to drum up some funding."

"Funding for what? Warn't you with Reacher?"

"You're looking at another victim of the downturn. After four years in Egypt, exploration fell out of favor with Reacher. They chopped my exploration group, and I quit."

"Good for you. Those sons o' bitches. Ya wouldna' believed the number of old hands that been screwed this last year. I imagine a lot of 'em 'll be here pressin' the flesh and peddlin' ideas."

"I look at it as an opportunity, Buddy. Before I left Egypt, I found an old mud log that documents a passed-up gas well. It's very exciting. The surest thing I've ever seen."

"Yeah, I hear ya. Ya got yoself a treasure map. 'X' marks the spot. I admire enthusiasm. Always have. Ya gotta have faith, son. Ya gotta keep going. Put your head down and stay after it and one of 'em 'll come in. Ya givin' a talk ya say? I'll be there. Right now, I'm meetin' a partner o' mine and I'm a bit late. Take care and good seein' ya."

They had walked several blocks to the convention center. He watched as Buddy disappeared through a revolving door. Looking up at the sky, already that deep, deep blue that existed in the Rockies, he turned and stared back up Stout Street. Hordes of people were walking to their jobs. Their permanent jobs.

Jake stopped at a coffee cart to buy a latte and leaned against a wrought iron railing. He thought about his early career. Out of school, the geology job market was nonexistent. His first "permanent job" was outfitter for a packhorse group leading tourists on trips through Montana's Bob Marshall Wilderness. Then he worked for a Canadian mining company in British Columbia. Staged in a tent camp at 9,000 feet in the Chugach Mountains, he was in charge of a four-man crew putting in exploratory tunnel, looking for gold and silver hidden in quartz veins. Six months of that convinced him there must be something better.

He opened a car wash in Vancouver with his paltry savings and a bank loan. Less than a year and fifty thousand cars later, he decided the car wash business wasn't heaven either. It rained frequently enough in Vancouver that most people merely waited for the rain to wash their cars for free. After that, Jake got a job teaching geology at a small college. He liked the hours, the coeds, and the fieldwork, but didn't like the academic politics and the parochial nature of the community. He finally stumbled into the oil industry in Denver.

"Excuse me." A young man making his way to the convention brushed past him. Jake looked after him, seeing himself twenty years ago. Confidence bordering on arrogance. Dreamy hope. Impatience for the next day. That mental state fled Jake during the later part of his career, but it was now back. He whistled as he turned and walked into the Convention Center.

"So, in summary, let me offer the following points. First, the Sinai represents one of the most under-explored hydrocarbon prone basins in the world accessible to western companies. Second, recent gas discoveries in central Egypt and Saudi Arabia, along with data in the Sinai, indicate a rich source rock exists which should have generated gas. Third, my work has high graded the vast interior of the Sinai, and I have narrowed potential drill sites down to the best location. Thank you for your time."

The applause was moderate. Not bad from a relatively small audience of seventy people. With the move towards increased exploration overseas, this session on emerging frontiers would normally have drawn a larger crowd. Unfortunately, another session on shale gas was running concurrently. That session was loaded with talks about the emerging technologies of horizontal drilling and hydraulic fracturing. He heard later that over three hundred people attended most of the talks in that session.

The house lights came up, and the session chairman asked for questions. A couple of people raised their hands.

The first question was a good one, the type a speaker loved to get. "Why is the basin so underexplored if it is so prospective?"

"Good question. There is just enough geologic data around to peg the Sinai as gas prone, and not oily. Gas is hard to transport and sell. A decade ago, the Egyptian government did not grant foreign contractors any rights to gas. If you found it, it went to the government. A few years ago, new concession agreements included gas rights, with the government purchase price pegged to internationally traded crude oil."

He pointed to another hand. A short and wiry looking gentleman with flowing silver hair out of proportion to his slight build stepped up to one of the microphones.

"Isn't it true most of the wells in the Sinai produce fresh water, and how do you rationalize that fact with finding hydrocarbons?"

Jake thought he detected a slight foreign accent.

"You're correct. There are precious few wells in the Sinai, but they do confirm that aquifers contain water fresh enough for irrigation. Although most oil and gas bearing rocks in the world contain salt water, there are a few exceptions like the Bighorn Basin of western Wyoming where oil or gas lie above fresh water within a rock layer. I see the Sinai as a similar area."

"But isn't it true," the interrogator continued, "that fresh water biodegrades oil? Basically turning it to gunk? Like the tar pits in California."

"Sometimes. Most deep aquifers are salty, and most hydrocarbons sit above salty water. Many shallow oil accumulations have turned into asphalt when they contacted fresh water circulating near the surface. The oxygenated water reacts with the oil to strip volatiles and turn it into paste. But if the system is isolated, normally at depth, this doesn't always happen. The Bighorn Basin and a good part of China are examples where oil has remained good quality, although the associated water is fresh. The Athabasca tar sands north of Edmonton Canada are an example where the oil has been degraded. But the Sinai is a gas province anyway. The effects of fresh water on gas are minimal. Fresh water does not present a problem to gas in the Sinai."

The next question came from a woman Jake recognized, but couldn't place. It was straightforward and simple to address. The session chairman thanked him, and following another short round of applause, the chairman introduced the next speaker, who would talk about Jurassic microscopic pollen grains common in Tanzania during the time of the dinosaurs.

Jake escaped the meeting rooms, walked through the exhibition hall, and bought a Corona from a cute young girl in a short cowgirl skirt. The hall was packed with vendor displays. An extremely high ceiling provided room for an actual drilling rig, albeit a small one. There were lots of banners and balloons done in red, white, and blue.

He stopped at the Schlumberger booth to hear about the latest down hole equipment. Wandering the exhibits left him unsatisfied. He didn't really want to learn about new technology and unlike the old boom days no one had cool giveaways. He left the hall and went back to the Brown Palace. He didn't feel like dinner.

CHAPTER 12

THE next morning Jake went to the hotel gym later than usual. He bought a hot dog from a street cart near the conference center, where he again toured the exhibit hall. Mid-afternoon he wandered over to the conference Bookstore where dozens of technical publications were displayed. He picked up a large book titled "Oil on Their Shoes", about some of the early wildcatters. The book was filled with old photographs of significant events in the early days of the business. As he flipped through the book he felt a hand on his arm.

"You would've made a great old time geologist, Jake Tillard." He turned around.

"Libby? Is that you! My God! How are you?" Jake bent down to hug his old buddy, literally picking her off the floor.

Libby Joyce, daughter of a Vegas gambler. Pure lightning and mischief packed into a petite and beautiful body. Libby and Jake had been office mates in graduate school, sharing the frustrations and rewards of that long two-year period. At the time they shared technical notes, personal thoughts, and some very wild times. Libby had been a holy terror, intelligent in a scary way, and independent beyond all reason. She was the creative half of their liaison. They were each other's confidants. They hadn't seen each other since grad school.

"I'm just fine. I've got two fast cars, three dogs, a house in the mountains, and an interest in two mines and an oilfield. I play ice hockey in the winter, and rock climb in the summer. What else could a girl want?"

"You haven't changed a bit. Except maybe for the piercings," he said, eyeing the small diamond stud in her nose and the multiple pieces of metal in her ears.

"If you like these, you'll have to see my tattoos. We'd need a few drinks and somewhere private though. How the hell are you Jake? What's with the ponytail?"

"Well. I'm in transition."

"OK let's have it. What's goin' on?"

"I'm a widower, for starts?"

"Oh Jake. I didn't know. Poor Paula. What happened?"

"Car accident. She went quick."

"Wow. I'm so sorry. I always thought you guys were the luckiest couple in the world. So well suited for each other, and so much in love. I really liked Paula. When did she pass? Are you OK?"

"A few years ago. I'm still working it out. Time helps. I've got one beautiful daughter, no job, no dogs, no house, and no oilfields or mines. But I do have one gas prospect begging to be drilled. Until this week I thought that was pretty good. But there must be a few hundred folks here with a prospect."

"Sounds like you could use a drink. Today's program's almost over. I know just the place. Guess?"

"Buckhorn?"

"You got it."

Libby looked the same to Jake. Flowing brown hair, petite, gorgeous figure set off by absolutely straight posture. Her facial features had always impressed Jake as classic, like something from Greek mythology. Her skin was an alluring olive, still as smooth as he remembered. Jake didn't care for the proliferation of piercings, but he was intrigued by the mentioned tattoos. Girls commonly fell for bad boys. Libby was a bad girl who attracted men.

As students they teased and flirted but never developed a romantic relationship. Jake wasn't sure why but it just never happened. He thought she'd had a crush on him but he felt her a bit too tomboyish. What they did do was share each other's lives, especially the pain, elation, and other emotions that accompanied their dating dramas.

Weaving through the exhibition floor and out into daylight, Libby led them a couple blocks to a dilapidated looking parking lot that Jake thought looked unsafe. She stopped in front of a Lotus and flicked the remote unlock device on her key chain.

"Pretty fancy Libby. Worry about the car in this lot?"

"Well maybe I should, but I own the lot, and figure if I can't park here who can? It looks ragged but it's temporary." She held up her thumb and index finger in a little pinch and pointed east. "I'm this close to getting the building next door. I'm gonna tear that down, merge the lots, and put up an office tower."

"You didn't tell me you're also a real estate tycoon," Jake said with a little envy.

"I told you things are goin' good."

They drove out of the lot and zipped across Speer Boulevard.

"Remember when I was pissed off at that mining company I worked for in Central America? I quit and tried some environmental work in South Dakota. That was a bore so I quit and moved to Billings to try the oil business. I struggled for a few years, begging at doors, selling small oil prospects like a Fuller Brush girl. I made a couple important contacts so when I did map the big one I could keep a chunk for myself. I drilled the discovery at Flintlock Field six years after starting in Billings. Three partners put up the money, a third of the cash for a quarter interest. The other quarter was mine, essentially free. As they say, the rest is history. Well, sort of. I got bored with oil and wanted to get back to minerals. So I moved to Denver and opened shop. We're here. I'll tell you the rest inside."

The Lotus eased into the parking lot of the Buckhorn Exchange, liquor license number one in the city of Denver. A landmark, it held the record for the longest continuous service of spirits in the entire state.

Libby and Jake walked through the door into the past. They had compared notes in the Buckhorn twenty-five years earlier when they were both job hunting. Like then peanut shells crunched beneath their feet as they found an empty table with a couple of mismatched wooden chairs. The walls hosted a cast of animal heads, ranging from buffalo and moose down to prairie dogs and the famed antlered rabbit, the Buckhorn's equivalent of the unicorn. Beneath the menagerie, the walls were littered with photographs and letters of the rich and famous who had dined there. A dozen presidents, scores of Hollywood stars, and innumerable sports figures, including rodeo greats.

A heavy and heavily made up middle-aged waitress took their order then disappeared into the kitchen. Jake picked a peanut out of the basket, cracked it, and popped it into his mouth.

"Remember our last time here, Jake?"

"I do. Neither of us knew what was next. We were interviewing like mad and it seemed no one needed geologists."

"Right. But we didn't care."

Jake got that sinking feeling again in the lower part of his stomach. "At least one of us did well. That's a pretty good result. Tell me the rest of your story Libby."

He looked into the sparkling green eyes of his old confidant. Always exotic, they were still full of self-confidence mixed with a little mischief.

"Well it took a few years but I got hooked up with some old school buddies trying to restart a gold mine in Nevada. I put some money into that and it's done well. The real fun though was finding and starting a rare earth mine near Mountain Pass, California. It's now the only operating rare earth mine in the US. It's us against the Chinese."

"Wow, you're a mogul. What about the personal side?"

"I live in Genesee, up the mountain. From my bedroom I can see Mount Evans and the Continental Divide." She laughed. "I even have a picture window in my shower."

"Don't you worry about peeping Toms?" Jake asked.

"No more than when we all went skinny dipping in the hot pools outside of Missoula. Back then my body was worth peeping at. Do you remember the Jerry Johnson springs up Lolo Pass? One pool after another all filled with naked bodies."

"Yeah, those were fun times for sure. From what I can see, your body doesn't look all that worse for wear. I'd peep."

"Age is not just a state of mind. I'm hiding behind expensive cloths. Anyway I did a lot of mountain biking until a couple years ago. Since they've repaved the neighborhood, I've been roller blading. It's a gas going down hills, but tougher than hell going up."

"No family?" Jake asked.

"No. A couple of guys along the way, but nothing stuck. I'll bet that doesn't surprise you. I almost got married to a guy that owned ten Subway franchises if you can believe that. He was a lot of fun and we had some very good times."

"So what happened?"

Libby laughed again, a different sort of laugh toned with wistfulness.

"It got so far as the rehearsal dinner. It was a great time at the Little Nell in Aspen. We had a load of friends there with the bar flowing. I think the excitement of it all did in my fiancée. One of my girlfriends grabbed me by the arm and dragged me outside. Seems she and her beau had an idea that led them out there but the spot was already occupied. By my fiancée and one of his old flames."

Jake didn't know whether to laugh or not.

"What did you do?"

"What do you think? I walked up to them, humping on the grass, and helped a bit."

After a gap in conversation Jake asked the obvious. Knowing Libby, he was almost afraid of the answer.

"Well, they were in the classic missionary position. Him on top. Her on the bottom. I drove the toe of my pump right into his balls. I think that pushed his dick as far into the little slut as possible."

Jake was aghast. Involuntarily, his knees came together under the table.

"Then what.

"I turned around and went back to the party. The slut stumbled in and got the manager to call an ambulance. My ex-fiancée went to the hospital. My guess is he'll never have kids. The rest of the party was a blast."

"I'm sorry, Libby."

"Oh, don't be. It dawned on me later that evening I had more fun without him than I would've had with him."

Libby drained the rest of her beer and ordered two more. Both of them were silent for a couple of minutes, lost in their own thoughts. Libby broke the silence.

"So tell an old friend about your gas prospect, if you trust me not to steal it."

Jake's attitude perked up immediately. It seemed like he was riding the emotional roller coaster these days, going from peak to trough in a flash, then back up almost as fast.

"It's a sure thing, Libby. It's there. It's been drilled. The only question is how much gas is there."

Jake went on for twenty minutes filling her in on the details. She listened to it all, nodding, asking probing technical questions, exploring the issues involved with playing the oil and gas game in a foreign country. Libby always impressed everyone with her insightfulness and inquisitiveness. In school she was a professor's dream. Pushing the envelope, looking at a problem in a different way.

She also contemplated the face of the man across the table, the unmarried man with one beautiful daughter. Jake didn't clue in to that part of the conversation. At the end he noticed her posture had changed from leaning forward with both elbows on the table to a reclining slouch with her arms crossed. He didn't think the body language was encouraging.

"What a story!" she said, bolting up in her chair. "This has elements of intrigue."

Libby's eyes rotated towards the ceiling and her lips pressed together. Jake recognized this look from twenty years ago as intense interest.

"Want to fund me Libby?"

She thought about it. She could do it. It might stretch her a bit but she could muster the funds. However she wanted something else out of this meeting.

"I'd love nothing better Jake. But the third world is not my playing field. I have a tough enough time dealing with the Bureau of Land Management, the Mineral Management Survey, the IRS, and the rest of the system here. I don't go near Indian lands because of the complications dealing with tribal councils. Sorry old buddy but I'm not your banker. If you get someone with the desire and money to believe you though, you should be able to sell this one. Just remember to keep a big piece for yourself."

"That's the plan. It could be tough. But I've got that feeling if it doesn't happen soon it'll happen later. I'm willing to wait."

"Hang in there. Tell me more about Egypt. I've always wanted to go there. I guess I've been working too hard to fit in much travel."

Jake was going up the coaster track again. He talked about the people in Egypt, their humor, their tragedy, his friends. He talked of the poverty, the inequity, and the strength of family. The more he talked the more he missed the place.

He talked through their steaks, through their desserts, through their coffee. Libby listened. Jake was so wrapped up he didn't notice her eyes tilt toward the ceiling and her lips press together again.

They ended up talking about Montana. Libby bought a small cabin north of Missoula on Flathead Lake. She said he must come to visit sometime, not that she was ever there.

Libby insisted on paying the bill, and then they walked outside. The sun was down and the temperature had dropped. Jake looked up at the Milky Way and considered that dawn was about to rise over his gas prospect. Libby deposited him at the Brown and said goodnight. She left some rubber on the road as she drove away. Jake just shook his head.

"**CAPTAIN MACKENZIE** again. We started our descent into the New York area but Air Traffic Control has us in a hold and predicts a forty-five minute delay. Fog's got Boston nearly shut down so traffic's re-routed around the Northeast. Sit back and relax. I apologize for the bumpy ride. We'll get you there as soon as we can."

Jake looked at the Oriental girl in the seat next to him. She had fallen asleep over Kentucky and hardly moved since. He had avoided staring at her legs before but let his eyes focus on them now. Her legs were still crossed, but as she had slouched in her sleep, the short skirt had remained where it started.

His mind snapped back to this trip and the meeting scheduled for tomorrow. After the convention he took a phone call one evening. A man named Jack asked if he was still seeking investors for the Egypt gas deal. Jake said yes and after further discussion agreed to visit New York to discuss potential funding. He wondered how they had heard of his deal.

When Jack had suggested Jake bring his wife and enjoy a weekend in the Big Apple at the company's expense, Jake explained his wife had passed away. The next day he received a FedEx envelope with first class seats, a prepaid hotel voucher at the Ritz Carlton Central Park, and five hundred dollars cash "spending money". Two days later he left Gussie with Layla and drove to the airport.

The plane was in its final approach. Even with this delay he would reach the hotel by six, in time to relax before dinner. He had wanted to keep the evening open but Jack had insisted on booking theater tickets for the two of them, saying they could become better acquainted.

"Flight attendants please take your seats."

Why did all pilots sound alike with that calm, John Glenn voice? If his plane was ever going down, he knew the pilot would reassure them that everything was under control.

The oriental girl woke up when the wheels touched, smoothed her skirt, and looked at him with a slight smile.

"Boy is my neck sore. How long have I been asleep?"

"A couple hours. You probably had the best flight of anyone onboard."

Jake stood up, got his carry-on from the overhead bin, and followed the girl out of the plane.

At the Ritz he discovered a suite waiting, with a cavernous marble clad bathroom, a sitting room with stocked bar, and a king size bed with ten assorted pillows. He threw down his bag, made himself a drink, strolled to the expansive windows, and looked down five stories at West Fifty Ninth Street. 'How many yellow taxis are in this city?' he thought as he heard the cacophony of horns accompanying the gridlock below. The sounds of evening traffic were interrupted by the phone. Jake located it on the desk.

"Mr. Tillard?"

"Yes this is Jake Tillard. Is this Jack?"

"No Mr. Tillard. My name is Osama abdel Fatah, a colleague of Jack. I will be your host in New York. Jack had to leave the country suddenly last night and sends his regrets. How is everything so far?"

"Good, Mr. Fatah. I had an uneventful trip and appreciate the fine accommodations you've provided."

"Our pleasure Mr. Tillard. Our driver will pick you up Monday at nine o'clock if that is acceptable."

"That will be perfect. Thank you very much." Jake started to hang up the receiver before blurting, "Wait!" into the phone. "Will you be accompanying me to the theater tonight in Jack's absence, Mr. Fatah"?

"I am afraid I cannot. My sincere apologies. But if you would not mind I have arranged for someone else to fill in. She will ring your room at precisely seven. Is that OK?"

Jake took too long to respond and the man said 'Fine, then goodbye' and hung up.

Jake drained his drink, looked at the desk clock, and decided he had time for a shower. He shrugged into his jacket just as the phone rang.

"Mr. Tillard?"

"Yes."

"My name is Satchi Uto. I'll be accompanying you to the theater this evening. I will wait in the piano lounge on the second floor if that suits you."

"I'll be down in a few minutes Ms. Uto."

He saw her the minute he walked in, seated by the piano. Tall, long dark hair, svelte body clothed in a small amount of black clingy material. Very long legs. She turned as he approached. Her skin was as white as the piano keys. She was gorgeous. Jake thought again of the girl on the plane.

The rest of the evening became a blur. Drinks at the piano loosened things up and it became obvious right away that Uto was not an employee of General Investments Ltd. This was not to say that she was not in their employ. The effect of seeing Miss Saigon with Satchi Uto was too much, and dinner at a new Thai restaurant drove in the final stake. They ended up back in Jake's suite, working hard to satisfy his fantasies of Asian beauties.

When his eyes opened the next morning, a note saying 'thanks for the good time' had replaced Satchi. Jake was about to become involved in Middle East whirlwinds again.

A quick phone call to Gussie assured him all was well at home before the limousine dropped him on the corner of 3rd Avenue and 51st at quarter past nine. Per instructions, he took the elevator to the 75th floor where the doors opened into a world of brown leather and dark wood. No modern glass or turquoise, this was a classic gentlemen's setting. Jake strode to the receptionist seated behind a large mahogany desk. No switchboard, no computer, no paper, not even the name of the company. Just a single telephone beside a leather blotter.

"Mr. Tillard?"

"Yes," Jake replied.

'Guess they don't get many visitors,' he thought as he found himself staring at an attractive blonde girl. Her features looked Dutch, with straight hair, fair skin, and a perfect toothy smile. When she rose to show him the way Jake couldn't help but look at her.

All three men in the paneled conference room were smoking. They rose as he approached. The oldest and fattest put his hand out. He was at least five inches shorter than Jake, balding, with a plump clean-shaven face.

"Ah, Mr. Tillard. Welcome to General Investments. We are so glad you agreed to visit us. My name is Osama abdel Fatah. Let me introduce you to Taha Shaarawi, and Aly Hakim. Please have a seat. Can I offer you tea, coffee? We are having Turkish coffee, if you would prefer that?"

Ordering a Turkish, he guessed his hosts were Egyptian, and thought that a good omen. Osama was fat and arrogant, probably from a rich background. He was obviously in charge and relished his position. Well built, athletic, and worried looking, Taha was probably the brains to the deal, possibly on the technical side. Aly looked like a thug, someone you didn't want to cross. He looked out of place in these refined surroundings. Jake believed all three were Egyptian but sensed they were different from the Egyptians he knew in Cairo. They seemed colder, more aloof, and more intense. Perhaps they had lived in New York too long.

Osama did most of the talking, deftly switching from pleasantries to business without Jake realizing it. General Investments Ltd was a holding company, the glue that bound together a film company in India, a flower and produce exporting corporation that supplied product from Egypt to Europe, a shipping business in the Pacific, and a world-wide spice trade. The owner of the private company wanted to do something new, while returning to his Egyptian roots. The idea of finding and supplying his motherland with natural gas appealed to him.

Although he asked leading questions, Jake could not discover the name of the owner. Osama evaded his inquiries with practiced expertise.

'What the hell', thought Jake, 'if a rich Egyptian wants to remain unnamed so be it.'

The bulk of the meeting was dedicated to the geology of the prospect. Taha's questions remained fairly general as time progressed.

"What have you learned from your fieldwork?"

Jake summarized his mapping of Cretaceous through Tertiary outcrops in the northern Sinai, explaining why the rocks on the surface bode well for reservoirs deeper down, and why the highly weathered surface samples couldn't shed reliable light on the quality of an oil source beneath the surface.

"Do you have any data on oil or gas shows in the Sinai?"

They discussed the lack of tests and hydrocarbons in the Sinai as a whole. Jake spoke about tectonic upheavals, which twisted the rocks in that area and formed the domes that he was sure had trapped natural gas.

Sometime in the late morning, after several coffees, Jake started to get an uneasy feeling, as the questions veered towards how he had found the mud log, where the prospect was located, and other details he was unwilling to divulge. He got the impression Taha was not well versed in geology. Although geologists were sometimes unrefined Taha was more than a bit coarse. Jake swung the conversation back to Osama and asked what the next step might be.

"Mr. abdel Fatah, I believe you now have enough information to decide whether to proceed. I suggest you talk with your organization and let me know if you would like to meet again. When might I hear from you?"

"Yes indeed Mr. Tillard. This has been most enlightening. We need two weeks before we can get back to you. Thank you for your time. This is just the kind of opportunity my superior is seeking."

Jake noticed for the second time Osama had used the word 'superior'. It had an odd sound to it, although English was a second language for the man. An old feeling welled up inside him, a feeling of caution, suspicion, and unease. It motivated him, and he decided to test the waters a bit further.

"Your superior, Mr. Fatah?" he said, deliberately leaving out the 'abdel' part of the name.

He noticed a slight flicker of Osama's eyelids before the man tried to hide his reaction by twitching his head.

"Why the owner of the company of course, Mr. Tillard."

Osama stood up a little too quickly after that comment and Jake knew he touched some sort of nerve. Was it organizational jealousy, a dislike of the big *'moudeer'*, or something else?

In any case, he stood up as well and extended his hand to Aly Hakim, the quiet behemoth who had said barely a dozen words.

"Shukran, Aly."

They shook hands all around and Jake left them in the conference room. On the way out he noted the slender blond was reading a magazine.

Jake sipped a drink at the Tavern on the Green in Central Park. The guilty feeling for running up his tab passed as dislike for the General Investments people grew. Maybe he was rationalizing a rejection already but he felt if they did not come back to him he wouldn't be disappointed.

He walked through the lobby of the Ritz, stopping at the front desk to pick up his key and ordered a bottle of Malbec sent to the room. The manager promised to send it right up, and handed Jake an envelope marked URGENT. He thought of Gussie with trepidation as he tore it open, fumbling with the paper inside. He breathed a sigh as he read. "Urgent you call at once. Gussie OK." But the unease re-emerged as he continued reading. "House broken into. Layla."

He thought about Egypt and wondered why he felt safer in the States? Houston was a far more dangerous place than Cairo. Pulling his phone from his jacket pocket, he dialed the house number. The phone conversation left him with a bad feeling. Layla and Gussie had been at a friend's house so Gussie could swim. When they returned home, Layla had noticed curtains in disarray, so she looked in the dining room window. Everything was in chaos, contents emptied from drawers and closets, cushions removed, books pulled from shelves. When she walked through the house, not a thing was in its place. She said the police now were at the house. Jake told her to book into a nearby hotel, and wondered how fast he could get home.

Jake had two thoughts.

'Thank God they're safe.'

And 'The mud log.'

CHAPTER 14

SIX hours after lifting off from LaGuardia, Jake pulled into his Houston driveway. A police car sat at the curb and the front door was wide open. Parking in front of the garage, he hopped the azaleas lining the flagstone steps and went through the front door. The grandfather clock lay to the left, its glass shattered, its pendulum protruding out the side at a clumsy angle. Both drawers of the English tea table were pulled out, their contents spread across the floor. Even the five foot tall antique Egyptian grain pot had been knocked off its limestone base, the three large pieces that remained looking like a giant broken egg. Everywhere he looked he saw pictures off the walls, furniture upended, and piles of belongings.

"Who are you?"

"Jake Tillard. This is my house."

"Oh. I'm sorry, sir. My name is Joe Collins, sheriff with the Tomball Police Department. Why don't we step outside and I'll answer any questions you might have."

Outside the sun was warm, the air was heavy, and the pine trees and roses appeared as if everything was normal.

"How bad is it? Who did this?" he asked the sheriff.

"Sir, as far as burglary goes this is as bad as I've seen. I can't say what's missing of course, but it seems they were lookin' for somethin' in particular. Mostly what we see 'round here they're lookin' for electronics or jewelry they can pawn. Usually drug addicts. Seems here they were tryin' to tear your place up searchin' for somethin' in particular. You got any idea what that could be?"

Joe was surprised by Jake's reaction. He'd seen women cry and men become infuriated and make crazy threats of retaliation. Jake's reaction was subdued. Jake developed the same ache in his gut that he had in the offices of General Investments.

"No disrespect, Sheriff, but is this in your league?"

"Actually sir 'bout mid-day I put in a call to HPD and asked for their Special Investigation Unit. They don't normally get involved in burglaries, but seems like they should take a look at this one. Detective Walker should be here any time now. You haven't seen the house yet so what makes you ask that question?"

"Your description of the house made me think this was unusual, that's all. Now if you don't mind I'd like to look in the house."

Jake walked straight to the office. The mud log was gone. With the sheriff in tow, he moved slowly through the dining room to the kitchen and breakfast room, drifting upstairs through the bedrooms, bathrooms, and Gussie's playroom. Jake didn't touch a thing. He knew nothing was missing except the mud log. Calling Layla from the bedroom he learned the scroll had been with them, Gussie and her friend coloring like mad, trying to finish it before 'Daddy' got home.

"That explains the mess," he muttered.

"What's that?" asked the Sheriff.

"Nothing," said Jake.

The Marriott became their home for the next week during which the police found no fingerprints, fibers, or clues of any kind. They reassured Jake the investigation would continue, but in reality knew it was a low priority. While mulling over the situation Jake noticed the message light on his room phone flashing. A man named Radisson had left a phone number to call with a Utah area code. It was only seven thirty there. He dialed the number. A female voice answered with a non-informative, "How may I help you?"

A half hour later, General Richard A. Radisson returned his call.

"Jake, thanks for returning my call. My name is Dick Radisson. I'm a senior investigator in the CIA. I understand you had a break-in at your house a few days ago."

"That's right. What's that got to do with the CIA?"

"Maybe nothing. I'd like to explain, but not over the phone. Where will you be the next couple days? I'd like one of my men to talk with you."

Jake hesitated. He had planned for months to attend his class reunion in New Hampshire the coming weekend but he was hesitant to leave Gussie again.

"Well, I'll be in Houston for two more days, then I'm supposed to be in Hanover, New Hampshire at a class reunion."

"I don't see any reason to cancel your plans. This can wait until you return to Houston."

"Mr. Radisson, I'd be happy to talk to your guy when I get home, but can you give me some idea of what this is all about."

"Sorry, no, Jake. I'll be in touch."

Radisson hung up the phone. He sighed and speed dialed '3' for Kawinski. A feminine voice stated that Stanley Kawinski was out and suggested leaving a message. Dick Radisson didn't bother leaving his name, but said, "check your email."

Before leaving for home he forwarded a network document to Kawinski's secure mailbox, a memo carrying a medium security classification from the National Energy Security archives, Middle East Section, Israeli Interest Desk, Miscellaneous Fact File. Ten men were detailed, with photos and resumes. Two of those men held 'Danger' assignations. Another was Jake Tillard. During routine telephone monitoring, Jake Tillard's name had come up in a conversation tied to the two dangerous men.

"**DAMN** it's pretty up here," Jake said, steering the rental through the picturesque Vermont valley.

When Jake searched for Radisson on the Internet, the best fit was a General who had graduated from the Air Force Academy and been stationed overseas and in Washington D.C. It seemed he currently worked for the government but it wasn't clear where.

Jake continued along Interstate 91, following the Connecticut River that separates Vermont and New Hampshire. June was his favorite time of the year here. Mud season had come and gone, the trees were a delicate green, the sky a dusty blue. After the previous week it felt comforting to be here, with memories of happy times and fewer responsibilities.

Passing Ascutney, he looked over the new townhouse developments and partially finished construction projects, searching for the ski hill he used to frequent. Rough economic times had hit New England, and there were signs of poverty everywhere.

At Norwich he slipped down the exit ramp and pulled over to gaze across the broad river at the campus of Dartmouth College, Baker Library's steeple rising above the pines and chestnuts. He continued across the low bridge into Hanover, reliving the years when he rowed crew. He coaxed the car uphill onto campus, parking in a space near the Hanover Inn. It was the perfect New England inn, its white clapboard exterior punctuated by deep forest green shutters. A long front porch was littered with green rocking chairs and cozy white wicker. Jake settled into one of the rockers, and gazed across the 'Green' to Dartmouth Row. Those four white brick buildings formed the early backbone of the College, founded in 1769. After checking into his antique-filled room, Jake spent the remainder of the afternoon walking around.

He came up a day before Reunion started to see how the college was doing. Although still dominated by undergraduates it looked different, like a mini United Nations. Kids from all ethnic backgrounds headed for their next class, laden with piercings, tattoos, and mismatched garments. Jake remembered cookie cutter male students, predominately white, middle or upper class preppies, with painter pants and Sperry Top-Siders. Times had changed.

Dinner the first evening was a solitary affair, at a corner table eating a garden salad, listening to a lone guitarist crooning 'Sounds of Silence'. After eating Jake wandered to Occom Pond where he had learned to create topographic maps his sophomore year. Without thinking he drifted down Fraternity Row to 'The Magic Green Cottage', walked up the front steps to his old fraternity house, and passed through the screen door. The house was in greater disrepair than when he was here three decades before.

The whole place looked like it could drink gallons of paint. Sporadic holes in the walls revealed slats behind plaster, and entire areas of molding and door trim were missing.

Stragglers from spring term were sprawled in the basement's 'Tube Room' watching classic television shows on Nickelodeon. Jake joined them before switching at some point to play beer pong on the decrepit ping-pong table soaked by innumerable spilled beers. That was the last thing he remembered before waking the next morning. He held his head as he rose, and stumbled into a bathroom that reeked from last night's activities. Or more accurately the activities of the last term. Outside, the sun hurt his eyes, which in turn sent a message to his head, which made it hurt even more. 'And the reunion hasn't started yet,' Jake thought.

As the weekend progressed Jake recognized old friends and acquaintances, talking to at least a dozen people about his gas opportunity, vaguely hoping to tap into the bank accounts of his more successful fellow alums. On the morning before he left, Charles Alfred Lister III sat next to him at breakfast in the class of '72 tent. They had crewed together. Not close in school, they knew the same crowd and could remember enough common events to rebuild a connection.

Charles had been an obnoxious guy as an undergraduate, and hadn't changed. He had the composure of a 'third', clearly coming from money and not embarrassed to let you know. These days he ran a venture capital company, doling out his friends' and associates' money to worthwhile business ventures. He had never entered the world of oil and gas, but seemed interested, until he stood to leave.

"Jake, enjoy yourself. I say this whole reunion thing is a tad surreal. On one hand it seems no time has passed since we were here. On the other it seems like another lifetime."

"Yea. Makes me wonder what I've been doing the last couple decades."

As he left the 'Hanover Plain' Jake was filled with emotions. It seemed as though the weekend had thrown fuel on his current fire. Remembering the wild times, the freedom, the fun, and especially the lack of responsibility made him wistful.

The drive to Boston was lonely and depressing, the flight to Houston worse. He drowned himself in gin and tonics and fell asleep somewhere over Kentucky, not far from the spot where the Oriental girl with the nice legs had fallen asleep several flights earlier.

CHAPTER 16

JAKE woke when Gussie yelled "Daddy, phone", before dropping the receiver to the floor. The person on the other end undoubtedly heard an unpleasant noise when the phone bounced on the tile floor. Jake didn't care.

He picked up the receiver, "Hello".

"Mr. Tillard, this is Osama abdel Fatah from General Investments. I've been trying to reach you for several days. How are you?"

"I'm fine Mr. abdel Fatah. I've been out of town. How are you?" He rubbed at his eyes, trying to wake up.

"I am most well, thank you."

A brief pause gave Jake more time to clear his head.

"I have reviewed your package with my top manager. We are definitely interested in pursuing your opportunity. We have funding set aside, and can now work towards an agreement."

Jake knew enough about the culture to tread carefully and to continue without jumping to conclusions about exactly what was being communicated. He sensed enough promises and sureties in Osama's speech that he suspected all was not yet tied up. It was time to clarify and confirm, something he had practiced ad infinitum in Egypt.

"Wonderful, Mr. abdel Fatah. I can't tell you how that makes me feel. My prospect is a good opportunity, and I'm looking forward to working with your organization. Can I ask if there is anything else you need before progressing?"

Jake would have put money on his hunch that the boys from General Investments were far from ready to ante up. The question was how to extract just what obstacles remained. Osama answered after a hesitation just long enough to convey that something indeed was missing.

"Nothing significant really. We would like one more person to review the technical data. An expert from the Middle East. A geologist familiar with the Arabian Gulf."

He noticed Osama's aversion to the more common term 'Persian Gulf'. Gulf Arabs made a point of this, but he did not think Egyptians would make that distinction. It raised another warning flag.

"No problem. I can meet him at his convenience. Just what would he like to see?"

The conversation continued dancing around the facts. Jake tried everything to pin him down, and finally took a stab at the mud log.

"The only thing I didn't show in New York was the mud log, the direct evidence for the gas. But I told you what it shows. It's not complicated."

Osama jumped on this a bit too quickly.

"Yes, the mud log, that would be important. I know our Middle East expert wants to see this with his own eyes. He thinks older mud logs can be quite interpretive. They need a practiced eye, someone with lots of experience. Do you have the mud log with you?"

Jake had not spoken about the whereabouts of the log during his visit in New York. Osama seemed too concerned with its well being.

"Yes, I do. Don't worry. I'm sure your expert will find it revealing. Shall I come to your office?"

Again a quick response.

"No. No. Actually it would be more convenient if this meeting could be held in Houston. Our representative is in Houston now for two more days. Can you find the time to meet?"

Jake thought about this, and decided to test a bit deeper.

"I'm afraid it would need to be either today, or if not then Friday. I am unavailable the next three days."

"I'm sure Friday would be fine. Our representative can extend his visit, no problem."

Jake pressed a bit further.

"I would be happy to call him this morning. Where is he staying?"

Osama sidestepped this question, not giving a hotel name. Jake had guessed correctly that no representative had yet arrived in Houston. He hung up after agreeing to meet Friday afternoon.

The phone took a ten-minute rest before ringing again. This

time Gussie shouted "Telephone for Daddy". By chance, she put the receiver down in such a manner that it stayed on the table, thus no loud sound made its way to the ear of General Dick Radisson.

"Jake, a colleague of mine will stop by to discuss some things. I hope you can wait for him. He'll have my recommendation. Let me know what you think."

The line went dead; Jake hung up and stared across the living room, that feeling starting in his gut again. He knew things were about to unravel. He suspected General Investments was part of the plot.

Gussie came running through the living room wearing a swimsuit, the palm tree on her bikini bottom swaying with every step as if caught by a tropical breeze. Jake watched it sway out of sight knowing he would be in big trouble in about five years. 'She's going to be gorgeous, just like her mom,' he muttered under his breath.

Layla ran after her as he thought again of the break-in and of what might have happened had they been there during the break-in. The phone rang once more. Charles Alfred Lister III sounded as arrogant over the phone as he did in person.

"Jake, Charles here. Jake, my boy, how was your journey home?"

Jake was in no mood for small talk. Trying to keep his irritation under control he became less interested with every passing minute. Gussie ran through again, almost wiping out an English tea table holding a Chinese vase, Layla again in tow. He was about to shout at her when Charles said something to catch his attention. Jake missed the beginning of the remark but caught the end.

"...two of my colleagues are intrigued enough to take a look at your deal."

"I'm sorry Charles, would you run that by me again. My daughter just ran through the room nearly taking out a Qing vase. I'm afraid I missed what you just said."

"Qing, very nice. Basically Jake, we are interested in your deal. None of us know much about oil and gas so we've hired a consultant to give us a hand. What's your schedule the next couple weeks?"

'When it rains it pours,' thought Jake.

He hadn't even shown the deal to Charles and his buddies but already felt better with them as potential backers. He had not been comfortable with General Investments from their first meeting and hoped he could soon give them the slip.

"Charles, I can meet anytime. You name it."

They made arrangements to meet in Saint Louis on Wednesday. Two of the potential investors lived there so it would be convenient for them. Jake was beginning to feel more optimistic. He didn't like the idea of leaving Gussie again so soon after the break-in but knew he needed to do this.

Just past noon the sun beat down through dense humidity. Walking to the pool where Gussie swam with a friend under the watchful eye of Layla, Jake hung his legs over the edge. Although Gussie didn't want him to leave again, she didn't seem too upset. Again he was thankful that Layla was there. At least he would be back by Friday for his meeting with Osama's expert. The front doorbell rang.

Grabbing a towel he padded through the kitchen and living room to the front hall, leaving a trail of wet footprints. Since the break-in he had made a habit of checking the peephole before opening the door. Staring through the tiny glass he saw a distorted police badge of some sort.

"My name is Stan Kawinski. General Radisson sent me."

Jake swung the door open and looked at Stan.

"Dick wants me to brief you on our current thoughts regarding your situation. He's worried. Perhaps you could rustle up some drinks and find a quiet place to talk."

They moved to Jake's study with a couple gin and tonics. Stan was overwhelmed by the clutter; African masks, an Indonesian gong, a collection of carved canes sitting in an extravagantly engraved brass artillery shell. The walls were peppered with antique maps and diplomas, interspersed with framed fabrics, Bedouin wedding veils, and photographs. The real clutter however was the pile of paper and technical journals.

"Still getting everything back in order or is this your normal office style?" Stan glanced around for somewhere to sit. The stuffed chairs held their own piles of papers.

"A little of both I guess." Jake moved some of the mess onto the floor and they both sat down. "So start at the beginning."

"Jake, I'll be honest. Dick Radisson is a very special person. He started in the Air Force, progressing through the ranks before moving to the State Department. His first post was in Iran as the Shah was being booted out. He was based in DC but was frequently stationed overseas. While in Syria he switched to the CIA, unofficially of course. When he moved back to the States the last time he went official."

"Dick thrived in the CIA. He's smart, composed, and exceptionally persistent. Cool as a cucumber, hungry as a shark. To top it off he has a photographic memory. His dedication and intensity paid off. As the Middle East blew up with the oil embargo, his regional expertise became invaluable. His counterparts knew a lot about the Cold War and the Soviet Union but that arena was winding down. Dick made it very near the top of the CIA before moving back to State under Christopher. So let's talk about you."

"Before we get onto me, what about you? Are you with the State Department?"

"No," replied Stan flatly. "I'm with the CIA, still an agent. I chose not to go management. I like the field too much. The whole illusion of international intrigue. Macho stuff. I tried a desk job, got bored, and took a lateral move back to field ops. Dick brought me back as his personal field supervisor and I stayed in similar positions after he left."

"One more question. What was Dick doing in an office in Utah?"

"Ah, the area code. That's a convolution dreamed up by Radisson years ago. For many spooks and muckity-mucks, the Fed maintains central numbers they can give out. One for friends, one for foes, one for emergencies. That sort of thing. Operators patch callers through to appropriate people wherever they might be. In your case, they would have put you through either to the Pentagon, Dick's house in Virginia, his cabin in the Smokies, or his cell phone. It's basically a switchboard and secretarial screening process. No one is really in Utah."

They sipped their G and T's before Stan continued.

"Has General Investments called?"

"Yes. I spoke with Osama abdel Fatah this morning."

"Are they in a hurry to see you?"

"They want me to talk with their Middle East geologist Friday. Someone from the Gulf States with experience in that part of the world. I got a funny feeling when I talked with Osama. They're too interested in the mud log."

At Stan's urging Jake relayed in detail the story of his mud log discovery and his efforts since to sell his prospect. He discussed his experience in New York and the mixed feelings he had about that group.

Stan leaned forward and put his glass down on the nearest pile of books.

"So. There is no General Investments Ltd. Last week I went to New York to check them out. The office you visited was empty. It was probably a staged production just for you. The phone had been pulled out and the number forwarded to an answering service. The building manager said he'd rented the space for a two-month period but after doing some remodeling and moving in, the tenant stayed only a week. A Middle Eastern male had given him cash for the rent. The name and address on file didn't check out. No one at the office remembers setting up the account."

Jake's gut began to throb again. He tried to fathom the implications of what Stan was telling him. He looked at Stan and started to say something but words would not come out.

"Dick is worried about you and your family. It sounds like you've realized the Middle East boys were not kosher. Dick believes they're after your mud log and were the ones who tore up your house. Did you tell them you still have it?"

The nightmare began to unfold in Jake's mind.

"This morning on the phone I told them I have it. Honestly I offered that up to see if they would bite. I suspected that's what they were after."

"And did they bite?"

"Oh, yeah. Big time. I don't get why they're doing this?"

"Hey it's your industry. People do bad things to get control of oil. We need to figure out who these jokers are and stop them. Can you pop into our office in D.C. and run through a few scenarios? You know, look at some pictures, and play with some computers."

"I need to be in St. Louis Wednesday."

"You could stop on the way. I can fly you to Washington tomorrow noon, giving us most of the afternoon and evening. You can then take a flight to St Louis."

Jake considered the timing. He would barely have time to pack and say good-bye. He hated leaving Gussie.

"Stan, is this necessary? I don't know what else I can tell you guys."

"OK. Let's forget the trip to DC. I might be able to get some data and photos to you here but there's another issue. Dick believes it would be best for Gussie to leave Houston. We don't think it's safe here."

The world began to unravel. Jake thought of Gussie on the run. He contemplated what he'd gotten them into.

"My dad has a ranch in Montana. Do you think Gussie will be OK there?"

Stan looked into Jake's eyes again.

"Does your dad know what's going on?"

"Of course not. I didn't even know till now. I mean he knows about my prospect. I've told him about the contacts I made and the funding possibilities. He knows I didn't much like the General Investments folks. And I just told him I'm going up to St Louis to try for funding from a fellow alum. But he doesn't know about the link of the robbery to the mud log."

"You need to tell him everything. If we protect Gussie in Montana, we're going to need at least a couple agents there. Do you think that will be a problem?"

"Honestly, yes. They don't get much tougher than my dad. He won't tolerate agents on his ranch. He'll want to take care of Gussie himself."

The pain in his gut grew bigger. After Stan left he made arrangements for Layla and Gussie to fly to Missoula. Layla wasn't the best with airplanes but he thought Gussie could take care of her.

CHAPTER 17

JAKE tried to ride up the Arch but tickets were sold out. The afternoon was sultry, almost Houston-hot. He was dressed in a golf shirt and khakis, trying to beat back the sweat.

A watercolor caught his eye in a gallery window just off Olive Street. It was a pyramid with a gusher coming out. Or so it looked to Jake. In fact it was highly abstract, a mix of burgundy reds, oranges, and muted grays. The gallery was one of those minimalist affairs, white walls and open space. There were only a dozen or so paintings in the whole place. All were abstract. All were big. All were in the same color pallet as the painting in the window. None were distinctly anything but they all reminded Jake of the Middle East. He saw veiled figures in one, a mashrabiya screen in another.

"Hauntingly beautiful isn't it?"

The girl by his side was clearly anorexic. Jake thought she resembled something in the paintings. She didn't return his look but continued to stare absently at the watercolor. She wore a thin white cotton dress with spaghetti straps and no bra. Her skin was white like the walls, her hair black like ink. Jake thought she might have been pretty if she wasn't so gaunt.

"I don't know if I would've used those words," he answered. "I find them stimulating. Inspiring."

"There aren't many here but I find myself absorbed all day long."

Jake wondered what she had done to herself.

"They remind me of the Middle East," said Jake.

The girl looked at him. She had sorrowful, dark eyes.

"Most people don't pick up on that."

"On what?"

"The artist is from Lebanon. She grew up in Beirut. Saw the city fall apart. After the Beirut bombing she moved to New York. Now she paints her past. Can't get it out of her system."

Jake considered that for a moment. He felt the same way. He disliked parts of the Middle East culture but couldn't get it out of his system. The fact that he wandered into this particular gallery confirmed it. He said good-bye to the ghost woman and stepped back into the heat. Feeling drained, he headed towards his hotel.

The taxi stopped in front of the St. Louis Club a bit after eight. Jake stepped out beneath a merlot colored awning that extended from the front door. A formally dressed doorman opened the massive brass door, directing Jake to a dining room towards the rear. It made him think of the private men's clubs of his father's generation, furnished with décor creating an atmosphere of understated elegance and old money. Cigar permeated the place. The maître d' showed him to a table where Charles Alfred Lister III sat, sipping wine. Dressed in a charcoal suit with currently fashionable wide lapels, Charles' tie appeared to be the only aspect of his attire that was not conservative. It was one of those wild concoctions designed by some old rock star for charity. The restaurant was dark and intimate, the kind of restaurant Jake hated. Stuffy waiters, bad lighting, poor ventilation, cigar odor, and French food. It was expensive but it was a private club and that was not his problem. He could feel the clientele staring at his graying beard and ponytail.

At eight thirty Charles' two colleagues joined them. Jake quickly sized them up. Chester Grant was old, perhaps eighty, frail, and conservatively dressed, not unlike an undertaker. Gary White was younger, maybe forty, dressed like an Italian; crumpled olive green suit, skinny Chanel tie, wavy black hair swept over his head.

'The odd couple to be sure,' Jake thought. 'Or odd trio if you include me.'

They spent the next couple hours drinking, eating, and talking. Charles had warned him this was to be purely social, and business never came up. Chester dozed off twice that Jake saw. No one else seemed to notice. Gary White had a never-ending litany of humorous family problems. When Chester was alert he talked of his three dead wives and their idiosyncrasies. Charles was quiet, allowing his partners to explore Jake's personality. As Jake expected the smoke was heavy and the food heavier. In his mind it was a barely endurable evening.

Leaving the restaurant after eleven, Charles drove Jake to the hotel in his Jaguar. As he got out Charles told him to get a good night sleep. They would meet at nine for the business review. It would be thorough and exhaustive.

The office of Lister and Associates was a surprise. Jake had expected a small well-appointed office with a secretary or two, and maybe a few financial types. Lister and Associates occupied four floors of one of the newer high-rises in the heart of Saint Louis. He took an elevator to the twentieth floor where a receptionist sat behind a large stone desk surrounded by electronics, computers, and screens displaying data. She appeared busy, in contrast to the one he had encountered at General Investments. In between calls she buzzed someone to retrieve Jake.

While waiting he looked past her through glass walls into a large bullpen, where people were crammed in, punching on computers, screaming into phones, and running around everywhere. It looked like a cross between what Jake thought a bond trading room would look like, and an advertising agency. He was mesmerized. This was a business. He didn't know what he had expected but this wasn't it. This was something he never expected in St Louis. Most of the workers wore tee shirts or golf shirts. Some were in shorts, others in suits. Posters were taped to the walls. A philodendron climbed up a column in the middle of the room, where someone had fastened it to the ceiling with tacks. It seemed to defy gravity, creeping along for fifteen feet across to the window where it hung down.

"Ready to sign up?"

Jake spun around and faced a young man in a light tan suit and club tie.

"My name is Tom Plumber. Mr. Lister asked me to show you around. His apologies, but your meeting had to be postponed until ten."

Jake looked at the clock on the wall and read nine fifteen. He had been concerned when he got stuck in traffic. At least his late arrival didn't matter. They shook hands.

"I'd love a tour," replied Jake. "This is not what I expected."

"Wait till you see it up close and personal. If you'd like, you can leave your briefcase with Leslie and she'll see that it finds you later."

Jake walked behind the reception desk and handed her his oversized briefcase. Leslie smiled pleasantly in return.

"Lister and Associates has four Divisions. The backbone of the company is the Link Division. They build computer modems. That's what created the company and it's still our bread and butter. The largest section in terms of staff is our Games Division which you are looking at now."

Jake peered again through the glass into the large room bustling with activity.

"Some years it's the most profitable, and other years it posts a loss. In my opinion it's the most fun, maybe because it's where I started. Not as much fun is the Commercial Division downstairs. They wear dark suits and spend their lives staring into screens, trading commodities, buying and selling businesses, and dealing with derivatives. Last is the Venture Capital Division. That's where you'll spend the rest of the day."

They entered into 'the funhouse' as the company referred to the bullpen of the Games Division. Tom explained their business mission as they wandered through the mass of creativity.

"Since it was formed ten years ago, their unwavering goal has been to create leading edge computer games. As the industry grew bigger they focused on the upper end market."

Jake noted that some employees seemed to be teenagers, which made sense when he thought about it. Tom stopped in front of a particularly odd looking young man with a very strange looking machine, if you could call it that. He introduced the kid, all of twenty years old, to Jake as a games genius. Standing on a rubber mat in Converse sneakers, he had a virtual reality helmet strapped to his head.

"Our newest technology," he offered.

After explaining how the setup worked he strapped the same helmet onto Jake, threw a switch, and stood back. Jake saw himself standing on what appeared to be a golf course.

"Where am I," he asked.

"You are on the first tee box at Pebble Beach. Normal green fees are around four hundred dollars a round. Of course you'd have to get yourself there, rent a car, stay in a hotel, and use a caddy. Add in meals, drinks, and miscellaneous, and you'd be lucky to get by for less than fifteen hundred bucks for your round. In a few months we'll have these contraptions scattered around the East Coast. You'll be able to play eighteen holes at Pebble Beach in an hour for sixty bucks. Don't like Pebble Beach? Try one of the other forty courses we've got from around the world."

Jake held onto the 'golf club' that Tom thrust into his hands, addressed the 'virtual ball', and took a swing. He looked up to see his ball headed off the fairway to the right. It bounced a couple times and rolled into a trap about two hundred yards out. Jake took a step towards the fairway and nearly got sick as the ground rushed under his feet. In a few seconds, he looked down at his ball. Turning around he saw the tee box over two hundred yards away. That explained the eighteen holes in an hour. The bottom of his vision field contained green LED numbers indicating he was one hundred eighty yards from the pin. He said 'four iron' out loud and the number four appeared next to the distance with a 'yes' beside it to indicate the computer agreed with the club choice. He felt the club vibrate and realized its length had changed, becoming shorter as the 'driver' became a 'four iron'. Jake swung again and watched his ball hook left over the hedge out of bounds.

"Wow, bummer," the geek said.

Jake removed the helmet.

"That's pretty neat," he said.

Tom said they expected to install two thousand of the machines within two years, with each machine netting at least eighty thousand dollars a year the first year.

"Do you give your profit projections to everyone," Jake asked.

"I've never been asked to give them to anyone before. Charles told me to lay out the welcome mat for you. Nothing out of bounds."

They walked through three Lister and Associates floors before ending up in a very large, if unspectacular, conference room. Leslie replaced Tom and brought Jake's briefcase to him.

"Is there anything you need Mr. Tillard? Coffee? Tea?"

"Coffee would be fine, thank you, Leslie."

"Yes, sir. Mr. Lister will be just a couple minutes."

He watched as she exited the door. Alone again he considered the morning. 'OK Charles, you have the money,' he thought. He had never doubted that. 'Why did you give me the million dollar tour? Were you really delayed?'

"Jake, apologies my boy." Charles came through the door with Gary White and two men Jake hadn't yet met. Chester obviously wouldn't be making it.

"Let me introduce our technical experts. Dave Potlatch is our geologist." One of the newcomers raised his hand in a small gesture. "Dave took a Ph.D. in geology from Cambridge, started with British Gas, worked twelve years for Exxon Research, five for Saudi Aramco, and formed his own company eight years ago. He's also from Houston."

"Lou Adams is our engineer-economist. With degrees from MIT and Imperial Lou has parlayed his talents into buying, improving, and selling producing properties in the western US and Canada. His expertise is project planning and facilities construction. He flew in this morning from Calgary."

The three ordered coffee from Leslie when she brought in Jake's cup. No small talk was invited, Dave requesting that Jake start at the technical beginning. As Jake discussed the regional geologic story behind the structural and sedimentary history of the Sinai Peninsula it became obvious from the infrequent but penetrating questions that Dave was very good and had done some research ahead of the meeting. He picked up on uncertainties, probing those areas that had relevance to the gas prospect. He was particularly inquisitive in all areas of major risk.

One major concern was source rock. Dave demanded to know everything Jake could tell him about the layer of rock which had supposedly generated and liberated the natural gas. Jake purported it was generated within the Jurassic Safa Formation, a layer of rock two hundred yards thick lying beneath the entire northern half of the Sinai. The Safa had been laid down about two hundred million years ago as a swamp. Over the next hundred million years it was heated and pressed beneath thousands of feet of younger sediments, transforming the old plant material into natural gas.

Dave focused on evidence proving Jake's hypothesis. The Safa Formation did not reach the surface in the entire Sinai, so geologists couldn't sample it directly. It had been penetrated within the Sinai by only three wellbores drilled back in the thirties, and data from these wells was questionable. The best evidence for source viability came from Egypt's Western Desert two hundred miles to the west. Wells there had cut through the Jurassic and recent discoveries were producing wet gas that could be 'typed back' to Jurassic source rocks.

The biggest challenge was proving that the swamp had extended across the whole Sinai. Even if it had, there was little evidence to show that the same thick section of organic rich source beds was preserved.

Jake did the best he could to show what evidence existed, weaving a story as intricate as that of a trial lawyer in a difficult lawsuit. It did not help that he could not show any of the original data he had left with Reacher in Egypt. After leaving Reacher, he went to the EGPC and got some data, but only a little. Dave would have to accept that his memory was good, and that he was honest.

They spent a whole hour on the source story. Before lunch they covered the deposition of the source, reservoir, and seal rocks. Eating while working they discussed the three consecutive structural upheavals that had contorted and pushed up the flat lying rock layers into domes, that could trap gas as it buoyantly tried to flow to the surface and escape.

Mid afternoon they switched to topics important to Lou. He wanted to know the composition of gas produced in the Western Desert, in order to estimate the type of fluid that might exist in the Sinai. Any liquid hydrocarbons would complicate flow through a single pipeline. If it contained any water, corrosion would be a problem. If it contained even small amounts of hydrogen sulfide, it could be deadly and would need special metallurgical pipe. If the liquid phase contained any waxy molecules, expensive chemical treatment might be required to keep it from solidifying in the pipe. Anticipated pressures in the reservoir would dictate what kind of compressors would be required. And on and on. They marched through areas Jake had considered when he was with Reacher Oil but never needed to answer himself. His engineer normally did this work. Jake began to feel that even if his prospect found gas it would be nearly impossible to make money.

At seven that night with only minimal breaks the experts ran out of questions. They very graciously thanked Jake and left without hinting at their conclusions. Jake was drained.

Most of the day he had been locked up with the two consultants and Gary White, who said no more than ten words. Gary walked out with Dave and Lou leaving Jake to pack up his displays and data. Charles came in and asked Jake if he would like to have dinner. Charles had to leave for Paris the next morning and wanted the opportunity to say good-bye. Jake was exhausted but famished. He agreed but was not encouraged. Neither the technical grilling nor Charles' demeanor suggested he would be getting good news from Lister and Associates.

This time, Charles picked an Italian restaurant on The Hill, with an atmosphere more to Jake's liking. Italian music and the smell of garlic filled the air. Waiters in black and white wove in and out of the crowded room, with big round trays of food and drinks. Simple wood chairs and crisp white tablecloths suggested a typical Sicilian roadhouse.

Jake was worried. Where would it leave him if Charles and his crew didn't buy into the deal? Charles ordered fried calamari and Chianti, served in a clay pitcher. Neither man smiled. Jake formed a mental image of himself in a canoe slipping over the edge of a waterfall.

"OK Charles, give me the bottom line please. Are you interested or not?"

Charles leaned back with his glass of wine and began his explanation, avoiding 'the bottom line'.

"Our technical experts advised us of a fairly long string of potential risks. You must remember that Lister and Associates has never entered into an upstream oil or gas exploration deal. This is new ground for us."

Jake had an empty feeling. Realizing just how much hope he had put with Charles he stared at the older man as he droned on in his arrogant voice about the unlikelihood of success and the risks associated with drilling this well. Jake didn't need this. He knew the risks all too well. It had been his life. He debated whether to argue or shout out how this prospect was different. That the well had really already been drilled. How it didn't get any better than this. He opened his mouth to speak. Before anything came out he shut it, the words coming out of Charles' mouth not what he had expected.

"After our experts scared the shit out of us, they recommended we participate to the greatest amount possible."

Jake thought he misunderstood. He paid closer attention to Charles, who now leaned forward with both hands on the tablecloth.

"We are prepared to offer the following. Lister and Associates will provide all funds required for exploration up to a cap of ten million dollars. You provide or hire all technical and operating expertise as you see fit. You have full authority to act as the operator, the COO if you will. We hold a sixty percent working interest leaving forty percent for you. Although we will carry you for the exploration phase, you become liable for your forty percent of costs after a discovery well is successfully tested. Of course we might be able to act as your banker in setting up loans at fair market rates. What do you think?"

Jake was stunned. 'I got it,' he thought. 'I got it. The money hunt is over.'

"I think that's great Charles."

Jake shook his head and laughed. He reached over, poured more Chianti, and took a sip, knowing the next part of the conversation was critical. The percentage Charles wanted was higher than what Jake had in mind. He had envisioned a fifty-fifty split. He needed to negotiate.

Neither man wanted to gouge the other. This attitude of seeking a consensus was not common in any industry but was particularly rare in the oil business. They finalized a deal in ten minutes. Lister and Associates would retain a fifty-one percent working interest, giving them an overriding vote. They would put up all exploration and development money, carrying Jake for his share, to be paid back from production profits. Although Jake would get only a modest salary until Lister and associates recouped all their investment, Jake was ecstatic. This was what he wanted. He would not worry about putting his own money at risk, even for the development phase that he would normally be expected to fund. Both men were happy with the deal. Jake got almost everything he wanted. Charles gave up less than he had the authority to give up.

Charles picked up the clay pitcher and again filled both wine glasses. He held his up in toast.

"To a successful endeavor and a healthy profit for both of us. Yahoo. I'm in the oil business." The 'yahoo', too loud, seemed out of character.

"To all that and more," said Jake. "Especially to getting the concession to begin with. The rest will be easier."

The remainder of the evening was icing on the cake. The pressure was off. Charles did most of the talking, recounting his entry into the world of big business. After graduating from Dartmouth he worked with a large discount department store chain, where a rapid rise into management left him unsatisfied. He noticed the mid 80's trend towards personal computing and guessed millions of people would need to communicate with other computers through phone lines. He formed Lister Industries to make modems, and one thing led to another. He became filthy rich.

For his part Jake spoke mostly about his exploits as a geologist. Helicopters, the bush in Alaska, the desert in the Middle East. He knew it sounded exotic to the average American and he had fallen into the habit of embellishing actual facts. It balanced out the fact that he was not rich.

They ended the evening with Charles promising to get a letter of intent drawn up the next day. The paperwork to actually form the partnership would take several weeks but the binding letter of intent would free up spending money for Jake and allow Lister and Associates to breathe easier knowing they had the deal captured.

Charles gave Jake a ride to the hotel. As he walked to the reception desk Jake did not notice the very large man sitting against the far wall to his right. Of Middle Eastern descent, he kept his face hidden behind a newspaper while Jake retrieved his room key, walked across the lobby, and pushed the button for the elevator. When the elevator swallowed him up the man lumbered to his feet and swished out the revolving door.

Getting into a blue sedan, the fat man elicited an amused stare from the doorman. Before the car door even closed the fat man and his driver began speaking in loud tones, gesturing emphatically.

They spoke in colloquial Egyptian Arabic and only they knew what was said.

The next morning Jake and Charles signed the letter of intent and shook hands for the last time. That afternoon Jake flew out of St. Louis, deal in hand, headed for his dad's ranch in Montana.

CHAPTER 18

ON windless days the pulp mill's yellow haze hung over Missoula
and the northern Bitterroot Valley. The Ford F250 from the Bar-J
Ranch headed south, fleeing the especially thick smog. To the west
rose the linear Bitterroot Mountain range, made of billion year old
granite rising more than six thousand feet from the valley floor. An
early US Geologic Survey effort mapped this ridge system as the
continental divide, defining in error the border between Montana
and Idaho. Years later another survey showed the true continental
divide near Butte, a hundred miles to the east. Nevertheless the
Bitterroot Range remained the divider of states.

East of the valley rose the less impressive but equally beautiful
Sapphire Mountains. Geologists believe the Sapphires, which
stretch more than sixty miles, slid off the Bitterroots on a slippery
layer of shale when the latter were uplifted fifteen million years ago.
As if God had not made the area magnificent enough, He added a
bit extra, putting a sapphire mine right in the middle of the range.
As a teenager Jake used to drive over Skalkaho Pass and pan gravel
for the semi-precious stones.

Jake grew up between the two ranges, his family ranch south of
Missoula near the town of Hamilton. There wasn't much around
then, the nearest neighbors four miles away. The last twenty years
saw an invasion by Californians looking for peace, beauty, and
somewhere to put their money while escaping state taxes. Rich ones
bought ranches. Others bought summer homes. The newcomers
were spoiled, pampered, and soft, unlike the old settlers and Native
Americans, who had a rugged spirit born from necessity.

Lester the ranch manager was driving the Ford. Neither of them
prone to ramble, they had caught up on events quickly while waiting
for luggage. In the car they drove in silence, giving Jake time to reflect.
The road followed the river on its west bank, where new log homes
had been built in what Jake knew was hundred-year flood plain.

Finally they pulled off the main road and stopped. Jake got out and looked up at a large stone and timber arch with the 'Bar-J' brand at the apex. He had helped erect this vertical welcome mat more than twenty years ago, the arch made of round Bitterroot granite boulders bigger than Jake's head. The brand was etched into a circular polished disk of granite, the inset symbol coated with gold leaf. The granite disk had been his dad's idea. The local mortuary dealer made it. The gold leaf had been his mother's. Early in the morning when the rising sun caught the gold just so, it reflected back as brilliantly as the sun itself. Whenever Jake saw it at sunrise he thought of his mom.

Gussie and the three dogs reached him first as he got out of the Ford. His dad, Layla, and the cook waited on the front porch. It was nice to be back at the ranch.

After chasing Gussie around the large open family room Jake settled into a worn leather chair with a Lucky Lager. It was more than a year since he had been to the ranch. He got along fine with his dad but neither was a talker. When they were together both tended towards silence rather than discussion. His father went to get two more beers.

The house hadn't changed much. The log walls held trophies of elk, deer, moose, and one grizzly shot by his mother. He smiled as he recalled that event. She was camping with the boys when the big bear came up from the stream into their camp. Jake had been only eight but could remember it like yesterday. His mom tried to talk with the bear, but that did not work. Standing on its hind legs, sniffing their scent, the bear charged as soon as his front legs hit the ground. Dolores Tillard had waited to see what the bear would do before shooting twice. The bear fell eight feet in front of them.

Below the trophies were framed photographs. They were all family; none showed the governors and more famous people that visited from time to time. There was Jake and his brother Tom with strings of rainbow, brown, and cutthroat trout. The family on peaks around the area and skiing the backcountry. His mom and dad lounging in the natural hot springs west of the property. They had all been close. Tom and their mom died when Jake was nineteen, killed instantly in a head-on with a pickup. In those days, they didn't wear seat belts. They did however drive drunk.

Gussie dashed in, climbed onto his lap, and spent the next five minutes filling him in on what she'd done in the last five days. It sounded like his childhood. Grandpa had taken her riding and fishing. They'd been around the ranch on treasure hunts looking for fiddlehead ferns, white quartz in the creek, and all sorts of plants and trees. Gussie had her own horse named Yipper and couldn't talk enough about all the farm animals. He tried to hug her but she was off again before his arms closed around her. Layla, as usual, ran after her.

"Son I've enjoyed immensely having my granddaughter here at the ranch. And I'm glad you could swing bringin' Layla. She's a gem."

"I know dad. She getting along OK here in the wild?"

"She's had to get used to some different ways, but I think she's enjoyin' herself."

The two men had another beer while the cook put food on the wooden table. The steaks were good but slightly overdone the way his dad liked them. It was nice to be back. To the US. To the ranch.

They spent the next week enjoying what God had provided. Jake picked a horse and rode every morning. The Bar-J had changed little in the last thirty years. Two thousand acres, it backed up on National Forest to the west where they ran cattle. The current ranch house stood in the southern portion with a small barn and corral to one side. The main stocks, barn, and ranch buildings were half a mile north. The original house still stood next to the main barn. Dolores had been insistent when they built their new house that it be at least that far away from the ranch workings. Although she loved the property she grew sick of the noise, smell, and men associated with ranching. Jake's dad didn't mind moving the house at all. Lester took care of almost everything by then and a little privacy did not bother him.

After totally relaxing for the first few days Jake decided it was time for business. He spent time each day putting together a bid document for the Sinai acreage block. Without notes from his Reacher days he operated on memory. Giving it his best shot he constructed a bid document for a basic production sharing agreement (PSA). He would agree to pay the government a signing bonus of one million dollars when they awarded him rights to explore. After signing the concession he had four years to acquire at least two hundred miles of seismic and drill at least one well. His commitment for that was five million dollars. He would have options to enter into second and third exploration periods of three years and two wells each. The total spend for all three terms could be as much as twenty million dollars. If drilling were successful, he would have the right to develop and produce oil and gas for twenty-five years. The Egyptian government would share the oil or gas stream, their percentage varying with the level of production. Basically, Jake's company would end up with about twenty percent of any production.

Production sharing agreements were common. The basic idea was simple, but they had very complicated details involving bonuses, periodic partial acreage relinquishments, taxes, penalties, and graduated production splits. Jake did his best, but knew he would need expert help. He called his old buddy Larry "Snake" Holt, lawyer and professional negotiator.

The "Snake" arrived Wednesday afternoon and Jake drove him from the airport directly to Luke's, a local bar already crowded at three o'clock. Toddlers ran around, a baby was crying at the bar, and two dogs lay along the wall. The clientele was scruffy, either cowboys or mountain types, with a few college boys in the mix.

Taking their longnecks and a basket of popcorn to the back room they noticed the pool table was open. Jake racked the balls and they caught up over a game of eight ball. An hour later they left Luke's, drove south, and stopped at the Bar-J entrance. The sun had just sunk below the mountain and stone arch. The sky was light lavender with scattered pink clouds. In less than a minute the magic had passed and the sky became that more common blue gray of sunset. They walked directly into the dining room for another steak dinner.

The "Snake" stayed only a day to finalize the agreement Jake would sign with Charles, and to suggest changes to the bid letter. He used his laptop to run through various production scenarios with possible terms offered in the agreement, optimizing percentages to give Jake the best financial return with the level of gas production he expected. Jake realized that flying the "Snake" to the ranch was one of the best decisions he would make in this entire deal.

After a ride and an early dinner he drove the lawyer back to the airport for the red-eye to Houston. Jake returned to the ranch after eleven o'clock, couldn't sleep, and worked on the bid letter. Two hours later he stared at the final version.

"You OK?" Marv was standing in the doorway.

"I'm great, thanks dad. See this?" He held up ten sheets of paper. "This is my future. I've got the money lined up. I've got my Egyptian partner. I've got the winning bid. All I need now is for the Egyptians to award the concession to me."

"Sound easy son."

"After the bid round the really hard part will start. We just need to be sure we get the concession."

"What d'ya think are the chances?"

"I think they're good but you never know. No one really likes the Sinai and I don't think anyone else will make an offer. If they do, no one would offer this much."

The next morning was spent with his family playing around the ranch with Gussie, Lester, and Marv. He considered how lucky he was to have his extended family. If only his mother and wife were still alive.

CHAPTER 19

Vince Mantero poured another cup of black coffee to go with his second Twinkie. He began to doze in the surveillance van as an alarm made him jump. One red light on the panel indicated the dining room window had tripped. Seconds later another light indicated motion in the living room. Someone was inside.

Vince shook his sleeping partner.

"Let's go. What the fuck," said Bruce.

"Two alarms up. Probable intruders."

Vince called for police backup, and then he and Bruce were fully armed and out of the van in less than a minute. It was dark as Hades. No stars or moon provided even a glimmer of light. They were nearly invisible, dressed in black, their skin smeared with charcoal. The van was parked around the corner from Tillard's house but they covered the forty yards quickly. Having reviewed the plan over and over, Vince headed for the backyard while his partner ran to the front.

Dodging a pine tree Vince flattened himself against white brick next to the tripped window, which was still open. Moving slowly he glanced inside, seeing no one. He swung his body over the sill without a noise and crouched inside. He tapped the microphone in front of his mouth two times, then one, hearing one tap in response. Bruce knew he was inside and knew he should stay positioned on the front porch.

Both had been in the house before and knew the layout. Vince moved from the dining room through the living room to the front foyer. Nine millimeter in his right hand and a small flashlight in the other, he slipped into the study. This was where they expected someone but no one was there. He finished inspecting the ground floor and told Bruce to come inside through the window.

"Upstairs," he whispered after they met.

Electronics magnified the sound so they could barely whisper and understand each other while not alerting anyone else. Bruce nodded, letting Vince lead. While Vince walked up the circular steps, his partner covered him from below. At the landing he could see a weak light within the girl's bedroom. He moved down the hall towards the light while Bruce came up the stairs behind him. Outside the bedroom he heard noises. A drawer opening. Boxes being moved. Bruce was right behind him. Vince motioned that he was going in. His partner nodded.

He peered around the doorframe and saw a figure, dressed in black, with a tiny headlamp strapped to his head. He was going through the closet. Off to one side was a wooden organizer with games and stuffed animals arranged in square cubbyholes. The man moved to the organizer, engrossed in his task of inspecting each one of the games. Vince put his flashlight into his pocket and took one step into the room. He looked to his right where he knew the light switch was located. As Vince reached his left hand over his right gun arm to turn on the light, Bruce saw a gun appear from the left. The gun fired at the same time Bruce shouted.

An instant later Bruce had taken two steps forward and put four bullets into the black shape holding the gun. He quickly turned and aimed the gun at the other man, firing a couple more shots as the second guy disappeared behind the bed. Bruce dropped to the floor and shimmied back out the door.

"Federal marshals," Bruce shouted.

No answer. He lay in the hall with his head and his gun inside the doorframe, the semi automatic pointed towards the bed. He knew the man would have to move. He blocked the best way out, the only other route being the window. To reach the window the intruder would have to come over, under, or around the bed.

He didn't know if Vince was alive or dead and wanted to find out quickly. He flipped a switch on his small radio pack to transmit to police band.

"This is Federal Charlie One calling backup. Do you copy?"

"Roger Charlie One. We are approaching. ETA one minute."

The voice came through the headphones clear but the intruder couldn't hear it. Bruce wanted to end this nightmare before backup complicated things. He responded to the backup making sure he was loud enough to be heard across the room.

"Roger backup. I have one officer down, one intruder down, and the other intruder cornered in the upstairs southwest bedroom. Will await your arrival in one minute."

The intruder launched onto the bed and dove towards the window. Bruce fired continuous rounds. He could see the man twitch slightly before he went head first through the window.

"Shit," said Bruce.

He got up, ran to the window, and looked down. The figure was draped over two azaleas fifteen feet below, twitching. He couldn't check on Vince without risking the intruder fleeing. Weighing the alternatives, he pointed his gun down and put two more rounds into the man.

Going to Vince, he ripped off his goggles, flipped on the lights, and bent over his partner, head floating in a pool of blood. Bruce couldn't see through the hair the one hole just above his left ear. Placing his gun down he moved the bloody head to a more natural position, his other hand feeling the neck. There was no pulse.

Bruce looked to his right to find the killer. As soon as his eyes focused on the shape he flinched. Even as he reached for his gun, he knew he had screwed up. His hand touched the cold metal just as the first bullet hit him in the chest. The Kevlar vest saved his life from this first shot but the impact shoved him back and knocked the wind from his lungs. Two more bullets ripped into him and the world went black.

Book Two
Competition

CHAPTER 20

SEVEN thousand miles away Jake touched down at Cairo's International Airport. One of the first off the plane, he went through the 'alien' line at Passport Control before claiming his luggage.

Outside the heat hit him like a furnace as he followed his limo driver to the car. The ride to the Semiramis Intercontinental was uneventful and Jake relished his new expense account.

In his room the porter placed his suitcase on a stand next to the desk. A five-pound tip was enough to circumvent the routine explanation of the minibar, light switches, and television controls. Alone at last he walked to the window and looked down at little black taxis, donkey carts carrying vegetables or garbage, and a snake-like stream of tiny people crossing Lion's Head Bridge. Straight out he could just make out the pyramids, all but hidden by the pollutants of twelve million people.

After a shower and change of clothes he was in a taxi, sweltering as it inched towards Giza. Listening to horns blaring, watching people dodge in and out of cars, Jake tried once more to figure out what kept this city going.

The taxi pulled into the circular drive of the Mena House, and a tall, turbaned, Sudanese valet opened his door, ivory smile set within a jet-black face. Jake did not mount the granite steps to the hotel proper but instead walked the other way, descending steps to the garden. He took a table and waited for his partner.

"*Salaam al aleikum*, Salah."

"*Aleikum al salaam, habibi. Izayak*"

"*Colo tamem, Shukran.*"

Jake noticed his Arabic vocabulary had deteriorated. His accent always atrocious, he now worried about being understood. If it got much worse he wouldn't be able to buy a mineral water on the street. Fortunately Salah changed to English quickly.

"You look good," the statuesque figure said.

He pumped Jake's hand vigorously.

"You look good too, my friend. But you're in danger of wilting. How can you wear a wool coat in this heat?"

"Appearances are everything. I am known by my sport coats. Ask anyone."

"I don't have to. I know it. I recognized you entering the garden before I saw your face."

Fighting jet lag, Jake insisted on meeting today. Although it was hot outside, tenting provided relief from the sun, and fans moved the hot air around.

"I love the Mena House garden. Where else can you eat kebab, smoke shisha, and look at the great pyramid of Khufu?"

"Nowhere else," said Salah. "But I prefer looking at the foreign ladies?"

The Garden Tent cafe was poolside. Salah was ogling the Italian tourists in skimpy bathing suits, isolated from the Islamic world beyond the perimeter.

"How is Hoda?" Jake asked as always. The same answer came back. Salah's wife had been sickly since the two men first met.

"*Lesseh aish* — still alive. As beautiful as the day we married."

"Have you been able to travel?"

"You know how it is. Hoda is on her deathbed until it is time to travel. If I suggest Paris, London, or Dubai, she makes a miraculous recovery. If it's places I do business, her condition deteriorates and I go alone."

They got down to business over nan, dal, raita, and vindaloo. In addition to typical Egyptian fare, the terrace was now serving Indian food from the famed Mogul Room restaurant.

"I have one piece of news," said Salah. "Apparently, interest is being shown in the Sinai block from a local investor. Rumor has it someone very connected."

Jake pondered this. Only fifty to a hundred men controlled most of the business in Egypt. Almost all of them started with "old-money" squirreled away pre-Nasser. He thought the new player must be one of those; however no local Egyptian had yet dabbled in oil and gas.

"Salah, what does this mean? Who do you think it is?"

"Well, it means we have a competitor. Who it is will dictate how serious a threat they will be. There has been talk about encouraging local business interests to participate in the petroleum industry, but no one I know in Egypt has the capability of being a serious player. There are people with money, but it takes more than money to find oil."

"Can you find out who it is?"

"It should not be difficult. There are few secrets in Egypt that cannot be purchased. We need time and a little money."

Jake followed Salah's gaze to the right, locking in on the rear of a blond walking away from them. She was wearing a G-string suit, common in Europe but unheard of in the Islamic world. From the lack of tan lines, it was obvious the girl did not often wear a more substantial suit. Jake saw as she turned and descended the ladder that her top was equally as revealing.

He saw a smile spread across Salah's face. He knew Salah was no saint, having been with him on a couple business trips to Europe. Like many Arabic men, Salah strayed far and wide when he could, over-compensating for the repressive environment in which he lived.

"Salah, you can put your tongue back in your mouth. She is up to her neck in water."

"Ah, how lucky is the water."

"Thinking too hard about things like that is not good for one's heart. Especially a heart as old as yours."

"Until my day arrives, I will continue to seek out beauty. Life should be savored in all its glory, my *khawaga* friend."

They chatted about other pool guests before Jake paid the bill. Walking out of the garden, he left Salah poolside to enjoy a new group of French ladies. He crossed the Semiramis' reception area heading for the entrance. The sounds of a wedding two floors up filtered to the open lobby. In his years in Egypt he never developed an appreciation of Arabic music. He was tone deaf so not a fair judge, but it never stopped sounding like bad percussion improvisation to him. Non-musicians pounding on cheap drums, blowing into second rate wind instruments. The only thing he remembered from weddings was not being able to hear anything at all for hours afterwards. He closed his eyes during the taxi ride back to his hotel.

Stepping into his room, he felt uneasy. Nothing in the room or bathroom looked out of place, but one peek into his suitcase confirmed his suspicions. Changing in a hurry before, he had pulled some things out of the suitcase quickly. Paula had always yelled at him for doing that. Invariably the clothes on top became a bit messed up. The clothes in his suitcase were now too neat.

Walking to the closet he opened his carry-on, which he did take great pains to organize, so he could always find what he needed on a plane in a hurry. Here too things were not right. Pulling out his laptop, he opened a hidden program that tracked usage. Someone had powered it on while he was gone. The system was not password protected, but it was set up so certain files could not easily be accessed. A casual intruder might not find these hidden files. Even an experienced hacker would need some time to get at them. No one had gained access to that area of the computer.

Jake thought about the intrusion over a minibar beer and finally gave it up as a waste of time. He was convinced they had not found anything worthwhile.

He spent the next hour working on one of those secret files, the official bid form he would submit with the document he had written earlier. He completed it, added a front fax page, and took it on a memory stick to the hotel business center, where he encrypted it before sending it to Charles in New York. The last line on the front page asked for Charles' concurrence.

He returned to his room, dead bolted the door, and for an extra measure of security propped a chair against it. Exhausted, he sank into the bed to watch BBC news. There was a human rights story, some sensationalism on an earthquake in China, and brief coverage of the Middle East peace process, including excerpts from an interview with Nabil Ben-Haim, Prime Minister Shapiro's chief negotiator. Ben-Haim had just emerged from an all day session in Taba, where Israelis and Palestinians were hammering out issues concerning Jerusalem. Jake fell asleep during the Elsa Klensch fashion segment.

While Jake slept, Karim Nabet received a delivery at his home in Zamalek, an island in the Nile in the center of Cairo. A smile spread across his face as he read a copy of Jake's fax. Finished, he looked up and peered out his living room window, on the tenth floor of a building his father had given him for his sixteenth birthday. He could see the Semiramis Hotel, and imagined Jake sleeping like a baby.

Karim Nabet started with a small fortune of family assets when his father died, pre-Nasser. Leaving Egypt in 1951 he fortuitously sold these properties before they were appropriated a year later. Writing off Egypt, he put the proceeds into Swiss, British, and American accounts, investing heavily in the post-war manufacturing economy. His investments grew exponentially while he enjoyed a playboy lifestyle from his flats in Paris and Mykonos. In the early nineties Nabet came home, outwardly reaffirming Islam. Investing locally, his personal playground seemed to be south of Hurghada on the western side of the Red Sea, an area developing into a world-class beach and diving resort. He was cashing in on the hotel and condo boom, and growing his fortune even more. His formation this year of Triton Oil was the latest in a long line of ventures.

Years ago Jake had traveled with his boss Barney to fish from Hurghada's newest five star hotel, the Barracuda. When their boat broke down, the hotel offered the owner's personal boat in replacement. Little did they know it came with the owner. The fishing was unspectacular, but the company was another matter. Karim, in spite of his obesity, was extremely personable and charismatic, hitting it off with Jake. They developed a relationship, seeing each other a couple times a year.

Karim picked up the phone and dialed an international number.

"This is Karim. Mr. Tillard is planning to offer more than I expected. If our other pressure does not convince him to back off, I will at least know what bid to submit. The pressure on Hesham at EGPC is getting the message to him. Whether it impacts Tillard we will see. Should we increase pressure?"

"Not yet. We can get nastier later. But only if needed. It is a shame we did not find that mud log in Houston. Without it we won't know what to do with the acreage."

"*Insha'Allah*, we will find it," muttered Karim, reaching for the Baccarat decanter filled with single malt Scotch.

"*Insha'Allah* indeed," replied Yosef Kettler in Jerusalem.

The next morning Jake picked up the envelope slipped under his door. Inside was the return fax from Charles with an encrypted confirmation to the bid terms. There were only twenty-five days left until the bid deadline. Salah would continue trying to find out who the other bidder was, butter up members of the EGPC bid committee, keep lobbying his upper level buddies in the Ministry of Energy about the export idea, and search out all the fringe players who needed to be stroked.

Lufthansa 432 to Frankfurt took off on schedule. Jake settled into his Business Class seat and drank a St Pauli Girl while looking at farms on the Nile Delta. In four hours, he would be in Frankfurt. A two-hour layover and another ten in the air would get him to Chicago. A four-hour layover would give him time for a Taco Bell, and another two in the air would plop him in Missoula. With luck, twenty-four hours from now, he'd be hugging Gussie at the ranch.

CHAPTER 21

"**MR. TILLARD**, my name is Dick Radisson. I work for the Federal Government. I'm phoning about your son, Jake."

He did not go into specifics as to just which part of the government employed him.

"Jake is currently over the Atlantic. I can't wait for him to land before acting on some disconcerting news. It's pertinent to the safety of your granddaughter, sir."

Marv considered the voice on the phone. It delivered short, clipped, efficient sound bites.

"I'm listening."

"Government agents have been watching your son's house in Houston. There was another break-in last night, with some fatalities. They were looking for something. I don't think they found it. I expect them to keep looking."

Marv wondered what kind of agents were staking out Jake's house, how Radisson knew Gussie was at the ranch, and a host of other things, but they seemed irrelevant at this point. He needed to know why this man felt the need to call him so urgently. He also needed to know if this guy was who he said he was.

"Mr. Radisson," he started. Radisson cut him off.

"Please, call me Dick. I'm aware of why Gussie is in your care. I wanted to alert you as to what transpired in Houston, and take additional precautions to ensure Gussie stays safe."

"OK, Dick. Do you really think Gussie is in danger here in Montana? On my ranch?"

"I do."

Marv was not convinced. Dick wanted to send agents to the ranch, but Marv refused, saying the ranch was pretty self-contained, and that they could take care of themselves.

"Mr. Tillard, I respect your reluctance to suffer this intrusion. When you hear from your son please ask him to call me. I'll update him on the Houston property."

Marv hung up and summoned his ranch boss.

"Lester, there's been more trouble at Jake's place in Houston. A fellow from Washington thinks a few bad guys might be interested in Jake, and thinks there may be a threat to Gussie. He wanted to send some agents to the ranch but I told him we could take care of ourselves."

"Damn right, boss. What do you want me to do?"

Marv had been pondering that very question.

"Stay close to Gussie. Put out the word for every hand to start carrying. Expect trouble. Be alert."

Lester hadn't expected such severe marching orders.

"Boss, do you really think there might be trouble?"

"Got me. Those government types are afraid of their own shadows, and always cover their asses. But this Federal guy sounded worried. So let's be on the safe side and be alert."

"I'll round up the hands and give 'em a talk. They'll pay extra attention. Gussie might not like havin' me around all the time boss."

"Of course she will, Lester. She's stuck on you like a tick to a hound. Just act normal and tell her you don't have much to do. Show her more of the ranch. Just bring your gun."

Marv knew Lester wasn't shy around Gussie, but the prospect of being with her all day had him flustered. It had been a while since they'd had children on the ranch.

"OK. I guess I can keep her busy enough."

Brad Marshall stood at attention before the big desk, arms at his sides, eyes looking straight ahead at the American flag. The stories about General Richard A. Radisson were legendary and he dearly wanted to get off on the right foot.

It seemed an eternity before Radisson looked up. In fact, Dick had ignored his visitor for thirty seconds while he finished signing a couple of orders. He apologized as he looked up, not one to waste anyone's time, from the President down to the janitor.

"Good morning, Agent Marshall. Sorry for the wait. Have you read the briefing document?"

"Yes sir."

"What is Jake's daughter's name?"

"Augusta, sir. Gussie for short."

"Agent, your job until you hear otherwise, directly from me, is to protect that little girl. If you save someone else in the meantime, great. If you kill someone, too bad. You understand me, soldier?"

"Yes sir".

Brad Marshall felt intensity emanating from the General. They had never met before and Brad couldn't tell if this case involved a personal interest, or if he was like this with every case. He sensed the former but wasn't going to ask.

"One more thing, Agent Marshall. Mr. Tillard does not want you on his ranch; so don't let him know you're there. Eight to ten ranch staff are there at any time, apparently all experienced. Don't let them see you."

Brad met the General's eyes.

"General, I have experience out west. That will not be easy. Agents Boots and Wilson will come along. Both worked with me in Idaho. If we have to jeopardize secrecy or effectiveness, which should we give up?"

Radisson's steel gray eyes bore into Marshall like a drill.

"You should be able to remember the primary goal son. If you can't, I can find someone who can."

"Yes sir," Brad replied timidly. "I'll protect the girl'"

"Don't screw up," Radisson shot back.

With that, the General picked up a sheet of paper and turned his attention to a situation developing in Qatar. Brad Marshall realized that the meeting was over. He thought about reaffirming his understanding, thanking the General, and saluting. None of these seemed appropriate, so he merely saluted, turned, and left the room.

As he passed the General's secretary, he didn't notice her smile. Most agents receiving their first orders from Dick Radisson came out with a similar look. She hoped Agent Marshall could deliver whatever Dick had asked of him.

Lester sent one of the hands to fetch Jake at the airport. As the returning ranch vehicle passed under the stone arch, agent Boots's eyes followed it with night goggles. She spoke into the microphone on her lapel and Brad Marshall acknowledged the message, seeing the truck two minutes later as it approached the house. The agents worked sixteen hours on, eight hours off, having set up a small army style bivouac a mile from the house, off of ranch property. So far, they had gone undetected.

Jake walked down the hall to Gussie's room, and had his hand on the doorknob when Lester entered the hall from the room next-door, shotgun in hand. The squeaking of the floorboards had alerted the ranch boss.

"Don't shoot Lester. What the hell are you doing with that thing?"

"You'll have to ask your father Jake. All I know is he asked me to watch over Gussie and to expect trouble."

Jake regarded him for a minute, and then went into Gussie's room. She was clutching Polly, her rag doll made by girls in a battered women's shelter outside Missoula. Before he had left for Cairo, they had gone up there with Marv, who was on the board.

Gussie's mouth was closed in a tight little pout, and Jake wondered what she was dreaming about. Her eyes were not quite closed, and he wondered how she could sleep like that, something she did quite often. He leaned over, planted a kiss on her cheek, and caressed her hair. Her eyes opened a little more, then widened as she recognized her dad. Her arms left Polly and went around his neck as they hugged.

"Daddy," she softly muttered while clinging tightly to his neck with tiny arms damp with sleep.

"I missed you, my Gussie-bear."

They lay side by side for a few minutes until Jake was certain she was back in a deep sleep. He planted one more kiss on her cheek, put Polly back in her arms, and went to find his dad. He passed Lester in the hall where he apparently decided to take up a position. Marv was in his bedroom reading when Jake knocked softly and entered.

"Gussie OK?"

"Fine as can be dad."

"Jake, that little girl of yours is somethin' special. Without you around, we've been able to enjoy her, and have her all to ourselves. I don't know where she got that many brains, but if you want to beat her at chess you'd better play her soon. She's brought back all kinds of memories of when your mother was still with us. Frankly she's a lot more fun than you were at that age. And not at all a pain in the ass."

Jake smiled at his dad's razzing, but switched to the bigger issue.

"Dad, what's going on? Why the hell is Lester guarding Gussie with a shotgun?"

Marv gave him the two-minute version, and told him to call Dick Radisson. Alarms went off in Jake's head when he heard that Dick thought Gussie was in danger. He went downstairs and dialed the number Dick had given him. Surprisingly Dick answered himself.

"Radisson," came the gruff greeting.

"Jake Tillard here. What's going on, Dick?"

For the next ten minutes Jake listened to the analysis of the Houston situation, cringing at the news of the stakeout, and the dead agent. The house didn't bother him but the last part of the conversation elicited panic and fear.

"After the shoot-out we had a more perturbing issue come up. Seems you're of interest to someone who doesn't play nice. Our intelligence surveillance people have discovered two different inquiries were made relating to you. One having to do with the diplomatic mission in Cairo from a high level World Bank type. We never would have found out, but the Chief Economic Liaison who received the inquiry is a personal friend of mine. The other one is more bizarre. Someone queried your IRS account."

Jake wondered why he had been the topic of conversation with a liaison officer in Cairo, but the IRS query peeked his interest even more, maybe because everyone in America has an innate fear of the IRS.

"How'd you find that one?"

"I've got a program that cross references government computers. Not many people are aware of this capability so keep it to your self. After the Houston fiasco I plugged in your name and searched back two months. Ten minutes later I had twenty pages of printout. Mostly boring stuff, except for the IRS query. The odd part is the request had been for just your regular income streams. The kind of stuff that comes from stocks, bonds, bank accounts, and real estate.

"Who accessed the system?"

"We don't know yet and that's surprising. It's tough to hide, but this person did."

Jake still had difficulty making the link to Gussie.

"What's the connection to Gussie? Why the paranoia?"

"Smells like pre-blackmail activities. I'm thinking someone wants that mud log bad. They wrecked your house and may be preparing to extort you. God knows how far they'll go. We've got to assume they're looking for leverage."

He updated Dick on the bidding climate in Cairo. Radisson was concerned and thought about enlisting his buddies in the Egyptian security agency.

"We give them over two billion a year," he said. "Should be no limit to the cooperation we get. But it's getting more complicated over there, more difficult to figure who you're dealing with. Can you talk your dad into accepting a few agents on the ranch? I promise they will remain completely in the background."

"I'm sure I can. When can you have them here?"

"Tomorrow morning."

Jake hung up and sank back in the overstuffed armchair. His eyes closed and he dreamed of times gone by. Paula was holding Gussie overhead, propping her up with a hand firmly placed under her diapered bottom, allowing her to explore the hand-hewn beams on the ceiling. Gus squealed with delight as her mommy pretended to drop her, Paula glowing with pride and happiness watching her daughter's joy. It wasn't that long ago they had been the perfect American family. What went wrong? Why did he stubbornly keep them in Egypt? And how on earth did he get into this current mess.

The knock came at eight, just as Jake walked down the stairs. Agent Marshall stood at the front door, hat in hand, giving his name to Layla, who had started to settle into a larger role at the ranch.

'Shit,' thought Jake. He had not yet told his dad about the agents. 'How did they get here this quickly?'

Brad Marshall did not look like he had been awake all night. A quick shower and a hot meal had revitalized his body, but his mind was trying to keep up.

"Jake Tillard," he said, stepping in front of Layla.

Introductions were made as Marshall came into the living room. Marv walked out of the kitchen to see what was going on, and Jake introduced the newcomer. He invited Brad to sit, while he took his dad aside to explain what was happening. He got no opposition from his father, who had evidently learned of the agents' presence within three hours of their arrival the day before. One of his ranch hands, an illegal Mexican from the high country in Sonoma, saw them. Marv had used binoculars and his favorite horse to check them out. Having decided they were not a threat, and in spite of Radisson having ignored him, he let them be.

Their first meeting was cordial and Brad was surprised. Marv even suggested one of the agents move into the ranch house, while the other two roam the grounds, saying if they were to be around they should try to be effective. Brad was not surprised they had been detected.

Brad decided he would move in since it was his responsibility to guard Gussie. Ensuring her protection would be easier if he was inside the house. At least he thought that would be the case.

CHAPTER 22

LIBBY arrived at the ranch a week later, having accepted Jake's invitation during the Denver convention. With so much going on, Jake had little time to anticipate her visit, but was thrilled she made the trip. He needed the diversion, and Gussie could use some female company besides Layla. Settling quickly into the ranch routine, Libby and Gussie spent hours on horseback. Libby and Jake spent hours walking and talking.

It had been a while since he had really kissed a woman. His meetings with potential dates over coffee seemed contrived and awkward. This time it was natural. Libby had been at the ranch three days when they were skipping rocks across the stream.

"Bet I can get more skips than you." Libby said, with a twist of her mouth, lift of her eyebrows, and a sideways glance.

"You're on. What's the bet?"

"A kiss."

She didn't look at him when she said it, but merely bent over and flicked a stone.

"Five," she said.

Jake picked around in the pebbles at his feet to find a flat stone. 'Do I want to win this?' he thought. 'Or should I let her win? Is there a difference? She never said who had to win to get the kiss.

"Five skips also," Libby said after he threw his rock. "That's a win for me."

"Why's that a win for you?"

Jake stared at her, sensing something was happening. She was so relaxed, with a wry little smile.

"Well, I'm your guest. And I'm cute."

Jake couldn't argue and just grinned. Before he knew it, she took a step towards him and pressed her lips against his. Her arms found their way around his neck, her tongue exploring his lips. They remained in that first embrace for an eternity. He found her soft all over, tongue, hair, and shoulders. Libby found the opposite true of him. Before he became embarrassed, Jake broke the embrace and took her hand.

"Walk with me Libby."

They moved downstream, away from the house. Finally, he took her hands and pulled her down on a mossy spot, beside the stream. They held each other for a long time, neither making a move towards more intimacy, but satisfied for now with what they had. The thought of the roaming agents did cross Jake's mind, but he discounted that as a non-issue.

She dozed, and he stared at her face. Her skin set off her long brown hair nicely, her cheekbones high set. Her nose was chiseled, her eyebrows thick, and her lashes long. But it was her delicate lips that set her apart. Not thick, but sexy. His last observation before drifting off was her eyelids quivering, responding to a dream that Jake was convinced included him. That same face greeted him when he woke. Libby had just washed her face in the steam, and beads of water remained.

"Good afternoon, sleepy-head. Did you have a nice siesta?"

Leaning over him, drops of cold water fell from her nose to his face.

"That's cold."

"Don't be a wimp."

Rising, he could see she was barefoot and had done some wading. Her legs had a pink glow created by the icy stream. His thoughts began to stray farther and before they got out of control, he took her hand and started back to the ranch.

Ten days after Jake got to the ranch, Gussie started fifth grade in the Bitterroot Elementary School, ten miles down the road. She would stay in Montana through fall term rather than return to Houston. Jake would return to Cairo several times, not to mention possible other trips. With his dad, Lester, Layla, the ranch hands, and the agents, Jake could not imagine a safer location.

Marshall's job was more difficult when Gussie went to school, but Jake wouldn't hear of any alternative. Brad followed the bus with his car, and during the day kept vigil from outside school grounds. Since they began their protection assignment, nothing extraordinary had occurred. But they were seasoned veterans, and knew better than to let their guard down.

Libby left the ranch the day after their foray downstream to see old friends in Whitefish. Not knowing how the visit with Jake would go after so many years, she had built an escape into the trip. Now she regretted the side trip, and as she drove past Flathead Lake, she was anxious to return to Jake.

With Gussie in school and Libby gone, Jake became lonely and sullen. Lester and Marv both noticed, Marv counting the days until Libby's planned return. He had always hated moping.

In his brooding state, Jake stayed in communication with Salah in Cairo and Charles in New York. Making plans to leave for Egypt on the twentieth, he hoped to return with oil and gas rights for a large chunk of the Sinai.

Libby returned as planned, Marv watching from the upstairs landing as she and Jake hugged at the front door. He liked Libby, who seemed rugged with a healthy dose of femininity. He sensed his son felt something even greater.

That night Jake asked Libby to ride west the next day into the high country, the National Forest. She was game, so he gave Lester instructions to outfit two horses and pack a picnic.

It took two hours and three thousand feet of elevation gain to reach the ranch boundary. Libby had no idea how he could identify the edge of the property, as there was no fence. She guessed it didn't make much difference, since the Federal land was identical to that of the ranch.

Growing up in the grasslands of South Dakota, part of the reason she chose geology was the lure of mountains and fresh air. She needed to get back to the mountains full time, and was still looking for a way. After another half hour, Jake jumped off his horse and tied it to an aspen. Libby did the same as he grabbed the picnic basket and a blanket.

"Where are you going?"

"Come," was all he said in response.

He led her a hundred yards through the loveliest aspen grove to a wide flat granite outcrop. The vista was immense, with a one hundred eighty degree view across the Bitterroot Valley to the Sapphire Mountains.

"God this is wonderful."

"Spectacular, huh?"

Jake held her hand as they just looked. Finally he broke the silence.

"The view's not the special part."

"What could be better?"

He grabbed her hand and led her away from the edge toward the trees. She had no idea what he was doing.

"Close your eyes."

She closed her eyes and tried to use her other senses. She stumbled as Jake guided her, smelling the trees and feeling the wind on her face, stronger as they approached a clearing. The only sounds were the rustle of leaves and the crunch of forest debris beneath their feet.

"Still closed?"

"Yes sir. But I can't keep them closed much longer. It's making me nervous."

She heard a new sound, faint but constant. It was the smell that finally registered. Water. Sulfurous water. Before she could help herself, she opened her eyes. Twenty yards in front of her was a hot spring, with the sound of cascading water. She had visited many hot springs in the American west. Some big. Some small. She loved them all.

Someone had improved this natural spring, but it still retained its charm. Hot water bubbled into sandy pools at the base of a very small cliff, then funneled into a PVC pipe that sent it cascading into a larger manmade pool. With its top at ground level, the pool was built of rock; in a square shape about four feet on a side. The water flowing out of the pipe created a virtual shower.

Behind the springs rose Mount Edward, named for an early British explorer. Their view was directly at the peak and its arête, which connected it to the next mountain. Beneath the arête was a beautiful glacial cirque and tarn. Several small birds chirped to their arrival.

"Jake, this is the most beautiful place I've ever seen."

"It's a very special place only a few folks know of. It's on government land, but it's tough to get here without coming through the ranch. So no one comes."

"No one?" she repeated, that sly smile returning.

Jake had worried how to approach this moment. Apparently, he worried without reason.

"Can we swim in it?" asked Libby.

Jake led her to the edge of the pool. He watched her unbutton her shirt, smiling as she arranged it on a big boulder. Her boots came off next. Then, sitting on a boulder, she eased off her jeans and turned around to lay them neatly next to her shirt. Jake looked at her from behind, mesmerized. His eyes got to her narrow waist before she turned to face him. Holding eye contact, she reached behind her, undid her bra, and removed it. Casually removing her panties, she flung them behind her onto the boulder, took two steps towards Jake, and gave him a peck on the cheek.

"Want to come?" she asked coyly.

Jake took off his boots and socks, then his shirt. She looked at his chest and whistled. It made him even more embarrassed.

"What about the rest?" she teased, cocking her head.

Libby perched herself on the edge of the pool facing him, legs dangling in the water. Jake could not help looking at her breasts, which seemed perfect. The moment of truth had come but not as he had anticipated. It seemed so natural for Libby. He never imagined he would be the one embarrassed. He had become excited the minute Libby unbuttoned her shirt. He began to take off his pants and turned away.

"Don't turn around."

He pulled his pants and underwear off, placed both on the rock, and walked to the pool.

"Well I guess you find me sexy, huh?"

Her hands took his as he got in. She put his hands behind her back and gave him a long, deep kiss. Their bodies came together and Jake moaned approval. Libby broke away, taking a step back to the pool's edge. He found himself staring directly into her full breasts with their large, caramel nipples. She smiled, put her hands behind his head, and pulled his mouth to her breasts. Soon after, she slipped into the water again, wrapping her limbs around him.

"Too hot for you?" she said grinning.

"Not re ... ," was all he got out before her mouth covered his.

The first time was quick. Whether it was the temperature or just the first time, he couldn't tell. Nor did he care. Afterward, they lay on a blanket beside the pool. Jake listened to the sound of the water and watched a Rough-legged Hawk hovering above. Libby dozed. Without any guilt, Jake propped his head on his elbow and looked at her body, taking in every detail. It seemed an eternity in paradise.

When Libby woke, they made love again, this time on the blanket. After they finished, they slipped into the pool. To dry they merely walked naked around the clearing, looking for wild flowers. They even ate naked, joking about Adam and Eve before the apple.

Finally, they dressed and returned to the overlook. Holding hands, Jake asked her to come with him to Cairo.

"That's a long way," she said after some thought.

"I know. I've done the trip a few times."

"I meant it's a big deal. I don't know if I can be away that long. Anyway, what would I do?"

"Well we could continue what we started here."

He grinned at her and was surprised that she blushed.

"I mean during the day."

"We could do it during the day and night."

Her blush deepened. They discussed it without coming to a conclusion. The ride down the mountain was exhilarating. Both felt that nothing could upset their sense of contentment. They rode fast, taking chances, jumping deadfall, dodging trees and branches. It was nearly dinnertime when the ranch compound came into view. They saw Gussie and Brad flying a kite in the clearing. It was one of those broad Japanese types with two strings and three tails. Brad was making it dive and almost hit the water before it swooped up again into the big Montana sky. Gussie cheered every time, her voice filtering up the slope they descended.

Lester and a hand were waiting when they got to the barn. Lester had his rifle, which he had begun carrying whenever he was out of the house. Even with the agents present, he took his protector role serious.

"Good ride, Jake?"

"Very good," answered Jake, stealing a glance at Libby. She shot him a look that said 'be careful, don't gloat'.

Lester smiled when he saw the look on Libby's face.

"I trust the mount was adequate, ma'am?"

"The mount was much better than adequate," she said.

Jake coughed back a laugh, Libby shooting him another piercing glance.

"Lester, she's a beautiful animal. I'd like it if I could take her out again."

"It would be my pleasure, ma'am."

A few days later, Jake packed for Egypt. He had managed to talk Libby into coming as far as New York for the weekend, where he was meeting Charles en route. She declined, however, to accompany him to Cairo, saying she would come after he got his acreage.

It was an emotional parting with Gussie, but Jake felt comfortable leaving her at the ranch. Besides, at his dad's suggestion, Libby agreed to return to the ranch after the New York trip to stay with Gussie for a day or two on her way up the valley. Marv had said he thought the womanly influence would do Gussie good. Jake had not expected her to accept, but was happy she did. He had noticed she was affectionate and gentle with Gussie, another good surprise.

CHAPTER 23

YOSEF KETTLER read the morning papers while sipping an espresso at Benny's Cafe in the Old City, the smell of just baked bread wafting down the narrow passageway. Between stories, he watched the steady stream of early risers pass, trying to get to work on time. This was his neighborhood, his world, and his routine.

Three stories occupied his attention this morning. In addition to their relevance to his current endeavors, he pondered more deeply how these activities would impact his daughters and grandchildren.

The first story, "Inflation Led by Energy", probed fuel price trends, in particular the cost of electricity. Over the past year, while the cost of gasoline inched down in line with world markets, the domestic cost of electricity had more than doubled. Some of this increase could be explained by an ever increasing living standard and more people using air conditioning, but most had to do with the price of imported coal and fuel oil.

The second was a letter to the editor from Simeon Friedman, one of Israel's top construction moguls. "More Brownouts Likely" predicted that electricity interruptions would increase. As demand increased, regional electricity companies were resorting to rolling brownouts to manage a supply/demand problem. Friedman felt it a sad commentary on the modern Jewish state that such procedures were necessary, and postulated it would hurt the building industry and the economy. Yosef agreed, in spite of not being very fond of the author.

The third article disturbed him the most. Israelis were used to hardship and sacrifice, so expensive electricity and intermittent disruptions in service were tolerable. Increasing violence and the potential for another war were not. "Palestinian Gasoline Rationing Debated" was in the liberal publication Ha'aretz. Gasoline rationing was a concept that Yosef just didn't really get. Gasoline was either imported or refined locally from imported oil. Prices were consistent with world markets, so rationing surely couldn't relate to supply restrictions. He was not sure what was behind the debate, but he had an uneasy feeling. He made a mental note to ask Daniel Ran what he thought. Yosef felt that an artificial gasoline shortage could lead to unrest and even war.

'It wouldn't really take much to create a war,' he thought.

But then, war had always been good for Yosef's business. Upon reflection, he decided not to contact Ran after all

JAKE and Libby had an uneventful flight to the Big Apple. Charles had booked them a suite at the St Regis, a beaux-arts hotel around the corner from his office. Their check-in was flawless, and Jake guessed from the looks of the lobby that everything else would be as well. He expected nothing less from Charles Alfred Lister III.

The suite was fantastic, with a bedroom, sunken sitting room, and marbled bathroom filled with Louis XIV style furnishings. The bellman deposited their bags in the sitting room, gave them a brief tour, and accepted his tip discretely. Less than a minute later, Libby began unbuttoning her pants.

"Not so fast. I know I'm irresistible," Jake grinned, "but we have reservations for a show in just over an hour."

By this time Libby had her shirt and bra off. She stood in front of him with hands on hips.

"Well, it's your choice of course. An hour is quite a bit of time."

He couldn't resist, shedding his clothes and following her into the bedroom.

"Hurry, we have a show in an hour," she mocked.

At the springs she had been quiet, biting her lip and whimpering. This time she was anything but demure. At first he worried about their neighbors in the suite next door, then his focus returned to Libby. More aroused than he could remember, he followed her peak and then lay with her. She smiled and gave him a kiss before jumping up and heading for the shower.

"We can't be late."

They met Charles and two associates after the play at a Greek restaurant in Midtown. The older gentleman seemed more alive this evening, probably because of Libby. Her black dinner dress with spaghetti straps showed off phenomenal shoulders, neck, and cleavage. More than once he caught his colleagues glaring at her. Even the conversation swayed towards Libby, the men suddenly enamored with mineral exploration.

"What was it like to be a woman in the mines in Central America?" Chester Grant asked as he ate a giant prawn.

"My first time underground I disguised myself as a man. They are very superstitious in Honduras, and believe that women underground bring disaster. That first week no one on the crew knew I was a woman. Lucky for me the first trip down I made a few suggestions to the face blasters that made their job a little easier. By the end of the first week word spread that I knew what I was doing."

"But you didn't stay long."

"No I didn't. About a year until I decided the job didn't give me what I wanted."

"What did you want?" Charles asked.

Jake had been halfheartedly listening so far but was reengaged by this question. He wanted to hear the answer.

"Two things. First I wanted to work in nature, but not a half-mile underground. It loses its appeal down there. The other thing I wanted was to discover something. In the mines I was only helping extract what someone else found. I wanted to find something myself. Did you know that only one in ten geologists ever find a producible ore deposit? In their lifetime. Their whole lifetime. I wanted that challenge."

"But you didn't continue."

"No I didn't. The industry was in the pits and I couldn't find a job. I had some lean years doing environmental consulting and odd jobs. But I knew something would turn up."

"Ah the optimism of youth."

That was Gary Greene's first comment since they had sat down at the table.

"Jealous, Gary?"

"Probably so Chester. Probably so."

Gary had been a holdout on Jake's project from the start. He was the one who required endless numerical justification and detailed cash flow projections. He was very risk averse, and found the natural resource industry intimidating.

"You have been a pain in the ass you old coot."

Chester let loose again with a wheezy chuckle. Libby looked to make sure he was OK.

"Excuse me Chester, we have a lady present," Charles said.

"A lady that's worked underground with miners. I'll bet she can translate anything I could muster into perfect colloquial Spanish. Am I right Madame?"

"I have to admit I've heard it all, sir. My ears are not easily offended."

She excused herself to go to the powder room. In polite fashion all the gentlemen half rose to acknowledge her exit.

"Nice lady you've got there Jake," said Charles.

"Would she consider a mature gentleman?" asked Chester.

"She's got me," said Jake, chuckling.

"I keep forgetting you're no spring chicken. Maybe it's the tan, the ponytail, and the muscle look."

Jake looked at the old man and caught a twinkle in his eye.

"Jake you need to visit us in the office tomorrow for half the day," said Charles. "Gary never did like this venture. Now he thinks our bid needs to be improved."

Jake looked from Charles to Gary and wondered if the conspiracy paranoia gripping Dick Radisson had hit his funders. He'd see tomorrow.

In the morning Libby and Jake had breakfast in the suite before leaving the hotel. The secretary at Lister and Associates recognized Jake, welcoming him with a smile as she rose. Taking his order for coffee, she led him to Charles' office. Chester and Gary were already there.

"Morning Jake," said Charles.

Typical to the northeast they traded pleasantries for about a minute before settling down to business. Gary started in sharp contrast to the night before.

"You know I never supported this venture. I don't understand the oil and gas business, nor do I like Egypt. Both of these are risks we don't need."

Jake started to respond to that simple risk assessment but Gary cut him off.

"Exploration risk is not the issue today. My partners overruled me and we are in this thing one hundred percent. That includes me. My concern now is political risk and safety. I've been doing a little research into recent bidding activity in Egypt and believe the bid you worked up is appropriate in today's environment."

"Excellent Gary."

"I also received information on recent attacks on your physical property."

"How'd you get that information?"

"I have friends in the government who are aware we are pursuing opportunities in Egypt. It seems apparent to them and therefore to me that someone bad is very interested in you. Apparently it has to do with this deal and your mud log."

"Jake, we are concerned," added Charles. "First of all for your safety. Secondly for our joint venture. We will do anything we can to help. It's an open offer."

Jake looked all of them in the eye and saw genuine concern.

"Thank you Charles. Thank you all. I am worried, however I've taken precautions and feel ready to go ahead."

"Good. Just remember our offer."

Charles was turning out to be one hell of a guy. Jake admitted his original impression had been wrong. Gary and Chester stood and shook Jake's hand before leaving the room, again wishing him luck.

"Jake," said Charles, "the way I figure, someone else wants this lease pretty bad. The first thing we need to do is make sure we get it. I don't like to lose. If I've understood you correctly, in Egypt the EGPC evaluates bids based largely on work commitment with a keen but somewhat subordinate eye to the fiscal terms. Correct?"

Jake nodded and Charles continued.

"Their main concern is the number of wells and amount of money bid for the block, because they like to publish very large commitment numbers in the local press. And they use figures for all periods, not just the initial one, right?"

"You have it correct."

"So, we plan to commit to one well in the first four year period, two in the second, and two more in the third, for a total of five wells and twenty million dollars. Of course at the end of any period we have the right to drop acreage and forego any remaining commitments. The later period commitments are meaningless from our point of view."

"True. Of course everyone else knows that as well."

"Right but it's a fine line between a good economically sound bid and a clearly outrageous bid that no one could deliver. I think we can increase our commitment with little risk to our potential economic return."

"I'm listening," Jake said.

"Add one well in the first period. Offset it by increasing our gas take from twenty to twenty five percent. That's the percentage of the gas we get. We'll drop our oil take to fifteen from twenty percent. Since we expect gas and not oil, this benefits us. These terms should play well to the government and the press. Increase the second and third period well commitments to three each, bringing the total publishable commitment to eight wells and forty million. Impressive from a publicity point of view but not much different from our point of view. Hell, if we miss on the first well we'll probably fold everything up and leave the country. We don't have to worry about ever coming back like major oil companies do."

"Sounds good Charles. Do Chester and Gary concur?"

"You leave that up to me. Let's have a drink."

He rose and walked to the bookshelf on the north side of the room. He pressed a button, opening a panel to reveal a fully stocked bar. Bending down, Charles slid another mahogany door aside and opened a medium sized refrigerator. With a pop he poured flutes of Dom Perignon.

"To a successful bid."

"The bid is just the first part," Jake retorted.

"But the only part I'm concerned about."

"You have that much faith in me Charles?"

"Yep. The best technical consultants money can buy helped convince us of that. You met two of them but we actually used four others in a blind test. Basically, they all wanted to know if they could get their own money into the deal."

"I should be insulted you used so many experts."

"Don't bother, it doesn't wear well on rich people. Which, with any luck, is what you're about to become."

Charles refilled their glasses and hoisted his in another toast. His last statement floated on air for quite a while before the small talk resumed. The meeting ended exactly three hours after it began.

Jake politely refused Charles' invitation to lunch and spent the next couple hours wandering the city. Near Delacorte Theater he grabbed a gyro from a cart. It seemed a million miles from the ranch.

"Got any change buddy?"

Jake looked at the person behind the voice and saw a haunted face. Grubby, unkempt, with a wild look in his eyes.

"Maybe. What will you do with it?"

"Depends how much you give me. A buck won't buy shit. Four'll buy me a pack of smokes. Ten'll get me a meal. A thousand'll buy me a used Harley."

Jake laughed along with the nameless homeless person. He opened his wallet and handed the guy a twenty.

"Do me a favor. Don't use my twenty for smokes. I hate smoking. Buy some food. OK?"

"You bet bud. God bless."

The ragged figure turned and walked off, cutting a straight path through a constantly parting sea of business people, some dressed in thousand dollar power suits.

That evening Jake looked back over his shoulder as he walked down the gateway onto the airplane. Libby returned his gaze, waving. His heart skipped a beat as he turned and stepped into the plane. He was still awash with emotion considering his future. Following an elderly lady down the aisle, he went three rows too far before realizing it. Fighting his way back up current, he plopped down in his seat.

He stared blankly at the faces of fellow passengers as they filed past. This time he wasn't just leaving Gussie but an old friend who had swept back into his life. Things appeared to be taking a turn for the better, and all he could do was wrestle with an anxious feeling. He motioned to the flight attendant and ordered a scotch.

Jake closed his eyes and regulated his breath, easing the tightness in his throat and chest. The image of Libby at dinner with his partners floated into his mind. Her laugh had captivated him as it captured his colleagues.

'My God,' he thought, 'I'm acting like I can't live without her.'

Maybe he didn't believe it was possible to love someone again. She seemed absolutely perfect and they had obviously taken to each other. What was the problem?

He daydreamed about the hot springs as the Airbus nosed up. He sipped his Scotch, thankful he was in Business Class.

The clientele at JFK airport was always diverse, but Libby thought this crowd downright scary. Walking back from the concourse, she examined the faces she passed. Each had a story; many looked like they'd had a tough life. Typical to New York, none of them looked at Libby, all engulfed in their private thoughts, immersed in their own troubles.

She didn't notice, but one person in the crowd did look at her. In fact, Moustafa Badry did not lose sight of her, following fifteen yards behind.

"Taxi," shouted Libby as an empty yellow cab rolled by.

It stopped five yards past, and she wondered why it was so hard to get a cab in New York. Moustafa watched as she got in. When it cruised down the ramp, he dialed a number on his phone.

"Hello."

"She's in a Yellow Cab."

"Fine. Get back downtown."

The phone went dead and he hailed another cab for the ride to Manhattan. In the couple of days he had tailed her, Moustafa began to appreciate her as a woman. She was a bit too thin for his taste, but he thought she was probably great in bed. Moustafa was a professional who did what he was told.

'It's a shame,' he thought in the back of the cab. 'Such a pretty woman.' He hadn't gotten orders yet to hassle her, but he knew his employer, and could predict that would change. Moustafa was expensive, and clients generally hired him when they needed more than just surveillance.

'*Malesh*', he muttered, 'Too bad.'

The cabby looked in the rear view mirror in response to his muttering. They locked eyes and the cabby quickly looked away. He didn't really like what he saw.

CHAPTER 25

THE Gezira Club occupies a decent chunk of Zamalek Island, in the Nile next to Cairo's central downtown district. Founded in 1882 as an elite golf course and social club for the British Army, it went downhill immediately after Nasser nationalized it in 1952. He turned half of the eighteen holes into public ball fields and changed its membership policy to allow a broad spectrum of locals to join. Combined with forty years of bad maintenance, that yielded a sprawling mess with a hint of faded elegance.

"What's wrong?" Jake asked Salah as they walked in.

"I need the toilet."

Taking a seat, Jake watched Salah walk across the terrace, weaving his way between the tables. His demeanor on the phone this morning had been odd. When Jake suggested meeting at a favorite kebab restaurant, Salah said he would feel safer at his club.

It was a typical August day in Egypt, hot and dry with a hint of a breeze, and a relentless sun. Most men in the club wore sporting shorts and short sleeve shirts. Most women were covered head to toe in long skirts, long sleeve shirts, scarves, or the black abaya. A few even had their faces covered.

'Perhaps Salah was right,' Jake thought as he waited for his colleague. 'Perhaps it is safer to talk here.'

"Things are not normal," said Salah as he sat down.

"Why, *habibi*?"

"Hesham Ibrahim has done everything but plead with me not to submit a bid. He told me the acreage is no good. He tried to convince me no one could make any money off this lease, even if they discovered something. He even told me he is worried I will blow myself up on one of the drifting plastic mines left by the Israelis."

"Hesham's paranoid."

"He is very agitated. For some reason, he wants me out of this deal."

"Why?"

"I do not know. Hesham and I were at the University of Cairo together. I attended the weddings of his three daughters. Perhaps he is looking after an old friend?"

"Sounds odd. I wonder if Hesham's involved with our competitors. Maybe he's on the take."

"No. This is not possible. Almost everyone in government takes bribes and favors. But Hesham and Maged are incapable. They are very religious with strong Islamic ethics."

"OK, forget about bribes. You remember that someone broke into my Houston house last month, right? A week later Federal agents shot two Middle Eastern guys. The US government has my daughter under protection. Maybe the same crooks have gotten to Hesham."

"My God."

"We need to know why Hesham's upset. Maybe he's run into our bad guys. Can you get an answer out of him?"

"That depends. I know him as well as anyone. Whether or not he will confide in me depends on many things."

"Yea, like what kind of pressure is being put on him."

"I can only try."

"We've got an appointment with EGPC tomorrow, right?"

"Ten o'clock. First with Hesham; then with Maged. I doubt Hesham will talk with you. Maybe I can meet him again later."

Jake decided not to tell Salah about the change in bid level until the last moment. He felt guilty keeping his partner in the dark but Salah didn't need to know.

When Jake arrived early at EGPC's office, Salah was already sitting in one of the plastic-covered chairs outside Hesham's office. He never understood the tacky plastic covering, which felt sticky to the touch after so many people had sat on them. Ibrahim came out of his office a bit after ten o'clock. "Nadia, please send in the tea boy."

As soon as they all settled into chairs in his office, an ancient, galabeya-clad gentleman appeared to take drink orders. Each ordered *'Ahwa mas boot'*, that thick, bitter, and extremely strong local coffee, mercifully served in a demitasse cup.

Salah and Hesham chatted in Arabic. Jake couldn't understand much of what they said, so he glanced around the office. Leather-bound theses cluttered the bureau, piles of papers everywhere. Framed calligraphies of Koranic verses.

"*Shukran, Abdou. Khalas, badi bokra,*" said Salah.

"*Tayib, habibi. Youm el gomma. Wa Hoda.*"

Jake caught the last few lines, when they made plans to meet later that afternoon. Hesham did indeed seem nervous.

"Now, *khawaga.* How is life in the United States?"

"Not as enjoyable as Egypt but we manage."

"Ah yes. How is your daughter?"

He and Hesham had never interacted socially, yet he remembered Jake had a daughter. He was forever amazed at the social memories of Egyptians.

"Fine thank you. And your family?"

"Fine also. My wife is doing much better this year."

Jake struggled to remember what had been wrong with the woman. Absolutely nothing came to mind so he just nodded.

The old fossil knocked on the door and came in with three small coffees and three tall glasses of water. Jake wanted to help before he tripped but the man managed to serve all the drinks and let himself out safely.

"So what can I do for you?" asked Hesham.

"We want to reinforce our interest in the Sinai block. We plan to put in a strong bid next week and have everything in place. Strong technical plans, solid money, and an aggressive commercial plan."

"You will see when the bids come in," said Salah, working to maintain his appearance of importance.

"I hope you are successful Jake Tillard. Few geologists know the Sinai as well. And Salah my old friend, this would be a perfect thing for you to do before you die. I am sure, *Insha'Allah,* that your bid will be the best. I told you before that there was another company interested in the block. The Sinai is suddenly popular."

"Which company is it," Jake asked, knowing that Hesham could not tell him.

"It is not a true company in fact."

Jake tried to keep a poker face, but his eyebrows went up with this news. The Egyptian smiled, relishing his power.

"What do you mean?" Salah asked.

"I'm told the bid will come from a local man relatively new to the industry."

"Who told you that," asked Salah.

"A Palestinian from New York. They must be working together."

Bells went off in Jake's head. He glanced at Salah but the New York connection had not yet registered with him.

"A smart guy, he seems to represent this local rich businessman. Or overseas money may be involved. There are lots of displaced rich Palestinians roaming the world."

"Would EGPC allow such a consortium to operate in Egypt?"

"Why not. Can we tell one foreign devil from another?"

'You mean you don't care if you go to bed with respected businessmen or terrorists,' thought Jake. 'Or you can't distinguish between them.'

Finishing another round of small talk, the two partners stood with Hesham Ibrahim and shook hands while leaving his office. As they thought, Hesham was not willing to divulge much in front of Jake. Once outside, the door closed leaving Jake to wonder again what went on behind that closed door all day.

After waiting fifteen minutes on another plastic-covered chair, they repeated the performance with Maged Khafagy, Chairman of EGPC. The meeting was shorter and Jake let Salah do most of the talking in Arabic. Their main take-away was that EGPC favored capable foreign interests over local slippery ones, although they would love to award a block to a local, just for the optics. After twenty minutes, they left Maged to his business. The partners parted for the afternoon; Jake to the hotel pool and Salah to grab a bite before revisiting Hesham.

Jake relaxed in a chaise by the Marriott pool, surrounded by palm trees, waiters in starched shirts, fat men in speedos, and girls in bikinis. He noticed none of these as he talked on his phone.

"Charles, things are going well."

He brought his chief funding partner up to date on the competitive atmosphere and their conversations with EGPC.

"I've come at this several times from different angles now. Maged Khafagy will ensure that the bid process is fair. I don't think we can expect any favors, but I do think we will get equitable treatment. That's something for a third world country Charles. We're not using bribes or graft. This is not Nigeria."

"Wonderful Jake. We'll know in ten days then?"

"We should."

"Wonderful. You stay safe over there, OK?"

"I'll try."

His eyes focused on the fronds high up in a Royal Palm. 'Time to call home,' he thought, dialing the ranch.

"Bar-J."

"Libby?" asked Jake.

"Jake is that you?"

"Yes. Direct from poolside in Cairo. I didn't expect you to answer. How are you?"

"Great. Your dad is so nice. And Gussie is one super kid. Remembering you in grad school it's hard to believe you could have produced her."

"Nice."

"Just teasing."

"Yeah, yeah."

"Jake how is everything there?"

"Really good. Salah and I just met with the government. We've got competition but nobody serious."

They talked for fifteen minutes before Libby corralled Gussie and put her on the phone. Three minutes later, after a record setting phone conversation with his daughter, he said good-bye and settled back to enjoy the afternoon.

Salah was not having such a good time. His old friend Hesham was in dire straits. He hadn't slept in days, and in stark contrast to when Jake had been present had begun a constant babble as soon as Salah entered his office.

"You must not bid," his whisper sounded like a low volume scream. There was desperation in the plea that sent chills through Salah.

"Hesham you must tell me what is wrong."

"I cannot. All I can do is beg you not to bid. Our families are in danger. Salah I am very scared."

"Have they done something to your family?"

Hesham hesitated a bit before answering.

"No, they are OK. *Insha'Allah* I want to keep it that way."

"Who has threatened you?"

"I don't know. I don't know. It is connected to the Sinai concession. My God, six months ago we couldn't have given away that worthless land. Now everyone wants it."

"Who wants it Hesham?"

"You for one my friend. I can't get you to back away. And you are the only sane one in all of this."

The two stared into each other's eyes. Hesham was clearly frightened. Salah thought they must have hurt someone, whoever 'they' were.

"Have you gone to the authorities?"

"No. That would be very bad. Very bad indeed. They warned me not to."

"I know someone high up in the Department of Security. I could call him."

"No. I do not know who is behind this but I know it involves men very high up. Very important men. Men who could destroy me. And you."

"Why. What do they want?"

"The same thing as you. They want the Sinai. They want to win the bid. They are willing to do terrible things. Back out now before it is too late."

Hesham's last words echoed in Salah's mind all the way up the Corniche. Salah had fought in two wars with Israel and had seen many atrocities. He did not scare easily, but he was getting too old for this kind of stuff.

The driver left him at the Marriott. He had to tell Jake what he found out, not that it would change anything. It would probably just make him more excited about the block's prospectivity.

Book Three

Complications

CHAPTER 26

IT was not really a noise, yet Marv jolted up from a deep sleep. His watch said almost midnight. He lay still. No noise. Nothing. He breathed quietly and listened. The sheers swayed gently with the breeze coming in the open window.

He was in the attic bedroom that had belonged to his son Tom. The room was much as it was when Tom was alive. Marv wouldn't let anyone disturb it. He had moved on but would never let go. He slept up here when something bothered him. Last night he could not fall asleep, troubled by Jake's predicament. He had one son left and didn't know how to help him, leaving Marv feeling old and inadequate. Marv was about to turn eighty and felt like it.

The moon was quarter full but bright enough to light the room, casting an eerie gray pallor. He got up, walked to the window, and looked out. The babble of the stream carried across the meadow to the house. A coyote howled in the distance.

Pulling on his robe, Marv began the journey down three flights of steps to the kitchen. After one flight he saw the first sign of trouble. Brad Marshall was asleep, propped in a chair, head on his chest. Marv chuckled a bit and looked forward to teasing the agent. Getting closer he became confused. It looked like Brad spilled a drink but there was no glass. Just a dark spot on the pine board floor, glistening in the light of the lamp down the hall. Then it registered. He rushed the last three steps to the agent. Pulling up the head, a wave of revulsion swept his body. Brad's head was nearly separated from his body, the neck sliced cleanly to the spine. Marv froze, staring at the insides of a neck, clearly discerning the trachea and arteries.

His mind cleared and his thoughts moved on. Letting the head fall he rushed into Gussie's room. Her window was open, her curtains also blowing. The bed was empty. Marv picked up her teddy bear.

"Shit. At least there's no blood," he muttered.

Layla was staying in the room next to Gussie's. When Marv went in he saw no signs of struggle or of Layla. He went to Libby's room next. She also was not there but her sheets and covers were dragged across the floor. A ficus plant was knocked over. There was blood on the pillow.

'Too little for a neck artery,' he thought, 'but too much for a bloody lip.'

In Lester's room, his heart sank as soon as he walked through the door. Nothing was disturbed, but Lester's body lay on the floor, in an unnatural position. Marv willed himself to continue to Lester's body. Lester had been with the ranch since Marv could remember, and was family. Tentatively he reached for Lester's neck, getting a pulse. He put his eye in front of Lester's mouth, and felt breath.

"Live you son of a bitch. Live."

Tears welled up in Marv's eyes. He snapped out of slow motion, moving into action. Backing down the hall to Brad he picked up his gun and radio. For all Marv knew the intruders were still in the house. A quick check on the radio told him the other agents were in trouble too. Neither one answered.

Marv grabbed a house phone to dial 911, and was almost surprised when he heard the familiar dial tone. An operator answered and he reported the situation as calmly as possible. The depth of questioning and time it took frustrated him.

'Dammit!' he thought, 'didn't she realize it was an emergency'.

He returned to Lester and tended to his friend as best he could. While waiting, he called his old friend Joe. Holding the Glock in front of him, Marv waited for what seemed an eternity before he heard the first of many sirens.

CHAPTER 27

THE house was thick with police, each trying not to disturb anything. Marv was in the upstairs hallway watching the commotion. An ambulance had taken Lester away, the EMTs hooking him up to monitors and IVs. They would not tell Marv much but they seemed concerned. Marv had methodically searched the house and all the out buildings for any sign of the three women. Nothing. It was an agony he had not felt since the car crash.

Moments later a deep voice boomed through the house as a large man entered.

"Who the fuck is in charge here?"

Marv looked into the great room below, a massive spruce beam obscuring the man from his view.

"I am," said a youthful looking police captain.

"You were son. All these guys with the Hamilton police?"

The young man nodded, seemingly anxious to relinquish responsibility. Hamilton was not used to homicides. Meth labs were as serious as it got here.

Joe Faraday showed his Montana State Trooper badge and brushed aside the younger man.

"Listen up everyone. Get the fuck out of this house. Now. I am detective Joe Faraday, Captain with the Montana State Police. I am taking charge. Everyone out and wait for me on the front porch."

Marv watched this display with detached interest. He walked down the stairs, stopping in the great room. Joe came over and put his arm around the anguished man, who was also one of his oldest friends. Black cowboy hat, weathered black leather vest, Joe smelled of cigarettes and horses.

"What the hell happened Marv?"

Joe skipped 'hello' and 'sorry'. He needed the facts. Marv went through the night's events, filling in background to explain why

Federal agents were on the ranch, and fitting Gussie and Libby into the picture.

"Shit, what a fuckin' mess. The Feds are gonna be crawlin' 'round here in no time. What about the other agents? Any idea where they are?"

Joe sat on the couch, resting his boots on the coffee table, and indicating for Marv to sit next to him. One of the policemen called from the front door, asking if Joe was coming out. Joe's voice boomed out again with more than a hint of annoyance.

"Course I'm comin' out. When I'm fuckin' ready. Now take a seat on the porch and wait."

"Yes sir."

The local officer-in-charge backed out the door and didn't come back. Marv answered Joe's earlier question.

"There's always one agent on duty outside, roaming around. The other stays in the bunkhouse. They overlap shifts. After I found Brad and checked all the rooms I used his radio to call them. No response. I haven't had time to check the bunkhouse."

"Wait here a minute," said Joe, who left the house while Marv walked to the window and watched the police in the meadow, flashlights sweeping the ground. He thought about the other agents. He had sized them up as professionals, not likely to screw up. Whoever did this was good. His mind wandered to Gussie again.

"Excuse me sir."

He looked up and saw the young officer. Andy was a good boy from down the Valley, the son of Gladys and Harry Prewett.

"Yes Andy?"

"Who is this Joe guy? He's throwing his weight around a bit heavy. I think he's got jurisdiction but I've got no orders to follow his direction."

"Andy, do whatever he says. Joe Faraday's a remarkable man who gets things done. You can learn a lot from him."

His mind wandered back to those days when he and Joe were footloose and invincible. Joe loved life and believed it should be lived at full speed. Marv loved life and wanted his to last as long as possible. Marv settled down and built his ranch business. Joe never settled, joining the marines, deployed to war, and then signed up as a mercenary in Africa just for fun. Marv looked at Andy and saw interest in his eyes.

"When Joe was in his late thirties he came home to Montana and joined the State Police. His career's been up and down. He's been cited a few times and has two medals of merit. He was also charged and acquitted twice of using unorthodox techniques. In both cases he found 'his man' dead. Technically, he probably should've been jailed. But this is Montana. A jury of your peers means something up here."

"What do you mean by 'unorthodox methods'?"

"Do you remember the Caitlin case?"

"The kidnapping near Butte?"

"Yep. It was a pretty famous case but most people don't know the real story. With rare journalistic restraint, the press agreed not to publicize some aspects of the case. The ones that might've ruined Joe's reputation. The beginning's well known. Amanda Caitlin, thirteen years old, disappeared from her ranch in the Crazy Mountain Basin east of Butte. A massive manhunt failed to turn up a single clue. Joe was the primary investigator on that case and he refused to give up. After three months they reassigned virtually every field officer to other things. Joe refused to do anything else."

"How did he get away with that?"

"They threatened to fire him. He offered his resignation. They didn't take it. He kept on."

"Man I don't think that could happen today."

"Son if you have convictions as deep as Joe Faraday, anything is possible. Joe kept looking and a bit later brought in little Amanda. He found her in the hills tucked away in a hut. He said she was there alone. He was a hero."

"So what was the problem?"

"Well, a week after Joe brought in Amanda, a hiker in the area came across four bodies chained to a tree, three men and a woman. Mind you they were almost a mile from the cabin. Each of them had apparently been wounded by a bullet. Not killed mind you, just incapacitated. A couple knee shots, one man in the groin, and the woman had a wound in her hip. Not a slug remained, each having been dug out of the bodies. Not with surgical precision."

"Sounds gruesome. Must have been a real wacko."

"Maybe."

Marv looked at Andy; a bit surprised he was not putting it together.

"None of them were killed by the gunshots. When the hikers found them a large part of each had been eaten by wildlife."

"You mean someone left them tied to the tree wounded?"

"That's the story. Think about it. Four bleeding people chained to a tree in the wilderness. You've got wolves, big cats, and bears. The autopsy found a whole range of animals had saddled up to the dinner table. We'll never know how long it took or how much they suffered."

The light bulb suddenly went off in Andy's head. Marv saw his eyes widen and he pulled back.

"Joe did that?"

"That was the State's position. Enough evidence was presented at trial to prove those four people were undoubtedly the ones who kidnapped and repeatedly raped Amanda. There was clear DNA evidence of that."

Marv's thoughts drifted off then returned to Gussie, feeling nauseous contemplating where she might be.

"Did he do it?" asked Andy.

"He was acquitted by a jury of his peers. Montanans. Ranchers some. A crusty bunch. Maybe there wasn't enough evidence. His lawyer spent a whole day detailing the treatment of Amanda, over recurring objections from the prosecution. You gotta love judges from Butte. He had a sixteen year-old daughter himself, saw exactly where the Defense was going, and was not going to stop them. His lawyer put Joe on the stand. Over three solid days he described the investigation, the link of the four men to Amanda, and the remoteness of the place where she was tormented over eight months."

"Didn't the prosecution protest?"

"I think every prosecution protest in that case was overruled. Joe said under oath he believed the four had done it and thought they got what was coming to them. He said he admired whoever chained them to the tree and said the taxpayers should give that person a reward for saving Montana millions of dollars in court and prison costs."

"But he didn't admit to doing it?"

"The prosecution asked him point blank if he did it. Joe said no. When the judge finally instructed the jury how to reach a verdict I would have bet my ranch on a unanimous guilty outcome. The jury took less than two hours to reach a decision. Everyone thought he was cooked. Joe was found not guilty on all counts, was reinstated to the State Patrol with full back pay, and became a god within the trooper ranks."

Andy seemed a bit shocked by the fact that a cold-blooded killer could be leading this investigation. Suddenly the police radio sprang back to life.

"I've found one of the agents. Dead."

"Don't touch him," Joe's voice boomed.

There was no agent in the bunkhouse nor did they find the missing man for another three hours. By one o'clock Joe had dismissed every one of the local police for the remainder of the day, wanting to avoid trampling the entire property and contaminating evidence. State police forensic teams were on their way and the FBI would arrive by early evening. Joe knew it would be prudent to let them continue the forensics. The state police were better prepared to do the initial investigation and the FBI would have even more sophisticated resources.

After the local police left, Joe and Marv were the only ones left in the ranch house. After calling his colleagues at State Police to check on their progress, Joe settled into a chair next to Marv, who fixed a bourbon for each of them.

"Tell me more about the Federal connection," said Joe.

"This guy named Dick Radisson's been leading the effort out of Washington. I've never met him, but he sounds competent. He called Jake within a day of when his house in Houston was robbed. Said they were working on a big case and he thought Jake's problems were related."

"I need to call him. I wanted to get the facts first."

"Joe, we're old friends you and me. I don't want Radisson involving us in some government thing. He's never met Gussie but he seems overprotective of her for some reason. I don't like it."

"Does seem odd."

"Brad told me that Radisson has a hard core reputation. He promised to bury Brad if anything happened to Gussie. He basically told him to break the law if necessary to make sure that little girl stayed safe."

"Sounds like a good guy. Let's give old Dick a call and see. You got the number?"

Marv pulled a slip of paper out of his wallet. A female voice answered on the first ring.

"Good morning."

"Who have I reached?" Joe asked.

The woman merely repeated the number he had dialed and asked whom he was calling.

"Dick Radisson."

She asked him a couple questions then said, "Hold please for General Radisson".

Fifteen seconds later a brusque voice came on the phone.

"Radisson."

"Lieutenant Joe Faraday here with the Montana State Patrol. General, I'm not sure if you're aware but we've got an incident up here at the Tillard ranch. At least two of your agents are dead and three females are missing."

"I'm aware but I appreciate the call Lieutenant. We should be there in about two and a half hours. Ill see you then."

"May I ask where you are now, sir?"

"I'm in route over eastern Montana. Hitched a ride with the navy out of Virginia."

"We're kind of remote here General."

A normal airplane flight from the east coast took over four hours in the air alone. Not to mention connections and land transport. This guy was in hurry to get here.

"We may not be omnipotent in my group but we can get from A to B Lieutenant."

"See you soon General."

"Call me Dick."

Joe looked at his watch. One forty-five. He set his timer. 'Let's see how long it takes to meet Dick face to face,' he thought.

State Police began arriving. Joe had a plan focused on giving the forensic experts the time they needed to shake down both the house and the grounds before the feds seized control. By two-thirty they found the missing agent, midway between the bunkhouse and the ranch house.

They went out to the body and Marv recognized Nancy Boots immediately. She had been garroted, her neck cut by a wire which was still planted in her skin. The forensic detective was just lifting a plaster print of a sole mark.

"Ordinary fence wire in her neck, Joe. The kind you find on any ranch. That's not going to lead anywhere. This is a weird sole print, though. Not the normal kind of shoe you see around here."

"Good work Doug. Let me know what you come up with."

When they got back to the ranch house, they ran into another team that had just come from the other agent's body.

"Pretty clean sir. Neck slashed with a knife."

"Looks like a professional team, well equipped. His agents must have gone down quickly at the same time. Means at least three of them."

"What do we have for prints inside?"

A mousy looking man with bottle glasses limped over.

"Gloves everywhere Joe. We'll keep it up of course, but I'll bet that's all we get. I concur, they were professionals."

"Great," Joe said with a healthy does of sarcasm.

Joe walked over to the window and looked up at the Bitterroots. Marv came and stood by his side. The mountains looked crisp and powerful, bathed in the late afternoon light.

"Most people like the light at sunset best. Just before the sun goes down you get that purple glow. Alpenglow. Cuz of the light spectrum. You know Marv this federal guy will want to run the show once he gets here. I wanted to run it, until I spoke to him on the phone."

"He has a persuasive voice."

"I suppose. In any case I heard commitment to match mine. I think it will probably work for me to lead the State part of the manhunt, cuz no one can do that better. But if it's agreeable with you

I think this guy is probably best equipped to coordinate the overall operation. 'Course I'll be on the job until your girls are back home. You have my word."

"Joe when I called you I wished for nothing more."

"Let's get us some more coffee."

Joe heard the 'whomp-whomp' of the helicopter from Gussie's room. He looked at his watch and glanced out the window.

"Holy shit. They're here. Look at that bird."

A fully loaded Bell Cobra attack helicopter was coming directly at the house. It screamed in, decelerating madly. Ten seconds later, sixty feet from the front door, a man jumped out and walked towards the house. Joe and Marv went down the stairs to greet the General.

They found what they expected, combat khakis on a tall imposing man, clearly over fifty. Clearly in good shape.

"Joe?" inquired Dick.

"Yeah that's me. And this is Marv Tillard. Impressive entrance."

Radisson ignored the comment.

"Nice to meet you both. Sorry about the circumstances. Marv we're here to do everything in our power to get your grandchild and the two women back. Please know this is a high priority and I'm personally committed. Joe what's new since we last spoke?"

"We found the third agent dead. We've got tire tracks and boot prints. One of our guys found a track that left the main road a half-mile north of the ranch entrance. Looks like there's a series of 'em, all the same tire. Their ages vary, the most recent one probably last night. One of the sole prints near one body is distinctive. Not your common Montana shoe."

"Good work."

Radisson asked if he knew why the agents were there, and was surprised to find Joe was well informed. Not one to beat around the bush, Radisson got to the sticky point right away.

"Let's talk about jurisdiction. I plan to take over control of the investigation. I want you to coordinate the local part, including State Patrol, local authorities, wilderness search, and other in-state activities."

"Sounds good to me. I think we can work together."

Radisson looked straight into Joe's eyes.

"I read a thick file on you on the way up," said Radisson. "We'll get along just fine."

Within the hour two troop helicopters disgorged twenty more Federal agents. Some were obviously Special Forces dressed in camouflage. Others wore suits. Joe was impressed again. He was also even more confused.

'Why,' he thought, 'does a kidnapping in Montana merit this extent of Fed activity? What the hell is Jake involved in?'

When all his men had been given assignments Dick returned to Marv.

"I tried phoning my son in Egypt," Marv began. "Apparently he's in the field and can't be reached."

Dick Radisson nodded and put his hand on Marv's shoulder. He took out his cell phone and speed dialed Stan Kawinski.

"Stan what's your ETA in Cairo."

"About four hours General."

"Do you have any questions on your mission?"

"No sir, I'm clear. Has anyone spoken to Jake?"

"We're having a problem contacting him. Hopefully before you land he'll be informed of the situation."

"Yes sir."

"I'll contact the Ambassador directly and have everything waiting."

"Thanks. I'm anxious to get there, sir."

Dick ended the call and turned back to Marv who had been listening to Dick's side of the conversation.

"Did you get the gist of that?" asked Dick.

"I think so. Let's hope someone can find Jake."

CHAPTER 28

SALAH stayed in Cairo to handle any last minute developments, while Jake watched the Sinai roll by as heat shimmered off the hot pavement, the road ahead dancing with the horizon. Traffic was light, the truck brigades from Gaza and Jordan apparently on holiday. Nahkl loomed in the distance, marked by a tall concrete water tower. The village consisted of four rudimentary concrete structures, two of which were falling to pieces. Jake chuckled, eased up on the gas, and pulled into the COOP station.

"*Salaam al aleikum.* Super, full."

"*Aywa. Zeit? Maya?*"

"Oil and water are OK. *Petrol bes.*"

"*Aywa.*"

He bought a cold Pepsi and a bag of hard candies in the small store. He would undoubtedly run into a bevy of kids somewhere, and candy went a long way towards making friends. Twenty minutes later, he pulled onto a dirt track leading to Mohammed's trailer. He looked around and saw a hundred shades of brown. The only exceptions were plastic bags that blew incessantly across the desert, amoeboid shapes of light blue, pink, and white, which would only stop when they met a fence or bush. The modern tumbleweed.

He drove up on two Bedouin children tending goats. They took the candies he offered, smiling and chattering in rapid Arabic he could not understand. Stopping on a small rise, he spied the trailer.

"There it is," he said to the wind. "Mohammed, you're not gonna believe what's gonna happen here."

Coming out of the trailer as the Mercedes drove up, Mohammed had a rifle, which surprised Jake, especially as it was pointed at him. Jake pushed the button to roll down his window, and shouted as he slowed down.

"*Sabah el Khair, Mohammed. Izayak?*"

"*Sabah el full, habibi.* May your day be filled with fragrant flowers. *Alhamdulillah.*"

Smiling broadly, he threw his free arm around Jake's shoulder as he climbed out of the car. Mohammed pulled a chair in front of the trailer door and asked Jake to sit while he prepared tea. Jake would have preferred to sit inside, out of the sun and the heat of the day. Odd, he thought to himself, but maybe it was even hotter inside the trailer. After a few minutes, Mohammed brought out a teapot with two glasses and a cup of sugar. He measured out four teaspoons of sugar for himself, and one for his guest.

"Ah, you remembered," Jake said in slow Arabic. "I'm flattered."

"I have been around enough foreigners to know one sugar is enough."

They laughed again, talking about tooth decay, the will of God, and foreigners with odd ideas. The small talk lasted for a half hour.

"Yesterday was a day of astonishment," said Mohammed nonchalantly, proceeding to take the next half hour to talk about it. Jake mostly nodded, asking a clarifying question every now and then, but mostly just listened.

"When the sun was high, a car came over the rise from Nakhl. It was blue, driving too fast. When it stopped near my trailer, a cloud of dust flew, and two men got out. They were odd-looking, dressed in blue jeans and white shirts, like rich Arabs. Both had trimmed beards and short hair. They walked slowly, waving."

"They spoke funny Arabic, like from Lebanon. They told me it was hot, and asked me if I lived here. I said sometimes."

"It sounds like they were pleasant."

"They were not friendly, but they were nice. At first. When we talked about the desert. How it was tough to live here. They told me they lived in the desert once, but moved to the city. There were nice things in the city. Plenty of water, stores with everything, electricity for lights, heat in the winter, cool air in the summer."

"I told them I saw Cairo once. I saw black air, smelled cars and garbage, heard the noise of a million people. I told them I didn't like it. I invited them into my trailer for tea. Inside, one of them sat, and the other walked around looking at everything. I asked if I could get him anything. That's when they changed."

"How?"

"The walking one became aggressive, asking how long I lived in this trailer. He opened cabinets and drawers. I told him to stop. The one sitting took a gun and told me to move to the bench."

"What kind of gun?"

Going into the trailer, he emerged thirty seconds later with an Uzi, regular Israeli issue.

"Mohammed, this is an Israeli gun."

"Yes I know. Like most Bedouin, I worked for both sides during the years of war. I recognize most weapons."

"How did you get this from him?"

"I will get there my friend. I sat down while the other man kept looking for something. I told him perhaps I could help if he told me what he was looking for. He told me to shut up. It's a small trailer, so it took only ten minutes to look everywhere. They found only one thing of interest."

"What?"

"I will show you. But first I will tell you the rest. When they didn't find what they looked for, they pulled me to my feet and demanded I show them where I hid the rest of the stuff. I told them I didn't know what they were talking about, and the one man hit me in the face with the gun. When I looked back he hit me again."

Jake looked at Mohammed's face, and saw a fresh bruise, which trailed from his left eye into his hair.

"I was lucky. The man was going to hit me again when I saw a red spray come out of his head, inches from my face. I heard the shot and window breaking after. Out front was another man with a rifle. By the time I fell to the floor, another shot sounded and the second man spun around and hit me as he fell."

Jake was not sure he had understood the mix of English and Arabic, and asked him to repeat. When he realized he had, he asked, "Who was it outside?"

"My cousin Abu. He went past me in the trailer. I heard another shot. The second man had reached for the Uzi, so Abu shot him again in the other shoulder and kicked the Uzi away."

"Yesterday?"

"*Aywa*. My cousin saved my life. He was in the Egyptian army during the war of 1973 as guide and sharpshooter. He had seen the car drive up, and the two men come into the trailer. I am most fortunate. He is a nomad and wanders the Sinai. But he is here this month, in the tent over there."

Mohammed pointed to a tent in the distance, next to a lone Acacia tree. Jake strained to make out a few goats, and what was probably a woman covered with a black abaya.

"My cousin came to my trailer with his army gun. When he looked in the window, he saw the man hit me with his gun. Abu doesn't like guns, or men who carry them. When he went to the war, he was filled with the excitement of youth. After the war he was changed. He shot the first man in the head, killed him instantly. The second one he wanted alive, so he shot him in the shoulder. That's why he started spinning and hit me as he fell down. His second shot got the other shoulder."

"Where are these men, Mohammed?"

"The dead one we buried over there," he pointed to a pile of rocks. "The other one is inside."

"Is he alive?"

"Maybe. My brother and I tried to find out who they were, and what they wanted. He was not helpful."

"Can I see him?"

"Of course."

The Bedouin opened the screen door and led Jake into the small trailer. The man was lying on the couch, both shoulders wrapped in bloody rags. His arms were at his sides, with silver duct tape wound around his body. Tape was also wound around his ankles and knees. He did not look alive.

"*Yallah*. Let's go, wake up."

Mohammed slapped the man's face and got little reaction. Another slap and the man's head turned towards them. Every part of his face was swollen, cut, or bloody.

"My God, did you do this?"

"Mostly Abu."

"And he didn't tell you anything?"

"No. He is stubborn."

"I guess so. Did he pass out?"

"Many times. Abu saw interrogators during the war get prisoners to talk. He says this man is unusual. Nothing we could do would loosen his tongue."

"Where do you think he's from?"

"His gun is the Jewish kind. He has money. I think maybe he is Palestinian."

"Why do you think that?"

Jake remembered on his trips to Israel that he couldn't tell the Arabs from the Israelis, the Moslems from the Jews. The two cultures descended from similar ancestors, and the two religions were derivatives of the same beginnings.

"He mumbled in his sleep about many things. Most did not make sense, but he mentioned Al Aqsa mosque. That is one of the holiest Moslem sites in Jerusalem. I don't think a Jew would dream of a mosque, do you?"

"It's a crazy world."

He looked at the body on the sofa. They weren't going to learn much from him today. He wondered if Mohammed knew more than he had told so far.

"Do you know anything more about him?"

"A little. We looked in his wallet, pockets, and car. This is what we found."

He took Jake to the counter, where a small pile of things had been swept into a corner. Neither of the two wallets contained useful information. Some Egyptian pounds, and a few receipts that Jake could not read. No driver's license, and no identification. There was a map, some manuals for the car, a Koran, and a couple of shirts. Spare ammunition for the Uzis.

"Mohammed, I'd like to have someone come out and look at this stuff, if it's OK with you."

"Sure, my friend. Do you know why they came here?"

"I think so. I'm sorry you're involved, but I think it's my fault. These two are probably from the same group that robbed my house in Texas."

Jake had debated how much to tell Mohammed, and had made the decision to tell him nothing. Now he realized that was the wrong decision. He motioned for Mohammed to follow him outside. He did not want the near-dead man hearing anything. They walked out the door, past his car, and twenty yards into the desert. He reached out and held his hand, a gesture of friendship.

"There's good news, and there's bad news."

He told Mohammed about the mud log, and that he thought it meant there was natural gas beneath the ground. He told him what he wanted to do, and what it would mean for the desert.

"I believed you would know what to do with the paper. You have been a good friend to me. If you say this is good, then it will be good."

Jake felt a heavy weight on his shoulders.

"Mohammed, most things are both good and bad. There will be many changes here. Some will help you and your family, and others will take away things you like. Part of you will be destroyed, but other parts will be woken up."

"Nothing stays the same," he said simply. Then, surprising Jake even more, "What can I do for you, *habibi*?"

The weight pressed down harder. Here was a proud Bedouin, descended from a long line of desert dwellers that had maintained their freedom, independence, and simple lifestyle in the face of invading Turks and Israelis, Egyptian socialism-capitalism, and Pan-Arabism. Now, Mohammed was entrusting his future and that of his family in part to Jake, and asking how he could help. Jake threw his arms around the man and thanked him. They walked back to the trailer.

"Mohammed, would you mind if I looked through the trailer again, to see if anything else strikes me as important."

"My home is your home, my friend. If you see anything you want, take it."

"Thank you."

There really wasn't much left from the original mud logging days. He progressed through the main part of the small trailer, looking again at the large bank of instruments along one wall, with drawers and spaces for equipment. There were still bottles of acid for testing if a rock was limestone. A stereoscope stood in a little space. He moved to the back room, where the mud loggers had slept. In some junk within the small closet, his eyes fell upon a Coke bottle. For years,

Coke was an Arab black list company, because of some ownership link to the Jewish community, and had not been sold in the Arab world. He picked it up and turned it over in his hand, his eyebrows suddenly rising.

"Is this yours? I mean, is it new? Did you drink it?"

"No. Everything in this closet was here before."

"Do you know where it's from?"

Mohammed took the bottle and looked at it.

"From Israel. This is the writing of the Jews."

'Bingo,' thought Jake. He had another link between the trailer and the Israelis. He had evidence that Israelis drilled the gas well years ago, and evidence that Israelis were involved in his current troubles. He walked back to the man on the sofa.

"Wake up."

Jake picked up his head and tried to rouse the man.

"Mohammed, please get me some water."

While the Bedouin was outside, Jake leaned close to the man's ear, and whispered into it.

"I am your friend. I can help you. I am American."

He got no visible response. Mohammed came back with a glass of water that he quickly splashed into the face of the prisoner. He got some coughing in return, but nothing that gave hope for an awakening.

"Mohammed, do you think he will ever wake up?"

"*Insha'Allah*, perhaps."

"I want to bring someone to interrogate him."

"You are most welcome, but this man's mouth will not cooperate."

"Don't injure him anymore, OK? We need him to be much more alert than he is now. Can you give him water and food?"

"I can try. As you see, he is not very good at taking it himself. But I will have my brother's wife prepare some tea and force it into him. When you return maybe he will talk."

"*Insha'Allah* I will be back tomorrow."

"*Insha'Allah*."

Jake placed the man's head back on the cushion, trying to show Mohammed the kind of gentleness he wanted.

The light outside caused him to squint. As he took one more look at the prisoner's rental car, the idea occurred to copy down the serial number. On the dashboard was a metal plate with the twelve-digit VIN number that Jake copied onto a business card in his wallet. Glancing at the interior, he saw nothing of note. A quick look in the glove box revealed some papers in Hebrew. There were a few receipts and some type of registration in Arabic.

"A professional needs to look through this," he muttered.

Turning to Mohammed, Jake thanked him, and told him he would return tomorrow.

"*Insha'Allah, bokra, habibi.* Please come for lunch."

Suddenly, a jet turned above them, lower than normal. Jake thought it was likely an Egyptian Air Force fighter plane doing practice maneuvers over the desert. The UN-enforced treaty for the Sinai specified that Egypt could not have any bases there, and Jake wondered if that covered aircraft presence as well. When it was directly overhead, it was close enough to see some English writing and a US flag. 'Very odd', he thought.

Jake passed at least a dozen Bedouin children on the drive to the main road and handed out the rest of the candy. Here, females wore the black abaya starting at age seven. The desert was a bastion of tradition, and a harsh place for any of God's creatures.

CHAPTER 29

THE drive to the Ahmed Hamdy tunnel, beneath the Suez Canal, was uneventful. Jake was anxious to return to Cairo, but as usual had to wait while traffic moved through the underground channel one way at a time. He stopped behind an ancient Fiat, turned off his car, and got out to stretch. Suddenly the pace car came through the tunnel from the opposite direction, signaling the change in traffic flow. He followed the Fiat at five miles per hour through the long passage, trying to breath as little as possible to avoid the noxious exhaust. Suddenly a thought occurred to him. At the top of the local socioeconomic ladder were perhaps a hundred rich Egyptians, one of whom he suspected had a hand in his recent misfortunes.

'Karim Nabet. Why didn't I think of him sooner? If anyone can give me an inside track, he can.'

"I'll give Nabet a call," Jake said out loud as he emerged from the tunnel. He took his reentry into daylight as a sign of good things to come.

The drive downhill into the Nile Valley and the smog of Cairo was a downer. He dodged deep potholes on the Ring Road and turned onto the Autostrade, heading for the Citadel and downtown. The press of humanity made him anxious, and he almost hit a man who ran in front of his car. At one intersection he shooed away a ragged boy selling boxes of Kleenex, a woman peddling necklaces of sweet smelling jasmine, and a legless man seated on a platform with wheels, begging for a living. After the Sinai, the metropolis of Cairo was unnerving.

Breathing a sigh of relief when he pulled into the Marriott, he valet parked, picked up his day pack, and walked to reception, where three envelopes were waiting for him. Riding up to the eleventh floor, he glanced at a young Arab girl standing next to an older gentleman. He wondered if she was his daughter, granddaughter, wife, girlfriend, or hooker. You could never tell. They got off on the fifth floor, and Jake watched her take his arm as they walked towards their room. He thought hooker.

In his room he opened the first envelope, dated most recently. The fax read, 'To Jake Tillard. From R. Radisson. Call ASAP.'

"Shit."

Fumbling for his wallet and Radisson's number, he stared out the window and dialed the number.

"Yes?"

"Dick Radisson please."

"Who is calling please?"

"Jake Tillard."

"One minute please."

The wait was longer than he remembered.

"Radisson's office. Is this Jake Tillard?"

"Yes it is. Who is this, please?"

"General Radisson's personal secretary, sir. Can you hold just a minute for the General?"

"Of course."

He looked out again at Lion's Head Bridge and the Opera House. From here Cairo looked like any international cosmopolitan city. And why not? The British built the bridge, the Japanese built the Opera House, and the Americans built the hotel.

"Jake?"

"Yes. Is that you Dick?"

"Yes. I have some extremely bad news. I'm at your dad's ranch. Gussie, Libby, and Layla have been kidnapped, and I've got three dead agents."

The shock hit him hard. He was finding it difficult to breath, and took two steps to find a seat on the bed. Dick stopped speaking after that one sentence, knowing Jake would need a few moments to process. He waited for Jake's response, expecting him to take a moment. Jake replied much quicker, and was surprisingly coherent.

"How about everyone else?"

"Your dad is fine. Lester is in the hospital in a coma. Everyone else was untouched."

"What do you know about my daughter?"

"Not much. Nothing in your daughter's room indicates any physical harm to her."

Radisson did not include Libby in that statement.

"What about Libby and Layla?"

"Apparently, there was a struggle in Libby's room, with some blood on her sheets and pillow."

"My God."

"Not a lot of blood, Jake. Forensics doesn't think it's a big deal."

"I'll get back as quick as I can Dick. Who the hell are these guys?"

"So far nothing here sheds any light on that. I've got a small army of folks trying to uncover something. If there's anything here, they'll find it. I would say, however, it appears that someone really wants your data from the desert."

Jake remained seated on the bed, rubbing his forehead while he relayed to Dick the events at Mohammed's trailer.

"You say the man talked about a Mosque in Jerusalem?"

"Apparently. Al Aqsa is one of the three most holy Islamic sites in the world."

Radisson didn't tell Jake his suspicions. The project he had been working for the past year was focused on rogue elements in Israel. For some reason Radisson couldn't yet put together, Jake Tillard seemed to be caught up in this mess.

"I want you to stay put in Egypt."

"No way. No fuckin' way! There is no way I'm staying here while my daughter is missing in Montana. Are you crazy?"

Jake rose from the bed and began pacing in front of the large window overlooking the river.

"Think about it, Jake. We've got an army of people here looking for them. There is nothing you can add. What you can do is work it from that end. Stay in Cairo. Go to Israel. Help me find the root cause. The real problem is over there. The men in charge are closer to you than to me."

"I can't do that Dick. I'm coming home."

He was working out in his mind the fastest way back, likely via British Airways through Heathrow to Chicago, and a connection from there to Missoula. He wasn't sure about the layover in O'Hare, but guessed it would take him at least thirty-six hours to get to the ranch.

"Dick, this is my daughter we're talking about. I'm going to scrap this whole deal."

"That's up to you, son. I can't tell you what to do with your business, but I can tell you these are bad people. You may hold the key to the girls' safety. If you bail on your deal, you may lose leverage."

Jake thought about making a deal. But with whom? No one had approached him. How could he make a deal?

Dick needed Jake to stay engaged. He had begun to look at him as someone he could trust to assist in moving his project in another direction. He tried one more tactic.

"Stan Kawinski will land in Cairo shortly. I'd like you to talk with him before you get on a plane."

"If he gets here before I leave, fine. Does he know where I'm staying?"

"He does."

"Are your people tailing me?"

"They are."

"Even here in Cairo?"

"Yes. I should praise our Cairo office. Obviously you have not caught on to their tail."

"No, I haven't. But I'm sure they didn't follow me yesterday across the Sinai."

"They followed you to where you left the paved road, but not any further. The locals would have made them, and perhaps told you."

"So they lost me after I left the road?"

"Not exactly. We didn't have you under direct contact, but checked on you every twenty minutes or so by satellite or jet."

He thought about the fighter plane he saw over Mohammed's trailer.

"How much did it cost the taxpayers to watch me yesterday?"

"Nothing extra. We just reallocated some fixed costs. Gave our operations folks something real to work on. Stan should be there in a few hours. Wait for him. Help him put together a plan. You can make flight arrangements, but talk to Stan before you leave. We'll hold down the fort here. We will find them, Jake."

"Yeah, sure."

He ended the call, and looked at the hustle on the Corniche below. Every one of the small forms was a human being, each with their own problems. He had always shuddered at the thought of the problems Cairenes had. Now he could shudder at his own predicament. He stood up, opened a beer from the minibar, and dialed a number.

"I am calling Mr. Karim Nabet, please," he said in his best, broken Arabic. "This is an old friend and business associate, Mr. Jake Tillard."

"Mr. Nabet is out of the country for the next two weeks. Please spell your name, and leave a phone number."

Jake did as asked and hung up. He called BA and made reservations on the next flight to Heathrow, connecting on to Chicago and Missoula. He had missed the daily flight, so he had almost twenty hours before he needed to leave for the airport.

CHAPTER 30

A BEARDED priest followed by a procession of teenage boys, all dressed in black, had passed minutes before. All that remained were ghosts of religious tradition. Incense permeated the air and Latin chants echoed through the small chambers and passageways separating Yosef Kettler from the devout group. Their footsteps becoming fainter, he could already hear another group of faithful approaching. It was a musty, dark, and ominous place. None of these factors made Yosef believe in a god, after his experience in Auschwitz. He believed only in himself.

Kettler remembered his first time in the Church of the Holy Sepulcher. Twelve years old and just off the boat from Poland, he had no mother, no father, and no relatives left alive. Having survived the Nazi death camp at Auschwitz, he had latched onto a pious rabbi who tried to make Yosef into a believer. They toured all the religious sites near Jerusalem. Jewish sites like the Western Wall, the Hurva Synagogue, and the Mount of Olives. Moslem sites like Dome of the Rock, Al-Aqsa Mosque, and Dome of the Chain. Christian sites like the Church of the Holy Sepulcher.

The Church was as eerie and ominous now as it had been then, a hodgepodge of architecture, somber and dark. The Greek Orthodox order controlled a room with an altar built above the rock where faithful believe Christ's cross once stood. Yosef remembered as a young boy reaching his hand down the small hole to touch this holy stone. Immediately adjacent was the Roman Catholic area of Golgotha, Calvary in Latin, where Jesus was stripped and nailed to the cross. Further into the Church's core were more altars, chapels, crypts, and chambers, crowded with oil lamps, candles, icons, and shrines to every apostle and saint known to man.

It was in the Chapel of Adam, adjacent to the Rock of Golgotha, where Yosef sat waiting. A very public area, he passed time watching the visitors. Most tourists possessed a look of awe if they were religious. The non-religious regarded the sites as they would the Pyramids. Yosef was smart enough to realize it was not that easy. You could not judge a book by the cover. Just like you could not presume to know what another person believed. That was another thing he learned in Auschwitz.

A young man glanced his way, after lingering a bit too long at a particularly uninteresting part of the chapel, waiting for several others to leave. Yosef stood and followed the man slowly, keeping a good distance behind. Down stone steps worn into polished bowl-shaped rocks by millions of shuffling feet descending century after century. He persisted past the Stone of Unction, with its glass lanterns hanging by massive chains. He felt a chill as he descended and the air became damp and cool. A musty scent permeated the candle lit space. He continued on through the rotunda, where he passed an Armenian procession. Finally, the man knelt at a small shrine in a quieter, more remote part of the Church known as the Arches of the Virgin. Josef allowed him to walk away before sitting beneath one of the pillars along the northern wall. Not a minute later, the Minister of Security joined him, the young man gone.

"Good afternoon," Yaroun Herschel greeted.

"*Vos makht ir?* How are you," Yosef replied in Yiddish. He could not rely on that tongue to prevent eavesdropping but it would reduce the probability of being understood. Most people in the Church were Christians, not inclined towards old Yiddish.

"What can you tell me?" the Minister asked in the same language.

"I'd like to tell a story if you haf de time."

"Of course. A Jewish fable, perhaps?"

"Not quite. A parable."

"Go on."

"Some years ago, de desert to da south was controlled by a different ruler. Dis ruler brought progress and change to a land beset by timelessness and tradition. A band of men set out to study de land. Dey made maps, took samples, and dug into dirt, looking for tings of many colors. Dey vere unsuccessful in dere quest, finding only a ting dey could not hold. It took mudder earth millions of years to create dis ting dat in dis place had no value. De men did not record dere discovery and it vas almost lost."

"Almost is a word that holds promise."

"Indeed it does," said Yosef.

The men sat at the base of the column until another group passed. In their wake, they left a stream of incense and lingering echoes of chanting.

"I found one who remembers de event. He cannot, unfortunately, remember vere it occurred. Ve tink dere exists a treasure map, but as yet ve haf not been able to get it."

"Can you tell me more?" asked the Minister.

"I can tell you as much as you vant to know, but I tink ve should probably moof to anader place."

"My car is outside Damascus Gate. A black Mercedes."

The Minister of Security struggled to stand up and straighten his limbs. As he walked towards the Rotunda, Yosef discerned a limp favoring the left side. He remembered the Minister had received a medal after the Yom Kipper war in 1973. Perhaps the limp was related.

Another pair of eyes followed the Minister. Above the spot where the two had talked was a small opening in the wall, behind which a narrow staircase led from the Arches of the Virgin to another altar in the Place of Sorrows. The tall black man who watched the Minister leave had been descending this stair after saying his private prayers. He would have gone right down the stairs but for the fact he heard archaic Yiddish. Surprised at that language being spoken in the Church the man paused to listen. His Yiddish was rusty but he made out talk of a treasure hunt.

After the Minister disappeared Yosef walked the other way, back past the Stone of Unction, and out the main door of the Church. The press of a diverse crowd brought him back to the real world.

Turning right he walked uphill along the Via Delarosa, or Way of Christ. Yosef looked at the wooden rosaries, olive wood nativity scenes, and other objects for sale. He bent to avoid the T-shirts and galabeyas hanging from awnings above the shop windows. At one point a group of Americans passed him, the man in the lead dragging a large wooden cross, the rest reciting prayers in Latin as they inched their way along the route Christ had taken. Yosef slid past small cafes serving thick coffee, tea, falafel, and shwarma. This was the heart of the Arab quarter of the Old City, and Yosef, quite frankly, did not feel comfortable.

Out the Damascus Gate Yosef entered the din of modern Jerusalem. He saw the Mercedes right away as he climbed the stairs towards Sultan Suleiman Road. The guard leaning against the small stone fence did nothing to stop him from opening the back door and getting in.

Two minutes later the Minister entered, and the car began driving. Tinted windows made Yosef nervous, in his mind targeting the car as worth blowing up.

"So Yosef, tell me the real story."

"Yaroun, vat detail you vant?"

"I want to know everything. I am committed to getting a new source of energy for Israel. Prior to the next election."

Yosef smiled. The Minister's motivation was personal gain. The rhetorical bullshit about clean energy for the State of Israel was just that. His lecturing about procuring a safe, secure, long term source of energy was posturing. It was his political ass on the line.

"You may get your energy. Or you may not. I found man vif Israeli Geological Survey during Israel's occupation of de Sinai. He is quite brilliant scientist, but frustrated one. He spent his life mapping rocks of Israel, hoping to find oil field. All he found vas a shitty little gas field in de Sinai, just across border from Gaza. Ve produced it a few years before it died."

"So this man is frustrated. That's not my problem."

"Actually, it's not true he only found one field. He found another gas accumulation in Sinai. Den it vas too far from anyting to hook up. Dey didn't even test de vell, abandoning it just before a new offensive vas launched in sixty-eight. Some equipment had to be left dere, and noting vas recorded of de find. My contact claims drilling evidence vas so strong dat he is certain gas could be produced. From his surface mapping, he tinks lot of gas. Vorthless back then, it might be vat you look for now."

"Interesting, Yosef. This gas is in the Sinai. Egyptian gas."

"Yes. Dat is vy plan is complicated."

The Minister smiled, happy that Yosef had focused so quickly towards the Sinai. Yosef told the Minister about the bid round in Egypt. How he had teamed up with a very rich Egyptian who would file for the Sinai concession, and eventually work out a deal to produce and export the gas to Israel.

"Yosef, a few years ago I discussed such export with the Egyptian Minister of Petroleum. Even in those days the Moslem fundamentalists would have screamed if Egypt sent its resources to Israel. Today there would be even more resistance for export to happen. They barely produce enough gas for their own domestic use."

"Economics, dear Minister. De whole world runs on economics. Politics and philosophies aside, it vill make economic sense to do dis. Ve vill see dat."

Yaroun agreed of course that economics would favor bringing the gas to Israel. He knew that Egypt's radicals would never come around. That was why a high-ranking US politician had visited him, and the US was a core part of the plan.

"Sinai gas is closer to Israel den to Egypt gas grid. It vill be cheaper to build a pipeline to us. Israel vill pay premium for clean fuel. Egypt can sell us gas at high price, and buy fuel oil at cheaper price to run power plants. Dey sacrifice air quality, but frankly, not concerned."

"Keep talking Yosef."

Yaroun tapped his chin with his index finger, and Yosef noticed the end was missing.

"Unfortunately, ve keep running into complications."

Yosef had laid out the idealistic plan for the project. Now came the time to discuss the nasty side of the deal.

"Dere is an American competing vif us for de acreage. Ve tink he has information on exact location of old Israeli vell. Unfortunately our Israeli geologist has Alzheimer's, and can't remember vere his discovery lies. Ve tried to get dis information from American, but failed. Ve are trying to dissuade him from bidding against us."

"He refuses to deal with you?"

"Ve attempted to partner him in beginning, using shell company in New York. He refused, and gathered necessary funds from an American consortium. Ve haf begun to use more invasive techniques."

"This is what you do not want me to know?"

"It might be better you not know details."

"I appreciate your concern for my well-being, Yosef. Politically I must be careful. I will leave the details to you. But remember how important this is to the State."

"And to your political future," Yosef added sarcastically.

"Not only my future. I suspect there will be trickle down benefits to at least ten of your businesses. Not to mention the profits you will make off the basic gas business. You will make money at the expense of both Egypt and Israel."

"Dere is profit to go around. Now Israel is committed to building a natural gas industry. Ve need a source."

"Yosef, it is no secret I don't like Egyptians. They are a stupid people, devious and dirty. But I like your idea. Do what you need to bring it about, and negotiate with those donkeys for all you can get."

Yosef did not expect such an attitude. He had always found his Egyptian partners shrewd, competent, and savvy. Several of his businesses were in Egypt, and he frankly enjoyed visiting Alexandria and Cairo.

Minister Herschel looked at his watch. He needed to hustle to make his appointment with Simeon Friedman.

"Where can I drop you, Yosef?"

The older man looked at his watch. It was still a half hour until his next meeting.

"The American Colony."

Minister Yaroun looked at him with raised eyebrows. The American Colony hotel was in East Jerusalem, an area generally avoided by Jews since the Intifada in 1987. The hotel was still popular with British and American journalists and expatriates, and was a favorite of Palestinian bigwigs. He wondered who Yosef was meeting.

CHAPTER 31

THE main building of the American Colony Hotel had been a pasha's palace. Yosef loved the limestone courtyard, which provided a respite from the noisy neighborhood. A hotel since 1902, it had been renovated several times, and was stunning throughout. Its stone floors, kilim rugs, Ottoman furniture, and a plethora of potted palms created a colonial, tropical atmosphere.

Yosef noticed that afternoon tea was being served in the courtyard under a canopy of lemon trees bursting with blossoms. Since he was early for his meeting, he took a seat and ordered Turkish coffee and sweet rolls.

Twenty minutes later a short, corpulent, balding man entered the lobby. Karim Nabet spotted Yosef and turned to join him, almost knocking over an elderly British woman.

"Tea?" Yosef asked.

"No, thank you. I thought we should go somewhere else."

Karim had called the meeting, knowing Yosef was leaving that night for Switzerland. Yosef finished his Darjeeling and threw some Shekels on the table. They walked out of the hotel, down the drive, and onto Nablus Road. Turning left, they passed the Tombs of the Kings, where a cue of tourists waited patiently to see the first century treasure.

They turned east, crossed Saladin Street, and plunged into the depths of East Jerusalem. The area had deteriorated greatly since Yosef had last been there. Old women in black abayas shuffled along, stooped from a lifetime of hard work and worry, while small children darted barefoot amongst them. Bricks, dirt, and trash were strewn about, long ignored by local residents and the government.

"*Sabah el khair*," Karim greeted the waiter as they sat at a small table outside a crumbling building that housed the small coffee shop. Although dirty, he thought nowhere in Jerusalem did the filth approach that of Cairo.

"*Sabah el full,*" came the reply. 'May your day be blessed with sweet smelling flowers'.

Yosef looked around and realized what an optimistic greeting that was. Karim whispered to the waiter, who promptly shooed away the men at the next table and reappeared with two small glass cups of tea. Karim Nabet was Egyptian but had family connections to this Palestinian neighborhood. As long as Yosef had known him, and as much business as they had done together, he realized they hardly knew one another.

"This is not a glamorous cafe Karim."

"But it is safe from wandering eyes. And ears."

"What do you want to tell me?"

The two men did not meet often, although they should have. Karim had been Yosef's Egyptian partner in many ventures, and would lead this gas venture through the newly formed Triton Oil. He knew nothing about the oil business of course, and would need to find someone to do the actual work.

"My man in EGPC tells me only two companies will bid. An Egyptian friend of mine will run our bid. He has ties to the industry, so it will not look strange for him to do this. If we are successful with our bid, I will pay him three hundred thousand US dollars."

"That seems reasonable. What about our American friend?"

"Your people have been ineffective. The American still plans to submit a bid. If it is the one I intercepted from his hotel, our bid will win. If not, then…." His right hand moved in a sideways wave. He let his voice trail off in a manner that irritated Yosef.

"We have only seven days until the bids are due. I want this acreage, Karim."

"Then get the American out of the way."

Yosef pulled his cell phone out of his pocket.

"Get me Osama abdel Fatah," he barked into the phone.

He looked out over the neighborhood while he waited. At one time the limestone houses must have been quite nice, with plants gracing the gardens. Now, an ubiquitous lack of upkeep had allowed the desert to encroach. The area was a mess.

"Osama, I need to talk now."

He told the Palestinian where he was, and gave him twenty minutes to get there.

"We will find out what is happening with the American. In the meantime, tell me what is new with you."

It was Karim's Mercedes business that brought them together almost twenty years ago. Thanks to a loophole in the laws of Egypt and Israel, created by the Camp David Accords, it made sense financially to bring Mercedes cars through Israel to Egypt. Yosef benefited from this convoluted import path, and Karim benefited from a volume arrangement with the German manufacturer. Since then, the two had done many deals and had become wealthy, influential men. Their business relationship was a symbiotic one. They knew little of each other; nonetheless a friendship of sorts had developed. Karim responded to Yosef's question.

"Right now, my nineteen year old son is my main headache. He's dabbled in drugs for a couple of years, and last week, I got a call from a friend, a police lieutenant, who had my son in his office. He asked if I could come down at once."

"Was he arrested?"

"Almost. My friend saw him come into the station, and had him diverted to his office. I went down immediately. Mohammed was selling drugs. Can you believe that? I give him money, and this is what I get in return."

"I assume you got him out?"

"Of course. It cost me a thousand dollars, but Mohammed's record is clean. Thank God."

"Children are difficult," Yosef said, "Or so I hear. I have not been fortunate enough to be a father."

They traded words about their personal woes until a car stopped across the street. It was a dark blue Mercedes with tinted windows. Yosef squinted into the now descending sun and watched Osama abdel Fatah get out. The short man crossed the street and pulled up another wooden chair.

"*Shalom. Sabah el khair.* I am sorry it took so long."

"Twenty minutes, exactly. You are early for an Arab."

Yosef glanced over at Karim, who failed to realize the jibe was aimed at him and his earlier tardiness.

"Who picked this hole? Palestine does have coffee shops that are not dumps."

Palestinian by birth, Osama grew up in the Moslem Quarter. East Jerusalem was not his cup of tea, particularly after spending the past five years in the United States.

"Karim knows the locals here. How this is possible for an Egyptian I don't know."

"This is not far from where you grew up, is it, Osama?"

Karim didn't like Osama abdel Fatah, and took every opportunity to needle him. Osama turned to Yosef, not taking the bait.

"I have come at your request, Mr. Kettler."

"I understand your operation with the American is not going well," Yosef started.

"We are doing everything.... "

Yosef, who obviously didn't like Osama's attempt to defend his efforts, interrupted Osama.

"Karim tells me he has everything under control in Cairo, except for the American's bid. Take three minutes to fill me in on what is happening. Assure me his bid will not be submitted."

Osama leaned back in his chair, took a deep breath, put his hands on the white plastic table.

"We have not recovered the mud log yet. Yesterday we kidnapped his daughter and girlfriend in Montana. Unfortunately there were casualties. We can safely hold the females for about a week, and then will have to kill them. Our operation in the Sinai was a bust. Two of our men were sent to the trailer of a Bedouin looking for evidence of the original well. They have disappeared, and it is too dangerous for us to go near that area again. In Cairo, our mole in the national petroleum company is responding to our pressure. After delivering his son's finger to him in a box, he will do anything we want. Unfortunately, he cannot control the American either."

Osama was proud of his ability to summarize the complicated operations in less than three minutes.

"You don't have shit," responded Yosef, his face red. "The US operation was not supposed to have casualties. You are failing, Osama."

"We still have time, sir. We have his daughter as the key card to play."

"Play it soon. As much as it disturbs me, I agree you cannot afford to let the women live. This was not the plan and I hold you personally responsible for each death."

"Yes, sir. I will see the American does not submit a bid."

Osama thought to himself, you don't care what happens to them as long as you can do your deal. He hated this Jew. All he wanted was to finish this operation, get his fee, and get out. This was turning into a nasty job.

'How did I get myself involved with an Egyptian and a Jew,' he thought.

CHAPTER 32

WOKEN by the phone, Jake looked at his watch. Just after midnight. Half asleep he flicked on the bedside lamp, knocking the phone receiver to the floor. Retrieving it, he brought it to his mouth.

"Hello."

"Mr. Tillard?"

"Yes, this is Jake Tillard. Who's this?"

"Never mind my name."

"What do you want?"

"We want to win the Sinai bid."

Jake shot upright immediately, trying to erase the sleepy haze from his mind.

"We have something in common then. I would also like to win that bid. I am the one who nominated the acreage."

"I must disagree. That block was nominated by my colleagues, who will not tolerate you bidding."

Jake was narrowing down the accent. Palestinian or Syrian.

"That is a pretty strong statement, my friend. One must tolerate those things over which one has no control."

"But we do have control in this case. We have your daughter."

Jake sprang out of bed. He knew this was coming but it stunned him nonetheless.

"If you've hurt her…"

"What, Mr. Tillard? I am afraid you are at a disadvantage. You do not know who we are, or where we are. We can do whatever we want with your daughter and your girl friend. And your housekeeper."

He thought about the women. What had they done to them already? What would they do?

"Rest assured they are now all fine, and are being treated very well in fact. I am sure you want that to continue. I assure you it will, as long as you do not submit a bid."

"How do I know you really have them? That they are fine?"

The man did not pause long, but seemed to confer with someone, while holding his hand over the phone. He came back with the reply Jake wanted.

"I can let your daughter talk with you."

"Please put her on the phone."

"Not now. I will call back."

"I'll be here," Jake replied as the phone went dead.

CHAPTER 33

THE phone rang again six minutes later. Jake stared at the telephone, willing himself to answer.

"Yes," he said tentatively.

"Jake, this is Stan Kawinski. I'm downstairs."

He breathed a sigh of relief, told Stan to come up, and went into the bathroom to splash water across his face. By the time he brushed his teeth there was a knock at the door. He looked through the peephole. Stan Kawinski looked like a man who had just flown across the Atlantic. Unshaven, blood shot eyes, shirt rumpled, he shook Jake's hand as he patted his shoulder.

"I'm very sorry, Jake."

"Thanks, Stan."

Stan sensed something had happened since he was briefed in Washington. Closing the door behind him, the big man plopped down in the stuffed armchair and waited.

"They called me. I asked to talk with Gussie, and they said they'd call back."

"When?"

Jake looked at his watch.

"Maybe an hour."

Jake told Stan about the first call. There had been a time lag, suggesting it originated overseas. Gussie wasn't right there, so there might not be a phone where the women were being held hostage, or perhaps the caller had just been in a different location. If it was in the US, there were not a lot of places without cell reception. Stan asked a clarifying question from time to time. After Jake finished, Stan reached into his bag, and took out a rather large portable phone. He walked over near the window and pushed a single button.

"S9," he said into the mouthpiece, then paused before adding, "Omega 6471."

Jake knew they had a good cell system in Cairo, but sensed this call was different.

"I'm with him," Stan said. "They've made contact and will call again within two hours. I suggest you tap and trace all satellite relays into Egypt."

"Who was that?" asked Jake after Stan had hung up.

"With the push of a button this gadget can direct dial twenty numbers from anywhere on earth, using our defense satellite system. It's got a Global Positioning System that shows exactly where I am. The only shortfall is it can't go through obstacles like trees or buildings."

"That didn't answer my question, Stan."

"That was Langley.

Langley was CIA headquarters outside Washington DC. Stan was not going to tell Jake who was on the line. Jake wondered if they could really listen in on every satellite telecommunication between the US and overseas and filter those coming to Egypt.

"Jake, I need to fill you in."

It sounded so impersonal to Jake that way. 'My God,' he thought, 'this is my daughter. My life.'

"Dick is personally taking charge. He feels this is linked to an ongoing investigation, and because of that he's got special authority. Ten Federal agents are in Montana along with local and state police."

"Dick's in charge. Is that normal?"

"The last time Dick Radisson took charge of a field operation was a decade ago. He's at the ranch sharing command with a State Trooper, though I can't imagine Dick Radisson sharing command with anyone."

Jake wondered why Dick had agreed to that. Clearly this matter was Federal jurisdiction. Jake had a thought.

"Who's the Montana guy?"

"Some maverick they tried to throw off the force a few years back. Story goes he ought to be in jail."

"Joe Faraday?"

"Yea, it's Faraday."

Jake drew a breath. He had known Joe Faraday since he was a little boy, and had even hunted with him. Joe was known as the half Indian, not because of any genetic connection but because of his outdoors skills. He could track anything, and used to guide hunting trips for money.

"You know him?" Stan asked.

"I do, and now I understand. I'm glad he's involved. I want to call him and talk with him."

"If you want to pass on your idea of a backwoods hiding place, don't bother. From what I understand, Faraday beat you to it. He's got packers in the mountains, police combing rest stops, cafes, and gas stations. He's even got bikers out running down clues."

"Montana's big country," Jake said.

Stan saw the angst in Jake's eyes. He knew how difficult this must be, and couldn't imagine anything worse for a parent. He tried to divert Jake's attention, suggesting they order room service and talk about what to do when the next phone call came. Stan told Jake to stretch out the call and ask leading questions designed to find out where they might be hiding. If they did not let him talk to Libby, he should ask Gussie if Libby is all right and if she could see her. Stan hooked his recording device to the extra phone in the bathroom.

Finally, it rang.

"Hello," Jake said.

"Hello, Mr. Tillard," Jake was sure it was the same voice.

"Have you thought about our last conversation?"

"I want to talk with my daughter and Libby."

"Speaking with the woman is impossible. I have the girl. She will be permitted just a few words. Don't ask anything or I will cut the line immediately. Do you understand?"

"Yes, I understand."

Stan noticed the satellite lag but the voice quality was clear. He listened for background noise, and heard something he could not place. There was a long pause and he was afraid the connection was lost when they heard Gussie's voice.

"Daddy?" she said faintly.

"Yes, sweetheart, it's me."

"Daddy, I'm scared." Her voice trembled with fear.

"I know Gussie. Are you OK? Are they treating you OK?"

"No. Daddy, come get me. I'm scared. It's cold at night. And it's dark up north in this big house."

Jake could hear the man telling her something. Jake was proud of his daughter for sneaking information.

"Gussie listen to me. Daddy will come get you. You need to be brave. OK?"

"Daddy, I want to come home! Now," she sobbed.

"I know Gussie. How are Libby and Layla?"

"I don't know. The three men won't let me see them."

Mohammed was agitated by that answer and yanked the phone out of Gussie's hand.

"Mr. Tillard your daughter is too clever. You can see she is fine. At least for now. Your girl friend is also fine."

"Let me talk to her."

"I cannot do that. Your friend would give you information the minute I put her on the phone."

"Why have you done this?"

"You already know that. Now listen. You will not submit a bid on the thirty-first. If you do, your girlfriend and housekeeper will be shot dead. Do you understand Mr. Tillard?"

"I hear you, but I don't understand."

"Then think about it until you understand."

"OK, OK. Please. I will agree to what you want. But I want Gussie first. You give her to me and I'll do what you want."

"Mr. Tillard I am not stupid. Your daughter and the woman are the keys to what I want. When I get what I want, you will get them back. Not before."

Jake was stalling at this point, trying to keep the line open as long as possible.

"How do I know you will keep your end of the bargain?"

"You don't. You have to trust me. Remember that if you submit a bid, you will never find your daughter's body."

Jake cringed.

"Who are you people?"

"Goodbye, Mr. Tillard. You will not hear from us again. If you do as I say, we will release the women on September first, the day after the bid round closes."

"Where will you release them?"

"Good bye Mr. Tillard."

"But I need to......"

The connection went dead. Jake kept the phone at his ear, hoping something else would happen. It was still there when Stan pried it from his hand. Jake was staring out the window. It was almost three in the morning, yet there were still a large number of cars and pedestrians milling about.

"Jake!" Stan was shaking him gently, trying to bring him back. "Jake come on, snap out of it. We have work to do."

"She said it was cold. And dark."

"And north," said Stan. "In a big house. Could mean they are in a stream valley without a lot of sun. I'll send the recording to Langley for analysis."

"I need to get back there."

"We need you here," Stan replied.

They looked at each other and spent the next half hour discussing Jake's leaving. Stan walked over to the minibar and pulled out a Schweppes Tonic. He didn't bother with a glass, but drained the little bottle in one long swig. Airplane flights made him dehydrated.

"Stan you look like hell. You need a nap."

"I'll make it. I want to visit the trailer in the desert and see if I can find anything you missed and ask the prisoner a few questions. I can sleep on the drive out."

"I'm going to Montana, remember?"

Jake started repacking his bag.

"How am I going to get to the trailer? And how can Radisson get hold of you if you're in the air? Most importantly Jake, what if the kidnappers call back? Think man."

He let Jake stew on this for a couple minutes.

"There's not much you can do in Montana. I know how you must feel, but think. Where can you do the most good? Where do you think the puppeteer is?"

Jake sat down and rubbed his head.

"You're right. I can't even get back to Montana for almost forty-eight hours. And I don't know what I'd do. I can play out this cat and mouse game with the bid submission. If nothing happens in five days I won't submit the bid."

"Jake, these thugs in Montana who took Gussie and Libby are just taking orders. Joe will find them and God help them when he does."

"I get it. So what can we do here?"

"Work with me Jake. Let's figure it out."

"Give me twenty minutes, and we'll leave for the Sinai."

"Make it thirty. I need a shower. I also need to put together a few toys for the trip."

CHAPTER 34

CRUISING up Mokattam hill east of Cairo, Jake and Stan left the congestion and pollution behind. Jake looked at his watch. Four forty in the morning. They would be at the tunnel before six when it opened. That would put them at Mohammed's trailer just after eight.

He looked at Stan, who had fallen asleep less than a mile from the hotel. When they discussed the hostage situation Stan believed they would never let the girls live. Based on past cases they assumed that Gussie and Libby would not be released no matter what Jake did. Jake had reached that same grim conclusion. They needed to find the head of the beast before that happened. The key was here in the Middle East.

As his mood intensified, Jake's foot pushed harder on the pedal, and the Mercedes passed a water truck as if it was standing still. It was crazy to drive this fast on the Cairo-Suez Road in the dark. Most traffic drove with their lights off, to preserve their batteries. He slowed down to sixty miles per hour, still passing other traffic.

A hundred and fifty miles later, Stan woke as they pulled into the COOP gas station in Nahkl. He stretched and Jake could hear bones cracking as he rolled his neck.

"Looks desolate," Stan said.

"It is. Wait 'til the sun's up and the hot wind sets in."

"Can't wait. Where's the bathroom?"

"Inside the café to the right. But I'd go around back. It's more pleasant."

Jake paid for the gas, bought two cold Pepsis, and leaned against the car. Stan returned and Jake handed him a Pepsi.

"We're going to win this Jake. We will find them."

Stan's look caused Jake to shiver.

As they rolled up to the trailer Mohammed was outside, rifle in his arms.

"*Salaam al aleikum, habibi.*"

Jake responded with multiple greetings in broken Arabic.

"Who is he?" the Bedouin shrugged towards Stan.

"A friend. With the US government."

"Police?" asked Mohammed, stroking his beard. He did not like police of any kind, a feeling developed from years of smuggling and an intense independence.

"Not exactly.

He knew Mohammed would not be satisfied until he understood exactly how Stan fit it. He decided the best approach with this wise Bedouin was with the truth.

"He's a spy," Jake said, continuing in Arabic. He had looked up the word for 'spy' last night.

Stan looked at Jake with an inappropriate wry smile.

"A spy," said Mohammed, breaking into infectious laughter. Soon Jake and Stan joined in, not sure why they were laughing.

"I love spies," said the Bedouin.

Jake looked at the other two men, who were now rolling with laughter. He wondered if Stan understood some Arabic.

Mohammed threw his arms around Stan, hugged him, and led both of his guests to chairs outside the trailer door. With cups of tea, they spent the next ten minutes talking about little things. The heat. The pollution in Cairo. The Peace Process. Mohammed put all these things at about the same level of importance. After a while he stood up and asked if they wanted to talk to the man inside. Stan replied he would.

Inside, the sight of the man frightened Jake. The gaunt figure looked worse than he remembered. Jake wondered if Mohammed was feeding him. Stan sat next to the man, whose hands were tied behind his back and fixed to a metal bracket on the instrument rack. His feet were also tied together but able to be swung onto and off of the couch.

"Has he told you anything?" asked Stan

"Nothing," Mohammed said simply.

A few Bedouin had tried everything they knew to get the man to say something, to no avail. For the last couple of days they had largely ignored the increasingly frail creature, giving him minimal food and water twice a day.

"Mohammed," Stan said loud enough for the bound man to hear. "Very little time remains. This man's friends have kidnapped Jake's daughter and lady friend. With your permission I'd like one last chance to get something out of him."

"He is yours. We have not found him good company."

"Thank you."

Stan went out the door, and over to the car. Opening the trunk, he got the small bag he had brought with him. In the trailer, he took out a handgun, fixed with a long barrel silencer. Next was a small machine with a batch of wires coming out of it, followed by small metal tools that looked like surgical instruments. Finally he took out a couple of needles and small vials filled with yellowish liquid. He arranged these on the table before walking over to the couch.

"My friend," he addressed the prisoner. "I need information. Only you control what I do to your body and mind to accomplish this. Do you understand?"

The man did not respond. Jake couldn't tell if he was still cogent. Stan reached out and put his right hand on the side of the man's head, pressing his thumb into the soft spot beneath his ear. The man cried out in pain, and looked at Stan with clear arrogance.

"Better," Stan said.

He went to the table and filled a syringe with liquid. Mohammed held him as Stan injected the serum into the man's arm.

"Now we wait a few minutes," Stan said in Arabic. "What did you do to try to get our friend to talk?"

"We tortured him."

Because Stan asked, Mohammed went over the techniques they had used, which were crude but normally effective. Apparently the man did not respond to pain.

"The drugs should help, but there isn't a drug that can break someone if they've been trained well and are mentally strong. I suspect we will have a tough time with this one."

Stan walked to the table and picked up the small machine.

"Jake, can you move the car closer to the door and hook this to the car battery."

When that was done, Stan sat next to the figure on the couch. He began talking to him about his home, trying to start a conversation about pleasant things in his past. He got a few words before the man realized he was talking. Then nothing.

"Hooked up," said Jake.

Stan took two wires from the machine and hooked the clips to the man's ears and toes.

"We'll find out how much pain he can endure."

Stan pushed a button and the body next to him jerked spasmodically. It kept convulsing for seconds after the shock raced through the body. His head flopped onto his chest, and Jake wondered if he was dead. Stan grabbed his hair and yanked his head up, the eyes opening.

"Who would you like to call?" asked Stan.

"My God," the man answered.

Stan sent another shock through the emaciated man, but he refused to say anything else. He did manage to nod his head when asked if he was ready to die.

"As I thought," said Stan. "We will not get anywhere with pain. Our friend is a professional, probably trained years ago."

"So what do we do?" asked Jake.

"We go to plan B."

Stan picked up another syringe, and injected liquid of a different color into the man. He needed no help this time holding the arm down.

"This is a last attempt, Jake. Quite a few don't make it through this part. The drug is rather strong."

Jake pondered the ethical aspect of what they were doing. He watched Stan administer this chemical torture, and observed Mohammed leaning against the wall, taking it in without blinking an eye.

"Where are we?" Stan asked the man in a quiet tone.

"Al Aqsa. Beautiful day."

The words were faint, but all three of them had heard. Al Aqsa mosque was in Jerusalem. Jake looked at Mohammed to see if he showed any sympathy for his religious brother. Nothing.

"Who is with us? I think it is your boss. But I don't know his name. Can you tell me?"

"Osama."

"Osama? What are his other names?"

Nothing

"I need to see him tomorrow," Stan continued. "I have a big job for him. For you. Where can I find him?"

"Old City. Saad Badry antiques."

With that the man's head fell down. Stan checked for a pulse and got none.

"Better than some sessions," he said standing up. He packed up his equipment and carried his bag to the car. When Jake joined him he was already on the satellite phone.

"What now?" asked Jake.

"We wait."

"For what?"

"Transportation."

Stan looked at Mohammed and addressed him in Arabic, asking him if he could get someone to return the Mercedes to Cairo in one piece. The Bedouin smiled and said he would be happy to do it personally. Stan took out some US dollars and peeled off a few hundred-dollar bills.

"This should cover petrol, your return trip, and any problems you might have along the way."

The two of them continued in Arabic for a while, Jake following the conversation in general, but missing the details. They talked about war, specifically the Sinai campaign in which Mohammed had participated. Jake was shocked Stan was fluent in Arabic. It seemed effortless for him.

They drank tea, ate cheese and bread, and chatted. After an hour Stan's phone rang. Saying only one word before terminating the call, he stood and stretched.

"Mohammed, would you help me with the body."

The two of them untied the body, wrapped it in a blanket, and dragged it outside. Jake heard the whomp-whomp-whomp of a helicopter. Looking up, he saw the Sikorsky HH-60 Pave Hawk approaching from the west. It came straight in, setting down less than fifty feet away.

"Let's go," Stan said.

Two US Marines ran over, picked up the body, and put it in the cargo hold. Stan put his arms around the Bedouin, kissed him on both cheeks, and waved for Jake to head for the chopper. Jake repeated the process with a tear in his eye. He loved this old Bedouin.

Struggling with the seat belt even as the massive helicopter lifted off, he finally managed to fasten it, and don one of the huge Clark headsets. Stan was talking to the pilot.

"...don't give a shit what they say. Tell them to contact US Operations Ben Gurion. I want this chopper in Jerusalem in less than one hour."

Jake glanced down at his watch. Just after eleven. It seemed like this morning had lasted an entire day.

"Stan," he asked. "What are we doing?"

"Following a lead."

The pilot broke in to say Israeli air control could not give them permission to enter Israeli air space.

"Give me frequency one-one-seven point four, and scramble," Stan instructed the pilot.

"Yes sir."

The pilot knew this frequency was today's top-secret red alert level frequency. A new frequency was used every day for ultra-high level, US military transmissions. He wondered just who this guy was, and how he knew the code.

"Chopper Zulu Charlie Two Nine Eight, you are on level five frequency. State your business."

Stan answered. "This is S9."

"Code, please, sir."

"Omega 6471."

After a few seconds, "What can I do for you, sir?"

"I am approximately forty minutes from the Egyptian Israeli border forty miles south of El Arish. I'm heading for Jerusalem.

Please give Israeli Air Control the proper instructions for our entry, and send escorts to meet us at the border."

"Yes sir. Anything else, sir?"

"No. Thank you."

The pilots looked at each other.

"Do you need any other instructions?" Stan asked, glancing towards the pilots.

"No sir. Heading zero three five and fixed."

Jake stared at Stan, while Stan avoided his face. Jake deduced this would not be a good time to ask questions.

"Zulu Charlie, this is Navy F18 Hornet Delta Alpha Two Zero Two. I have you in sight, above you at two o'clock. We are off the Carrier Minnesota with instructions to escort you to Jerusalem. Israeli Control is not yet sure about this, so there are two of us here to show you the way.

Jake looked out the window and saw two F18s closing in slowly on the helicopter. He was worried about crossing into Israel with Israeli Air Traffic Control being 'not yet sure' about them.

The trip went without incident and the helicopter set down at twelve sixteen on a military strip near Jerusalem. As they stepped out of the helicopter, two black SUVs drove up and stopped. Two non-military looking young men carrying Uzis got out and waited. The rear door to one of the vehicles opened, and a woman in a charcoal outfit walked towards the helicopter, one of the armed men accompanying her. Meeting halfway she extended her hand first to Stan and then to Jake, addressing them both by name.

"Welcome to Israel."

"Thank you, Madam Secretary," replied Stan.

Jake wondered why US Secretary of State Nancy Clancy was here to meet them, at an Israeli military airstrip outside of Jerusalem. He suspected it was not totally because of his daughter.

CHAPTER 35

"**EIGHT** ball, far corner."

Joe took his time, pulled the cue back, and shot just hard enough to bounce the black eight ball off the purple four, into the corner pocket.

"Shit," proclaimed 'Hickey'. "Ain't never seen you play this good, Joe. Not never."

Joe had known Hickey for at least thirty years, their fathers being acquaintances of sorts. He got the nickname 'Hickey' during junior high school, for the obvious reason. No one called him by his real name. In fact almost no one knew it.

The three hundred pound Hickey came around the pool table and put his arm around Joe's neck. After three straight defeats he'd had enough, and was ready to pow-wow. They moved to a wooden table in front of the bar. Several Hell's Angels followed but didn't dare pull up chairs.

"What brings you back to Luke's?" asked Hickey.

Luke's was a typical Montana bar, the kind normally found along remote roads, or just outside town limits. It was, however, in Missoula proper. The decor was early lumberjack, with a wood floor, wood paneling, wood chairs and tables, and a wood bar. Initials were carved everywhere.

"I need help," answered Joe.

Hickey looked at him and cocked his head. Joe hadn't expected this to be easy. After all, he had put Hickey's dad behind bars not once, but twice. He knew the boy was basically good, and Faraday believed he was a good judge of people. Evidence was nice, facts were useful, but he could feel in his heart if someone was good or bad, guilty or innocent, just by talking with them. Hickey was good.

"You still with the State Police?"

"I am."

"Then you come to the wrong place, man. You gotta be nuts even steppin' foot in here."

"Well, you know me Hickey. I never did what everyone expected. Your dad and I were friends once. It pained me to take him down. But we've been through that before."

"You need personal help or official help?" Hickey asked.

"Help with a case."

"Fuckin' eh. Why the fuck would I help the police?"

"Let me buy you a pitcher of beer."

He ordered several, one for the table, and a couple for the other bikers.

"These are on me, not the State. OK?"

"Your nickel," the big man mumbled.

"Hickey, think back. Do you remember Amy?"

"My daughter? That's a stupid question. What's this got to do with her?"

"Nothing, directly. But stay with me. Think of her smile. Her hair. Her little body always ready to play with her daddy. The way she came running. The life she had in front of her."

"I try to forget Joe. Not remember. What the hell?"

Hickey's eight your old daughter had drowned a few years back. Jake knew the loss had all but destroyed this tough guy.

"Hickey, your little Amy is gone. There's nothing we can do about that. Hopefully you'll see her in Heaven. I'm trying to help a different little girl. A girl who's not yet in Heaven. I'm lookin' for her and I need your help."

Hickey's interest aroused, Joe poured another couple beers before launching into the kidnapping. He took out a picture of Gussie and played on the emotions of the man with the ragged beard, unkempt hair, and black leather outfit.

"It's been three days since the kidnapping. We've got some clues and we've got a lot of manpower. But really we got shit all. We don't have the kind of network you have. Your guys can get into places we can't. Places the Feds will look out of place."

Joe looked into Hickey's eyes. He almost had the biker.

"Look at it as a challenge. I've talked this up with a couple of folks. Frankly nobody thinks you guys can do it. I agree but I'm not sure. These guys are as professional as they come. Middle Eastern bad asses. Badder than you."

Joe figured the best way to hook a biker was to tell them you didn't think they could do something.

"I'd like to see if you can flush them out without getting yourselves, or the hostages, killed."

Hickey stared at Joe for several minutes before responding. "The big boss approve of this?"

"Not exactly."

"What the fuck does that mean?"

"It means I didn't ask," said Joe.

Hickey laughed.

"So, we are under cover, but no one knows. What if we get into trouble? Who's gonna bail us out?"

"Nobody," Joe answered.

He knew Hickey could not pass up this challenge. He dropped the final bomb.

"You guys afraid?"

The leather-cloaked man rocked back, straining the hind legs of the chair. Hickey let go a great belly laugh, calling to several of his buddies, ushering them over.

"Wait'll you hear this one. Joe here wants us to do a favor for the State Police. He needs our help on a case."

There were a few nervous chuckles. Not too many though, because they weren't sure yet where their leader was heading.

"He wants us to ride around the state and find some bad ass ragtops. Middle East dudes who kidnapped a little girl, a gorgeous lady, and a nanny."

The chuckles subsided a bit, replaced on some faces by smirks, on others by wrinkled brows as the seriousness of the situation began to set in.

"So here's how I figure. We got two options. We can wimp out and let the fuzz continue flopping around. Or we recognize they can't do it, that they've coming crawlin' to us for help, and we can show 'em we got what it takes."

Joe looked at the faces that were studying each other, trying to gauge which way the wind was blowing. One thing you didn't want to do if you were part of a gang was take the wrong view. Motorcycle gangs, like school children, labor unions, and hedge fund managers, acted with a lemming mentality. They typically left the thinking to their leaders. This was how Jamestown happened, and why there were cults. Joe hated groupthink, but understood it and harnessed it whenever he could.

The group discussed things for the next half hour before unanimously deciding to show the cops they could play. Most of them did not look at it as a matter of good or bad. It was an ego thing. Hickey had his three main guys stay.

"Joe what do you know?"

"At this point only a few things which might help you. We're sure the guys are from the Middle East."

"God damned rag heads," blurted out one of the men. "I hate filthy rag heads."

"These guys may not look the part. They may look like they fit in here. When they were in New York, they looked like they were straight off Wall Street. My guess is you won't recognize them as being out of place. We've got a set of tire imprints we've plastered, from a Michelin HXV 16/24 high speed, high heat, and high performance tire. Not the kind you'd put on a pickup, and not the kind you see a lot in Montana. If we were in California that'd be useless. But not here. We assumed a rental car, and searched from Helena west to Boise, Jackson Hole north to the Canadian border. Hertz is the only outfit that has these, and they only put them on Mercedes, BMWs, and the oddball luxury car."

"That don't narrow it down very much," another biker noted.

"Fifty two of these were rented during the two weeks prior to the kidnapping. Only eighteen are still out."

"Shit. That ain't many. You sure?"

"It took five hours to get this information, from the time we sent a fax of the tire print from the ranch."

Even Hickey raised an eyebrow on that one. Joe wanted to impress them. Let them know they were now playing in the big league, while showing them the sense of urgency needed.

"Of the eighteen cars, thirteen were rented to people we've already talked to. Three others were rented to people who checked out, although we haven't located them yet. Two remain. One used a hot credit card, belonging to a woman named Cutler from Lincoln, Nebraska. She checked out fine, and wasn't even aware her credit card was missing. I assume this car is already stripped, and the parts are in seven states. The last one was rented to a man by the name of Cecil Karmourian, from New York City. The credit card checked out OK, but we couldn't find Cecil anywhere. When we checked out his New York place, we got a bit of a surprise. Cecil Karmourian, of New York City, died two months ago."

"Fuck me," said Hickey. "So this is the one."

"Probably."

"So what's the car?"

"A dark blue Mercedes, model E-350. Tinted windows, top of the Hertz line. License plate AFP-452. We've been unable to find it in the last thirty-six hours. If we find the car we'll find the hostages."

"Then we'll find it," said Hickey. "We'll find these assholes too. Then we'll cut off their dicks and stuff 'em in their mouths."

"Right on the first part," Joe said. "You'll find them. Wrong on the rest. These assholes have a ten-year-old girl, a fortyish American woman, and their thirty-something Egyptian nanny. They'll kill 'em if you knock on the front door. I couldn't give a shit if you cut these guys into little tiny pieces but I want those girls alive. If you fuck up and get 'em killed I'll personally cut you up into little tiny pieces."

"No shit, man."

The biker tried to sound tough, but there was something in the eyes of Joe Faraday that convinced him to stop.

"When you locate the car, don't stop to look at it. Don't even slow down. Get your ass to the nearest phone and call me. We've got a special forces crew to do the rest."

No one said a word. Joe had their attention. As well as their interest and commitment.

"Another pitcher," he shouted above the jukebox to the bartender. When it came he poured another glass for each of the men.

"Gentlemen, welcome to case 5377, State of Montana homicide. Three lives may depend on you."

As he said this Joe threw a couple photos on the table. One showed Gussie, brushing a horse. The other showed Libby, rather seductively sitting on a railing, dressed in a terrycloth robe. Her hair was wet, and her smile was inviting.

"Ain't no rag head gonna bang this American beauty," said the same biker who voiced the earlier comment on Arabs. He slammed his fist on the table, sloshing beer out of the pitcher. "God damned filthy sons o' bitches."

"What's your name son?"

"Willy Stroh," the twenty-some year old said.

"Be careful Willy. One more thing boys. Don't tell anyone what the fuck you're doing."

Joe threw down a few business cards and walked out the front door. Joe kept two sets of business cards. His official one was standard issue with the normal name, title, address, and phone numbers. The other, which he used for cases like this, was unorthodox. The Arab hater picked it up and read it. The top line stated simply 'Joe Faraday'. Underneath was written 'Friend of Amanda Caitlin' and a phone number.

"Amanda Caitlin," Willy wrinkled his brow as he looked up.

It took only a few seconds. Hickey watched Stroh as it sunk in. There wasn't a Hell's Angel in the United States that didn't know the story of Amanda Caitlin and how the State Trooper strung out those people to be eaten by local wildlife. Bikers were a macho group and didn't like men who mistreated women. Every Hell's Angel idolized Joe Faraday, and would give their left nut to work alongside the legend.

"That's right boys," said Hickey. "He wasn't kidding when he said he didn't care if you cut those Arabs up into little pieces. Truth be told it'll piss him off if he don't get to do it himself."

"Holy shit," said Willy.

"Let's get started. It's gonna be a long night, and a long day tomorrow. We're gonna find this Mercedes."

Chapter 36

"*SABAH al khair,*" the short, rotund, secretary bellowed with a smile.

"*Sabah al full,* Nadia."

"How are you?"

"*Alhamdulillah.* How are you?"

"I am good."

"How is your family?"

"God's will, we are all fine. And yours?"

"They are fine as well. It's been too long my friend."

Salah and the older woman exchanged an endless string of greetings. Bucking the trend to veil, Nadia wore her hair as she had for the last thirty-some years, pulled back to display huge gold earrings. Salah had known her a very long time as she followed Hesham Ibrahim from one position to another.

Salah looked around, smiling as he noticed the new PC on her desk. It was the latest and greatest but he bet she didn't use it. In the Ministry the mere presence of the machine on her desk indicated position. Who cared if she needed it, much less knew how to use it.

"Hesham is worried," Nadia continued. "He came in yesterday fine, just like any other day. By the afternoon something happened. I don't know what. He will not tell me."

"Maybe it is too personal," Salah offered.

"Not for me. I know everything."

"Surely not everything my little busybody. Yet I'm sure you must have some idea."

"Not at all." Her brow wrinkled, her tired old eyes showing sadness. "Really, I am worried."

"You were born worried. I'll bet you came out of your mother with a headache and a well worn set of worry beads."

She smiled. The phone on her desk rang, obviously Hesham. The conversation took less than a minute.

"Hesham was with the Minister. He said make yourself at home in his office for ten minutes. What will you drink?"

"*Ahwa mas boot*," he replied.

Salah made no move towards Hesham's office. It would have been unnatural to trade a spot next to a live human for an empty office. They continued chatting for the next twenty minutes. He with nothing else to do. She with nothing on her desk that was more important. Finally Hesham came around the corner and put his hand on Salah's shoulder.

"My friend why are you talking to this old woman? Did she not invite you into my office? Nadia shame on you."

Hesham looked at her desk and the empty glasses.

"At least she moved her body to order a coffee. God willing some day I will get a secretary who is useful."

"Someday you will be dead Hesham Ibrahim, and you won't be able to torment a secretary."

As soon as they settled onto the sofa in Hesham's office, Salah could tell at once that Nadia was right. Something was bothering his old friend. Hesham could not hide it.

"Hesham what is wrong? Are you all right?"

"No. I am not. I told you before that you and your American partner were in dangerous waters. You wouldn't listen to me and now you see."

The phone rang and Hesham jumped. He didn't answer it but burst into tears, his worry beads slipping through his fingers.

"Tell me Hesham?"

"They sent me a finger. They sent me my son's finger."

"What are you talking about?"

"A box was delivered to my house. My wife received it. What if she had opened it? She would have killed herself."

"What happened?"

"I came home early that night. We had Koshri for dinner. She almost forgot about the package, and gave it to me after Umm Ali."

"Did you open it at the table?

"No, thanks to God. I took it to my study. No one but me is allowed in the study. I opened it. A letter was on top. It said 'Keep your son's finger. You can bury it with the rest of him next month unless you help us.' My God. My God. This is my son they have chopped up".

Hesham sobbed uncontrollably. He was now off the couch, pacing with his fists clenched.

"Hesham, do you know who they are?"

"I have an idea but am not sure. I have only seen the man who serves as contact. I suspect his boss is a rich Egyptian with ties to Israel. You have to stop this man or they will kill my son."

"What have they said to you?"

"If they lose the lease they will send my son to me. In pieces."

"What is the name of the man who contacted you Hesham?"

The tired and worried man did not want to divulge this information but Salah was relentless. With persistence he finally got the name.

"Itzak."

It was a single name. Salah knew no more. No address. No phone number. Nothing.

Salah was late to his next appointment but being Egyptian didn't give it a fleeting thought. Announcing himself to Maged Khafagy's secretary he took a seat. He did not get along with Amani, although she had been around as long as Nadia. While she went into Maged's office Salah sat on a plastic covered chair. After several minutes Maged opened his office door and walked over to greet Salah.

"How are you?"

"Fine, and you?"

"Half and half," the Petroleum Minister replied. "My wife's mother died yesterday. I shouldn't be here at all."

"Why are you?"

"Meetings. I am leaving for the mosque in a little while."

It was very unusual for a man to be in the office on such a day. Granted it was only his wife's mother, not the father, or an important brother. Still he should be with his wife.

"My sympathies. Where is the funeral?"

"Al Hamra mosque. It starts at twelve for midday prayer. She was old, her life full. May I live to be seventy-five."

Salah waited until Maged exhausted his personal grief, then brought up the Sinai block and the bid round.

"What are you saying Salah?"

"I'm saying not everyone is playing fair."

"So what else is new my friend? No process is fair in Egypt. There will be bribes. There will be deals. In the end we will do what we think is the best for the country."

"This is different Maged. There are things happening which go beyond anyone's morals. If the truth gets out it will be embarrassing for the Petroleum Sector."

"Salah what you are talking about. And I hope you have some proof to back up what you will tell me."

It took some time, but Salah el Gindi finally finished telling Maged Khafagy what he knew. At the end Maged's first comment at least told him the man had listened.

"You are insane. You can't expect me to believe you."

"It is the truth. American police are trying to find Mr. Tillard's daughter. You must know someone here who can call them and check."

"I know someone," Maged replied.

He picked up the phone and asked Amani to reach General Mohammed Latif. He turned back to Salah.

"You better be telling the truth. I do not have time to waste chasing tall tales."

Khafagy turned to stare out the window once more. Salah waited. Expecting him to say something, he sat patiently in the chair in front of the Chairman's large mahogany desk.

"Let us assume I confirm your crazy story. What then?"

"Then you must do something about the bid round. Throw out the bad elements. At least delay the closing date."

"Does your American friend feel the same way?"

"We have not discussed this."

"You two do not discuss such issues? You just told me all about his daughter."

"Yes but we did not talk about delaying things."

"Then my dear friend I must conclude he does not want the

closing date extended. I will bet no one involved in this bid round wants to delay it. Certainly not the government."

Salah did not know what to say. Maged was basically telling him he would do nothing about the bid round.

"Then it is hopeless?"

"Not hopeless dear Salah. There is always hope. That is all we have besides faith."

"Then may God be merciful."

Book Four
Politics

CHAPTER 37

RADISSON was irate. Clarissa knew better than to open her mouth. She had seen him like this and attempts to calm him usually backfired. He asked her to call yet another three people and get them to the meeting. It was just after midnight.

"Yes sir."

Her air of formality was designed to provide him feedback on his mood. He looked at her and she cringed, thinking she had made a bad decision, until he smiled.

"Am I being a real asshole?"

"Yes you are," she smiled back.

The two of them had worked together for a long time.

"Good. Maybe I'll get some results."

Radisson pushed into the conference room, stopping conversation immediately among the dozen or so people. He had grilled them all for over four hours and his brief absence to give Clarissa orders was the first respite they'd had. Now after only five minutes he was back, standing at the head of the mahogany table, with his fists down in front of him.

"Let me summarize once more. Nothing." He paused for an uncomfortable amount of time. "That's what we've got. Nothing."

The sound reverberated through the medium-sized room.

"This is supposed to be the best God damned intelligence network in the entire God damned world. We've got the CIA, FBI, and every branch of the Service working on this. I can't think of anyone not involved. It's been over six months and we've got fuck-all."

Radisson glowered at the men around the table. There were no women here.

"Lindsay, why do you think we've got fuck-all?"

Rick Lindsay had not expected his boss to call on him. As Radisson's go-fer, he usually melted into the background, taking minutes.

"I don't know sir."

"Then I'll tell you. Because this group of good-for-nothing girls hasn't come up with one productive lead in six months. Let's go through it one more time. From the beginning."

No one said a word. Tired faces stared down at the table, or at the clock labeled "Washington DC", mounted on the wall.

"Lindsay if you would."

"Yes sir. The CIA and Mossad have followed a group of high placed Israelis for the last couple years. The group's fundamental goal is to create the ultimate Jewish state in Israel, purge all Arabs and non-Orthodox Jews, and make a land grab for territories they used to control. They want to build a fence around this geography and tightly control ingress and egress. Their goal is not that unusual but their strategy to achieve it is unique."

Lindsay went on in some detail about the group and its actions. Everyone in the room knew these details, but he kept up the summary.

"Six months ago a disturbing development emerged. Some members of the group stated they favored limiting Israel to Jews, but wanted Jerusalem open access to both sides. This was just a Trojan Horse. Their real goal was widespread destabilization across the Levant in order to secure long-term US aid."

"OK," Radisson broke in, "get to the current issue and Tillard."

"A month ago a Mossad agent working routine phone surveillance was listening in on a member of the faction. He was talking to a new voice, apparently an Arab. The Arab talked about geologists and the Sinai then mentioned the name 'Jake Tillard'. Mossad passed this information to CIA, and we started tracking Mr. Tillard."

The red blinking light on the phone in front of Radisson told him Clarissa was holding a very important call.

"Pardon me ladies."

The men diverted their eyes, stared at one another, and shook their heads. Radisson picked up the phone.

"Yes. OK."

Clarissa connected him to Paul Wheaton, a Jesuit Professor of religion at Catholic University, whose specialty was pre-Nicene Christianity.

"Dick Radisson," he said politely into the phone.

Rick Lindsay was the only one looking at Radisson, sensing something was up. Radisson nodded, interjecting an infrequent 'yes' or 'really'. Suddenly he asked if the man would mind coming downtown. There was a pause.

"Yes I know it's a bit late."

Another pause.

"Thank you very much. No. No. I'll have a car pick you up. Probably twenty minutes. The driver's name will be Sid."

Radisson hung up and sat back. His gaze seemed to be fixed somewhere between the far wall and Maryland. Lindsay was intrigued. No one said a word.

"Gentlemen this may be the break we've been waiting for. Let's take an hour to freshen up then meet back here."

Lindsay cringed when he heard a groan emanate from one of the younger men from the White House staff. The General was halfway to the door, but turned around before ducking through.

"If anyone needs the rest of the night off, feel free."

He let about five uncomfortable seconds go by.

"Just don't come back. I don't like whiners."

He spun again and was gone.

"Shit," the groaner said. "Who the hell does he think he is?"

Three or four unpleasant looks shot his way. Most of the men there had known Dick Radisson for a long time. Most respected him, a few even liked him, but none would cross him. As cell phones didn't work in this area of the building, a few found phones to tell their wives they wouldn't be home tonight.

Paul Wheaton stood up after a very brief introduction. The three men Clarissa had summoned sat in the shadows against the wall, distanced from the others. Rick Lindsay was the only person besides Radisson who knew them. No one asked who they were.

"Two mornings ago I got an odd phone call from a fellow Jesuit living in Rome, which you know is the hub of Christianity."

The youngster wanted to groan again but refrained. He was an agnostic, perhaps even an atheist. The whole idea of someone throwing their life away by joining the Jesuits was beyond his comprehension.

"The hub of Christian power and information. Where you would call if you were a Christian with important information you didn't know what to do with."

Several faces around the table looked up. One of the men against the wall lit another cigarette, ignoring the no smoking policy. The Jesuit stood behind his chair, pushed it towards the table, and leaned on the back, clearly used to lecturing.

"My friend received a phone call from a fellow we both met last year at a conference in Khartoum, organized for the preservation of the Coptic Christian tradition. This fellow is an Ethiopian Copt, an old order of Christian servants that persists south of Egypt. Undoubtedly, you know Egypt has its fair share of Copts. Cairo itself is almost ten percent Christian. Our mutual friend is now assigned to the Ethiopian mission in Jerusalem, and spends quite a bit of time at the Church of the Holy Sepulcher near the Ethiopian mission."

He sensed he was beginning to lose a few of them, and inserted another attention seeker.

"All of which explains how he came to overhear the conversation. He didn't know who the second man was, but he did recognize the Israeli Minister of State Security."

Paul Wheaton, religion lecturer to masses of students plagued with terminal ennui, paused for effect. He had them hooked.

"The Minister of Security has a fairly distinctive face, rather gnarly from too much time in the desert sun. Moreover, the Minister has a slight limp, favoring his left leg. I honestly can't remember if it was one of the wars, prison camps, or what. Anyway, the conversation he overheard is interesting on several levels. First, it was in archaic Yiddish, not the most common language spoken in one of the holiest Christian sites in the world. Second, the Minister of Security was without his bodyguards, which is very rare. Third, the other man seemed to be an equal. He was old, probably well off, and probably well connected."

"But you don't know who he is?" asked one of the men.

"No. The Ethiopian did not recognize him. He looked Eastern European, but his Yiddish was Israeli."

"You said your Ethiopian friend was new to Israel, yet he speaks Yiddish?"

"He speaks fluent Amharic, English, French, Arabic, Urdu, Yiddish, and Persian." Wheaton smiled. "You'll find many of the world's priests speak a number of languages."

"Go on, Mr. Wheaton. Get to the conversation in the church."

It was the first time Radisson had spoken since the Jesuit started. He was getting impatient.

"Right. Well, the older man started telling a parable, something about men searching for riches in the desert. Drawing treasure maps, digging holes. Looking for gold, or some other metal he thought, although it was never explicitly stated. Apparently they were searching for something, but it wasn't clear what."

Paul paused again to catch his breath. The youngster from the White House yawned and looked at his Baume and Mercier. His mind drifted to his girlfriend's legs and what he wanted her to do with them. The man who asked the last question asked another.

"Is that all?"

"There's not much more really. He mentioned an American, but said they didn't get anything useful from him. Something about a stump, or log."

A few heads tilted up.

"The Minister seemed very interested in this information, inviting the other man to his car, then left. The older man lingered for a few minutes, then left as well."

"How did your friend hear all this without being noticed?" This time the question came from the smoker against the wall.

"He was behind a stone lattice. Coming down a private stairway reserved for resident clergy. I seriously doubt the men even knew there was a stairway there."

"That would be the Place of Sorrows?"

A few of the men at the table looked around at the man in the shadow against the wall. They could see his face, but not very clearly. Wheaton was clearly taken aback.

"Why yes, that's correct. At least that's what those in residence call it. The official name is the Altar of the Blessed Virgin. You seem to know your church, Mr. ummm."

He did not think he would get a name, and he didn't.

"Does that stairway have a locked gate?"

"I really don't know. It's been quite a while since I was in Jerusalem. It seems as though you might have the advantage."

"Thank you Mr. Wheaton." Dick Radisson had taken the floor. "My secretary will show you into my office, if you would be so kind as to wait for a short while."

Radisson waited for him to leave. He looked at his colleagues and shook his head.

"Why don't you all discuss this new information? Generate some options. I'll be back in a half hour to hear what you've come up with."

Five seconds later he was gone. The men stared at each other, except the three men against the wall, who exited through the back door.

The five men sat around the table in Radisson's office.

"Was he sure it was Minister Yaroun?" Tom asked.

"Without question," replied Wheaton.

"Tell me again why this Ethiopian bothered to call someone."

"It makes perfect sense. Two men are speaking Yiddish in the Church of the Holy Sepulcher. They pause their conversation whenever anyone walks by. They talk about treasure maps and resurrecting some kind of search. One of the men is the Israeli Minister of State Security without his normal cadre of bodyguards. Makele Abebe is very bright and thought something was fishy."

"Moreover," Wheaton continued after a pause, "there is one more piece to the puzzle. As an Ethiopian, Makele appreciates that Israel has not been universally kind to his countrymen. Simply put the Minister of State Security is racist and has spoken out against the black community. Ethiopians have been unable to make headway and Makele does not like the Likud Party or anyone associated with it."

Radisson intervened, filling in blanks as he put together the rationale behind the communication.

"So your friend thinks if he can get this information out of Israel he may crimp Yaroun's style. He's not sure but it sounds like there's something dirty going on. He'd like to implicate the Minister."

"Exactly. But Vatican security wasn't interested. They have their own priorities and this didn't fit. Thinking it could be interesting to the West, they called me."

"Paul thanks for your help and for coming down this late."

Radisson had deliberately put an end to his visit and didn't think the other gentlemen needed to know why Rome had called Wheaton. He was in fact protecting Paul Wheaton, who had a long-term relationship with the CIA. Very few people knew he regularly shuffled data and queries between the US and the Vatican.

Tom Billington lit another Marlboro.

"Do you buy the story?"

"Langley called me before Wheaton did and corroborated it."

"The story started in some archaic language and has run through a number of filters. Remember the old telephone game, where the message at the end barely resembles the original."

"That's the nature of our business. However the way I see it, anyone who can remember esoteric scripture in several languages probably has a good chance of getting it right."

"So what do you think it means?"

"I'm not sure. It sounds like the Minister's into something up to his eyeballs. Somehow this fits into the case we've been working for six months. It also links to Tillard."

"So where do we go from here?" asked Tom.

"We call a friend, which is why you're here. Tell me about our Ambassadors in Israel and Egypt."

Tom Billington espoused on the relative merits of the two men, in two of the most important US Embassies. Both were career diplomats, hard and seasoned. Cairo and Tel Aviv were not the kind of posts you sent a former campaign manager. Those people were sent to London and Paris.

As descriptions and histories flowed out of Billington's amazing memory, Radisson chose the Ambassador to Israel as the better candidate to approach. He was ex-Air Force, graduating from the Academy as valedictorian.

"Dial up Ambassador Foley," he said.

"Yes sir."

Tom Billington picked up the secure phone on Radisson's desk and dialed a number from memory. He gave the required code to the operator, asked to be put through to Foley in Tel Aviv via a US military satellite link, and handed the phone to Radisson after introducing him to the Ambassador.

"You're up rather late," the Ambassador said in a baritone voice.

"It's been a long day Mr. Ambassador."

"Then call me Gordon. What can I do for you?"

'That was something you didn't hear very often in government circles,' thought Radisson.

He took the next ten minutes to brief the Ambassador and suggest how he might help.

"I believe the Egyptian Petroleum Minister is meeting tonight with his counterpart in Israel. As I understand it they will be talking about energy cooperation, past and future. Egypt used to supply Israel with more than half its oil imports, until they couldn't produce enough. Israel is guaranteed by treaty the right to bid for oil and gas produced in the Sinai, but there isn't any production there. They get over ninety percent of their oil now from the Caspian. The future's about gas and that's what these talks are about."

"Where will Egypt get the gas to export? I didn't know they had a lot of it."

"They have enough for internal use, with some surplus. Most of the new discoveries are in the offshore Nile Delta. There is a tiny pipeline along the Med on the north coast of the Sinai, delivering some gas to Gaza and Israel. Four times this past year, terrorists bombed a hole in it. It takes about a month to fix it, before they bomb it again."

"What about producing gas in the Sinai itself?"

"White elephant I understand. A few optimists believe it could produce some gas. Most of the scientific community downplays any real potential."

"Ambassador I believe the Israeli Minister of Security has gotten himself peripherally involved in the upcoming Egypt bid round, and have good reason to believe he is teamed up with some nasty folks."

They talked a while longer and hatched a plan to put some tension into the system.

CHAPTER 38

ACROSS town in the Oval Office the President was being briefed on a situation in Asia. Before the briefing ended the Commander in Chief asked his staffer if there was any news from the Secretary of State's courtesy visit to Israel.

"Secretary of State Clancy is in Israel now Sir, meeting with President Shapiro. She's planning to discuss the energy sector given the issues Israel's had with electricity shortages.

"As long as she stays away from that Project Stable business," said the President. "That was a stupid idea six months ago and it still is. Work a status report into your daily briefings at least weekly OK? And let me know if anything goes off the rails."

"I will Mr. President. Good night Sir."

CHAPTER 39   *Jerusalem*
                                              August 28

JAKE slept poorly although the King David was everything one could ask for in a hotel. The insomnia was a result of both his desperate personal situation and his meeting with the Secretary of State. When Nancy Clancy met them at the airstrip last night she divulged little, promising to put things into perspective when they reached Jerusalem. That had not happened.

Jake spent most of the night wondering what Clancy would say. He was beginning to feel like a pawn but could not identify the game. Throughout his career he had dealt with plenty of government officials and egotistical leaders who created a bad atmosphere. Jake was beginning to smell a stink.

The city's rising din filtered through the French doors of Jake's suite overlooking the gardens. He took another bite of cheese and looked out at the Tower of David, the gold top of the Dome of the Rock, the Al Aqsa Mosque, and the Church of the Holy Sepulcher.

A bird alighted on his balcony, a sparrow of some kind. He tossed it a small piece of croissant but the bird flew off.

'Must be Moslem,' he thought. 'Damned thing would rather die of hunger than take a gesture of friendship from the wrong side.'

The phone rang.

"Hello."

"You're up," Stan said.

"Been up for a while Stan. What the hell is going on? I don't believe you're in the dark."

"Honest Jake. I have no idea."

"Right."

He hung up and stared over the Old City again. The entire world seemed topsy-turvy; he couldn't believe anyone anymore.

Forty-five minutes later Jake and Stan were enroute to the Secretary of State. The black Mercedes with heavily tinted windows and bulletproof doors weaved through the morning traffic. It passed the central bus station where a bomb the month before killed three people and injured fourteen. Jake looked at the open area where at least a dozen buses waited for passengers. The local population lived with the constant threat of being blown up. It was a way of life.

The car climbed towards north Jerusalem into an orthodox neighborhood. Men walked briskly, dressed in black suits with wide brim black hats. The Mercedes stopped in front of a beige sandstone house indistinguishable from others on that block. Stan and Jake got out, walked through the gate, rang the front bell, and were greeted by a young man wearing a shoulder holster. The gun in his hand was pointed at the visitors.

"Kawinski," Stan offered.

The young man looked at both of them. He nodded and stepped aside, keeping his eyes on the front porch as he closed the door. Only after he locked it did he put the gun away.

"This way please."

Jake noticed a second man behind a column, holding a semi-automatic. The décor was plain and functional. Clancy rose as they entered her office.

"Good morning gentlemen," she offered her hand. "Mr. Tillard I trust you had some rest last night?"

"A poor rest Madam Secretary."

"I can understand. You've been through hell. You're wondering why I have entered your world. Let me tell you."

Jake was surprised by her blunt approach.

"Please."

"Mr. Tillard you've managed to entangle yourself in international events that affect the US and other foreign governments. Your predicament has implications far beyond your personal interests."

"OK," Jake responded. "You've got my interest. But I already figured that out."

"This is all top clearance information of course. I can bring you in on certain aspects of this operation, but in return you must consider yourself part of our team. Seconded if you will to the US Government and therefore subject to our oversight."

"I'm not sure what that means," Jake answered.

Jake looked into Clancy's eyes and saw nothing. He knew he
had to take the offer but when push came to shove he would not
let anything stand in his way to help Gussie and Libby. He wasn't
sure how to play it with Clancy, how to negotiate for the most
information.

"What can you tell me?" Jake asked.

"Put simply the best chance to save your daughter and friend is
ferret out the root cause."

Clancy in turn looked into Jake's eyes. What she saw made her
wonder if she was doing the right thing. Clancy expected fatigue and
helplessness. She'd seen these qualities before in men's eyes but didn't
see them in Tillard's. She saw something different. Determination
and purpose.

"I'm on your team Madam Secretary. Tell me what you know."

Jake stood and thrust out his hand, Clancy clasping it firmly.
Each wondered exactly what that handshake really meant.

"This will be a sharing session," replied the Secretary. Let's each
review what we have."

Stan Kawinski had been surprisingly quiet, as if he had merged
with the furniture. Now he was evident again, surprising Jake by
starting the dialogue.

"We have several major threads. The New York people, the
mysterious other bidder in Cairo, the house break-in in Houston,
the abduction in Montana, the Bedouin's intruder in the Sinai, and
the assassination in Tel Aviv."

"Wait," Jake interrupted. "What assassination?"

The Secretary of State answered.

"Two days ago a car bomb exploded in Tel Aviv's south side. The
Exploration Manager for the Israeli National Oil Company went up
in flames. His house was constantly guarded, and his guards looked
under his car each time before he started it. Obviously someone was
paid off. One guard was also blown up, but two guards are missing."

"What does this have to do with me?" Jake asked.

"I think you knew Vasily Kirchoff, the Chairman of INOC.
A tough Russian from the old school. His love of political ideals
died when he left Russia and joined the growing Israeli economy.
For the past year he was trending back into some nasty ideological

movements. The Exploration Manager that got blown up was feeding us information on this issue."

"You mean we have spies in Israel?"

"Of course. We do what it takes everywhere to get intelligence. Israel is no different. You seem surprised."

"I am. I thought our ties with Israel were so strong we wouldn't need that kind of thing."

Jake was not at all surprised. He had lied to buy time. Assuming he would get only what information they thought he needed, he was trying to pull out a bit more.

"Israel is not that different from other countries," the Secretary continued. "They even spy on themselves. This is an unstable region."

Jake nodded, looking to Stan to continue.

"Those are the major threads. At this point we're most concerned with our mysterious bidding consortium in Cairo."

"It's incredible you can't find out who they are," Jake said looking at the Secretary of State. "Surely we must have very good connections in Egypt?"

Clancy ignored his question.

"Mr. Tillard. You are under extreme pressure to bail out, yet you haven't. Is the Sinai that important to you?"

Jake thought before replying. He looked at the Secretary of State. There was something she was not telling.

"The Sinai is not more important than my daughter or my friend, of course. But they won't kill Gussie before the bid round. If I bow out now they might kill her right away. If I stay in they will keep her alive as a bargaining chip."

"Mr. Tillard if I were you I would bow out now and hopefully get your daughter back."

"I don't think that's the best option," said Jake.

"Then I hope you know what you are doing."

An uneasy silence followed before the Secretary continued.

"I can give you a bit of highly classified information that may help you. We've been running a program for almost two years aimed at better understanding a couple of groups within Israel. We believe these groups have high-level participation to destabilize the area. The Sinai may play into this. As you know Israel controlled that area once. I'm afraid the forces at work here are way above your level of operation."

Clancy offered nothing more. Surely she had other information, but Jake could not figure out what it was. The Secretary stood up. It was just before one o'clock.

"If you'll excuse me Mr. Tillard, I have another appointment. I appreciate your time."

"Thank you Madam Secretary. It's comforting to know your full resources are looking after my daughter."

The sarcasm cascaded out before Jake could check it. He was frustrated and knew Clancy had additional information that wasn't being shared. He realized as the sarcastic remark came out of his mouth that he had made a mistake. Clancy looked at him one last time.

"Good luck to you, and I pray for your loved ones."

Those last words struck Jake like a bullet to the chest. Clancy saying them caused a chord to break within his soul. They changed Jake. He now knew he was largely on his own.

The Secretary of State had already broken her gaze with Jake, but Stan was looking right at him, and saw the change in his eyes. He sensed things would be different from now on.

The Mercedes dropped the two men at Yod Vashem, the Jerusalem Holocaust Museum and Memorial. Neither had said a word since the Secretary of State left them. They strode up the long paved path, past the building dedicated to Holocaust research, past the underground room where mirrors produced millions of candle flame reflections, each one symbolizing a Jewish death. They walked silently to a small monument overlooking the Western suburbs of Jerusalem, a cliff in front of them, and an olive grove behind. Stan broke the silence.

"You've decided something."

"I have."

"You've decided to play?"

"Yes."

It was what Stan had been waiting for. The acknowledgment that he was truly part of Dick Radisson's fold and willing to go the extra distance, making up the rules as they went along.

"What don't I know, Stan?"

"A few things."

The men sat on the short sandstone wall. From time to time their conversation stopped as a tourist passed, but for most of the next hour they talked.

Stan gave him the details of the car bombing and filled him in on character profiles they had dug up. In particular he spoke about the characters that fronted General Investments Ltd in New York. He saved the best for last.

"Radisson called me before we left the hotel. The Israeli Minister of Security, Yaroun Herschel, is on the wrong side of this."

He told Jake the CIA had opened a case more than a year ago to investigate certain US-involved movements inside Israel. Their intelligence hinted at a group aspiring to start a war with Egypt. He replayed the story of the church conversation to Jake. He ended with their suspicions that Minister Yaroun was involved, but didn't know exactly how.

"Why didn't Clancy tell me about this? Since I am fully on board and all."

"She doesn't know."

"The US Secretary of State doesn't know?"

"Radisson didn't feel it was necessary."

"You're kidding right?"

"No I'm not. If an Israeli Minister is involved then who knows who else is as well. Dick suspects US involvement and doesn't trust anyone at this point."

Jake let the significance of this statement sink in. Was Radisson implying that Nancy Clancy could be involved in international terrorism?

"So where does that leave me? What do we do next?"

"It leaves us with a lot to do. Not all of it pretty."

Jake had been having a tough time understanding how the kidnapping played into international intrigue. Now it started to make sense. Power hungry fanatics in Israel wanted to establish supremacy and boost the economy by instigating a regional disturbance. A war.

Out the window he saw a boy about the same age as Gussie holding his father's hand. The boy and his dad both wore the black orthodox outfit, white shirt, black hat, long sideburns hanging down like the curly fries he got at Chili's. He looked at them and saw a different costume but the same human emotions.

CHAPTER 40

SUNLIGHT streamed through the window, oblivious to the evil pervading the house. Libby opened her left eye and peered at the bedside clock. Almost six. Someone was walking down the hall. She dreaded the face that would appear.

Ashraf had arrived a week before the other three Palestinians to familiarize himself with western Montana, and in particular the Bar-J Ranch. His first goal was to find a safe house.

The Kolkhorsts were decent people. After twenty-nine years in the bleaching section of the pulp mill, Stefan was enjoying retirement. Hunting, a bit of fishing, and a lot of puttering around the cabin. It had taken time for Eva to get used to him under foot, but they had achieved a happy stability in the last year.

Stefan and his sons had built his dream cabin from tall, straight lodgepole pines on the property. It took six years to put up the shell, another two to rough out the interior, and a final year for contractors to do the finish work. The three bedroom, two-story cabin had a view of the Jocko Valley and mountains beyond. It was at the end of a primitive dirt road, at the base of Pritchard Peak, with nothing around for miles.

Of three possible safe houses, Moustafa Badry chose this one at the last moment, the day before the kidnapping. Ashraf had been very quick, entering the cabin through the back door into the kitchen. Eva was listening to Chopin and never heard him. One bullet to the head pushed her upper body onto the kitchen counter, where she had been fixing breakfast. A second bullet seconds later put Stefan solidly into his Lazy-Boy.

The Palestinian dragged the bodies into the backyard, where he drenched them with gasoline and set them aflame next to a very healthy clump of rhubarb. The next day he dug a hole big enough to accommodate the bones and remaining pieces of both Kolkhorsts.

He looked up after he was done, and thanked his God for a successful venture.

Libby closed her eyes when Moustafa appeared.

"Do not pretend. I know you are awake. Called by the light of another day. Get up. Enjoy the company."

He laughed as she opened her eyes and looked at him. She was thankful it was not Ashraf.

"Put your clothes on and come down to breakfast."

He turned and walked down the hall. When his steps faded she saw Ashraf's face at her door. Predictable. He was her guard, and stalker, and stuck to her like glue.

"Get dressed."

He stuck to her out of more than job responsibility. He stuck to her by lust. Every time she changed her clothes, took a shower, or went to the toilet, he was there. She had protested vehemently and demanded privacy, but quickly realized there would be none. The best she could do was turn her back while changing. And keep her legs together when peeing.

She swung her legs out of bed, the University of Montana Grizzlies tee shirt barely covering her panties. Ashraf's stare bored into her backside as she walked to the bathroom, and when she sat on the toilet, his face appeared at the bathroom door.

"Bet you'd like to wipe, huh?"

She realized immediately it was the wrong thing to say. The ugly man came into the bathroom and bent over her, reaching for the toilet paper. She could see his gun in his left hand, less than two feet from her eyes. He pulled off several sheets of the paper and stood in front of her, his hand in front of her face. He bent a bit and slowly traced the paper up her legs. Starting at her knees, which were tightly pressed together, he dragged the paper along the valley where her legs met, until the paper tickled her hair.

"Open up."

"In your dreams."

The stubble-faced man moved swiftly. She saw it coming but couldn't react. The gun caught her on the cheek. Because she flinched it was just a glancing blow.

"Bitch," he shouted.

Ashraf stood up while Libby felt her cheek. A small cut, a bit of blood.

Ashraf turned and walked out of the room. His footsteps stopped as he took up his position by the door.

Libby wiped herself and stood up. 'Another close call with the pervert', she thought, hurrying to pull on her jeans. Careful not to make more noise than necessary, she went back to the bathroom and washed her face, brushed her hair, and hid behind the bathroom wall, while she put on a bra and pulled on another tee shirt. She looked at herself in the mirror and noticed Ashraf peering around the bedroom door. As she walked to the main living area, she could sense his stare.

"Ah, I trust you are hungry," Moustafa said as Libby entered the kitchen.

"Libby," cried Gussie.

The child slid out of her chair and came over to hug Libby around the legs.

"How are you today Gussie?"

Libby tried to act calm, as if nothing extraordinary were going on. The past couple days were very difficult for them both.

"OK I guess."

"You're not sure?"

"I just want to go home."

"And so you shall my little one," said Moustafa.

He patted Gussie on the head as he walked over to Libby with a pan full of eggs. He put a pile of the eggs and buttered toast on her plate, motioning for her to sit. That's when Libby noticed Layla's face.

"What happened, Layla?"

"It's nothing Miss Libby."

"What did you do to her," Libby asked Moustafa.

"Nothing to concern you. Our sister was not being helpful last night."

"I'm OK miss Libby, really."

Libby looked at her black eye and the cut on her forehead before sitting down next to her. Picking up her fork, she said the blessing.

Libby had never been church going but thought it might buy her extra respect if they believed she was a devout Christian. To her there was no difference between Christians, Jews, and Moslems. Same God. Similar histories. Similar atrocities. So far she had seen no evidence her piety bought special favors. She ended by crossing herself.

Ashraf slid into the place next to her at the table, and Moustafa put a plate of food in front of him. She watched as he shoveled it into his mouth, faster than a dog. When he finished he sat back, and Libby looked at the bits of food clinging to his beard. A wave of desperation swept over her. She wanted to vomit.

She carried her plate and Ashraf's to the sink. To occupy herself she had taken to sharing dish duty with Layla, which sometimes gave them a chance to share a few words. Not today. She was running water over the dishes when she heard Gussie giggle. Libby looked around and saw Ashraf with his hands wrapped around the eight year old, in an all too friendly way. She walked over and grabbed his arm.

"Leave her alone."

"Maybe you'd rather me bother you instead?"

"I'm sure you could find a sheep outside that would appreciate you more."

He slapped her across the face.

"No," screamed Gussie.

She pulled at Ashraf's shirt, trying to get him away from Libby. Ashraf turned and pushed her. Gussie slid backward and tripped over the chair, landing on her back.

"Shithead," Libby said as she bent over Gussie.

Ashraf was just about to grab her by the hair when Moustafa caught his wrist. He pulled the other man around and spoke to him in Arabic.

"*Enta magnoon? Mafish Mohk.*"

Ashraf responded with a look of consternation. Moustafa was the only one he would let call him crazy and brainless.

As soon as Moustafa left the room to answer a phone Ashraf put a hand on Libby's shoulder. His other hand squeezed her ass. For Gussie's benefit Libby did not respond. Instead she migrated around the table and cleared more dishes.

Mustafa ended the call and walked around the house to the backyard. Ashraf was there, smoking a Marlboro.

"New orders," Moustafa said.

Ashraf tilted his head back and blew a big puff of smoke; two rings swirling up towards the clouds. Moustafa watched them as they dissipated. Ashraf was patient.

"We are to kill the two women."

The news was not as bad as Ashraf had expected. He smiled.

"When?"

"Soon. I will decide the best way and the best time."

"What about the little girl?"

"We keep her."

"That could be difficult," Ashraf said. "The woman keeps the girl calm."

"I didn't think this would be a problem for you."

"It's not."

Moustafa looked at the other man, taking the easy way out.

"I have business east of here that will take about twenty-four hours. We will do it when I return."

Ashraf smiled again. Killing the two women did not bother him, but the girl was an issue. She would not understand, and might not act predictably.

While Moustafa was packing a small bag for his trip, Ashraf paid a visit to Libby's room. He found Gussie there, playing cards. He told the girl to go to her room. Libby nodded her head at Gussie to go.

"Would you like the good news or the bad news first," he said after he had taken Gussie to her room.

"Why don't you give me the good news," Libby answered. She made no attempt to move away from him.

"I have been ordered to kill you," he said bluntly.

Libby could not comprehend what she heard. The words entered her ears but did not register.

"What?" Her voice a little too high.

"I am sorry. It must be done."

She sat up straight and pulled away from his hand.

"Do you want the bad news now?" he added with a smile.

"Bad news?" she parroted.

The ugly, ill-shaven man paused. She smelled his bad breath as his face closed in on hers.

"I will rape you before I kill you."

Libby could not speak. She could not move. Ashraf just sat there waiting for her response.

"No," she finally whispered. "No. No. No."

Ashraf's face broke out with a huge smile. He had hit the nerve he sought. Finally he had reached inside her and squeezed her heart. She was broken. His smile left as quickly as it had appeared, literally knocked off his face by Libby's left uppercut. It was strong enough to break one of his teeth.

"Bitch," he shouted.

His first punch hit Libby below the rib cage, knocking the wind out of her. As she was gasping for breath he slammed his fist into her again, landing it on her left breast, pushing her onto the bed. He came down on top of her, his leg grinding into her pelvic region. His hand grabbed her left breast and squeezed the area he had just punched, her bra affording little protection. She still could not catch her breath enough to make a sound.

"I will return to inspect this bruise," he squeezed her breast with all his strength. "Tonight, after dark. Bruises always look better by candle light."

As he got off the bed Libby looked down and saw he was excited. 'Oh God,' she thought. 'This pervert is getting off on this.'

He left her alone, gasping. The thought of that man alone with her made her chest tighten. She vomited, her gasps replaced by sobs. Her breast began to ache.

Ashraf stood outside her room listening to the sobs. His thoughts were of tonight and he grew harder thinking about what he would do to her.

Gussie gazed out the open window of her room. Ashraf had pushed her in and closed the door rather than staying with her as one of them normally did. It was too high to jump from the upper floor to the ground so her plan to run away had to wait. The sun blinded her when she looked up to see a jet in the sky. Gussie had seen a few jets fly overhead, maybe going to Missoula, when she had an idea.

She grabbed the cosmetic mirror from the bathroom and brought it back to the window. Gussie tried to reflect sunlight towards the jet. She knew SOS in Morse code from Brownies and tried to move the mirror to give three reflections at a time. After two more jets went by she gave up.

CHAPTER 41

SALAH could no longer ignore the phone. At five in the morning it was usually a wrong number, someone who had been out all night at a belly-dancing club. Usually after a dozen rings they hung up. Not this time. Salah rolled over and reached for the phone.

"*Aywa.*"

"Mr. Salah el Gindi?" a cute voice asked.

"Yes. Who is calling?"

"Hold please for Mr. Karim Nabet."

Salah sat up, rubbed his eyes, turned on the light and winced at the brightness. Bending his neck from side to side, he listened to his vertebrae crack.

"Mr. el Gindi?"

"Yes this is he."

"I am sorry for the hour, but I start work early to avoid distractions. I try to do my important tasks first. I hope you do not mind."

"Not at all Mr. Nabet. What can I do for you?"

Salah did not know what to think. He knew of Nabet but had never met the man. What could he want?

"Let me be honest Mr. El Gindi. You are involved in a plan to explore for oil in the Sinai. I am also ready to invest money in that endeavor. Our interests interfere."

"I am merely a local facilitator Mr. Nabet. You might want to talk with the principles in our company."

"You underestimate yourself. Your partner Mr. Tillard tried to phone me a few days ago. I prefer speaking with you. If you help me win the Sinai bid I could make you very rich. I have the connections to put a pipeline through the Sinai and into Israel. Mr. Tillard will not be able to do that."

Salah was on the bed sitting and listening. How could Nabet know all this?

"I need time to consider," said Salah.

"By all means, Mr. el Gindi," said Nabet, giving a direct number to Salah. "Information is everything. It's what made me rich and it is why you should join the winning side. Please keep this conversation between you and me. Call me tomorrow. Good day."

Karim Nabet hung up before Salah could say anything. 'Arrogant son of a bitch,' he thought.

The sun cleared the building next door, throwing light on Salah as he sat on the bed, pulling on his calf high nylon socks. Buttoning his white long sleeve shirt, tying his club tie, and donning his sport coat, he was ready to attack the day. It would be another scorcher. Halfway to the kitchen the phone rang again.

"Good morning," Salah said in English, expecting Jake.

"*Habibi. Izayak?*"

It was not Jake. Salah could not place the voice, which continued in Arabic.

"You don't know me and my name is not important. Listen carefully. You are in a position to do something with what I tell you."

The sense of déjà vu began to creep up on Salah.

"The bid round is corrupt. Two bid committee members have been bribed. Each with fifty thousand US dollars and one hundred thousand more if their group receives the bid."

"Where did you get this information?"

"If I told you they would kill me."

The phone went dead before Salah could say another word. He vaguely recognized the voice but a name did not come.

He thought of the dozen men on the committee, and was sure some of them would do dirty work for fifty thousand dollars. Maybe most of them. He wondered how he would react if someone offered him that much money to vote one way or another. The possibility of one hundred and fifty thousand would be most attractive indeed.

Salah went to the kitchen and prepared a cup of espresso. For five years now, since visiting ENI in Italy, he prepared a single cup of espresso each morning. To him, espresso was a more refined form of the local Ahwa mas boot. He took the tiny cup and walked across the living room. On the balcony he listened to the city waking up, the cacophony of downtown activity. Car horns and the shouting of pedestrians was a fraction of what it would be in an hour. The smells of a polluted city had yet to cook under the August sun. Venus still shone in the same sky as the new sun. It was time to call Jake.

"*Shalom*. Good morning. King David Hotel. How may I direct your call?"

"Mr. Jake Tillard please."

He was amazed the operator spoke in English except for the 'Shalom' at the beginning. The on-hold Muzak was Andrew Lloyd Webber but Salah could not place it.

"Good morning," said Jake.

"*Sabah el Khair.* How are things in Israel? I heard about the bus bombing yesterday. Did you see it?"

"No Salah, I was nowhere near the bombing. You probably heard of it before I did if you were watching CNN."

"I was watching BBC. It was awful. So many people killed and injured. I was worried about you."

"Don't worry my friend. I'll be here for another day at most then I'll be back in the safety of Cairo. Is everything still a 'go' on the bid package?"

"Jake, I give you new information."

He replayed the conversation with Karim Nabet, and told him of Hesham Ibrahim's problem with his son's finger. Salah also told him about the last call about the bribery. Jake listened and made notes on King David stationery.

"Well that's why Nabet never called me back," Jake said.

"It is very strange he would phone me," answered Salah.

Jake instructed Salah to meet Maged Khafagy at EGPC and follow up on the bribery angle. Salah protested the best thing to do with the bid committee problem was to leave it alone, but Jake disagreed. One part of him hoped Maged would try to find out which of his apples was bad, but another part was certain Maged could do nothing about it.

Jake looked at his watch and said he had to go. He and Stan were going to the Ambassador's residence again.

When Salah called, Maged Khafagy was not in his office.

"I must reach him," Salah said.

There was a brief pause before Amani told him in the strictest confidence that her boss was home taking a sick day.

"But he is not sick," chuckled Amani. "Do you have his home number?"

"You are a true flower, Amani," he said after she gave him the number. "Try to have a nice day without the boss."

Salah reached Khafagy at his home number. Without revealing much he convinced the Chairman they needed to meet at once. Maged asked him to come to his house in Zamalek.

Salah took one last sip of espresso before heading for the elevator and the heat of the day.

Maged Khafagy was more receptive than Salah had expected, meeting him in his sitting room wearing a robe and slippers. Salah mentally agreed with Amani's assessment that Khafagy was not at all sick. The Chairman listened to the corruption accusations Salah laid out. He seemed to take it all in and Salah was encouraged, before his host popped the bubble.

"Mr. el Gindi. I am certain your contact gave this information to you just as you have relayed. There cannot be even an element of truth in it."

Salah was incredulous. He had been called a liar before, and even a cheat. But never naive.

"The truth is that what you were told cannot be correct. We have safeguards against this. We are not from a farm in the Delta. His Excellency the Minister is well aware that oil concessions are valuable, so strict rules exist to be followed. The process is foolproof."

The soliloquy went on for another ten minutes but never changed direction. The EGPC Chairman remained adamant his organization could not harbor such corruption and that his bid committee was above reproach. At the end Salah left dejected.

After Salah left the high-rise, Maged picked up his phone and dialed the private telephone number of General Mohammed Latif, his friend in the State Department. A secretary said he was in a meeting. Maged knew better and called the General's home.

"*Aywa*," a woman answered.

Mohammed was out of Egypt the next four days, unreachable.

'Strange,' thought Maged.

CHAPTER 42

AFTER tossing all night Maged hatched a plan to squelch this latest round of corruption. He was unwilling to allow such action. Though he had indicated to Salah it was impossible for corruption to exist within EGPC, he knew better. Corruption was the norm in all facets of Egyptian culture. He phoned his secretary before leaving his house.

"Amani set up appointments for me, starting at two o'clock. Every thirty minutes with one member of the bid committee."

"Yes sir. Can I tell them what the meetings are for?"

"No Amani you may not. In fact you cannot tell them anything other than to show up. Do not alarm anyone and do not take no for an answer. I do not want them to know that each of them is being called in one by one. I do not want anyone to know anything. Right now you and I are the only ones that know anything. It must remain that way. Do you understand?"

She knew this was an unusual request. She understood enough to curtly reply, "Yes."

"Thank you Amani. I will be there before two."

He looked at his watch. Half past twelve. He asked his butler to have his car and driver waiting. With reluctance Maged Khafagy took his robe off and laid it on the back of the wing back chair.

At exactly four o'clock, Ashraf abdel Amr came through Maged's office door. Maged started with tea, exactly as he had with the previous four, none of which had borne fruit. Before the tea arrived the two old colleagues exchanged pleasantries, each asking about the health of everyone related to them. When tea came Maged began his allegory.

"I used to have two cats, Ashraf."

"I didn't know you had cats."

"Cats are clever creatures. Smarter than dogs, don't you think?"

Ashraf did not know what to think.

"I have always thought highly of cats," the visitor said tentatively.

"They are cute," Maged continued, "and highly praised for their independence. But they have egos. An ego invites arrogance that can lead to a loss of self-image. A warped idea of where one fits in the world."

Maged paused to sip his tea.

"Take my brown cat. She became quite full of herself. Do you know why?"

"Please tell me," Ashraf said.

Maged leaned closer.

"I had three bowls on my kitchen floor. One for my brown cat, one for the gray cat, and one for my small dog. Twice a day I fill each one. Of course the dog gobbles his food immediately. The cats on the other hand sniff, eat a bit, go away, and come back later to eat some more. It is a system. I think it is fair. Perhaps they do not. I can't tell."

Maged looked at Ashraf abdel Amr and saw the other man's eyes shift to avoid his own.

"The system worked for years. Then the brown cat sneaked bites out of the other bowl. I'm not even sure the gray cat knew. But I knew. It wasn't fair. I looked more closely at the cats, and the brown one was definitely fatter. They may have always been like that, but now I had reason to dislike the brown cat."

"Anyway I ramble. The point is the brown cat was acting poorly. There I was, with three pets. Two trustworthy; the other greedy. Brown cat was very full of himself. What would you do, Ashraf?"

"I don't know," Ashraf replied.

"Would you ask the fat, brown cat if he was cheating?"

"But cats can't talk so what good would that do?"

"Exactly. It would do no good. No good at all. The cat cannot speak to me, but even if he could I suspect he would not. Do you know why that is?"

Maged was looking directly into Ashraf's eyes when there were two quick knocks on the door. He saw his guest's body jerk before he glanced around at the door.

The tea boy came in to collect the cups. Ashraf sighed with relief. He had been anxious and wondered if Maged had noticed. When the tea boy left Maged continued.

"I will tell you."

Ashraf struggled to remember where Maged was in the conversation and hoped the man did not ask him a question. Ashraf shifted again in his chair.

"He knew very well he was doing something wrong. His ego affected his reasoning and he thought he deserved the extra ration."

"I don't see the point in all this," Ashraf said.

"Ah. You will help me come to the point. What would you do with this fat cat? How would you handle the situation?"

"There is no situation Maged. This is not a critical thing with your cat. Why are you telling me this?"

"Because you need to know how I dealt with this cat, Ashraf abdel Amr. You need to know I killed it. "

Maged had lifted his hand and banged his fist down precisely when he said the word 'killed'. Ashraf jumped back at the noise and the Chairman could tell by this time that Ashraf abdel Amr was one of the corrupted committee members.

"I don't like cheaters," he said.

He let the silence pour in around them, and the body language of Ashraf was pronounced.

"I need something my little friend," Maged whispered through clenched teeth. "You should be thrown in el-Mahkoum prison. But I am willing to make a deal. I know there are two of you among the bid committee that sold out for a dirty pile of money. I have enough information to ruin both your lives but I require more to put one of you in prison. The first one who supplies what I need gets a pardon. I need a signed letter accusing the other of accepting bribes, the name of the person who offered the bribe, and information that will lead to the real power behind this betrayal."

Ashraf was aghast. It was not supposed to turn out this way.

"I don't know who the other is. Give me paper. I will write down what I know."

'One down,' Maged thought. Ashraf was in tears.

"I cannot stay. Here is what you must do. Go home. Write what you can and bring it to my house as soon as you can. Give it to me or to my wife, and no one else. I will judge who has given me the best information and who has given it first. Good-bye my friend. You are in a race now for your life."

The next interviewee, Rashed Ghaly, passed Ashraf in the parking lot, both unaware their already connected lives were about to become more entwined. They did not know that the other had accepted the same bribe. Indeed Ashraf's main concern in composing his confession document was that he did not know the identity of the other man.

Khafagy went through the rest of the interviews one by one, without succeeding in breaking anyone else. By the time he got home after eight o'clock, there was an envelope waiting for him from Ashraf abdel Amr. His wife said he had looked very nervous, sweating and in a hurry.

The envelope contained a signed confession from Ashraf containing a brief history of how he was approached, and how his corrupt bargain was structured. He was to vote for Triton Energy.

"So," Maged said to himself. "Triton Energy. Who is that?"

The document contained other information like the fact that Ashraf couldn't identify the other corrupt member of the committee. That Triton first called him at home and made an offer he could not refuse. That subsequent meeting with the contact from Triton had occurred at the Cairo zoo. There were no telephone numbers but there was a Swiss bank account number. Ashraf had called Switzerland to make sure the money was there, and learned an anonymous person had deposited it as cash. There was no way to contact the people who paid him. All he had was the name of the contact at the zoo. Itzak. It also mentioned the pardon that Maged had offered. Maged doubted he could obtain such a pardon.

Maged considered the name Itzak, which Salah had also given him as the man who had sent a severed finger to Hesham Ibrahim. Maged looked up the telephone number for Salah el Gindi, picked up his phone and dialed.

Ten minutes later Salah el Gindi dialed Jerusalem and got the same nice greeting from the King David. Jake's room phone rang five times before the English voice came back, asking if it could take a message. Salah asked for Stan Kawinski instead. Same five rings. Same offer to take a message.

"I must get in touch with one of them. Did they leave any phone number?"

"Could I please have your name sir? Hold one minute."

Muzak played for an eternity before a different voice came on the line. A male voice speaking in Arabic.

"How are you Mr. el Gindi? I am an employee of the King David hotel. How may I help you today?"

"I am a business associate of Mr. Jake Tillard, who is traveling with Mr. Stan Kawinski. I have extremely important business information I must get to one of these gentlemen, and was inquiring if they left a phone number."

"I do have a number for Mr. Kawinski, sir. You are authorized to have it."

Salah pondered the formality of getting this forwarding number as he wrote it down on a pad of paper. It had a US country code, but then had fifteen digits, more than Salah had ever seen before. Minutes later he was talking to Jake on Stan's satellite cell phone.

He relayed the information from Maged. After hanging up Salah again stared out the window, wondering what linked the problems of Hesham Ibrahim and Jake Tillard.

In Israel Jake was listening to Stan give the latest information to Dick Radisson in Washington. Dick instructed both of them to go directly to the United States Ambassador's residence in Tel Aviv. It was going to be a long night.

CHAPTER 43

JOE FARADAY finished a late lunch in his temporary office at the Bar-J before calling Dick Radisson with the daily update.

"I followed up on that FBI data you ordered when Jake took the call from the kidnappers."

"What turned up?"

"More than I'd hoped for. I focused on public phones first. On August 25 there were 53 calls from Montana public telephones to Egypt. That's a hell of a lot more than I would've expected. Who the hell calls Egypt from public phone booths in Montana?"

"The calls initiated all around the God-damned State. Most were from Billings and Helena, with a few out on the eastern plains. Only seven were from west of the Divide, where we're pretty sure our little group is hiding. I had Troopers check out every one of those phones. Four are in pretty busy places and one was in the Missoula County courthouse. The other two are remote, the kind they might use. One was a rest area on Interstate 90 just east of Missoula. The other was outside an abandoned gas station north of Missoula. That's on Flathead Indian land. There are some pretty isolated houses up that way. Lots of dirt roads. Not a lot of traffic. It's a really big area."

"Anything else?"

"Air Traffic Control in Missoula says a couple pilots reported seeing a mirror reflection, maybe a signal from the ground. Could have been an SOS. We get these things every now and then from lost hikers or hunters. It ain't hunting season. Both sightings were within a few minutes, in the same location. We've got it down to several square miles in the Jocko Valley, not far from that public phone."

"What's your plan?"

"I'm keeping the Troopers away from that area except for routine highway stuff. I've got bikers doing a sweep of every dirt road and track in a thousand square miles. I've just focused them to that specific area."

"A Mercedes rental can't just disappear."

"Maybe it's in a garage or a barn," Joe answered. "Maybe it's at the bottom of a lake. Who knows. If it's out there, we'll find it. You get any satellite intel?"

Radisson had put a top priority satellite reconnaissance team on the project, diverting a high-resolution satellite from its normal swaths over China. Two photo analysts and continuous multi-band coverage for the past three days had turned up five leads, which checked out false.

"Nothing. I'd put more faith in your Hell's Angels."

'Hickey' Fischer got the word about the Jocko Valley from Joe over his walkie talkie. He and Willy Stroh rode up the wide Jocko floodplain with mountains set back half a mile on either side. They were not the sheer rocky kind of mountains, but rather the gentler, tree-covered kind.

The valley floor was native grass spotted with pastures, some aspen groves, and cottonwoods along the river. The second haying was over and the stubble of feed crop looked pretty in the afternoon sun. The entire scene was brown except for the strip of clear water meandering down the middle.

The two men had been checking out houses along the river, riding their Harleys down the graded dirt road. There were some fine homes in the valley, built by professors from the University, lawyers from Missoula, or richer Flathead who had parlayed their Native American heritage into a fortune.

Hickey got off his motorcycle to relieve himself, standing at the side of the road on a sand track leading off to the right. His big belly poked out towards the mountains. A mixture of sand and mud, the track contained ruts from vehicles slowing down for the sharp turn. Hickey pointed at the ground.

"What?" shouted Willy.

"Lookit them tracks," Hickey yelled back.

Willy didn't get it. Shutting down his machine he got off and knelt down to get a closer look.

"You asshole," said Hickey, shaking his head. "Do those treads look like a big old pickup went through here?"

"Shit I don't know. I'm not a fuckin' tire salesman?"

"That print looks like the one Joe showed us. They could be up there somewhere."

"Well let's go see."

"No way man," Hickey said. "I think I remember this place. There's a few log cabins up there strung out on a ledge under a cliff. Great view of the valley and anyone who's drivin' up this fuckin' trail. The cliff's gonna make our bikes sound like the fuckin' Red Bull race at Indy."

"So let's park 'em here and walk up."

"My ass. We're gonna do just what Joe said."

"But we ain't seen nothin' yet."

"You seen the track. This could be the place. They got Feds up the ass on this case and I'm not screwin' up anything. Let's get to a wider place in the valley and try the walkie talkie."

The two men turned their bikes downstream and rode three miles before shutting them down and calling Faraday. When Hickey activated the send function, he also activated the built-in Global Positioning System. By the time he told Faraday what his thoughts were, a latitude and longitude had popped up on Joe's digital readout.

"Thanks Hickey. Now get out of there. Ride to Highway 93 and the gas station in Arlee. Wait there for me. I need to hear whatever you can tell me about the road in and the house."

Faraday picked up a less technically impressive walkie-talkie and announced a code yellow to the dozen or so of his crew on the ranch. He gave the coordinates and one of a half dozen sets of pre-determined plans to his assistant and walked out of the house. A four man Montana SWAT team met him at the helicopter. Two minutes later the rotors were turning and twelve minutes after he announced the code yellow they were heading north at over a hundred miles per hour, at an altitude of five hundred feet.

Faraday looked to the west and saw the bottom half of the sun cut off by the Bitterroots. 'Finally,' he thought, 'a break'. The SWAT team worked much better in darkness. He tried not to get his hopes up. Hickey told them he had no direct evidence that they had found anything.

"Please take her to her room," pleaded Libby. "Please. Let her stay with Layla."

"I want to stay with you Libby," cried the ten year old.

"Gussie do as I say. I'll see you later OK?"

Libby was having a tough time keeping calm and could not keep her voice down with Gussie. She wanted the girl out of this room when Ashraf came at her.

"But I don't want to leave you. I'm scared."

Gussie looked at Ashraf and the other two men with tears in her eyes. Ashraf was not letting Gussie run to Libby.

"See, what did I tell you," sneered Ashraf. "She wants to stay. I think that chair would be a good place for her."

Ashraf had come into Libby's room right after dinner, walking up to her as she stood with one hand on the post at the foot of the bed. Libby thought he was going to kiss her. She decided to knee him in the groin.

Without warning, before she could get her knee started, he punched her in the stomach, knocking the breath completely out of her. She knew she had to fight yet there was nothing she could do. Before she could get the first good breath in, he pulled her onto the bed by her hair and tied her hands to the posts. They were seven foot tall posts of solid cherry, with a carved pineapple on top.

The other two Palestinians appeared with Gussie.

"So should I tie her to that chair?" repeated Ashraf.

Gussie was now both scared and mad.

"Don't do that," Libby said.

"You plan to cooperate then?"

"Yes."

"Libby please."

"Don't worry Gussie. You'll be fine. Just think of the ranch. We'll be back there soon."

"Mohammed," Ashraf said, "take the girl to her room. Stay with her. And make sure the Egyptian woman is quiet."

As Ashraf turned to the other man, Gussie broke free from Mohammed and kicked Ashraf full force in the shin.

"*Kess Ommak*," shouted Ashraf reaching for his leg. He followed with a roundhouse that knocked Gussie onto the floor.

"Get her out of here," he yelled at Mohammed who dragged the struggling and kicking Gussie out the door.

To the other captor he shouted, "You watch the front of the house. It'll be dark soon. I don't want those motorcycle idiots coming back without our knowing it."

When Hickey and Willy stopped at the beginning of the two-mile driveway to the house, Ashraf had clearly heard the sounds of their engines. There was nothing by the river here to stop for, yet they had stopped.

"I do not want to be disturbed."

When he said this he had a big grin, which grew as his glare shifted to Libby. She thought his eyes were becoming crazed, and glanced down as he used his hand to shift the front of his pants.

"Yes boss," Mohammed said, his face knowingly reflecting Ashraf's grin.

The helicopter set down beside the road intersection fourteen minutes after takeoff. They could have arrived quicker if they flew a direct course but the pilot had flown an average of fifty feet above the river. The landing was dramatic although Joe guessed the pilot did not push the limits of the machine in order to keep the noise down. By the time Joe had undone his seat belt all four SWAT members were outside prepping their gear. Each had a small backpack and was loading gear onto small, compact quadrupeds. Hickey and Willy strolled over to meet Joe.

"Nice chopper," said Hickey.

He had been in Viet Nam but was nonetheless impressed by the efficiency of these men. They wore stretchy black body suits, black shoes, and black hoods that left only their blackened faces and ears exposed. The only thing not black was their eyes.

Ten minutes after landing the helicopter took off. The pilot used his night scope to locate the house they thought was the target then found a landing zone on a ridge across the valley. With the sun setting anyone at the house might hear a helicopter for a half-minute but would hopefully not think much of it.

Hickey's briefing had been quick and complete. He could not remember much about the few houses up the road, but his recollection of the terrain was detailed. The SWAT leader Randy was impressed.

"When can we come in?" Hickey asked Joe.

"You can't. We appreciate all you've done but right now I need you to go find a bar up in Polson."

The bikers watched as the four men mounted their little electric ATVs, Joe sitting behind Randy and wrapping his arms around the SWAT leader. All of a sudden the men were gone. Hickey and Willy looked at each other.

"They're gone," said Willy.

"There was no sound. How the hell can you make one of those things go with no sound?"

"Let's get the fuck outta here."

When Gussie's cries became muffled Ashraf turned his attention to Libby. Lying on the bed, her hands were still bound to the posts with ropes. She watched through watery eyes as he came at her. He was the ugliest of her captors, with short hair, a big round face, and yellow crooked teeth.

"It's time."

Libby kicked out at him but missed, slipping halfway off the bed. Her arms were pulled in an unnatural way, and her left shoulder twisted in pain.

"I thought you were going to cooperate?"

"I lied."

"Well I won't lie. You cooperate or I'm going to do all these wonderful things to that little girl."

"You wouldn't. Even you're not that perverted. And I know that you don't need me but you need Gussie"

"I need her alive but I don't need her a virgin."

"You filthy animal."

Ashraf reached out and grabbed her face with his big hand. He squeezed her cheeks, her mouth forming an 'O'.

"Let's start with a kiss."

She closed her eyes as his face closed in on hers. She felt his beard scratch her cheek. He took his time teasing her then finally his lips were on hers. Libby could smell garlic. She gagged and tried to fight him off.

Ashraf slapped one cheek, then the other. Her cheeks stung but she didn't care. For Gussie's sake she couldn't actively resist but she didn't have to participate. Libby looked at the dresser and focused on the items on top.

Ashraf stopped kissing her and moved his hands to her breasts, squeezing roughly. Several buttons popped as he ripped her shirt open. She had no bra.

"This one has a bruise," he muttered.

His mouth was on her left breast, lips biting the nipple.

Libby concentrated on a photo in a silver frame, of an older couple, she guessed the owners of the house. Moustafa had told her that Ashraf killed the couple and burned the bodies.

He switched breasts, biting harder now. It hurt.

Libby bit her lip and stared at an elegant brass lamp with a wide base, sitting on the dresser.

His hands were on her pants, undoing the buttons. One hand was inside her panties.

Libby turned her gaze to another picture. The same couple on skis when they were younger.

He pulled her pants off. They were tight, and her panties rolled down with them. Libby closed her eyes.

The group ditched the ATVs fifty yards short of the house picked by the helicopter pilot, who had seen someone walking back and forth on the front porch. They had been guided by their night goggles and earplug communications with the helicopter pilot on the ridge a mile away, equipped with long range infrared capability.

The pilot watched the team approach the house, guiding them through the topography. Working with hand signals the SWAT team moved in. One man climbed up a power pole to tap the phone line. He attached a device that would cut the phone and electric power when he pressed a remote.

Another member unpacked a helmet camera that linked with the helicopter, a Glock with a silencer, a couple of smoke bombs, and four percussion grenades.

The two remaining SWAT members, with Joe, moved towards the house, avoiding as many sticks as possible. The pilot told them someone was on the front porch smoking a cigarette.

Thirty yards from the house Randy asked if everything was a go. The pilot said the man on the front porch was still there, the power pole man clicked OK, and clicks by the road lookout told them the roads were clear. Randy motioned for Joe to stay put and the three SWAT members came together.

They started out slow, careful not to move too quickly in case anyone was watching. Two drifted north, the other south. Joe Faraday sat where they left him, behind a tree. He looked at the moon sliver and waited to hear something through his earphone.

"I promise you I'll fuck the little girl if you don't cooperate," Ashraf whispered into Libby's ear.

He squeezed her breasts until the pain caused Libby to cry out. He spread her legs and grabbed a fistful of pubic hair. He tied a rope around her ankles and fixed each to a bedpost.

Libby fought back the shock and thought of alternatives. Maybe if he untied a wrist she could get free and deliver a chop to his windpipe.

"Now don't do anything stupid," he said.

Undoing the rope that held one wrist to a post, he put his hand in her armpit. She thought he was going to climb onto her. Instead he rolled her onto her stomach. One arm was now behind her, still bound. Her legs were awkwardly crossed, tied to opposite posts.

"Wait," she said.

Libby squirmed, her body trying to jackknife. Ashraf slapped her ass and retied the ropes holding her limbs. Libby could now hardly move at all, on her stomach, her body stretched out, her legs spread like a wishbone.

"Now," he said, "Isn't that a sight?"

She felt his hands trailing along the insides of her legs. Starting at the ankles they passed over her calves, swiveling inwards at her thighs, sliding onto her ass.

"Your ass is very smooth and round. And white."

Libby's head was on the bed, a good portion of her weight on her chest. She could see herself in the mirror above the chest of drawers. She watched her tormentor bend over her, his head between her legs. She closed her eyes and said a prayer out loud, as his hot breath reached her.

CHAPTER 44

DARKNESS fell over the Corniche as the sun set over the Mediterranean. Crescent shaped beaches still hosted bathers taking advantage of the warm weather. Stan dozed in the back seat, still jet lagged, but Jake could not relax.

Veering inland the car pulled through an iron gate. Israeli guards suggested the residence of a government official and US Marines indicated the resident was American Embassy staff. Royal palms lined the drive to marble steps and an imposing front door. Roses flanked the entrance along with two marines. Stan woke up when the car stopped.

"Have you met Ambassador Foley?" he asked Jake.

"No but I've heard him speak. Seems an intelligent guy."

"He's a respected player in the Middle East. Did a stint in Tehran before Turkey, and now Israel. Speaks several languages. Graduated from Princeton. Foley played a big role in the recent negotiations with the Palestinians on Gaza."

The door opened before they reached it. Gordon Foley was a tad over five feet, bald with wire-rimmed glasses. Homely perhaps, but impeccably dressed.

"Come in gentlemen."

Jake found his voice rather whiny.

"I'm very concerned about your daughter Mr. Tillard. I want you to know I will do anything I can to help. Allow me to introduce Irma Levi, assistant to the Israeli Prime Minister."

Irma, even shorter than Foley, took Jake's hand in hers, and shook it with her other hand on top.

"Mr. Tillard, the Israeli government will lend whatever assistance it can to help extricate your daughter, Ms. Joyce, and your Egyptian housekeeper. I relay this from the Prime Minister himself."

Irma was well on in years with grey hair, a wrinkled face, and piercing blue eyes. She did not let go of Jake's hand until he thanked her. He liked her immediately.

The Ambassador led them down a long hallway to his study, where another man was sitting in a brown leather armchair. Jake recognized the smell of Egyptian cigarettes.

"General Latif, I'd like to introduce two men. Stanley Kawinski. Jake Tillard. Gentlemen this is General Mohammed Latif, second in command at the Egyptian State Department. The General answers directly to the Foreign Minister."

Latif hoisted himself out of the chair. He was as imposing as Foley was diminutive. "Mr. Tillard I believe we have a mutual friend. Maged Khafagy."

Jake understood that Latif was establishing his command of the situation and shortcutting the process to win Jake's trust. It was a typical Egyptian thing to do.

"I have the utmost respect for Mr. Khafagy," replied Jake. "But at this point I'm not sure I know who to trust."

"You are in a delicate situation," said Ambassador Foley. "You need to trust a few people and a good place to start is Dick Radisson."

Jake took note of the reference given to Radisson. There was however something about men like Radisson that made them dangerous to trust.

"General Latif's another good guy," Foley continued. "We have a long history. After Camp David we worked together on Sinai handover issues. Jake, you are involved with a corruption ring we've been investigating for over a year. We've been unable to catch this group with anything definitive, but think we've now got a chance to snare the beast. We need you. General Latif will explain."

"Mr. Tillard I love my country with all my heart but I do not love everything about it. Like all countries, including your own, Egypt has good elements and bad."

General Latif paused to light another cigarette, took a big drag, and exhaled a cloud of smoke. It hung in the air along with the General's words.

"Egypt has three significant sources of foreign income. The Canal is the biggest. Tourism is big but variable. Oil was big but is falling. We understand the corruption involved with the Canal. It is run by a very small group of people who skim off a little money. This is acceptable. Tourism is quite the opposite. Its revenues are widely dispersed and therefore impossible for anyone to control. All we do there is make sure no one gets too big. The oil sector is unlike the Canal or tourism. Most oil comes from the Gulf of Suez or the Western Desert. Five foreign companies pump eighty percent. This is a small number of companies for a highly profitable business. It has all the fundamentals for gross corruption and I have been investigating the Petroleum Ministry itself."

"I'm afraid you're out of my league General," replied Jake. "I've dealt with managers at EGPC but haven't dealt very often with the Ministry."

Jake knew he must tread delicately. One couldn't tell who was telling the truth and who was bending it.

"The stream of corruption flows from the Ministry downhill to the EGPC," said Latif. "I know you have dealt with my colleagues in the Ministry because I've got a printout of every meeting you have had there in the past few years."

"I'm not sure what this has to do with my daughter."

That was the card for which Latif had been waiting. The general glanced at the Ambassador who gave him a slight nod, which was not lost on Jake.

"What I am about to tell you is sensitive," the Ambassador started. "Normally you would need Top Secret clearance but we don't have time for that. I've done my own background check on you and will bend the rules. We have reason to believe that certain officials in both Israel and Egypt would like to start another skirmish over the Sinai."

Jake looked at them one by one. No one was smiling.

"I'm not sure I follow".

"Let me continue. Ms. Levi is here if you have any need for confirmation or clarification, but let me assure you that what you are about to hear has been vetted extensively with Prime Minister Benjamin Shapiro. Simply put we think a group of individuals is trying to start a war between Israel and Egypt. Possibly to create a new profit opportunity. Possibly for some twisted personal reason.

Possibly for revenge. At this time we won't discount anyone from involvement but we have our eyes on a handful of individuals."

"Daniel Moses Ran is Israel's Minister of Infrastructure. A lifelong politician, after three years in this position he has done little to distinguish himself. Ran sits over the Israeli Energy Branch and would like nothing better than to have some internal resources to develop. In previous jobs he has shown himself to be quite ruthless in achieving his goals."

"For the last three years Vasily Kirchoff has been the Chairman of INOC, the Israeli National Oil Company. A Soviet trained engineer, Vasily was number two in the Russian Oil Sector before immigrating to Israel. He is an old school product of the Soviet era who would love to have oilfields to play with. He thinks the Sinai is the answer."

"Yaroun Herschel is perhaps most culpable. He's been Minister of State Security for a decade. Internal strife continues, random bombings take their toll, while underground Palestinian efforts are increasing. Yaroun fought in three of Israel's past wars. He saw what victory did for old war heroes and is searching for a legacy. He has no wife, no children, nothing to lose."

"If one becomes creative in looking for motive, the business world has some candidates. Yosef Kettler, one of the three richest Israelis, is well connected politically. He is getting old and also looking for his legacy. A firm Zionist, he would do anything to progress the independence and wealth of the mother state. An early settler post 1948, Yosef has seen it all. I'm sure he could look past any nasty business to realize a noble goal."

"Ruth Karsh is a billionaire who inherited one of the largest conglomerates in Israel from her father. Istravco LLC is in the leisure business including hotels, cruise ships, tour companies, and travel insurance products. Her father built many of the original roads, hotels, and restaurants in the Sinai during Israeli occupation. Known as "Ruthless" for the tactics she uses to achieve success, she was indicted but never convicted for extortion and bribery. I'm sure she'd love to get the Sinai family businesses back."

"All well and good Ambassador, but it sounds like you're playing a game of Clue. You know, Colonel Mustard with a lead pipe in the study. How does any of that involve me?" Jake asked.

"We have a plan that I will share after dinner. I'm afraid I've been a terrible host. You all must be famished. And by the way, I loved Clue as a child."

With that they followed their host into the dining room where Jake could hardly contain his curiosity.

CHAPTER 45

ASHRAF got off the bed and Libby closed her eyes. Several minutes passed before she opened her eyes and found herself looking directly at her captor's face. With a big smile he stood and slowly unbuttoned his shirt, flinging it onto a chair. Ashraf wore a ribbed wife-beater, his thick black chest hair sticking out wherever it could. He pulled the white cotton shirt out of his pants and over his head. The sight of him repulsed Libby.

"Now you will see what I have for you."

He undid his belt and dropped his pants to the floor. His blue boxers had a small dark spot at the top of a big bulge. Libby closed her eyes again.

"Don't you want to see it before it goes inside of you," his voice quivered with excitement. "I would have you open your mouth but I am afraid you would bite down by mistake."

He laughed as Libby opened her eyes. He was no longer in front of her. She could not see or hear him. A minute went by with absolute silence then she yelled as the belt dug into the left buttock. She saw him then in the mirror, swinging it again, and it hit her right side. He alternated from side to side and every so often in the middle.

"Now your ass is not as white," he chuckled.

He was kneeling on the bed between her legs. She could see his hairy body in the mirror. His erection looked huge as he bent over her. Libby cringed as he straightened up.

"Are you ready?" he asked.

Randy crouched beneath the window wearing night goggles and watched as the man brought the belt down on the woman. The girl and the nanny remained unaccounted for. His colleague used the cabin log overlaps to scale the exterior, entering the top floor through an open window he had seen from the ground. A sound sensing microphone led him to Gussie's room where he could see that Gussie and Layla were safe but overlooked by a captor with a gun. All commandos communicated to the pilot. The key lay in coordination and timing. The pilot gave instructions.

"On three simultaneously take out front porch watch, man in bedroom, and man in girl's room. Then sweep house for other threats. Team leader confirm."

Randy clicked his radio twice.

"Action authorized. Proceed on three. One. Two. Three."

The SWAT member at the edge of the porch shot the smoking man with a silenced rifle. The left side of his head exploded and he went down with a thump.

Ashraf reached beneath her. His hand tickled her belly, and then moved lower. Seconds later Libby felt his penis between her cheeks. She bit her lip, trying not to scream, to not give him that satisfaction. She heard a slight 'pop' and a tinkling, followed by Ashraf screaming in Arabic. Ashraf bounced off Libby and onto the floor.

On three Randy had fired a silenced gun through the window, hitting Ashraf in the shoulder with a hollow point. At precisely the same time another SWAT member burst into Gussie's room and Tazered Mohammed.

Randy went through the glass window right after the bullet. Before he could get to Ashraf the SWAT member from the porch had him on the floor, twisting his arm behind him. A puddle of blood formed underneath him.

"My shoulder," shouted Ashraf. Randy's shot destroyed most of the shoulder but did not penetrate any critical organs. They pulled his arms behind him and put handcuffs on as Ashraf screamed even louder. Randy kicked him in the side and told him to stop screaming like a baby.

Randy had watched the last few minutes of Libby's torment and wasn't in the mood to coddle. He went to the bed and cut the ropes.

"Gussie?" Libby managed.

"She's fine ma'am."

Upstairs the man in black cuffed Mohammed, bent over Layla who had fainted, and told Gussie he was a friend of her father. Gussie stayed in the corner, in shock.

"Who are you?" asked Libby downstairs.

"The rescue team," said Randy. "Tell you more later."

He helped her dress and led her to the living room couch where they also brought Gussie. Randy left instructions to guide Joe Faraday to the back bedroom when he arrived.

As Joe entered the bedroom they heard the whomp-whomp of the helicopter landing on the front lawn.

"Who are you?" Ashraf asked.

"That's not your concern sir. I need information from you and I need it quickly," Joe said.

"I know my rights."

"You have whatever rights I want you to have."

"This is America. You are with the government. I have rights. I know. Take me to a hospital then get me a lawyer."

Ashraf looked at them with a smirk of contempt. Joe drew his pistol and shot Ashraf's knee. He screamed again, his eyes large with disbelief.

"I've shattered your knee," Joe said. "You will never walk again without advanced medical help. I will say this only once more. I need some information quickly."

The SWAT members in the room looked at each other, wondering if they should intervene. None did.

"This is not a normal case. You understand that, right? I need to solve a problem and that's what I intend to do."

"You can't do this," Ashraf shouted.

Joe had taken out an eight-inch commando knife, anticipating one more bout of protest. He squatted down and plunged the blade to the hilt in Ashraf's pulverized knee. The bearded man screamed in pain, rolled onto his side, and passed out. Joe stood up and asked for smelling salts. When the man came to, Joe sat him up.

"Who do you work for? I want names, addresses, and phone numbers to start."

Clearly in pain and heading for shock the man had reverted to Arabic.

"Can the Egyptian woman come help us?" Joe asked.

When Layla arrived leaning on a commando, Joe realized she was dealing with shock. He asked if she was OK to help out.

"I'm OK," she said. "Just let me sit."

Ashraf continued screaming in Arabic.

"He's saying that he needs medical attention," Layla said. "He thinks he is bleeding to death."

Joe held Ashraf's face in his hand and spoke clearly at the man.

"Yes you are. You will bleed out if you don't get care quickly. You'll get the best medical attention in the world as soon as I get what I need. Or else you will die. What is your name?"

Ashraf spat in Joe's face, saying in English "Go to hell." Joe directed his next comment to Randy.

"Please ask Ms. Joyce to join us. And bring the other prisoner as well."

Randy returned with a handcuffed Mohammed, Libby trailing.

"What is your name", Joe asked the man.

"Mohammed," the man replied. He was shaking, his eyes huge.

"Do you speak English?"

"Yes".

"OK then. Pay attention Mohammed. If I lose this man here, I will have to rely upon you for my information. What is his name," he said pointing to Ashraf.

A slight hesitation caused Joe to draw his pistol again, shaking his head slowly from side to side, never taking his off Mohammed who looked downright petrified.

"Ashraf."

"And the dead man on the porch?"

"Sami."

Mohammed seemed more agreeable so Joe decided he could take more risk with Ashraf. He would not draw this out.

"Ms. Joyce. I am very sorry to bring you in here again. I'm having some difficulty extracting information from your assailant. I've already had to shoot him in the knee. I thought you might have some idea of what to do next."

Libby didn't answer. She walked over to Ashraf and kicked his bloody knee, sending Ashraf reeling again. Randy gently grabbed her shoulders and pulled her back. Joe applied the smelling salts again.

"Pig. Child molester," she shouted at Ashraf. "If I could, I would cut off your penis and shove it down your throat."

"OK we can do that," said Joe.

Libby looked at him, eyes wide. Ashraf's eyes also widened as he tried to cross his legs. This resulted in more screaming.

"My policy going forward is to not repeat myself," Joe said. "Are there any other members of this team?"

Ashraf did not know how these soldiers found them. He did not know how much they already knew.

"There is one other man," he said.

"Where is he?"

"I don't know."

"When will he return?"

"Tonight."

Ashraf figured what the hell, what could they do about it? He was sure had lookouts. It was not as though Mustafa would get through anyway.

"Good so far," Joe said. "Now how about that name and phone number for your boss."

"Fuck you," Ashraf yelled.

Joe pulled surgical gloves out of his pocket and put them on. He took his knife back out.

"Ladies you might want to leave now. I don't believe I'll need any more translation."

Libby and Layla went back to where Gussie sat and hugged the little girl. A blood-curdling scream penetrated the house. Libby closed her eyes, wondering what she had done.

Five minutes later Joe joined them.

"How did you find us," asked Libby.

"Some good investigating and a lucky break. Did you use a mirror to signal an SOS to some jets?"

"No."

"That was me," whimpered Gussie. "I didn't think it worked."

Joe laughed, and kneeled down in front of Gussie."

"Well it did little lady," Joe said. "You're the hero today. And a very brave person. You saved your life and Libby and Layla's as well. Time to go."

He stood up and put his hand on Gussie's shoulder but removed it as she flinched.

"Sorry Gussie. Come on. Let's get you back to the ranch."

As they walked to the helicopter Libby asked him if they got the information they wanted.

"Yes ma'am we did."

"I didn't think he would ever give you what you wanted."

Joe looked at her and stopped walking.

"He didn't."

She looked puzzled. Joe took her hand in both of his.

"Ashraf was clearly dedicated to whatever cause he served. The other man gave us the information we needed."

She saw Mohammed being led into the rear of the helicopter, as two large black plastic bags were loaded into the cargo hold. After the helicopter took off another landed. Joe helped both Libby and Gussie into this chopper. Gaining altitude she could see a number of blue and red police lights spinning beneath them en route to the house. Twenty minutes later they touched down on the Bar-J front lawn.

In the house Joe stared at one old man, one pretty woman, one Egyptian woman, and one little girl, underneath trophies of elk, deer, and moose. Joe knew once more why he did what he did. For the first time since the Caitlin case a tear rolled down his cheek. He wiped it with his finger but another one took its place.

CHAPTER 46

AMBASSADOR FOLEY excused himself from the dinner table after the butler whispered in his ear, asking Stan Kawinski to accompany him. Jake and Latif drank coffee and traded pleasantries, not wanting to discuss anything substantial until the Ambassador returned.

In his study Foley read a confidential fax. When he looked up he wore an odd expression.

"It seems our Montana operations were successful. All three women are safe, two kidnappers are dead, one is talking, and the last one is still at large. Apparently the Egyptian women gave us some valuable information that she overheard in Arabic. She remembers them referring to their boss as Osama abdel Fatah. They had also mentioned an Itzhak in Cairo. With interrogation starting we expect more information soon."

"Jake will be relieved to hear this news," Stan said.

"Yes he will. But I don't want Latif to know. At least not yet. No real need for him to know. It might come in handy to keep the Egyptians in the dark on this for a couple days. You tell Jake in the car after you leave."

Dinner had taken too long for Jake's liking but finally they moved to the study and continued their earlier discussion.

"The General and I have spent days consulting with various agencies in three governments," said the Ambassador. "We've come up with a way forward. Our main goal is to apprehend and convict corrupt politicians. A subordinate outcome might be the salvage of your daughter and friend."

Foley glanced at Kawinski, seeing only a stone face. Mohammed Latif lit another cigarette, smoke rising toward the ceiling. Jake felt he could not trust anyone but knew he had to trust someone.

"What's the plan?"

"We want you to submit a bid," Latif began. "We will not interfere with the process in any way. Our group of misfits will hopefully outbid you. Over time as they begin to put activities in place, we should be able to track them. The difficult part will be to put them away before they can implement their strategy. We think their plan depends on an Israeli consortium getting control of the Sinai deposit. Trying to develop it will create enough tension between the two countries to precipitate a war."

"How will this help my daughter?"

"There's a chance that when the bids are in we will be able to trace who's involved with the kidnapping. It's a long shot."

Jake did not believe for a minute this would work.

"That seems impossible," he said.

Jake thought everyone around him was evil. It did not seem a sound plan but rather a desperate last attempt.

"There must be more you're not sharing with me," he said.

"No, I am afraid there is not," the Ambassador replied.

"OK I'll work with you."

As Jake said this, a smile crossed his face. Hearing his willingness to cooperate, General Latif and Ambassador Foley sat back from the table and smiled as well. Only Stan Kawinski did not smile. He had spent enough time with Jake to know better. Jake was too much like himself. He did not like being played.

In the car going back to the hotel Stan told Jake the news. A great wave washed over Jake.

"I've got to phone them Stan."

"Use my sat phone."

Jake felt tortured when the phone rang three times before Marv finally answered.

"I've been trying to track you down son. We're all so relieved. It's over. Gussie, Libby, and Layla are all safe."

"I just heard dad. Thank god they're safe. Is anyone hurt?"

"They're OK son. No real physical harm. The injuries are mental. I'd put them on, but they're not here. They're both with Joe at a crisis center in Missoula. Gussie's pretty shaken up but they've got her talking about it. She's gonna be fine. All three of them are pretty strong women."

"I know they are dad. Take good care of them till I can get back. Right now I'm gonna help find out who's behind all this shit."

Jake was operating on gut feel now. He wasn't sure where he was going, but now that Gussie and Libby were safe he was certain it was in the right direction. Now he could take charge of his destiny.

GENERAL LATIF and Stan Kawinski watched two Mossad agents drag Saad Badry out of his small store in the Old City. Careful to keep their distance they left to meet the agents at the local police station.

"These were transmitted from your office in Washington," one of the Israeli agents said, placing three photos in front of Latif and Kawinski.

"These are the thugs who kidnapped Jake's daughter. Ashraf, second in command, and Sami, position unknown, are both dead. This one, Mohammed, corroborated the involvement of Osama abdel Fatah. Your men have not yet captured the leader, whose name is Moustafa Badry. Moustafa's brother is Saad Badry, the man we just apprehended."

The agent threw down a fourth photo.

"This man, Osama abdel Fatah, might be a cousin of Badry's. According to Mohammed, Osama was the key contact for their team."

"What do you know about Osama?" Stan asked.

"Very little. He has loose connections with Hamas. He's got a record but nothing too bad. Mohammed said they got instructions by phone, he thought from Israel and New York. We're going to see what we can get out of Saad, who has no record whatsoever."

"The New York angle is interesting. Can we get a copy of Osama's face to Tillard? I've got a hunch."

Another agent joined them.

"There's no love lost between cousins. Saad Badry has not seen Osama abdel Fatah in years. He says they are not related anymore. One of those Arab-disowning things. He readily provided an address."

The agent held up a piece of paper.

"Mind if we join you," Latif asked.

"Not at all, sir."

Osama abdel Fatah was dead in his apartment. His body badly beaten with multiple gunshot wounds, his head deformed from repeated bashing with the bloody cricket bat lying next to the body.

"This trail didn't lead very far," Stan commented.

"Most trails have many branches," Latif answered as the agents began going over the apartment. He was holding a photo showing the dead man with a group of elderly men. One of them looked familiar.

CHAPTER 48

JAKE couldn't remember Salah ever meeting him at the airport. At midnight the air was heavy. Arrivals from Europe and Saudi Arabia crowded the international terminal. Jake was glad to exit the crush. The drive to Salah's flat was quiet, neither wanting to discuss anything in front of the driver.

"What have we gotten ourselves into," Salah asked as he poured drinks for both of them.

"Some pretty ugly business, my friend. But it's almost over. The worst is behind us."

"I hope you are right."

Jake updated Salah on what he knew. He suspected the apartment was bugged, and wanted to plant one final seed.

"Today you'll submit the bid, Salah. Five wells over the entire period will be enough to win."

Jake made sure to speak very clearly, slowly, and loudly.

"I have it ready Jake."

"I want you to submit it during the last hour of the day, so no one can see it and increase their own bid."

"OK. *Insha'Allah* it will win."

In a nearby apartment, Karim Nabet looked up at the heavens and put his hands on his head. The bug in Salah's apartment worked well, and Karim had exactly what he needed to submit a winning bid. He took off his headphones, poured a red wine, and sat back to enjoy the view of downtown Cairo at night.

"God is great. The world is great," he said to himself.

Nabet then made a call to Israel. There was no answer, so he left a message for Osama to phone back. It was strange Osama didn't answer, but Karim was not overly concerned. He thought a moment and placed another call to Israel.

After hearing the information Yosef Kettler leaned back in his chair and also smiled. He looked at his dinner guest and held up his glass. "To victory in the Sinai."

Nancy Clancy touched her glass to Yosef's and repeated those words.

Book 5

The Bid

IN the mid afternoon heat, Jake intercepted Salah coming out of his apartment, wearing a trademark wool suit.

"Do you have the bid?"

"Right here," Salah patted his briefcase.

"Replace it with this one," Jake said, handing Salah a large envelope.

Watching for a reaction, he saw none. Salah put his briefcase on the hood, took out a sealed envelope, and gave it to Jake. He placed the new envelope in the case.

"Our investors had a small change of heart overnight. Something to do with world market conditions."

Salah didn't ask any questions, but inferred this new bid was less robust. The world's oil price had been falling all month.

"Are you still optimistic we will win?"

"*Insha'Allah*, my friend."

Salah felt less hopeful.

That evening, Hesham Ibrahim walked into the dining room at the Maadi Club, where the maître d' seated him at Maged Khafagy's table. The Chairman offered Hesham a drink, and he ordered a guava juice.

"Would you care to join me for dinner?" asked Maged.

"That is most kind but not tonight."

After a suitable amount of time asking about family, Maged asked Hesham how the bid round was proceeding.

"We've received ninety-six bids on the twenty-one blocks offered, from sixteen companies. Four companies are new to Egypt oil and gas, and two of them are Egyptian. Four majors, who are the most active companies already, submitted 54 bids. It will take at least two weeks to analyze it all."

"That is a good showing indeed." Khafagy leaned forward and spoke in a quieter voice, "What about the Sinai block?"

Hesham looked ill.

"As expected we received two bids."

"Did you look at them?"

"You know I am not authorized to open anything. The bid committee will start that process tomorrow.

"When you review them start with the Sinai bids. Let me know about that block tomorrow evening."

Maged waved his hand and Hesham took his leave. Afterwards Maged walked to the terrace and lit a Cuban cigar. It was a sultry evening, thick with the smell of citrus blossoms. He was alone as he dialed General Latif.

"Have your men trailed him?"

"Yes. But I'm afraid something happened and we had to bring him in for questioning."

"And?"

"He has agreed to continue playing his role and wear a recorder. Of course he insisted on immunity afterwards."

"Excellent. How did you accomplish that so quickly?"

"It was just normal business," replied Latif. "Aly Hakim is his name, but he goes by Itzak. In fact he rolled over very quickly. Before we started with any intrusive methods."

"Will it be a problem hiding him afterwards?"

"I suppose that depends on who is involved. If he stays in Egypt it will be impossible. We may get help from our American friends, perhaps even put him into their witness protection program. No guarantees, but this would be the only way to keep him alive."

"Do what you can but don't use up any favors."

Maged didn't care one way or another what became of Aly Hakim. He had little time for anyone who dealt in dirty laundry.

"When will we hear something?"

"Aly will fly to Israel as soon as he gets the results of the bid round. We'll make sure the wire is working, and should hear something soon after he lands there."

DICK RADISSON phoned Jake around noon Washington DC time.

"Gussie is doing really well Jake. She's meeting with a psychologist from the University who makes the daily trek to the ranch. Libby is at the ranch and Layla's in the Missoula hospital recuperating."

"I'm taking the next flight back," said Jake. "My bid is in, and it's a waiting game now."

Jake wondered if anyone except Lister and himself knew the scale of the bid he actually submitted. There was really no way they could, he decided.

Radisson's next call was to Stan.

"Things are getting screwy Stan."

"What's up?" said Stan.

"I'm not sure," Radisson replied. "Clancy phoned me and asked some odd questions relating to Montana. It was unusual for her to phone me. She said the Montana operation might be relevant to a project I'm not cleared for. Something's fishy."

"Is there anything I can do Sir?"

"The Israelis have identified a couple guys in those photos from Osama's apartment in Jerusalem. One of them is Barney Wilcrow, Jake's old boss. On a fishing trip with Osama and Yosef Kettler. See what you can find out on Wilcrow from over there."

ITZAK rang the doorbell of Ashraf abdel Amr around one in the morning. Ashraf came to the door in a robe, looking at his caller like he was out of his mind.

"Sorry for the late hour, Ashraf. This will be the last time you see me. I wanted to make sure you still plan to vote for Triton. If they win, your Swiss account will receive the additional one hundred thousand US dollars. If not I suggest you move and hide."

"What are you saying?"

"I am saying that you need to find a way to make sure Triton wins that bid. Hopefully they will have the best offer. If not, you need to work it with the committee. Perhaps say that things are not black and white, that there are confusing terms, time periods, whatever. Just make sure the ultimate decision is in favor of Triton."

"I meant what did you mean when you talked of me hiding?" Itzak looked at the man before responding.

"This is big business, my friend. There are big rewards but also big consequences for failure. Failure is not an option for you."

With that he was gone and Ashraf was left looking out his front door with a most unpleasant expression.

Itzak paid a similar visit to Rashed Ghaly. After closing his door Ghaly ran to the toilet and was violently sick.

Late that afternoon Hesham Ibrahim was seated across the desk from Maged Khafagy, who wore a most unpleasant frown.

"You are certain the Triton bid is not the winner?"

"Not in total well count nor monetary commitment."

"Then you and your committee need to get creative Hesham. I cannot tell you why but you must announce Triton as the winner. Is there anything else?"

Hesham knew better than to continue. Jake Tillard's bid was clearly the best. He left Maged's office, not sure what to do.

Maged Khafagy placed a call to a satellite phone number.

"Tillard's bid was the winner but Triton will get the block," he said.

"Thank you Mr. Khafagy. That will help immeasurably."

Dick Radisson ended the call and took another sip of Bourbon.

WHEN he emerged from the jet way Gussie ran to him, almost knocking him down. Both cried as they squeezed each other. It was hard to let go.

Libby and Marv waited until Jake reached them. Jake looked at Libby, seeing bruises but realizing the worst was not observable. Marv took Gussie, giving his son a chance to embrace his friend. It was an emotional homecoming.

Dinner that night was simple, beef from the ranch, salad and potatoes from the garden. It was the best meal Jake could remember. Avoiding the kidnapping they talked about anything else. Jake told them about Egypt and the bid round, confident that his consortium would prevail. Marv talked about Libby and Gussie getting back into riding. Gussie didn't say much. They all realized it would take time.

Since being freed Gussie had slept with Libby but tonight she pleaded to sleep with her Daddy. Jake was overwhelmed by emotions of love, concern, anger, and guilt. He tucked her into the quilt-clad bed, removed his shoes, and climbed in next to her. She looked like an angel, peaceful and serene. He reached out and took her little hand in his. She sighed and he wondered if he would be able to leave her to finish the deal. When she was fully asleep, he gently got out of bed and crept to the door, leaving the light on as he left.

Libby and Jake spent the rest of the evening on the porch swing, wrapped in a wool blanket, talking about her ordeal. He couldn't fathom what they had been through and learned he owed a great deal to Joe Faraday. He let her talk, asking questions infrequently. Holding her for hours and listening was the best thing he could do. Libby cried from time to time. It was three in the morning when Jake could no longer fight off sleep. Libby solved one problem by telling him to sleep with Gussie. He knew Libby needed comforting as well but that would have to wait.

"I need to go back to Egypt in a few days and I want you to come with me," he said over breakfast of flapjacks and bacon.

"I don't know Jake. It's a long way and if you're leaving Gussie needs me."

"I want Gussie and Layla to come too. Might help you all."

They had a few days to figure it out.

"Bid evaluations should take another couple of weeks then I need to be there."

"Let me think about it."

JAKE glided fifty feet below the surface, using flippers to follow a lazy group of jack fish. The fish were not particularly skittish but were aware of him and kept their distance. They rose a bit and he followed up to thirty feet. Jake rolled onto his back and looked up, following his bubble trail to where Libby snorkeled.

The bubbles obscured her a bit, and backlighting from the sun made it hard to see her clearly. Jake kept his flippers moving, and slowly veered off to one side. As his visibility improved, he could see her waving. He waved back and rolled over. The jacks had disappeared and he declared his dive over, although eight hundred psi remained.

They walked over the reef table to the beach where Layla and Gussie had built a sand castle.

Back in the hotel suite Jake caressed her body as they kissed on the bed. Libby smiled as she pushed him away, reminding him that Gussie was in the next room and they had dinner reservations in an hour. Jake knew it was still too early for Libby to want sex but teased her a bit anyway.

"That's enough time," he said.

"No it isn't," she replied.

The waiter led them to a table on the edge of the terrace, where they had a view of the silver, mirrored ocean. Moonlight provided a dreamy illumination of the glistening waves tapping the sand. A soft breeze and candlelight added atmosphere. They stared at the beach before turning towards each other.

For the first time Jake confided that he had upped the ante at the last minute. Only he and Lister knew.

"So you think that will get you the block?"

"I can't imagine anyone submitting a bigger bid."

Libby raised her glass in hopes Jake would win, knowing from experience that you never knew until it was announced. The ceviche was wonderful, the grilled grouper even better.

HESHAM IBRAHIM sealed the last envelope, gave them to his secretary, opened his bottom drawer, and took out a bottle of Glenfiddich. He swallowed the first glass then sipped the next while looking out his window at the brown landscape. Each envelope would give a bidder the results for the blocks they bid on. The scotch was not to celebrate the end of the process, but rather to prepare him for Maged Khafagy. The Chairman would be happy with the results of the round as a whole. Egypt would take in over eighty million US dollars in bonus and look forward to minimum committed work programs of over two hundred million in seismic, studies, and wells.

He felt that Maged would not be happy with the Sinai outcome. After finishing the second tumbler and gargling with old tea, Hesham popped several mints into his mouth before walking down the hall to the Chairman's office.

Maged showed little reaction when Hesham explained what they had done with the Sinai block.

"When does the public announcement come out?"

"Companies get the results today by courier. Newspapers will have the release by the end of tomorrow, and will run it the next day. Results may leak earlier if companies release information. Something may also surface on the Internet. Things are not like they used to be."

"Good work Hesham. Take the rest of the week off. Spend it with your family."

Maged stared out the window after Hesham left. It was another sunny day in Cairo. 'Always a sunny day,' thought Maged Khafagy. 'Thanks to God to live in Egypt.'

LYING poolside under the mid day sun became unbearable so Jake and Libby retreated to their room, where Layla handed Jake an envelope that was slipped under the door. The note inside invited him to pick up a couriered package at the front desk. Watching Jake walk away with a big smile, Libby bit her lip, hoping it would be the message he wanted. She picked up the phone to order an iced bucket with Champagne but replaced the receiver before dialing. 'Just a feeling,' she told herself. Instead she asked Layla to take Gussie to the pool cabana for an ice cream.

Libby was sitting in a wicker chair on their terrace when Jake returned.

"Well what does it say?"

"I don't know. I thought we could open it together over a glass of Champagne."

He got a half bottle of Moet Imperial Champagne out of the mini bar, not checking the price list. Pouring two glasses, he held his up and said, "Salut."

Libby raised an eyebrow as they both took a corner of the manila envelope and tore. He pulled out the papers and started reading, Libby putting her arm around his shoulders. She watched his face, seeing the smile evaporate before he threw off her arm. He swatted the chair with the papers.

"Problem?"

"You could say."

She waited patiently, having seen enough disappointment to know not to rush things. She knew how much this meant to Jake and how much work he had put into it. Moreover she knew how firmly he believed he would win.

"They gave it to Triton."

Libby stayed silent.

"Nabet put in a higher bid. Three wells in the first, second, and third terms. No one could be serious about a bid like that."

Libby watched and waited.

"It's a sham. They might drill a well or two and then walk away if they come up dry. No one would drill three wells without hitting on the first one or two."

She let him think, taking a sip of Champagne. She knew he was trying to sort out what had happened, and was possibly thinking about what to do next.

Jake could not figure it out. His competitors knew about the low bid he did not file because that is what he leaked. No one knew what he really submitted. No one except Wintham. Could Charles be double-dealing, and if so, why.

Libby's hands kneaded the tension in his shoulders. He looked at her and saw sympathy and understanding.

"I just don't get it. Only Charles and I knew what we bid. We fed Nabet information on the original lower bid. I expected Triton to outbid us, but they could not have known what we really submitted."

"Maybe they are just more bullish than you."

"Maybe something is rotten in Cairo."

ALY landed at Ben Gurion airport and cleared customs. After security he saw a man holding a board with his name.

"I'm Mr. Hakim," Aly informed the uniformed driver.

"Any luggage Sir?"

"No. Is the car far?"

"Very near. Would you like to walk or should I pick you up at the door?"

"Walk," replied Aly.

He was in no mood to talk. He was nervous and wanted to get on with it. When he got into the car he asked the man to turn up the air conditioning. He was perspiring and wondered if his anxiety was apparent.

Hakim squirmed in his seat. Before clearing customs he'd been taken to a very secure looking room, where a man taped a wireless voice transmission system to his chest. It was all he could think about.

Normally Aly would have just phoned the information to Osama abdel Fatah, and that would have been the end of things. With Osama dead, he had been directed to deliver the results in person to Osama's boss, a man he'd never met. His message was positive yet he didn't feel good about this trip. He went through with it because he would make enough money from this deal to let him stop dealing with these people.

As the limo pulled into the King David, Aly breathed a sigh of relief that they would meet in a public place. The tape holding the wire in place was pulling on his skin, just below the left armpit. He closed his eyes and prayed that sweat would not give him away, fearing that any suspicions would lead to a body search and certain death.

"Check at the concierge for a message," his driver advised. "You will stay here tonight. I will pick you up tomorrow morning at 9:00 for the airport. Your plane to Cairo is at 13:00 and you need at least three hours to clear immigration."

Aly exhaled again. He retrieved an envelope from the concierge, followed the written instructions to the reception desk, and checked into a pre-paid room. Without going first to the room he walked through the lobby into the courtyard, where the maître d' asked if he was Mr. Hakim.

"Yes, that is me."

"Please follow me sir."

The gentleman at the table was not young. Aly had no idea who he was. Yosef Kettler didn't stand but motioned for Aly to sit. A fit young man wearing a suit, with a coiled wire near his ear, pulled out the chair for Aly.

"Thank you for coming so quickly Mr. Hakim."

"My pleasure Mr. Ahhhh."

"What do you have for me?" Kettler said without giving his name.

"Sir I mean no disrespect, but I don't know who you are. I am reluctant to deliver this to anyone without some assurance that they are the correct party."

"A reasonable request. Suffice it to say I know you work for Triton, you have company information you are hand carrying from Cairo, and I am the next courier."

This is neither what Aly was expecting nor what the purveyors of the wire wanted to capture. He had to think of a way to get an identity from this man.

"I have the letter from EGPC to Triton relating the results of the bid round."

"Then please give it to me and I will pass it along."

"I can't do that without at least your name sir." Aly felt the sweat increase. "What if I am asked later who I gave the envelope to? I would feel stupid saying I didn't even know the man's name."

"You can say you gave it to Osama. And that, my friend, should satisfy you. Give me the package and go enjoy your room this evening. There is a wonderful dining room here, very expensive. Charge it to the room."

Aly sensed the threat in the man's voice. Considering his options as the man reached across the table, Aly handed him the envelope, got up, and without another word walked back to the lobby. Looking over his shoulder, the older man was no longer there. Neither was the man with the earpiece. A chill ran down his neck as he got in the elevator.

"We got nothing with the wire. No identification, no admission."
Ambassador Foley stood up and punched the air.
"Sometimes that happens," replied Stan Kawinski. "Irma?"
Irma Levi had been fiddling with her cell phone as the wire conversation came to closure.
"He was meeting with Yosef Kettler. Mossad is tailing Kettler now."
A few minutes later Levi again looked at her phone, reading another text message.
"Kettler is heading for the city center. It will be most interesting to see who he meets."

A PRIME MINISTER shouldn't be short and paunchy with flyaway grey hair, and a shirttail hanging out. At least that was Ambassador Foley's opinion, but the last couple decades had taken its toll on Benjamin Shapiro. Before being elected Prime Minister three years ago, he spent twenty-five years with jobs in the Knesset, the military, Mossad, and foreign service. Foley knew that much public service could make anyone stooped and pooped.

The Prime Minister's security detail had wanded and frisked Foley when he entered the Kibbutz. Normally the Ambassador avoided this hassle but he knew Ein Geddi was a unique place. Possessing a large cadre of ex-military security staff to ensure a no-fail, safe environment, its remote location overlooking the Dead Sea was a good choice for a clandestine meeting. It also provided the option for a relaxing mud bath.

Approaching Foley, the Prime Minister held out his hand.

"Thank you for coming all the way here Ambassador."

"Nasty business, Mr. Prime Minister. We're happy to help."

"Yosef Kettler left the King David two days ago, after receiving information on the oil bid in Egypt. He went straight to a meeting with our Minister of Security Yaroun Herschel, who in turn phoned Vasily Kirchoff, head of the Israeli National Oil Company. None of these meetings in themselves are damning and the conversations we listened to were inconclusive."

"So you have nothing on them?"

"I wouldn't say that. I've known Yosef forty years and I'm not surprised it's come to this. He is very wise but unfortunately has trended to the radical right. He's an important figure in Israel but not beyond the reach of justice. On his way home, after meeting with Yaroun, he was kidnapped by hooded men in an unmarked van. I'm sorry to say his two bodyguards will be unable to continue in that line of work, or actually, any line of work. Although old, Yosef was given the opportunity to ponder his future. In exchange for legal immunity in Israel, he provided information that will enable viable cases against a number of others."

"You will put up with him?"

"Actually the Swiss will. We will give him immunity in Israel but extradite him to Switzerland, where we are working to freeze most of his assets."

"So who will go down?"

"I can only help dictate justice for Israel. Yaroun Herschel is in custody and faces a most unpleasant future. Vasily Kirchoff is being extradited to Russia as we speak, where it seems the FSB would very much like to host him in Novosibirsk for the rest of his years. Apparently Yaroun hated Vasily and was quite anxious to help us in that regard. I'm still not sure how big a role Yaroun played but it's irrelevant. Ruth Karsh and Simeon Friedman are more difficult, as they are prominent private sector players. I am certain Ruth will be convicted but we may need to cut a deal with Simeon to make this happen."

"Is she more at fault?"

"Who knows? Perhaps not. In any case she has overstepped the line too many times. We think she funded much of this, including the escapade in Montana. This fiasco is a good opportunity to rein her in."

The two men drank tea and let time pass. Foley broke the silence.

"For our part Mr. Prime Minister, the FBI has several people in custody. Mohammed Tawik and Moustafa Badry in Montana, and Taha Shaarawi in New York. They are also pursuing possible links to oilfield service companies in France and China. I predict several high ranking executives in these companies will be indicted. It seems inciting a war in this area can energize a host of players. Finally, General Latif has been busy in Egypt, where Karim Nabet is being strongly interrogated."

Both men leaned back and sipped their tea. The sun was setting behind them as they stared across the Dead Sea into Jordan.

"So who do you think was the leader of this sordid affair," Foley asked.

"I don't know," sighed the Prime Minister. "You and I are talking in part because of our own suspicions about your government's involvement. Let us see how that evolves."

"We need to ensure that this aspect does not reach the press. There is no need to mention a US plot to destabilize the region."

"Yes, your Project Stable. Quite shocking really. It would be most embarrassing to leak that. I suspect I will have a conversation down the road with your President."

"Indeed."

"Press releases have already been issued on Yaroun and Vasily. Yaroun has resigned for health reasons following a heart attack. Vasily is being extradited to Russia to face charges of tax fraud in the years after the fall of the Soviet Union. The only suspicious release, which almost no one will notice as such, will be an apparent reversal in bid award. I can't imagine that will draw much interest."

Neither man booked a mud bath and each left just after their conversation. Each was satisfied with the outcome. Neither could have predicted what transpired next.

"WELL, well, well," Jake said, leaning back in his chair.

Libby looked over the top of her Egyptian Gazette and stared at him, puzzled. Since losing the bid, he had been withdrawn and hadn't shared many feelings. Now reading the International Herald Tribune, he looked animated.

"There are three interesting articles buried on page four. I'd put money on a connection."

Libby waited for him to continue. He had a smile on his face.

"It seems Israel's had some internal problems. The Minister of Security stepped down, reportedly due to a sudden heart problem. The Chairman of the Israeli National Oil Company was deported to Russia the same day. And apparently there was a clerical error with the Egyptian bid round. Two of the bids are being re-evaluated."

"What makes you think any of those are related?"

Jake knew Vasily Kirchoff. They had shared stories from their past over shots of vodka in the old town of Jerusalem. Vasily loved Russia more than he loved Israel. There is no way he was involved with fraud against Mother Russia.

Jake was putting together a mental picture. As a geologist, he spent his career linking disparate clues and making logical conclusions. He used this deductive reasoning to link the Houston burglary, the mess in Montana, the incident at Mohammed's trailer, the interactions with the CIA, his bid submission, and these news articles.

"I knew it. I've been played Libby. This whole mess has to do with international politics."

That was enough to make Libby put down her newspaper.

"You think Middle East politics had something to do with Gussie and me being abducted?"

"And with my house in Houston, the guy in the Sinai, and me not winning the acreage. It's all connected."

Libby knew it ate at Jake that his bid wasn't successful, but she also knew that bids failed all the time. She thought him a bit paranoid. She saw an odd expression on his face.

They returned to their room to change into bathing suits and take Gussie to the beach. Libby was in the bathroom when Jake heard a knock on the door. He opened it to find a trim Egyptian in a white hotel uniform holding an envelope with Jake's name on it. Having no sender information, Jake was paranoid enough to think of anthrax. He went to the kitchen, got a knife, and slit the seal. Inside was another envelope, this one with a return address for the EGPC. He sat holding the envelope until Libby came out of the bathroom.

"You look great," he said, staring at her.

"What's that?"

"An envelope from EGPC."

She looked at him, turning over the possibilities.

"Are you going to open it?"

"I was waiting for you."

"It seems you can't open an envelope without help."

Jake ran the same knife along the top of the EGPC envelope and took out a letter, three pages thick. Libby watched as he read it and put it down, staring into space. His face gave nothing away. Finally the tension got to her.

"What does it say, Jake?"

Jake looked at her, pausing before answering.

"It says EGPC has awarded the Sinai block to our company."

Libby smiled, and couldn't understand why Jake did not.

"Jake that's good isn't it?"

"It's very good Libby."

Jake still had no expression on his face.

"Then what's wrong?"

"I'm not sure but I intend to find out. Something's still out of place. This whole thing was way too personal to just let it lie."

Jake made three phone calls. He told Salah the news and asked him to arrange a celebration the next night in Cairo. He told Salah to line up a nice private place for dinner and gave him a guest list.

His call with Stan Kawinski took longer.

The third call to General Latif took even longer.

After making reservations for the trip to Cairo Jake led Libby, Gussie, and Layla to the beach.

'One more day in Paradise,' he thought, 'before the shit hits the fan'.

IT was a dark night, one day off a new moon. The street was not really a street, more like an alley, with a dirt surface. The team of eight Mossad, all in black, surrounded the two story concrete hovel. When the signal came through their earpieces, two men entered the front door as two entered the rear. The remaining four stayed in position.

Shots were fired as the men entered. A bullet hit the chest of the first man, pushing him back against the wall. Even with his Kevlar vest the pain was intense. The second man dropped, rolled left, and fired.

The men who entered through the back found themselves in a kitchen. They moved quickly towards the opposite doorway, where the lead man collided with someone coming the other way. The agent was quick enough to grab the other man's arm, and point the gun away as it fired. Five seconds later the shooter was on the ground, face in the floor, arm twisted, with a knee in his back.

"Osama abdel Fatah, this is not your lucky day."

When Dick Radisson heard that the raid was successful he boarded a plane to Israel. Arriving the same day at a heavily fortified military facility, he was briefed by Irma Levi and the interrogation team, which had used a barrage of techniques to obtain precious little information. Yes, the man was indeed Osama abdel Fatah. Yes, he had been in New York City pretending to be the head of General Investments Ltd. No, he did not know whose dead body they found in his apartment. And so on. He revealed nothing about his bosses, or anything they did not already know.

Dick sighed, and asked Irma to try harder.

"We don't want to kill him," she replied.

"We need more than you've got so far."

"OK. Go to your hotel. I'll let you know."

Levi went with her agent in charge to the room where they held Osama. Dismissing the two men guarding abdel Fatah she sat facing the man and lit a cigarette. Osama's face was colored and puffy with blood running down one side. He was grimy with sweat.

"I want to know who started this whole mess," Levi said.

Osama looked at her and smiled. He spit towards Levi, but what came out just dribbled down the front of him.

"You don't know me, Osama. This is the only time you will ever see me." Irma paused and looked at the man. "I have your wife and child. Your little boy is very cute, your wife not so much. But I assume it works for you. You have exactly one minute to tell me what I want to know. If I am not satisfied, I will have someone do to them what your colleagues planned for Libby Joyce. Well, perhaps not exactly the same thing with your little boy. Some things don't translate from female to male. But we can adapt."

"You can't do that. You are bluffing."

"You are incorrect," she said simply.

Without warning Levi reached out, grabbed Osama's left ear, and with a swipe of a knife, cut it off. She put it on the table in front of Osama as he screamed.

"I don't know who started this," Osama said. "I had nothing to do with that woman and the girl."

Levi took it as positive that Osama was screaming and talking. His emotions gave him away.

"I'm not interested in explanations Osama. At this point I am only interested in who started all this. If you don't know anything that interests me, your family will suffer. If you don't tell me, your family will suffer. If I'm not satisfied with the answer, your family will suffer. I will find justice."

"But Montana wasn't my doing."

"Less than thirty seconds left, Osama."

After ten of those seconds, Irma Levi sat back and listened as Osama talked.

Fifteen minutes later, Levi stood up, nodded at Osama, and walked out of the room, leaving the ear on the table. She said nothing as she passed through the rest of the building.

Levi stopped at Radisson's hotel and told him what she had found out.

"Wow," is all he could say.

Radisson made a phone call to Stan and added two names to the invite list for Jake's party.

CHAPTER 60

THE Gezira Club was not grand but exuded a faded elegance. Not known for its cuisine, and dry in adherence to Islamic law, it was an odd venue for the meeting. Salah had obtained a special waiver to serve alcohol, but the real advantage in using the Club was the ease of providing security.

United States Ambassador to Egypt Dick Steer raised a glass to toast their success. Stan had expressed doubt he could get the Ambassador but Radisson had insisted. Steer was the main security risk and the reason why both US Marines and Egyptian security forces were highly visible. Jake, Libby, Salah, and the handful of dignitaries joined in the toast.

"To your success Jake. May your first well be a big one, and production start soon thereafter."

"Thank you Mr. Ambassador. Friends and colleagues. It's been a long and tortuous road. I never anticipated the pain it would bring. Who could have. I wanted to have a small gathering this evening to mark a beginning. My company has a long road ahead of it but I'm certain our Sinai venture will be exciting and successful."

Jake noticed that Stan had left the room, holding his satellite phone to his ear.

"There will be more times along the way to celebrate our progress. At this point let's just enjoy ourselves, and enjoy the fine food my colleague Salah has ordered."

A few minutes later Stan pulled him aside and whispered that Dick Radisson and General Latif would arrive within the half hour. They should proceed with hors d'oeuvres but delay dinner.

Jake exchanged small talk with the Ambassador, getting the impression that he did not know why he was attending. Jake didn't know Steer, but thought the man seemed cold and distant. Steer was a career diplomat who had spent the last dozen years in Egypt or Jordan, with an assignment in Israel prior to that.

Libby was very popular at the gathering and Jake enjoyed watching her. She looked sexy, dressed conservatively in a simple black dress, black pumps, and pearl necklace. He noted how easily she engaged men in conversation. She was now chatting with Maged Khafagy, both of them laughing and smiling. He felt a rush of admiration.

As the sound of a helicopter grew louder, Stan announced their two remaining guests had arrived. Dick Radisson and General Mohammed Latif entered the room, looking a bit rumpled. They made the rounds quickly before everyone took their seats for dinner. Hummus and kibbeh were followed by a creamy lentil soup. The main course was garlic infused lamb with Nile Delta wild rice. Dessert was a platter of sweet pastries and fresh fruit. Everyone was content when Dick Radisson finally stood up.

"I'd like to thank Jake for inviting me, and Ambassador Steer for joining us. Now please sit back, relax, and listen to an abridged yet incredible tale of how Mr. Tillard came to control an oil and gas lease in a most unlikely spot. The journey was more convoluted than he could have dreamed."

Dick surveyed the group that had become very quiet. Jake's eyes swept from side to side, trying to gauge the atmosphere. He knew where Radisson's talk was going.

"Most of you know the basics. Some of you have pieced together a bit more. I suspect, however, that only two of you know the whole story."

Heads swiveled, trying to decipher what was going on. Jake looked about and considered each person in the room. He'd put together most of the story while in Sharm el Sheikh. He and Radisson had fleshed out the rest yesterday by phone.

"Back in the early eighties, Barney Wilcrow, Jake's boss at Reacher Oil, spent a few years in Israel building commercial skills while starting a couple of small businesses. I might mention that his father Thaddeus Wilkrowski had emigrated to the US from Poland in the early part of the century. The surname was abbreviated to Wilcrow at Ellis Island. Barney wasn't a great student, so he visited an uncle in Tel Aviv and started making money instead. His first business was window washing, where Barney started small and worked his way up. It was tough at first. Most people and stores had little money to pay for window washing, so Barney got the idea that dirty windows might convince potential customers to engage his services. It was fairly easy to make windows dirty. For more reluctant customers, a broken window sometimes provided the incentive they required. And so on. After a couple years business was booming, and Barney farmed it out to competent and strong willed employees, moving on to the import/export trade. He moved consumer goods between Israel and Egypt, lots of black market trade. You can guess the rest. In all of those ventures, his partner was a fellow kibbutznick of his uncle. A man named Yosef Kettler."

Jake noticed the Ambassador fidgeting in front of him.

"The two drifted apart and Barney left Israel. He returned to the US, finished university, and began a successful career in the oil industry. Yosef went on to make a fortune in Israel. This being a small world, the two had a chance meeting in the late seventies on a flight from London to Houston. By that time Barney was well established in the oil industry. Within a year they collaborated on deals with oilfield parts and services, and lubricants. Yosef was ruthless and they each made a lot of money. I would think Reacher Oil might be interested in how much they overpaid for services during this period."

Jake noticed Stan slip out of the room.

"It turns out Barney believed in Jake's geology from the start, especially his theory that the Sinai was a winner. He saw the potential with Israel next door, the market for clean fuel being enormous. With Yosef to help, he envisioned hundreds of millions of dollars coming his way. Barney orchestrated things within Reacher Oil to get Jake out of the way."

The group remained very quiet.

"Barney approached his old friend Yosef to work a deal, his motives strictly financial. But his idea fit in with a larger agenda already churning in certain political circles. The US State Department had approached Israel's Minister of Security Yaroun Herschel to help with an effort to destabilize the region and give a jolt to the stalled Peace Process. I can't say more about this larger plan, but Yosef and Herschel saw a perfect fit with the Sinai opportunity. Yosef's import/export profits in and out of Egypt had shrunk. Destabilization would reenergize this business and satisfy the larger goal."

Dick reached down and picked up a water glass. He took a long drink while looking around. Stan had returned to his seat, and several husky Marines had repositioned themselves.

"The Sinai gas deal could provide something that had been missing, namely unstable activity within Egypt. Yosef and Yaroun believed if an Israeli company got the license, there would be protests and outrage on the streets of Egypt, a tinderbox of social unrest. They anticipated Egypt could not avoid its treaty commitment to offer Sinai oil and gas to Israel and the protests would turn violent. Yosef took this plan to his US contact for tacit approval and Ambassador Steer concurred."

The Ambassador stood up pointing a finger at Dick.

"This is ridiculous. The Egyptian political situation was not connected to any of these pos...."

"Please be quiet Ambassador. I'm sure you and your colleagues were pleased when the situation developed a life of its own."

"You're crazy Radisson. I for one am not interested in any more of your preposterous tales."

He whirled around and began to leave, only to find himself surrounded by two Marines who held the Ambassador's shoulders, while his aid handed him a piece of paper. Steer read a concise note from the US President, temporarily relieving him of duty and placing him under house arrest. An investigation team was en route to Cairo. He was to remain within the embassy until further notice.

"This way Mr. Ambassador," said his aide.

"You can't do this," he said with teeth clenched. "I am the Ambassador here."

"You were," Dick replied.

With the Ambassador struggling, the Marines led him out the door. The remaining guests looked at Radisson in disbelief.

"Now I'd like to propose that toast I promised earlier."

He held up his wine glass and waited while the rest of the group slowly did the same. Most did not understand what had transpired and did not know what to say. Dick looked straight into Jake's eyes and a very big smile grew on his face."

"To Jake Tillard. We hope his success will increase cooperation between our strategic allies Israel and Egypt."

THE well reached its total depth of eight thousand four hundred feet below the surface in late September, drilled without incident, ahead of schedule. The porous limestone reservoir layer was exactly where Jake had predicted. It was thicker than predicted with four hundred feet of almost pure methane capable of feeding a pipeline with minimal processing. Beneath the reservoir layer, the well penetrated a hundred feet of the Jurassic Maghara Group shale, with total organic carbon in excess of three percent. Jake had not predicted such a rich source rock. If the source layer was consistently this thick and rich it would have generated much more gas than he had originally predicted.

Jake sat under a large white tent with Maged Khafagy to his right, and Charles Alfred Lister III to his left. Government officials from Egypt and Israel as well as press took up the rest of the front row. In the row behind were Salah el Gindi, Libby, Marv, Gussie, and a host of others. Lister's Saint Louis office was linked by satellite, as was the EGPC office in Cairo. Jake stood and faced the others.

"This seems anticlimactic so I won't clutter the moment with extra words. I'll just thank you all, and give the signal to go ahead."

He pressed a large red button signaling the driller on the rig platform to begin the test. Nothing happened for a few minutes, and then a small flame appeared to the left of the rig, at the end of a twenty-foot pipe pointing northeast, towards Israel. Within a minute the flame grew to forty feet, and the group could feel the heat. There was no black cloud since the gas was so pure. There was, however, a roar similar to a jet engine. The group left the tent, migrating behind a wall that gave protection from the heat and noise.

Champagne corks popped and the politicians talked about future export to Israel. Later the unofficial indicated production rate would be announced as ten million cubic feet per day. Assuming ten wells in the field, and a price near four dollars per thousand cubic feet, Jake quickly calculated a monthly revenue well over ten million dollars. After costs and taxes, there would be plenty left.

Libby squeezed Gussie's hand and whispered, "Look at your dad and remember this day Gussie." She gazed at Jake who stared at the flare.

Before boarding helicopters for the flight back to Cairo, Jake gathered a small group together for a status update. He told them the pipeline plan was almost approved by the Egyptian People's Assembly, as well as the Knesset. Irma Levi revealed that Yosef, in spite of immunity for his part in this debacle, was being charged with embezzling funds from the Holocaust Fund for Survivors, of which he was a Board member.

"Did he really do that?" asked Jake.

"I'm not sure but it doesn't matter."

"What about Barney," Jake asked.

"Our government is deciding between three options," replied Radisson. "To try him in Delaware for ethics violations connected with his business dealings. To extradite him to Israel to stand trial for terrorism. Or to extradite him to Egypt, in conjunction with conspiracy to circumvent Egyptian law relating to proper preservation and use of Egyptian natural resources."

"Which do you think will happen?"

"I don't care," said Radisson.

"He should hope he is not given to Egypt," said Khafagy.

"Israel would be no better," added Levi.

IRMA LEVI was staying at the Royal Horseguards Hotel near Westminster. Enjoying a light breakfast in her room prior to rejoining the Conference on Middle East Stability, she heard the BBC announcer say something that caught her attention.

"No reasons were given as to why the US Secretary of State has stepped down, but speculation is mounting to matters in Asia. US relations with North Korea have soured since Clancy's summit with newly installed Kim Jong Il."

Levi sipped her coffee, turning off the television. She thought back to when she first learned of Project Stable, more than a year ago. Wondering if thwarting it sooner could have headed off a lot of trouble, she concluded that letting it run had allowed them to surgically extricate several bad apples from the system. Rising to dress for the conference, she thought she would do nothing different if she had the chance to do it all again.

JAKE, Libby, Gussie, and Mohammed set off on horses into the South Sinai Mountains for a four-day camping trip. Mount Sinai rose to the south. To the East they could see the Gulf of Aqaba, its intense azure blue set off by rich desert browns. They noticed little life until Mohammed began pointing it out. Some grasses here, a bush there, a scorpion that blended perfectly into the brown sandy floor. Most animals in the Sinai are nocturnal, and all are very well camouflaged. The sole exception is the Sinai Agama, a normally drab lizard except during mating season, when the males turn a brilliant blue. They felt especially privileged when Mohammed pointed out a normally elusive Nubian Ibex, the largest animal in the Sinai.

The second night they camped at the edge of a small cliff, where they watched the sunset, ate dates, and drank sweet tea.

In the morning Mohammed walked his guests a short distance to a pile of rock cylinders, each about two inches in diameter and up to two feet long.

"I thought you might know what these mean," said the Bedouin.

Libby looked into the piercing eyes of the dark, handsome, ageless man, and smiled before picking through the pile.

"These are cores taken for mineral exploration," she said.

Jake looked at the cores and glanced at Libby.

"Do you see what I see?"

"Looks like a classic epithermal mineral suite to me," she said, her smile growing.

"Is it good?" asked Mohammed.

"Gold and silver is always good," Libby replied. "Perhaps our stay in the Sinai will be longer than expected. Mohammed, do you have any idea who drilled these cores?"

"It was a long time ago," he said simply.

Jake looked at the tall lean man with the handsome, tanned face. Mohammed gazed towards the north where his family had lived for generations. It was another sunny day in Egypt.

THE END

Acknowledgements

I wish to thank several people for their editorial suggestions and encouragement. Don Orsi, wonderful friend, world traveler, voracious reader, and unfailing supporter. Bob Lamarre and Laura Wray, longtime friends and lifetime learners. Jared Orsi, an educator at Colorado State University who gave more feedback than one should expect from someone they've never met. Dick Orsi, who had a list of potential publishers along with advice to never give up. Maryanne Rhoades who devoirs this genre of novel and was encouraging from the beginning.

To my wife and best friend Lesa, thanks for tolerating the seemingly endless time this project required. Thanks to my mom, alive when I conceived this project, who believed I could do anything I wanted. Sarah Heller did a great job on the maps and tables; Clare Slade provided great artwork for the cover. Thanks to Reza Fassihi, friend, colleague, and Distinguished Advisor, for oil industry expertise. A hearty thanks to Robert Etheredge, without whom this book might not exist, or certainly look as good.

Other individuals read various drafts and provided encouragement. Thanks—you know who you are. Many people and organizations I encountered along the way provided colorful examples of character and mannerisms that crept into the narrative. Too numerous and fleeting to mention, they were indispensable to the book.